WHIRLPOOL

Tweed faces the most desperate emergency of his career. Europe is being sucked into a whirlpool of terror. Bombs are detonating all over the continent – inside Russia. *Glasnost* is being blown to smithereens. Who is the new enemy?

Bob Newman faces tragedy in Suffolk, England. Bent on revenge, he seems to run wild. He learns that within twenty-four hours of the tragedy, his girl friend's estranged husband was killed in far-away Finland. Is there a link between these events?

What game is being played by the devious Peggy Vanderheld? How involved is Evelyn Lennox, sister of Newman's girl friend? What are the aims of Franklin D. Hauser, formidable owner of the world's largest bank?

Struggling on all fronts, Tweed is faced by a fresh problem. Sinister secret police chiefs from ex-Communist states are vanishing. Is someone recruiting them into a new deadly force? If so, for what purpose?

The action sweeps to Sweden and Finland, close to the powder kegs across the Baltic. As a heatwave smothers Europe, Tweed's team explores the mysterious Institute in Lapland, north of the Arctic Circle. Does this hold the key to chaos?

And who is the professional assassin who is eliminating one witness after another?

Paula Grey, Tweed's personal assistant, is kidnapped. As Tweed grimly tries to save her life the turmoil escalates. Under his ruthless direction, the action turns full circle.

This is a novel for today – and tomorrow. The climax – the surge of the whirlpool – is literally the most explosive Forbes has written so far.

WHIRLPOOL

Colin Forbes

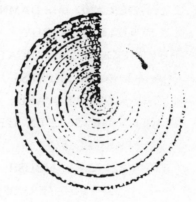

PAN BOOKS
London, Sydney and Auckland

A Pan original

First published 1991 by Pan Books Ltd,
Cavaye Place, London SW10 9PG

9 8 7 6 5 4 3 2 1

ISBN 0 330 31703 2

© Colin Forbes 1991

Photoset by Parker Typesetting Service, Leicester
Printed and bound in Great Britain by
The Bath Press, Avon

AUTHOR'S NOTE

All the characters portrayed are creatures of the author's imagination and bear no relationship to any living person. Also, the corporation, The International Continental Union Bank, US, again has no equivalent in real life anywhere in the world.

FOR JANE

CONTENTS

Prologue

Dawn came up like a warning.

Bob Newman, foreign correspondent, frowned as he drove his Mercedes 280E across the loneliness of Suffolk in February. Ploughed dark soil, crusted with frost, hemmed in the deserted road on either side. The weird light of dawn intensified his anxiety as his headlights now provided uncertain illumination. What was it his girl friend, Sandy Riverton, had said when she called him in the middle of the night?

'Bob, can we meet urgently? At the old church near Yoxford where we first met?'

He could have sworn her teeth were chattering with fear.

'Of course we can.' Stretched out in bed, he had suppressed a yawn. 'But why there? Is something wrong?'

'I can't explain over the phone. You *will* come? I've something I must tell you, something I should have told you before. It will help your investigation into INCUBUS. I must go. Can you make it there just after dawn? So no one will see us?'

'Sandy, what is this all about? Why that remote place – at that remote hour, for God's sake?'

'I can't linger. Do come, Bob. Please. I must go now. I will see you there?'

'Yes . . .' He had woken up. 'Where are you calling from?'

'Tell you when we meet. 'Bye . . .'

She had rung off before he could say another word. He

1

had jumped out of bed, washed, shaved, dressed very quickly. A correspondent learned to do that, even if he no longer needed to practise his profession – the best-selling book he had written years ago had given blessed financial independence.

There were no villages, no farms in sight as he slowed down, afraid that he might drive past the narrow track leading to the abandoned church and its separate bell tower. He had the heaters full on: it was a raw morning with a bitter wind blowing from the east, from the distant North Sea.

Not even a hamlet along this stretch of the road, he recalled. 'Near Yoxford' was an over-simplification of the position of the old church. It was in the middle of nowhere. So why would Sandy choose such a desolate rendezvous – at such a desolate hour? Because she was frightened, he thought grimly.

The cold bleak light was growing in the cloudless sky. Over to his left he caught a glimpse of a Georgian mansion huddled a quarter-mile off the main road. A deep central window was arched at the top. More Queen Anne than Georgian. And a curious coincidence – Livingstone Manor was the English country home of Franklin D. Hauser, President and Chief Executive of INCUBUS Inc., the giant American organization Sandy had worked for until recently.

He recalled another phone conversation with Sandy three weeks earlier. She had resigned from INCUBUS. No real reason given. When Newman had pressed her she had become vague.

'I just felt I was doing the same old thing, week after week, month after month. Time for a change, I suppose . . .'

She had left London without seeing Newman, telling him in a letter she was staying at her sister's place in Southwold further up the Suffolk coast. So why this

2

mysterious meeting close to Hauser's lair?

Newman spotted the track leading off to the right and swung away from the main road. This was an area of sloping fields and the track mounted a gradual incline. The daylight was strong enough now for him to see the tower of the ancient stone church silhouetted against the horizon, perched on a ridge. The bell tower came into view, a square slim block of stone separated from the church by a dozen yards. He found his anxiety growing.

He had realized in January how very fond of Sandy he was, that he'd reached the stage where he might well ask her to marry him. She was so very different from his first wife, foully murdered during the old Cold War years in Estonia on the Baltic. He increased speed, impatient to reach his destination. The ton and a half of car rocked, driving over the ice-hardened ruts carved out by farm tractors in kinder weather.

He glanced automatically in his rear-view mirror, catching a glimpse of himself. In his forties, his hair was fair, he was clean-shaven and with a strong face. Normally his expression was droll, with a hint of humour about the mouth and eyes. Bob Newman was a man generally liked by both men and women. He breathed a sigh of relief as he bumped over the crest. Sandy's red Jaguar was parked behind a dense hedge, the twigs so close together they formed a visual barrier from a distance.

Parking his Mercedes alongside the Jaguar, he got out. His hand touched the Jag's radiator. Anxiety flooded back. The radiator was cold. She must have been waiting for some time. Where?

The only shelter he could see was the church, but it would be like an ice box inside. Slipping on his gloves, he saw out of the corner of his eye the sun rising above a belt of dark blue. The sea. A much smaller flash of light caught his attention. From the large arched window at Livingstone Manor.

3

The sun was reflecting off the window. In which case the reflection should still be there. It had vanished. Reaching into his car he hauled out the powerful pair of binoculars he always carried. Of medium height and build, he crouched behind the car, perched elbows on the roof, focused the binoculars. The window at Livingstone Manor came up close. A silhouette showed behind the net curtains, a silhouette aiming a pair of field glasses.

Probably an early-rising servant wondering who could be visiting the church at this hour. He laid the binoculars back on the passenger seat, turned to face the church. To reach the ancient Norman edifice with its pointed windows he had to pass through the bell tower, open to the world at both ends. Beyond, a curving path led uphill between gravestones to the church entrance. He turned up his coat collar, walked forward.

Both tower and church were sadly in need of repair. Doubtless at the time of the wool barons the church had a full congregation, but the economic tide had long ago receded from this part of the world. He walked inside the bell tower.

Afterwards he was haunted by the sound his footsteps had made in the brooding post-dawn silence, the crunch and crackle of his shoes breaking ice.

In one corner of the tower lay the bell which had fallen at some time in the past. During the great storm, the locals said. He was walking out of the tower when he glanced up, stopped, froze as he stared at the horror above his head.

Sandy was suspended by a rope attached to an old beam next to the ladder leading to the tower. The rope was knotted round her neck which hung sideways at a bizarre angle. Her lifeless eyes stared down at him, her tongue protruded from her mouth. Her neck was broken. Her long gold hair hung down her back over her red wind-cheater. Her long legs were clad in denims. She looked like some grotesque statue in a pagan ritual.

Newman choked, grunted, then forced himself to move. He climbed the ladder, testing each rung carefully. Two of the rungs had been replaced by fresh wood. He stood near the top, alongside her corpse.

Reaching out he gently touched her pallid face. The skin was cold, felt like wax. The rope from which she hung was old. It was exactly like the remnant attached to the bell. He began talking out aloud, to himself.

'No. It's not possible. This is a mad dream. I don't believe it. I'm home in bed at my South Ken flat . . . This is a crazy nightmare . . .'

But he knew it was true. A part of his trained reporter's mind began to function, to observe. Could she have committed suicide? No. Why? Because she hated heights – she suffered from vertigo. He looked down at the yawning drop below. No!

He hated leaving her there but he descended the ladder because there was nothing else he could do. The odd thing was his first thought was her husband, Ed, must be told – Ed whom she was on the verge of divorcing. He must know.

Ed Riverton was a top executive in INCUBUS, the great American banking syndicate which was spreading its tentacles across Europe, investing in just about every type of company which existed. That was how Newman had met Sandy.

Travelling to Finland, he had interviewed Riverton in Helsinki. It had been a strange conversation: Riverton was nervous, evasive. Due to the fact that his marriage had been heading for the rocks? No, Newman had detected something he couldn't account for.

His mind returned to the dreadful present. Before he left the bell tower his eyes were drawn upwards. The view was hideous. She was swinging slowly from side to side, like a pendulum. Had he disturbed her rigid stance by touching her? Or was it the east wind blowing in through the open bell tower with renewed force?

What the hell did it matter? He had an awful premonition he would always remember her like this – that he'd never recall her cheerful buoyancy, her glowing smile when she had teased him. Yes, he'd always have this ghastly image imprinted on his mind – a grossly obscene caricature of the real Sandy.

He stumbled near the exit from the tower, recovered his balance. His mind was working on two levels. There was grief and shock, but another part of his brain was functioning – the reporter's. He forced himself to stare upwards again.

Above the beam round which the rope was tied was a platform where the top of the ladder rested. Carved in the platform was the hole through which the bell-rope had once hung. He calculated it was not possible for Sandy, kneeling on that platform, to reach down to the beam, impossible for her to have attached the rope from that perch. She stood – *hung* – five feet four inches high. Too short to have killed herself.

PART ONE

Profiles of Death

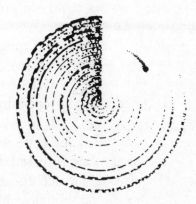

1

'Why – thank heaven – didn't you resign as you said you would?'

Monica asked Tweed the question while they waited for Newman to arrive. Tweed, Deputy Director of the SIS, stared out of the window of his first floor office at Park Crescent, London HQ of the Secret Service.

'Porridge-grey – and damn cold,' he commented on the weather.

Monica, middle-aged, her grey hair tied in a bun, his personal assistant for many years, leaned forward over her desk and studied Tweed. Of medium height and build, indeterminate age, he wore horn-rim glasses and was the man you passed in the street without noticing him. It was an impression which had often served him well. Clean shaven, his hair was still dark and behind the lenses his eyes were alert and penetrating.

'You haven't answered my question,' she prodded him. 'After seeing the PM you took a long leave and then came back. So what happened.'

'She wore me down,' Tweed admitted. 'When I did get back she had a very strange and dangerous problem which she dumped in my lap, assured me I was the only man she could trust to handle it. We talked for two hours and,' he threw out both hands in a gesture of surrender, 'at the end of it she, yes, wore me down.' His manner changed, became brisk. He walked behind his own desk, settled himself in his ancient swivel chair. 'I wonder what's worrying Bob Newman? When he phoned, asked if he could come and see me, he sounded edgy and shaken. Not like him. Wouldn't give me a hint over the phone.'

'Well, we'll soon know. He's due any second. And what is the strange and dangerous problem?'

'INCUBUS is part of it. The International Continental Union Bank, US – United States. I do wish the Americans hadn't this love of trainloads of initial letters to designate an organization. You've heard of Franklin D. Hauser, President and Chief Executive? Who hasn't? They say he's as powerful as the President in Washington. An exaggeration, of course. It's the people he's employing who are worrying both Washington and Moscow. I can't go into details, but it's a curious situation.'

'Curious?'

Tweed paused. 'Can't tell you much. But I've been asked by the PM to co-operate with a special operative of the CIA. And an unknown member of the KGB. Now that I call curious.'

He gazed towards the window as the phone rang. Monica took the call, said to send him up right away, put down the receiver, looked at Tweed.

'Bob Newman has arrived. You did want to see him . . .'

'Yes. I'm curious about Bob, too . . .'

He broke off as Newman entered, closed the door, nodded to Monica and slumped into the chair in front of Tweed's desk.

'What on earth is wrong, Bob?'

Tweed was startled by Newman's appearance. Normally he was relaxed and had an easy-going manner. Now he looked haggard, grim faced.

'You look as though you haven't slept,' Tweed remarked.

'I haven't – not a lot. I was woken in the middle of the night by a phone call . . .'

Tersely, he recalled his experiences of the past few hours. He went on to explain his interview with the police as Monica slipped out to make him some coffee.

10

'They had a Scotland Yard man at Southwold Police Station. From Homicide. He just happened to be there after solving another case. All the senior police officers were down with flu – so the Chief Constable asked for his aid. A Chief Inspector Roy Buchanan. Very intelligent, very persistent. In his quiet way he really grilled me about Sandy.'

'I once met Buchanan,' Tweed said quietly. 'I agree with your description. A highly competent, dogged type . . .'

'Dogged is the word.' Newman paused as though unsure how to phrase his next words, then burst out: 'Buchanan thinks I murdered Sandy.'

Tweed waited, saying nothing, tapping a pencil as he watched Newman while the reporter drank black coffee from the large mug Monica had brought him. He drank the steaming liquid in gulps.

'Buchanan said that to you?' Tweed asked eventually.

'Not in so many words. But he made the point there were no signs that Sandy had struggled for her life, that she must have trusted her murderer. That thought had occurred to me before I was hauled off to Southwold police station for the interrogation. I could tell what he was thinking from the way he questioned me. Flicks at you verbally with a rapier.'

'Sounds like Buchanan.' Tweed stared at Newman. He had shaved, but it was a rough job: a piece of sticking plaster at the side of his face showed where he had cut himself. 'I see you cut yourself shaving?'

Newman's eyes blazed. 'Exactly the same question Buchanan asked me. He even suggested maybe I'd like to show him the cut. I ripped off the plaster. I suppose he hopes the pathologist who butchers her will find skin tissue under her nails. Mine.'

'Drink some more coffee,' Tweed advised.

'I have to make a call to Helsinki,' Newman snapped.

11

'Sandy was divorcing her husband, Ed. But the least I can do is to call him, let him know.'

'The phone is all yours.'

Tweed leant back in his chair, glanced at Monica while Newman checked his notebook, dialled a Helsinki number, waited and then stared at Tweed.

'It would help my concentration if you could stop tapping that blasted pencil.'

Tweed, still unruffled, nodded, placed the pencil on his desk, took out a handkerchief and began polishing his glasses.

Newman gripped the phone tightly, listening to the ringing tone. Would they never answer the bloody thing? A girl's voice came on the line, repeated the number in English.

'I need to speak to Edward Riverton urgently. I'm calling his home because he told me he was rarely in his office.'

'Who is this speaking?' A tremble in the girl's voice.

'Sorry, this is Bob Newman. I interviewed Mr Riverton in Helsinki a few weeks ago . . .'

Newman had a grip on himself now. His voice was perfectly normal, Tweed noted.

'Oh, God, Mr Newman,' the girl exploded. 'This is Evelyn, his sister-in-law. You know Sandy, I believe. She was talking about you on the phone recently. I've just had terrible news and I can't reach Sandy. Her phone rings in Southwold but no one answers.'

'Slow down, Evelyn.' Newman's tone was soothing, controlled. 'I remember you well. Especially that marvellous dinner you cooked. *Gravad lax*. Some of the best salmon I've ever tasted. Now, tell me the news.'

'It's unbelievable. They dragged Ed out of the North Harbour just after daylight twenty-four hours ago. I was at the Turku office and there was some delay in telling me . . . We only get four hours' daylight in winter . . . It's horribly

12

cold. The harbour is packed solid with ice . . .'

She was babbling, on the verge of hysteria, even a nervous breakdown. Newman spoke slowly.

'Just take your time telling me. I'm a good listener. How did it happen?'

'The icebreaker *Otso* was clearing a passage for ships through the ice. One of the crew spotted Ed's body wedged inside a crevasse. They saw him just in time before the icebreaker crushed . . .' Her voice broke. Newman waited, heard her take in a deep breath. 'They took him to the mortuary and called me.'

'Who is "they", Evelyn? Give me the facts.'

'The Protection Police arrived and took him off the *Otso*. A man called Mauno Sarin phoned me. I knew there was something wrong from his voice. Can I get a drink of water?'

'I'll hold on.'

Newman looked at Tweed, sitting erect in his chair, while he held the phone to his ear, his other hand over the mouthpiece.

'There's the devil to pay about this business. Tell you in a minute . . . Yes, Evelyn, I'm still here. You said you could tell something was wrong from his voice. That was *before* he told you the news?'

'No, afterwards . . .'

She's gone over the edge, Newman thought. He cleared his throat. 'Just tell me what happened next.'

'I insisted on knowing everything. Sarin didn't want to tell me, then he said I'd know soon enough, and better from him than over the radio. Ed didn't slip into the harbour. For God's sake, Bob – he had been garrotted.' Her voice rose in pitch. 'With some kind of wire. The head was almost severed from the neck. Oh, God, Bob, how am I going to tell Sandy that?'

'Take another drink of water, a good big one, then we'll talk some more.'

13

Newman was ice cold in an emergency. How could he handle this? Tell Sandy's sister she was dead, hung by a rope inside an ancient bell tower? Horror piled on horror. But something was even more wrong than Sarin had realized. In the course of about twenty-four hours Ed Riverton had been brutally exterminated in Finland – and his wife had been eliminated with equal brutality in East Anglia, over a thousand miles away. He swallowed the rest of the coffee, managed to grin at Monica, then Evelyn was back on the line.

'I know you and Sandy are—' She broke off.

'Yes,' Newman replied in a monotone.

'I know I'm being a coward about this . . . should tell Sandy myself . . .' Babbling again. 'But I can't bring myself to do it now. Bob, could you possibly tell her yourself?'

Newman paused. Beads of moisture were forming on his forehead. Tweed was watching him closely, pencil gripped in his hand but motionless. How the hell can I tell her after what she's just been through, Newman asked himself. But someone had to.

'Evelyn, are you sitting down? With a full glass of water?'

'A jugful. Bob, what is it? I can tell from your tone something else is terribly wrong. Bob . . .' A deep intake of breath he clearly heard over a thousand miles away. 'Bob,' she repeated, 'I've got a grip on myself – and I am sitting down. Just tell me.' Calmer now, self-controlled. Temporarily.

'I've just had a similar shock, Evelyn. It's going to be a lot grimmer for you – on top of what you've just told me. And it is about Sandy. Like Ed, she's dead. It happened in the early hours of this morning.'

'I see.' Very controlled, too controlled, her voice dull. 'How did it happen, Bob? Car accident?'

'No. I said like Ed.' He paused, she burst out.

14

'Oh, my God! Not garrotted. Please, not that . . .'

'I phrased it badly. I mean like Ed she had been murdered. Want some more water?'

'No! No! How did she die? Tell me, damn you! I'm flying straight home. I'll just phone INCUBUS and say I'm leaving them . . . I had a job with them – *have* a job at the moment . . . Not in the same department as Ed . . .'

'Don't phone INCUBUS,' he warned. 'Just catch the first flight home. You have the phone number of my apartment in South Ken? Good. Phone details of your flight number and ETA. If I'm not there leave a message on the answerphone. Use a different name. Identify yourself as Jackie. OK?'

'How did Sandy die? You said she was murdered . . .'

'The details can wait till we meet. Don't forget to phone me that flight data.'

'Bob, I must go.' Suddenly there was a note of urgency in her voice. It alarmed Newman. 'I've got to get out of this place. While we were talking I was checking a timetable. I can just catch a flight if I rush. Have to pack. *Must* go now.'

'Evelyn . . .'

Newman slowly put down the receiver. She had broken the connection. There had been a note close to panic in her voice. As though she had seen something which disturbed her from the window of the apartment. He remembered the phone was perched on a window ledge in Riverton's Helsinki pad. He lit a cigarette, took a long drag. Tweed waited patiently.

'It's incredible – and sinister,' Newman began. He relayed to Tweed and Monica the gist of his conversation. Nothing in Tweed's expression betrayed his reaction as Newman concluded.

'Incredible,' he repeated. 'Two murders which took place within about twenty-four hours. One in Suffolk, one in Finland. The victims were man and wife. I know Sandy

15

was estranged from Ed, was thinking of divorcing him, but . . .'

'Were they still on speaking terms?' Tweed asked. 'Is there a chance Ed phoned Sandy and told her something important – something so important someone thought it was dangerous that she went on living?'

'Shouldn't have thought so.' Newman threw out a hand in a helpless gesture. 'Not impossible though. I really don't know.' He sounded at the end of his tether, all the adrenalin summoned up for his phone call now evaporated.

'And yet there's a common link,' Tweed pointed out. 'All three were working for INCUBUS – or had been until recently. Ed, Sandy – and *Evelyn*,' he added. Newman jerked upright, stared at Tweed, the picture of anxiety.

'So you think I was right?'

'Right about what?'

'To warn her not to tell INCUBUS she was leaving them?'

'There could just be an element of risk involved for her. Why, I have no idea, but the coincidence is very strange.' Tweed was doodling on his notepad as he spoke. He found he had drawn a noose, remembered how Sandy Riverton had died inside the old bell tower, scribbled it out before Newman could see it. 'What do you propose to do about it?' he enquired.

'Step up my investigation into the activities of INCU-BUS and its chief, Hauser, in Europe. Incidentally, Hauser has his British residence in an old Georgian mansion not two miles from that bell tower.' He stifled a yawn. 'Checking into that organization may take months. I've decided to fly to New York – main HQ of INCUBUS, then on to Boston where they have another top secret outfit. Meantime I'm going back to my apartment to get some much needed kip, then I'll meet Evelyn at

Heathrow. She might just be the key to what I'm looking for . . .'

'Robert Newman is our only lead in our enquiries concerning the murder of Sandra Riverton.'

Chief Inspector Roy Buchanan made the statement to Tweed in the Park Crescent office. His tone was non-committal, gave no indication as to his own suspicions. Six feet tall, in his forties, his manner was detached, his grey eyes watchful. He sat in the armchair recently occupied by Newman, his long legs crossed.

'What brought you to my doorstep?' Tweed asked amiably.

Monica watched the two men, fascinated. Under the surface of an everyday conversation a duel of two astute minds was taking place. Buchanan had balanced the cup of coffee Monica had provided on his crossed knees. He drank a little coffee before replying.

Seated in a hard-backed chair, Buchanan's assistant, Sergeant Warden, several years younger than his chief, watched in silence, his clean-shaven face devoid of all expression. Tweed had earlier asked him to pocket his notebook.

'You don't take notes here unless I request it,' he had informed Buchanan in an amiable tone.

'I had Newman followed here from Southwold,' Buchanan replied eventually. 'He said he was going back to his flat in South Kensington. I suppose it was discretion that led him to omit he was visiting General & Cumbria Assurance.'

A brief smile crossed his face as he repeated the cover name for the SIS engraved on the plate outside the entrance. And normally, Tweed thought, you'd never have got away with that. It confirmed the state of shock Newman was in – combined with no sleep.

17

'So, now you're here, how can I help you?' Tweed enquired.

'The Sandra Riverton murder has a macabre element.' Buchanan paused, hands inside his trouser pockets, very relaxed. 'I don't know whether Newman told you – the victim was hung from a rope inside an old bell tower. It suggests to me either an act of personal revenge or, alternatively, a demonstration to encourage the others, as the French say.'

'Really?' Tweed sounded only half interested. 'And who might be the others?'

'I wish I knew – always assuming that is the case.' A second pause. Tweed began to think the pauses were a Buchanan tactic – to emphasize what he said next. 'Newman did inform me that Riverton had recently been employed by the INCUBUS organization. They seem to be buying up half Europe . . .'

The observation seemed irrelevant, but Tweed doubted whether the man from the Yard ever said anything without a purpose. He kept silent, forcing Buchanan to continue. 'An odd coincidence is the fact that Franklin D. Hauser, chief executive of INCUBUS, has his English home in a mansion not two miles from that bell tower.'

'Probably just a coincidence,' Tweed remarked, 'as you suggested.'

'I paid a call at Livingstone Manor, Hauser's place. A butler, very English, the old school, told me Hauser was abroad. He showed great reluctance to reveal his where-abouts.'

'So you left without finding out?' Tweed's expression was so innocent Monica put up a hand to hide her smile.

'No.' Buchanan finished his coffee, twisted round to hand the cup and saucer to Monica. 'I enjoyed that coffee. Thank you.' He turned back to Tweed. 'I told him this was a murder investigation, that I'd adopt other

18

methods to trace his employer. That remark unsettled Jeeves. He then remembered Hauser was in Finland.'

'You didn't tell him that you have been asked to investigate INCUBUS. Never gave him the slightest hint.'

Monica made her comment to Tweed when Buchanan and Warden had left after a few more minutes' conversation. Paula Grey, a raven haired girl in her early thirties with strong bone structure, had just entered the office. She sat at her desk, crossed her shapely legs, rested her hands in her lap and listened. Tweed's close confidante, she often worked with him in the field.

'No, Monica, I didn't.' Tweed clasped his hands behind his neck. 'That's SIS business. Buchanan is clever. He was here on a fishing trip – trying to find out if Newman had told me something that might help his own investigations.'

'But Bob did just that. He told us that Ed Riverton, who had a top job with INCUBUS, was dragged out of Helsinki harbour,' she shuddered, 'after he had been garrotted.'

'In case everyone has forgotten, I'm still here,' Paula interjected. 'All this sounds a bit grim. Care to bring me up to date, anyone?'

Tweed swivelled to face her, gave a concise résumé of what had happened, including his own new directive from the PM and Newman's visit. Paula listened, watching Tweed, memorizing every detail.

'When do you start this weird co-operation with Washington and Moscow?' she demanded in her direct manner.

'This is very much under wraps.' He threw out his hands in a someday gesture. 'I don't even know who is coming from the States. Just one man – the personal representative of the President and operating entirely on his own. Same with Moscow. The Soviet President's personal choice – also operating on his own. This is the tightest undercover programme ever devised.'

'And the time factor?' Paula pressed.

'Again unknown. Could be weeks, months away. I'll be contacted when the time comes.' Tweed frowned. 'I find the whole business mysterious. It has an almost ghost-like character.'

'But Bob Newman won't stand still,' Paula commented. 'Not after the horrific killing of his girl friend. *He'll* be investigating on his own account.'

'Which may prove invaluable to us,' Tweed pointed out. 'He is the free agent. If he feeds me the data he uncovers it might put us ahead in the game before the battle opens.'

'Would you let me help him?' Paula suggested.

'Have to think about that.' Tweed stood up, began pacing round the office. 'Let's face it – he may not want help of any sort. You know how he is – a lone wolf. That's what made him a successful foreign correspondent.'

'I might be able to persuade him . . .'

'And you might not,' Tweed warned. 'He's in a grim mood about the murder of Sandy Riverton . . .'

'Which may just be connected with the almost simultaneous murder of her husband in Helsinki,' Paula insisted. 'It really is stretching the long arm of coincidence to breaking point – a husband and wife, both recently employed by INCUBUS, both murdered within twenty-four hours of each other. What is Bob's first move?'

'To meet Evelyn, the sister, off the plane from Helsinki. She may just have vital information that will give Bob the lead he's looking for.'

'I can get in touch with Bob at his flat,' Paula said, reaching for her phone.

'No, you can't.' Tweed's tone was brisk. 'First, he

needs sleep. Second, what he's proposing is dangerous. I've got to think about whether I'm going to let you try to link up with him.'

'So I twiddle my thumbs, go through more files?'

Tweed smiled drily. 'No, you don't. You start building up a dossier on all known facts about the International Continental Union Bank, US. With special attention to the man who created that colossus – Franklin D. Hauser.'

2

The headquarters of INCUBUS Oy. in Finland was a new twenty-storey glass block on the western outskirts of Helsinki. The glass was a deep blue colour, opaque, so the outside world could see nothing of what went on inside the heavily guarded building.

On the top floor Franklin D. Hauser was addressing executives inside the large board room. Ten Americans and one Englishman sat on either side of a long gleaming wooden table. Hauser paced slowly back and forth at the far end behind his empty chair as he spoke.

'I have brought you folks here from all over Scandinavia because some of you are fresh from the States and this little old continent is different from back home. That doesn't mean you have to start over again. No, sirree. We're here to establish INCUBUS solid in Europe and we'll do it the American way . . .'

He paused to drink ice water. Swivelled round in his seat to the right of the empty chair, the Englishman, Adam Carver, tall, slim, in his late thirties, watched his chief's performance with concealed amusement.

Hauser, six feet tall and heavily built, in his fifties, wore the uniform of the American executive. A chalk grey suit, a new starched white shirt, a tie with diagonal stripes, the shirt with a button-down collar. Even Hauser's face was standard: plump, clean shaven, pink, smooth as a baby's. Only the ice-blue eyes betrayed the man's ruthless will. He was, Carver thought, in his most folksy mood. I could have written the script, he mused, as Hauser continued.

'But first I'd like to say a few words about myself. I have an estate in Arizona outside Phoenix with forty acres of land and a nice house. I have an apartment on Fifth in New York. I have a mansion and twenty acres in Suffolk, Britain. Wouldn't you say that was all a man needed?'

But you haven't got a wife any more, Carver observed to himself. She ran off with a younger film star. Hauser was talking again after removing his jacket, placing it carefully over the back of his chair.

'So why do I go on expanding the company instead of putting up my feet and shooting the breeze?'

Hauser stood still, arms folded across his powerful chest. Sunlight reflected from the snow outside flashed off his rimless pince-nez perched on the bridge of his strong nose. His executives sat bolt upright in their chairs, gazing at him, anxious to convey the impression they were hanging on his every word. There was not a man present who had not stepped over bodies of rivals to claw his way to his present position. One wrong move and all that in-fighting was on the line, would be thrown away.

'I'll tell you why,' Hauser continued, beaming his famous smile. 'I'm doing it for you people so one day you'll all have what I have. But you'll have to give it all you've got.' The tone had changed, there was an edge to his voice. 'If INCUBUS is going to become the biggest organization in Europe, you're going to have to hit it twenty-five hours a day. You'll have to sleep and dream INCUBUS. It's going to be a full-time job to drag Europe into the twenty-first century. You people are going to do that job. Now I'm going to talk to you later, meantime you go down to Level Five and stay there until you've come up with a plan to infiltrate Finland. You'll have to be cunning, devious, smart. Already I've heard a Finnish businessman say in The Palace restaurant "Those God-damn Yanks are coming." He's behind the times. They're here. Work out a plan to convert this tiny country into a major base for our operation . . .'

His tone had been abrasive, challenging. He took off his pince-nez, perched them higher up his nose, looked down the table.

'Level Five. Get to it. Unless,' he ended in a decep-tively soft tone, 'there are any questions?'

There were no questions. The hard-bitten men round the table knew better than to make that mistake. They had been *told*. Carver watched as they gathered up their files, left the room in single file. Hauser's large hand descended on Carver's shoulder.

'You stay. We'll talk. You can go down later and whip up some action. Twelve hours in Level Five should con-centrate their minds, wouldn't you agree?'

Carver agreed. Level Five was underground. No view of the outside world. A labyrinth of rooms and corridors which had all the welcoming atmosphere of the interrog-ation centre in the Lubyanka in Moscow.

Hauser hunched his large body in his chair and gazed into the distance. His parents had named him after Franklin D. Roosevelt and he had carefully built up a similar outwardly benevolent image. It disarmed his opponents and the image impressed the outside world.

'I have a dream, Adam . . .'

He paused. Echoes of Martin Luther King, Carver thought, but not quite the same meaning to the stirring words. He waited, sensing his chief was in a reflective mood.

23

'I have a dream,' Hauser repeated, 'a vision of a world-wide homeland stretching from the Pacific coast of the States to the Urals. That politico, Gorbachev, is an amateur, a provincial hick who thinks he's made it big. And he talks of a European home from the Atlantic to the Urals. Well my vision is bigger than his. Adam, we're going to take over Europe and the Soviet Union. Dracon is working on the strategy.' He glanced at Carver. 'Frank Galvone is taking over from Ed Riverton.'

Hauser inserted a cigarette into an ivory holder, lit it. Carver, a good-looking man women fell over to meet, kept silent. He wasn't reacting to that ploy. Hauser thought the only way to keep his top men on their toes was to play one off against the other: to hint now and again someone else was after their job. Hence the reference to Galvone.

'A pity Riverton had that nasty accident,' Hauser continued. 'We'll all miss Ed.'

'That Finn, Mauno Sarin, you asked me to handle when he arrived here, said Ed had been garrotted before someone threw him into the harbour,' Carver commented.

'So crime is rearing its ugly head in little old Finland.' Hauser puffed at his cigarette. 'The penalty of growing affluence. Once upon a time the only crime in this neck of the woods was domestic. A jealous husband using an axe on his wife. Sometimes the wife used the axe. Times change. You satisfied this Sarin?' Hauser asked casually.

'He's chief of the Protection Police, so it's odd he was the one to come here. They're political – a small counter-espionage unit. Forty men, maybe a few more.'

'But you satisfied him?'

'I got rid of him. For the moment. I had the feeling he could be back. Don't underestimate him. Sarin is both cynical and shrewd.'

'So he comes back, you see him again. Take him out to dinner, pour champagne down his throat, and later in the

24

evening mention the little titbit that I'm friends with the Finnish President. If that doesn't turn the trick, offer him a nice car. Do it the American way.'

'That won't work with Sarin. He's incorruptible.'

'Adam.' Hauser laid a hand on Carver's arm. 'No one is incorruptible. With some you have to grease the wheels more liberally. And Evelyn Lennox has resigned, taken a walk. I had her followed to the airport. She took a flight for London. *Uno* has her address. Go and see her in a few days. By then our insurance outfit, Fraternal & Equality, will have visited her, offered her a big fat pension. Tied to the usual conditions, of course.'

'Who is going to see her?'

'Papa Grimwood will head the team.'

'Then why do I need to see her?'

'To make sure.' Hauser tilted his large jaw. Carver was familiar with the pose: borrowed from Roosevelt. 'To make sure she's accepted the pension – and the conditions. Her work was of a sensitive nature.' He gave another beaming smile. 'They don't call you The Charmer for nothing, Adam. You'll have her eating out of your hand.'

'What is Frank doing these days?' Carver enquired. 'Haven't seen him around here for a while. He used to spend most of his time in Finland.'

'I'm surprised at you.' Hauser's tone was mild but his dark thick eyebrows lifted. 'Asking questions outside your sphere of operations. And just after you've arrived back. Frank Galvone is still based with Dracon outside Boston.' He smiled again. 'But if you're anxious to see Frank he may be over here soon. It's time you two learned to get along. And now, I guess, you'll want to check up with *Uno* about the Lennox girl.' He opened the briefcase resting on his trouser leg, extracted a piece of plastic. 'There's the new combination. Let me have it back soonest.'

25

It was dismissal time. Carver took the plastic rectangle, nodded, left the room and headed for the elevator. *Uno* was the master computer located below ground level. It recorded every detail of past and present employees of INCUBUS. He was glad Mauno Sarin had no idea of its existence. And he hoped Papa Grimwood would handle the Lennox girl with finesse – assuming the old villain knew what the word meant.

Evelyn Lennox had checked flights to London. She found she could just catch a direct Finnair flight if she hurried. She packed a bag, looked at the phone, checked her watch. No time to call Newman: she would miss her flight. In the street outside her Helsinki apartment she hailed a cab.

'Airport, please. And could you hurry? I'm late for my flight.'

She was so absorbed with not missing the plane she didn't notice the pale faced girl with an aquiline nose and a scraped bone look. The girl started the engine of her Saab and followed the taxi. She was immediately behind Evelyn when the English girl bought her one-way ticket to London.

Aboard the plane as it climbed and headed out over the Gulf of Finland she sat in a daze. Earlier she had, despite Newman's warning, made a brief call to INCUBUS headquarters, leaving a message for her boss that she'd left for England.

Unlike her sister, Sandy, Evelyn was tall and had red hair. She wore a gaberdine suit of dark blue, a white blouse, and her sheepskin was tucked away inside the baggage compartment above her head. Staring down through the window, she gazed at the icefield which was the frozen Baltic. Not the best reason for flying home, but oh God, she was sick of the subzero temperatures, the

26

fact that the sun rose at ten in the morning and set at two in the afternoon. Endless dark which got to you, created a feeling of permanent depression.

Soon she fell fast asleep, worn out by the news Bob Newman had given her, by the earlier experience of the horrible death of Ed Riverton, by having to visit the mortuary to identify him, by the rush to the airport. She woke when the machine bumped something.

Staring out of the window she was astounded to realize she had arrived at Heathrow. She had slept for almost three hours. As the plane taxied along the runway she sighed with relief. No ice, no snow. It might be a sullen grey sky but it would be daylight for hours yet . . .

'That's the Lennox girl, Steve,' said Papa Grimwood, checking the photograph he had obtained from INCUBUS HQ in the West End. All British employees' details were on file. Evelyn was carrying her case to a waiting taxi.

'I have to collect the car from the multistorey,' Steve reminded him.

'So the timing is excellent,' replied Grimwood. 'We have her address in Wandsworth. We'll arrive on her doorstep within fifteen minutes of her getting there. Splendid timing,' he repeated, 'she'll be off balance from her extended flight. And very receptive to our methods of persuasion.'

Evelyn asked the cab driver to stop at the small supermarket near her house, bought the bare necessities for a drink of tea and something simple to eat. She had missed the meal served on the plane. The doorbell rang a few minutes after she had opened the lid of her case and returned downstairs to make herself a cup of tea. She frowned: no one knew she was back. Must be someone selling something. She opened the door and stared at the grotesque couple.

'Mizz Evelyn Lennox?'

It was a gnome-like little man who asked the question after removing his trilby. His face was ruddy and lined and he had a nutcracker nose and chin. He stooped like a hunch-back. Difficult to guess his age – between forty and sixty. Wearing a new sports jacket and grey flannels under his open raincoat. He had squirrel eyes which darted about and he took a good look at her legs beneath her short skirt.

'What is it you want?' she asked, tired from the flight.

'Fraternal & Equality . . .' The gnome's companion showed a printed card, keeping a firm grip on it. 'We're going to make you safe for life, lady.'

'This is Steve,' the gnome introduced. 'I'm Papa Grimwood, senior representative of the company. If we could talk to you inside for a few minutes you won't regret it.'

She hesitated. Steve was six feet tall, heavily built and his clean-shaven pale face showed no expression. Grimwood was smiling in an oily manner. Evelyn had vaguely heard of the company, a subsidiary of INCUBUS. Grimwood edged forward, still smiling.

'We make arrangements for all ex-employees. Financial – for life.'

'Ex-employees of who?'

'INCUBUS.' Grimwood lowered his voice and she had the impression he revealed the information reluctantly. She was too exhausted to resist and showed them into the living room. They waited until she had sat down and then Grimwood hauled a chair closer to her, seated himself. Steve chose a chair to her left so she had to twist round to see him.

'First, we'd appreciate it if you'd sign this document – a small formality,' Grimwood assured her in his most Uriah Heep tone. 'Then you'll receive your pension from

28

Fraternal & Equality. Five hundred pounds a week in cash – for the rest of your life.'

'I don't sign documents without my solicitor checking them.'

As she said the words her mind was calculating. Five hundred a week was twenty-five thousand a year. Grimwood leaned closer. His accent was a peculiar mixture of Cockney and American. Midatlantic. Maybe he'd spent time in the States.

'There are conditions, of course,' Grimwood went on, ignoring her remark. 'You agree never to discuss your work for your recent employer with anyone. Never,' he repeated. 'With no one. Not a whisper.'

She drank more tea. She was damned if she was going to offer refreshment to them. She put down the cup, crossed her legs, clasped her hands on her knees.

'And supposing I did talk to someone about my job?'

'Oh, my dear . . .' Grimwood shook his head mournfully.

'I'm not your "dear",' she snapped.

'My profound apologies. As I was saying, that would certainly not be in your best interests.' Grimwood shook his head again. 'Dear me, no. Your very generous pension would stop at once.'

'And that would be the least of your problems.'

It was the first time Steve had spoken since they'd entered the house. His voice had been harsh, menacing. She swung round to face him.

'What does that mean?'

Steve spread his huge hands, strangler's hands – the thought flashed in Evelyn's mind. He stood up, walked towards her, leant his hands on the arms of her chair.

'Just a few people did make that mistake. They talked. It wasn't good for their health. To take one example, a man was killed in a car accident. Fraternal & Equality always take a great interest in the health of their clients.'

29

For a big man he had a curiously quiet voice, sibilant. He went back to his chair.

'Are you threatening me?' Evelyn asked.

She was frightened, but she was furious, and her brain was ticking over now. These people had turned up with uncanny speed. There had to be some link with Helsinki. Again she began to think about the murder of her brother-in-law.

'Gracious me!' Grimwood leaned closer. 'Papa is concerned about what you've said. Steve was just recalling a little history. Sign the document now and forget about it. Think instead of five hundred pounds – in cash – sent to you by special delivery every week. For the rest of your life . . .'

He broke off as the doorbell rang. Evelyn uncrossed her legs, got up slowly, began to walk to the living room door. Grimwood spoke quickly.

'Get rid of whoever it is. This is your only chance for a pension most people would give an arm and a leg for . . .' He was talking to himself. Evelyn was heading down the hall for the front door.

Newman slowed down as he approached 495 Greenway Gardens, Wandsworth. He thought the name singularly inappropriate: either side was lined with a wall of Victorian terrace villas. Bay windows on the ground and first floors, postage-stamp sized front gardens behind railings, nothing remotely green in sight. He parked a few doors from 495, walked the rest of the way, pushed open the black, freshly painted grille gate, noted the heavy net curtains masking the bay windows, stepped inside the quarry-tiled porch and pressed the bell.

The upper half of the front door was a stained glass window which seemed to emphasize the cloistered atmosphere of the deserted road. Within ten seconds he saw the silhouette of someone approaching beyond the glass. The door was opened and Evelyn stood framed against a long hallway.

Newman grinned and then frowned as a mixture of emotions flashed over her face. Surprise, fright, overwhelming relief. She put a finger to her lips and gestured inside.

'A spot of trouble?' he enquired in a whisper.

She nodded, reached out a hand to usher him inside. He was wearing a trench coat, military style with wide lapels, the collar turned up, belted. He slipped his gloves into his pockets as he followed her over the threshold and she shut the door.

'Two men. From the INCUBUS insurance outfit,' she whispered back. 'The tall one, Steve, threatened me if I refused to sign a document.'

'Let's take a look at them,' he suggested.

She ushered him into the living room, which overlooked the front street and had a large couch in the bay. Chintz furnishings, walls painted magnolia, decorated with framed pictures of water-colour landscapes. Newman's trained reporter's eye took all this in in a glance. He stopped in the centre of the room, staring at the two men.

The crouched gnome-like figure remained seated, gazing at the visitor. The tall heavy, dark-haired with thick brows too close together, stood up and balanced himself on the balls of his feet. A man ready for a fight. Evelyn waved a hand.

'Bob, these two gentlemen are from Fraternal & Equality, an insurance company. This is Mr Grimwood – apparently known as Papa. And this is Steve. No idea of his other name. And this is Robert Newman.'

'Ah!' Grimwood rose slowly to his feet, smiling his oily smile, extending a hand. 'Mr Robert Newman, the famous foreign correspondent. I recognize you from

31

pictures in the papers and news magazines. A pleasure to make your acquaintance, sir.'

Newman ignored the extended hand, looked at the man called Steve who had tucked his right hand inside the lapel of his buttoned jacket. He moved suddenly, took three paces forward. Steve began to slide out the hand holding something. Newman raised his own right hand in a diversionary gesture and whipped up his right foot. It connected savagely with Steve's kneecap. The tall man screamed with pain, slumping forward, Newman's hand came down, nails jabbing into the back of the half-withdrawn hand. Steve yelped and Newman grabbed the gun he was holding. He backed away, looked at Evelyn.

'A Walther PP., 7.65 mm automatic. Who are these people?'

'They are from Fraternal & Equality, the insurance subsidiary of INCUBUS.'

'Really?' Newman held the automatic in the palm of his hand. 'A new way of selling insurance?' he asked the gnome.

'I must apologize profoundly, sir.' Grimwood glanced venomously at Steve who was still doubled over, nursing his kneecap. 'My associate can be impetuous. I think he feared he was about to be attacked by you . . .'

'Answer the bloody question. Is this a new way of selling insurance?'

'I was about to explain, sir. You see, often I carry large sums of cash and need protection. Especially in these days of violence. If you read the papers . . .'

'Forget the papers. Evelyn, what happened before I arrived?'

'They tried to force me to sign that document . . .'

Grimwood grabbed for the bulky sheaf of printed paper but Newman had hold of it. 'Tsk! Tsk! Don't snatch – it's bad manners. The last thing an insurance salesman should display.'

32

'I'm not a salesman,' Grimwood bleated.

'And the only violence so far has been caused by your friend – pardon, your associate – Steve. I wonder if he has a certificate to carry a weapon? Maybe the police would be interested in checking that point? But first things first.' He turned to Evelyn. 'What is this document these two are so anxious you should sign?'

'That's company property . . .' Grimwood had hauled his bulk out of the chair, his manner quite different. 'I must ask you to hand that back to me.'

'And I must ask you to shut your gabby mouth. I was asking my friend here.'

'It's a big fat pension for life,' Grimwood persisted.

'With conditions,' Evelyn snapped.

'So I see.' Newman was skip-reading the second page which, like the first, contained clause after clause. He read one aloud. '"*If at any time the aforesaid beneficiary divulges to anyone details of her confidential employment with INCUBUS then the aforesaid beneficiary will forfeit all further claim to any pension rights hitherto granted whatsoever . . .*"'

Newman folded the document, put it in his pocket, looked at Grimwood. 'That's a new one on me. I don't think you're very nice people.'

'And,' Evelyn interjected, pointing at Steve, who had sagged into an armchair, hugging his knee, glaring at Newman, 'he threatened me. Talked about it not being good for my health if I refused to sign. He also told me about another ex-employee who'd had a fatal motor accident . . .'

'Steve didn't finish his story,' Grimwood whined. 'After the man involved died we paid a large lump sum to his—'

'I'm sure you did,' Newman said sarcastically. His voice changed. 'Get out! Both of you. Now!'

'My knee . . .' Steve began.

'Give you a helping hand,' Newman assured him

33

cheerfully. 'Open the front door, Evelyn.' He grabbed hold of Steve by the scruff of the neck, half lifted, half dragged him to the front door. At the entrance he shoved hard. Steve sprawled on to the pavement as Grimwood hurried down the hall.

'We shall complain. That is an act of violence.'

Newman pulled the Walther automatic out of his pocket, held it on his palm, closed his fingers when Grimwood reached for the weapon. He nodded towards the doorway.

'Shove it. Don't come back.'

3

As Evelyn closed and locked the front door Newman hurried back to the living room. He stood to one side of the bay window and watched beyond the net curtains. Grimwood was half supporting Steve who had clambered to his feet, making their way further along Greenway Gardens.

When they had passed the house he stood in the bay and watched their progress. A large grey Volkswagen van was parked about four houses along the street. Grimwood stopped by the van door, extracted keys, opened the door and helped Steve inside. Grimwood slipped behind the wheel, closed the door, started the engine and slowly moved off.

'They've gone.' Newman turned to Evelyn who stood white faced. She looked even more attractive, her wide mouth a slash of red lipstick, her good bone structure tapering to a pointed determined chin. Her thick red hair

34

rested just below her shoulders on the blue gaberdine and her grey eyes stared back at him. Her expression was grave, so very different from Sandy.

'I could do with a tot of brandy,' she said. 'How about you, Bob?'

'No. Hot tea with a little sugar. You're in a mild state of shock. No wonder. And no alcohol.'

'You're right. Come into the kitchen with me while I brew up . . .'

The kitchen was a surprise. At the back of the house, overlooking a small garden with sour soil and moss-infested lawn, the kitchen was long and galley-like with all the latest equipment. Well laid out, so far as Newman could see while she made the tea. He perched on a stool before asking his question.

'You ignored my warning, didn't you? You phoned INCUBUS before you left Helsinki. And you didn't phone me.'

'I'm usually pretty sensible, but I panicked,' she admitted. 'I didn't have time to call you before catching a flight – but I felt I had to call INCUBUS. I couldn't just walk out on them after three years with the organization. At least that's how I felt then. Now I feel they can get stuffed . . .'

She recalled briefly what had happened after she arrived home. It was only after they had returned to the living room that she asked the question as she poured tea.

'How did Sandy die?'

'Drink some tea.' She was sitting down on the couch with Newman beside her. He waited until she had put down her cup and saucer. 'Sandy's murder was a shocking business. I'll tell you the details later . . .' She gripped his arm to protest but he was firm. 'I said *later*. What was it about your job in Finland which was confidential – to quote from this?' He pulled the sheaf of papers from his pocket.

Newman knew exactly what he was doing, that he was being ruthless – determined to extract information from her during her state of shock when she might talk more openly, when she was very hostile towards her previous employer after her recent experience.

She poured them more tea and he kept silent, anxious not to disturb her present mood. Drinking half her cup she put it down, twisted round to face him, her chin resting in her hand, and told him a strange story.

'As I told you when you came to dinner with Ed and me at his apartment in Helsinki, I'm a trained psychologist – like Sandy. I worked for what INCUBUS called the Profiles – Psychological Research Division. P–PRD. The Americans love initials. The key word is *Profiles*. Let me give you an example. There was an electronics outfit owned by a Finn in Turku, the second largest city. On the Baltic coast and the port where ships come in from Sweden. It was all very hush-hush – that was emphasized from the beginning.'

'What was significant about the electronics outfit?'

'INCUBUS's Finnish subsidiary – INCUBUS Oy. (or Ltd.) – was making a secret bid through another company to take it over. Most of its export trade is with Russia. High-tech stuff – they have Swedish high-flyer scientists working for them. A man called Timo Metsola owned the company outright. I was told to produce a complete profile of him.'

'What sort of profile?'

'The emphasis is on character.' She gazed into the distance and spoke as though reciting a lesson. 'The profile's strengths – strong will-power, physical endurance under pressure, reaction to intense pressure. Then his weaknesses – alcohol, drugs, any physical weakness such as being a diabetic. Any special fears such as

36

vertigo, fear of drowning, dislike of flying, etc.'

'This is weird,' Newman commented. 'Didn't it strike you as a strange technique?'

'Gradually, it did. I eventually became worried and then frightened. I was told the data was needed for the Medical Division – among a host of other activities INCUBUS owns a number of pharmaceutical laboratories. The profiles of outstanding men who'd achieved a lot were supposed to give data for the development of new drugs. After studying Timo Metsola I began to think that was all eyewash – that the profiles had a more sinister purpose.'

'Why?'

'Because I learned by accident INCUBUS was trying to take over his company – and exactly the same thing had happened with another industrialist I'd been asked to draw up a profile for.'

'How on earth did you obtain this information? I realize you're a trained psychologist but give me some details.'

'By trickery and fraud and subversion. That was when I began to question to myself exactly what I was doing. Give you an example? INCUBUS also owns a big business magazine in the States called *Leaders of Mankind*. One of its features is a portrait of some top businessman anywhere in the world. When I first went to see Timo Metsola I had to represent myself as a reporter from that magazine. I had all the credentials.'

'When you first went to see him? You went more than once?'

'It was a series of interviews. Even these big men are flattered at the idea of a major profile in *Leaders*. I'd been trained by the P–PRD Division. What approach to use, which questions to ask, what to look for while I was conducting an interview. While I was talking to Metsola one day he swallowed some medicine. We had got to

37

know each other pretty well by then. He said it was a preparation he had to take for diabetes. I noted that in the detailed report I handed in later.'

'Sounds weird, but hardly sinister.'

'But with the other Finn I interviewed there was something sinister.' Evelyn was playing with a lace handkerchief as she talked, plucking at it nervously. 'He was a shipbuilder – yachts. There's more than one of them in Finland.'

'Tell me about him,' Newman coaxed.

'Let me finish first about Timo. He had no intention of selling his company to anyone. Three months after I'd submitted my profile he sold out to INCUBUS. I built up the same sort of profile about the shipbuilder. And he didn't want to sell. But during the course of the interview it came out his brother was anxious to sell – he was addicted to gambling and owed a lot of money. Also he was the heir. Can you guess what's coming next?'

'Never guess,' Newman replied casually and lit a cigarette.

'Could I have one, please? I've given it up but I need one now.' She looked at him sideways. 'Light it for me.'

It was the first indication Newman had that she was interested in him. Watch it, he warned himself. He lit the cigarette, handed it to her. She took a deep drag, smiled at him, laid a hand on his arm.

'That tastes especially good.'

'What came next?' he asked brusquely.

'The yacht builder was killed in a supposed accident. He'd asked me to go and see him in the evening to continue the interview. There were lights on in all the windows.' She shuddered, took another drag. 'I found him. They'd had a huge fork lift truck on the roof where they stored materials. The truck had toppled off the roof just when he was walking underneath it. The two huge spikes were rammed into his body. They decided the

38

brakes had been defective, that the high wind that night had tipped it over.'

'You believed that?'

'Yes. Until his brother took over the firm and promptly sold it to INCUBUS Oy. And his habit of arriving back late in the evening after dinner to do more work was recorded in my preliminary report. I began to wonder if I was creating profiles for murder. Sounds crazy?'

'Depends. Did you talk to anyone about this?'

'Yes, to the only man I could trust. Ed Riverton, Sandy's husband. He was on the banking side.' She moved closer to Newman.

'As you know, I interviewed Ed during my Helsinki trip – about the banking operations. I got the impression he was being evasive, which roused my curiosity. That's the nasty thing about reporters. You told him all you've told me?'

'Yes. He didn't know anything about Profiles– Psychological Research Division. He was intrigued. Said he was going to investigate it.' Her lips trembled. 'A couple of weeks later they dragged him off the ice in North Harbour.'

'Sounds as though I was right when I decided to poke into the activities of INCUBUS – and Hauser . . .'

He stopped talking as he glanced out of the window. Newman put a finger to his lips to warn her not to speak. Standing up, he walked behind the couch into the bay. The Volkswagen van was back. Parked in the same place as before. The cunning sods had pretended to drive off – in case they were being observed – and had then reversed the vehicle into its original position. There was one difference in its appearance. A large aerial had appeared, projected from the roof, an aerial similar to those used by Post Office vans detecting people who didn't pay their TV licence.

Newman frowned at Evelyn to make her continue

keeping quiet. He began a swift and expert search of the room. A Swiss he had once known had taught him how to locate bugging mechanisms. He switched on the radio, continued looking. The bug was attached to the back of the TV set. He held it in his hand, put it back, twiddled the radio knob from pop music to atmospherics, turned up the volume.

'They bugged you,' he whispered. 'Now we'll feed them some disinformation. Be ready to play along with what I say.'

He turned the knob back to pop music, turned the volume down to almost nothing, began talking to Evelyn.

'So you have this aunt in Ambleside you're going to visit?'

'That's right, Bob. I just want to get away from my normal surroundings.'

'Ambleside in the Lake District is a good choice. Of course it's small – everyone knows everyone else and what's going on. But that kind of local gossip will ease the tension out of you. You've decided then to leave today?'

'I just want to leave London as fast as possible,' Evelyn replied, playing along.

'I'll give you a hand with the packing. Then I'll drive you to the station. That way I'll make sure we're not followed. If we are, I'll spot them . . .'

He turned up the volume loud, turned the knob to atmospherics, walked quickly to the window. Within two minutes the automatic aerial was retracted and the Volkswagen drove off.

Newman sat down, deliberately choosing the armchair Grimwood had occupied, leaving Evelyn on the couch.

'What was all that about?' she asked, the anxiety clear in her voice.

'They bugged you, as I said.' He opened his hand. 'They're making them smaller and smaller. It's called progress – the advance of science.'

'When could they have done that? I opened the door to them. I was with them all the time . . .'

'Not when you answered the door to me,' he pointed out. 'I am sure one of them attached this little blighter to your TV set in the short time you were showing me in. They're a crafty couple. Professionals. When they reached their van they drove off a short distance in case I was observing them. Then they backed the vehicle, elevated the aerial, listened in and tape-recorded our conversation; that would be my guess. We have to recall what we said, what they now know.'

'And Ambleside?'

'To protect you. They'll be convinced you're off to the Lake District today. That bit I put in about knowing if we were being followed when I drove you to the station will stop them trying to do just that, will keep them away from here. And I handed it to them on a plate. Ambleside. A small place. Everyone knows everyone else. They'll think you'll be easy to find there. They'll scoot off to the Lake District and search round for days.'

'It might work.' She brightened up. 'It *will* work.'

'And they'll be slowed down because they'll have to be discreet. I kept Steve's Walther – I might report that to the police. My guess is a quite different couple will be sent to track you down.'

'They found me here quickly enough,' she reminded him. 'I was back here and less than half an hour afterwards they were on my doorstep.'

'Let's think how they worked that one.' He frowned. 'It suggests some high-powered organization. First, you made the mistake of phoning INCUBUS before you caught your flight from Helsinki . . .'

'I'm sorry . . .'

He dismissed her apology with a curt wave of his hand. 'Let me go on. How they recognized you is what puzzles me. At Heathrow, I mean. I think they followed you here

41

from when you left the airport. What sort of records do they keep at their headquarters for this country in Norwich?'

'You mean about employees? Very detailed. Including photocopies of birth certificates, mortgages – even when they're your own, like mine. And photographs . . .'

'That's it. Those two had a photo to watch for you coming off the plane – which means you must have been followed to Helsinki Airport. Nice people.'

'You said we must think about what they know from bugging us while we were talking after they'd gone.'

'That's important. They know you have talked to me about your secret work. They know I'm investigating the octopus called INCUBUS. That will make my future investigations a little more difficult, but I can handle that. Now I know that they know.'

She stood up, carried a hardback chair close to Newman, sat down, placed a hand on his knee. 'Now. How did Sandy die? I need to know.'

'She was hung up with a rope round her neck. Suspended from a beam in an old bell tower in Suffolk where we'd planned to meet early in the morning . . .'

'Oh, dear God! Sandy . . .'

Newman went on talking fast. 'I was the one who found her. And that makes me number one suspect for her murder . . .'

As if he had triggered off a signal the doorbell rang. They looked at each other. Newman moved her hand, stood up and pressed his own hand on her shoulder to keep her seated. He went to answer the door himself, his right hand gripping the Walther automatic. He had paused in the hall to double-check the magazine was loaded.

Beyond the stained glass window he could make out two male silhouettes. Both tall. At least Grimwood & Co. hadn't returned. He opened the door.

Chief Inspector Roy Buchanan, with Sergeant Warden beside him, stood gazing at him. Buchanan raised an eyebrow before he spoke.

'Well, well. Mr Robert Newman again. We musn't keep meeting like this. People will talk.'

4

Adam Carver had spent longer than he'd expected with *Uno*. The computer was located inside a vault at Level Five – well away from the windowless conference room. Due to an appointment with a major client, he had returned late in the afternoon. Earlier, using the password, he had flashed on the screen all the data on Evelyn Lennox. What had startled him was that she had a sister, Sandra Riverton, who had worked for INCUBUS in Suffolk.

Uno. The nickname had been coined by Hauser himself and Carver found it childish. The President of INCUBUS, shrewd and ruthless, had a naïve streak. Carver had tapped keys and up came the data on the Lennox girl. He stared at it,

Age: Twenty-eight. Nationality: Brit. Description . . .
Occupation: Trained psychologist. Employed Finland.
Division: P–PRD. Rating: A1. Track record: Ultra.
Defects: Related to Sandra Riverton (Sister), employed
INCUBUS, Suffolk, Brit. Zone.

There was a a lot of other stuff he skip-read. It was the final word which caught his attention. *Cancelled.* Followed by a date three weeks earlier. Carver pressed more

43

keys and signed off. The screen went blank, unlike his mind. He sat quite still for ten minutes, thinking.

His mind was in a whirl and he was worried. He then lifted the phone to call Peggy Vanderheld, Hauser's statuesque and hard-bitten personal assistant. When giving interviews to the press Hauser liked to paint a picture of himself as the company's father figure.

'Just because I happen to be President of this company I don't play the Great White Chief,' he was fond of saying. 'My door is always open to any employee who has a problem. Night and day I'm available to the folks who work for us.'

It was a load of crap – like his speech that morning to the executives. His only concern was their future, to help them higher up the ladder? Bullshit. Carver was the Senior Vice President, Banking Loans. A qualified accountant, his official job was to raise funds, find more money. And there were twelve more Senior Vice Presidents across the far-flung empire of INCUBUS. Some were more senior than others.

'Peggy? Adam here. Level Five. I need to see Franklin D. When can he fit me in?'

'That could be difficult. He has a tight schedule . . .'

Damn! Adam had a date with a promising Finnish brunette for that evening. He was confident he'd brought her to the stage where he could lay her. Strike while the iron is hot.

'He asked me to check data on a recent employee. I've checked. He wants me to take action. There are queries before I can do that.'

'Which employee?' Peggy's American voice was a whiplash.

'Evelyn Lennox. Just mention that name to him. Plus I have questions to ask.'

'Hold it . . .'

Adam swore again while he waited. He'd booked a

good table at The Palace. His date had a Finnish boy friend but he knew he was prising her loose. With women you had to keep persisting before they sank into your arms.

'Carver!' Peggy was back on the line. 'Can you come now? Good. Move the butt.'

The connection was broken. Arrogant bitch. They said she carried inside her pretty head more secrets than *Uno*. That she was the only woman Hauser trusted. Had he something on her, Adam wondered as he closed the vault and headed down the corridor walled with stainless steel for the elevator.

Hauser was sitting in his de luxe, specially designed, black leather swivel chair behind a huge mahogany desk in his private office. The walls were panelled in mahogany except for the fourth wall behind him. This was solid glass with a panoramic view over a forest-fringed lake, which was really an arm of the sea.

He took the cigarette holder out of his wide mouth and beamed at his visitor, his Roosevelt smile, warm and toothy. Carver knew for a fact that Hauser had a collection of Roosevelt film clips, that he studied them to perfect the famous American president's mannerisms.

'Your timing is perfect,' Hauser announced. 'Frank has just arrived. Straight from the airport. He's on his way up now. Isn't that nice. A while since you two got together.'

He's playing with me again, Carver thought. Frank Galvone was also a senior vice president. Information and Planning was his division, whatever that might mean. And he was the last person Carver needed just now. The door opened. No respectful knock. Frank Galvone walked in, clad in a snow-covered sheepskin which trailed his ankles, the fur thick with snow. Beyond the window Carver could see a blizzard creaming down, blotting out the sea.

'Hi!' Galvone shook snow from the sheepskin, took it

off, dumped it in a chair. 'Almost as bad as New York here,' he remarked in his low husky voice.

'Frank, you've messed up my beautiful carpet,' Hauser told him mildly and smiled.

Galvone glanced down at the wall-to-wall shag carpet, shrugged. He pressed a button next to the door.

'We have peasants to vacuum the place. Make them work – if you don't want them to spend the day, and your money, sitting with their feet up.'

Peggy Vanderheld, clad in a navy blue form-fitting suit, came into the room. Galvone gestured at the carpet. 'Clean up this mess – and fast. We have a meeting under way.'

She glared at him venomously but went out, came back with the machine, sucked up the snow, left without a word. Carver spoke quickly, nodding towards Galvone's back as the American stared at the blizzard. He said this was something private.

'If it's the Evelyn Lennox problem, go ahead, Adam,' Hauser encouraged him. 'After all, we have no secrets from Frank. By the by, he called in at London on his way from New York.'

'Just a brief stopover,' Galvone said, turning round.

Carver nodded. Why had Frank found it necessary to provide that bit of information?

Galvone was a first generation American with his roots in Italy. Shorter than Carver – five foot seven – he was heavily built with wide shoulders and stocky legs. Clean shaven, his hair was black, as were his thick brows. His face was very bony, cadaverous. His cheekbones were prominent, his nose was long, his chin was aggressive, skeletal. Carver had never seen him smile. His brown eyes were blank.

'Now,' Hauser said genially, 'I have my two top men with me. I always feel comfortable in your presence.'

Carver said nothing: Hauser was up to his usual tactics

46

– playing off one man against the other. He frequently referred to Carver as 'my potential successor. In a few years he'll have developed a big enough ass to occupy my chair.'

But then Carver had heard that on other occasions he used the same language about Galvone. And he suspected Galvone took the rivalry very seriously indeed.

'OK.' Hauser settled himself more comfortably in his chair. 'Adam, tell us about Evelyn Lennox.' He looked at Galvone. 'He's going to check her out in London. Left the company at a moment's notice, flew back there. We just want to be sure everything is hunky-dory.'

'Why shouldn't it be?' Frank asked.

'Adam will tell us.'

Frank remained standing as Carver was ushered with a wave of the hand to sit down. 'Evelyn Lennox had a sister, a Sandra Riverton, who also worked for us,' he began slowly, staring at the floor. 'Is there a connection between these two?'

'Leave it there,' Hauser said amiably. 'You have to concentrate on the financial side. All you need to do is to make sure she's happy with her pension. Get her general reaction to life. What she's going to do next. You know the sort of thing.'

'I'm not sure I do.'

'You're The Charmer,' Frank interjected with a sneer. 'We all know you have the ladies in the palm of your smooth hand. Wouldn't do to send me.' He made a sound like a sly chuckle. 'I might end up knocking her teeth out.'

'I wouldn't put it past you,' Carver snapped.

'Now that's not a nice thing to say to a fellow vice president. Lost your sense of humour, Adam? It was a joke. J-O-K-E – you do know what a joke is?'

Hauser settled himself even more comfortably. There was nothing he enjoyed more than seeing a couple of his

47

subordinates at each other's throats. Better than a bull fight.

Carver looked at him, caught his fleeting expression, made a great effort to cool it. He nodded to Frank.

'OK. It was a joke. Fair enough.' He turned to Hauser. 'While I was checking the computer I came across a reference to the P–PRD. That's a division I'd never even heard of before. What the blazes does it stand for? What sort of work was Evelyn Lennox engaged on? And why is it coded with initials? All the other divisions have their functions spelt out. Like Frank's. Information and Planning.'

'What the hell has that got to do with you?' demanded Frank.

Carver turned to look at him, showing no particular reaction. Inwardly he was surprised by the vehemence in Frank's voice. Vehemence? Almost vicious fury.

'If I'm to talk to Evelyn Lennox,' he said calmly, 'I need to brief myself in advance with anything she might throw at me.'

'You've got no goddamned right to go poking around in that computer,' Frank snarled.

'Now, boys,' Hauser intervened, 'a bit of push and shove is OK, but you're shoving too hard, Frank. If you can't control your temper you'd better go down to the canteen and help yourself to a drink. Of mineral water.'

There was a snap in his tone and Carver watched as Frank struggled to compose his features. His opponent made a throwaway gesture with his hands, gave a sheepish grin which was more a grimace.

'Sorry, Chief. Those long flights can get to you. Jet lag can creep up on you. Think I'll sit down, rest the body and just listen while Adam tells the tale.'

Jet lag? From a three-hour flight, at the outside, when he'd only flown from London to Helsinki on the last lap? Carver was careful not to comment on the thought. He looked back at Hauser who started talking rapidly.

'I take your point, Adam. Why Sandra Riverton resigned from the company I've no idea. That kind of detail just doesn't reach me. I can't afford to get bogged down in the weeds. But at least you know she did leave. Maybe a coincidence, maybe the two girls talked on the phone, decided they'd both had enough. As to Ed Riverton, all we know is what the police told us. And you have the advantage, Adam, that you talked with this Mauno Sarin. Now, you're briefed, as you put it.'

'Not quite. What sort of work were these girls doing for us?'

'Women are a damned nuisance and I could do without hiring a single female. Their job is at home, in bed and then doing the cooking. But sometimes because they are female they're more suitable for interviewing men susceptible to so-called feminine charm.'

'You mean they were call girls?' Adam enquired.

'Hell, no!' Hauser pounded his huge fist on the desk and glared. 'They were secretarial types – like Peggy. Adam, you've got what you need. Catch the earliest flight down to London, check up on the Lennox twist. OK?'

Hauser waited until he was alone with Galvone, stubbed out a cigarette savagely, lit a fresh one. He took several puffs and Galvone was careful to keep quiet. It was unusual for Hauser to blow his top. When he spoke he seemed calmer and under control.

'You have a job, Frank.'

'Which is?'

'Board the same flight Carver takes to London. Go Economy and make sure he doesn't see you. Follow him, observe him, report back to me personally. Travel Section will tell you the flight he's on.'

'May be difficult to make sure he doesn't spot me.'

'Difficult? Disguise yourself. Fresh clothes. A ski outfit. Goggle glasses. Anything!' He stared at Galvone.

49

'Hell, you've had experience very recently of handling some tricky situations, taking instant decisions, and they came out just the way we wanted them. That's it. Tail Carver.'

5

Inside the living room at 495 Greenway Gardens Buchanan sat in the armchair Grimwood had occupied, legs stretched out, crossed at the ankles. He faced Newman and Evelyn on the couch in the bay. Sergeant Warden sat in the hard-backed chair, notebook at the ready. The conversation continued.

'Would you mind telling me how you heard your sister, Sandra Riverton, had been murdered?' Buchanan asked Evelyn, his grey eyes watching hers.

'I phoned her from London,' Newman said quickly. 'Which is why she flew back immediately from Helsinki.'

'I was asking Miss Lennox.' There was an edge to Buchanan's tone. 'Perhaps you would be good enough to let her answer for herself.'

'You do realize she's not obliged to put up with an interrogation?' Newman rapped back. 'We could show both of you the door. Unless you're charging her with something. That, as I understand it, is the law.'

'I do know my law,' the Chief Inspector replied equably. He rattled some change in his pocket. 'Do you wish to show me the door, Miss Lennox?'

'I am rather upset . . .'

'She's undergone some pretty awful ordeals,' Newman persisted. 'Do you normally question people when they're in no fit state to think clearly? I'm sure it would be best if you both went, deferred this interview until a more suitable occasion.'

'You own this house? Or part-own it?' Buchanan asked in the same mild tone.

'No . . .'

'Then kindly let Miss Lennox take whatever decision she may wish without prompting from you.'

'I really am very upset at the moment,' Evelyn replied, taking her cue from Newman.

Buchanan swung his gaze to Newman. 'A moment ago you referred to *several* ordeals. What did you mean by that?'

'For God's sake! She had just heard in Helsinki her brother-in-law has been hauled out of the frozen harbour. With his throat garrotted, in case you'd forgotten. Then she hears her own sister has been murdered under horrible circumstances. Hence, Chief Inspector, the use of the plural.'

'I have an excellent memory. I had not forgotten about Mr Riverton's death. I hardly would – you told me only a few minutes ago.' Buchanan was speaking in a monotone. 'But you made it sound like more than *two* ordeals.'

He clasped his hands in his lap and waited, studying Newman's reaction.

'I can't help what it sounds like to your tortuous mind. I was referring to both murders. Period.'

'Which is a weird coincidence – since both crimes appear to have been committed within about twenty-four hours of each other.' He look at Evelyn. 'And you said your sister had a similar job to yourself. What was the nature of these jobs?'

'Oh, we were just secretaries. Chief Inspector, I'm flaked out now. Could you leave this for a few days until I'm fresher?'

'Of course.' Buchanan stood up, putting on his coat as

51

Warden stood at the same time. 'I'll try and phone you before we come next time. Please don't bother – we can find our own way out.' At the door he turned and spoke to Newman. 'As for you, I would remind you I am conducting a murder investigation.'

Newman smiled grimly. 'And I'm hardly likely to forget that. Especially after the grilling you gave me at Southwold.'

The hint of a smile appeared at the corners of Buchanan's mouth, a cynical smile. 'And you appear to have calmed down very quickly, Mr Newman.'

On this parting shot he left. Newman followed them as they closed the door. He locked it. 'What did that mean?' Evelyn asked as he came back into the room.

'That he's a very shrewd and dangerous opponent. I'd pretended to lose my temper and he spotted it.'

'Why didn't you tell them about that ghastly couple – Grimwood and Steve? I gathered you weren't going to tell him, so I kept quiet too.'

'Which was smart of you. It would just have confused the issue.' He looked at her. 'That's not quite honest – I want to follow up that investigation myself. I would have told him if I'd thought there was a cat's chance in hell he'd have provided a guard for you – a constable on your doorstep.'

'And he wouldn't have done that?'

'Definitely not, on the evidence of what happened. No one physically attacked you, thank God. These days the Met. are always moaning they're short of staff. Too busy joy-riding in their nice shiny patrol cars to hoof it on the beat.'

'Bob.' She was standing close to him, he caught a whiff of expensive perfume. 'Couldn't you stay with me for a few days in case those men come back.' She paused. 'You could sleep in the spare bedroom.'

And how long would you expect me to stay there?

Newman was thinking. It simply wasn't on. His mind was full of Sandy, of the memory of her hanging like a rag doll. The idea of risking bedding her own sister was repugnant. He shook his head.

'That's not a good idea, Evelyn. I want to devote all my time to finding out who murdered Sandy. The longer I wait, the colder the trail will get. Buchanan could have told you that. Do you know a good locksmith?' She nodded without enthusiasm. 'Then get the locks changed on that front door. Deadlocks. Chubb or Banham. If I call you on the phone I'll ring twice, put down the receiver, do the same thing again. When the phone rings a third time answer it. That guarantees it will be me. Otherwise don't pick it up, no matter how long it rings.'

'Why would they call me?'

'They probably won't. But they just might to make certain you're not here – that you have left for the Lake District.'

'All right, you're going to be busy. So am I. There are the details of Sandy's funeral to be attended to. No, don't offer to help – I can manage on my own. I'm the only family she had left. Will you be attending?'

He refused to be roused by her anger, suspecting she was furious he'd turned down her invitation to stay. As he put on his coat he smiled.

'If there is any way I can help, all you have to do is to call me. And here is my card. Don't forget, Evelyn, I was very fond of Sandy. I was on the verge of asking her to marry me.

'Perhaps in that way she had a lucky escape.'

For the second time he ignored an insult. She was flaked out, as she'd said. Too much horror in too short a space of time.

'Think it over,' he urged her. 'But above all, be careful.'

* * *

'Now I have another problem,' Tweed announced as he took off his Burberry in his office. 'Since the INCUBUS investigation looks like taking some time to get off the ground I can at least devote my attention to this new one.'

Paula Grey and Monica exchanged glances. It was evening and Tweed seemed excited. He had just returned from a fresh session with the PM at Downing Street. He settled himself behind his desk, wearing his heaviest grey suit. Outside it was a raw bitter February night.

'Why is the INCUBUS problem going to take time to get to grips with?' Paula asked.

'Because it involves a lot of research – maybe months. I have people working on it already but it's a world-wide organization and the structure is complex. Maybe deliberately so, but that's only an educated guess.'

'So what is this new problem?'

'Europe, as you know, is like a boiling cauldron. Frontiers which have held for over forty years are no longer sacred. The Communist apparatus is collapsing everywhere, thanks to Gorbachev. But this leaves some very dangerous and experienced experts without a job. Can you guess?'

'You often say guessing isn't good enough in our work.'

'True.' Tweed smiled at the gentle rebuke, then became grave. 'The experts I'm talking about are the ex-members of various secret services and police forces. Suddenly – overnight – they're not wanted. Worse, from their point of view, some of the top-flight agents *are* wanted – so they can stand trial. Are you with me now?'

'Yes.' Paula looked rueful. 'You're playing a favourite trick . . .'

'Teasing,' Monica interjected. 'Tantalizing us while you lead up to something.'

'A number of the most efficient Communist agents – therefore the most sought after to settle accounts with – have disappeared without trace.'

'Disappeared?' Paula was startled. 'Couldn't they have been secretly shot?'

'No, they've escaped. From several Balkan countries in turmoil. And from what used to be the iron state of East Germany. Western agents – including our own – have verified they have simply vanished. It's worrying the PM and the more reports I study the more my anxiety grows. It has all the hallmarks of a master plan.'

'What on earth could they achieve? They're discredited and have nowhere to go,' Paula protested.

'Can we be sure of that? Supposing they are being formed into a new secret police – with the aim of destroying *glasnost* and *perestroika*? They would be a formidable group – men and women trained in the skills and methods of STASI, the old East German secret police, the Romanian *Securitate*, etc. Europe is in a state of turbulence in the East. Fertile soil for professional activists.'

'Have you any names – specific individuals?' Paula pressed.

'I can give you one which will send shivers up your spine – Ion Manescu. And a Romanian woman in London swears she saw him in the street as he dived into a taxi. A few days ago.'

In Lapland the Lear Executive jet began its radar-guided descent to Rovaniemi airfield in the dark. North of the Arctic Circle, it was always dark in February. Endless night. There were eleven men and one woman inside the cabin. None of the passengers had spoken a word to each other since taking off from Helsinki.

As the jet continued its descent they began to muffle themselves in fur against the subzero temperature on the snow- and ice-covered ground. Fur hats with ear muffs, heavy fur coats, fur-lined boots.

The thin-faced man with a Slavic face in the seat nearest the exit door at the front already wore specially made fur boots of a curious design with pointed toes. He ran a hand over his smooth face beneath his hooked nose.

Ion Manescu felt naked without the curved moustache he had shaved off. He was the first passenger ready to disembark as the jet landed, slowed to a halt. He peered out of the window at the moonlit landscape. Scrubby bushes festooned with ice crystals which gleamed. A barren prospect: more like a moonscape, but the airfield was many kilometres away from the town of Rovaniemi, an airstrip in the wilderness.

The steward opened the exit door when the plane was stationary and dropped the retractable stair ladder. Opposite Manescu a German, Helmut Ziegler, ex-STASI chief in Leipzig, rose to leave the aircraft. Manescu put out a hand to halt him.

'After me, if you please,' he said in German. 'Better that we establish priorities of rank from the start.'

He stood, his bulk barring the progress of the German, who glared. Then, in the light reflected from the snow, he saw Manescu's dark eyes gazing back at him. A veteran of the STASI, he shivered – partly from the icy air flooding inside the machine, but partly from Manescu's expression.

'Please,' Manescu continued and descended the ladder.

The file of other passengers followed him across the iron-hard snow to where a queue of strange vehicles waited for them, engines ticking over. Each vehicle had two enormous thick tyres at the front, two more at the back. In the weird glow of Arctic moonlight they looked like a cross between powerful motor bikes and beach buggies. The maker's name was inscribed along the chassis: Suzuki.

Within two minutes all the passengers were aboard their allotted transport and the cavalcade of machines, engines purring and sputtering sparks, moved off. It headed away from the distant airport building, a single-storey edifice, away from the main road to Rovaniemi, heading east cross-country into the wilderness.

Manescu adjusted his snow goggles as white flakes the size of cats' tails began to drift down. He was satisfied. He had asserted his authority. Always you must begin as you mean to go on.

6

Adam Carver walked out of London Airport and joined the taxi queue. He had travelled Business Class from Helsinki. As he stood in the drizzling rain he welcomed it: the contrast in temperature was huge compared with Helsinki. Here the weather had turned mild. As he waited several women looked at him. One said to her friend in a whisper:

'He's a handsome bastard. I wouldn't mind at all.'

'You're wicked,' her companion responded and giggled, gazing at Carver.

A late arrival came out between the automatic doors, stared at the queue, walked back inside to join the uniformed chauffeur who had been waiting and holding a card. *Mr Shade.* The chauffeur was carrying the passenger's bag but his client had insisted on carrying his executive case himself.

'The car is in the short-term car park. I'll take you to it, sir.'

'Then move. He's in the cab queue. My guess is you've got five minutes,' snapped Frank Galvone.

He had travelled aboard the same flight from Helsinki but in Economy Class, not an experience the Vice President of Information and Planning had enjoyed. He wore a leather beret to conceal his black hair, tinted wraparound glasses and a coat turned up at the collar which masked the lower half of his face.

Information and Planning, he was thinking as he walked up the ramp, shoulders stooped to further alter his appearance. Inside the Dracon think-tank building near Boston off what used to be known as Space Highway, the Division was known to the favoured élite who worked there – academics and strategic researchers – as Information and Action. That was where the master plan was being perfected.

'That guy just getting into a cab,' he said five minutes later as the chauffeur drove out of the car park. 'Follow him, don't lose him. But your first priority is don't get found out.'

Which is one hell of an instruction, Charlie Bone, the chauffeur, thought. Typically American. He was careful not to argue the point as he followed Carver's taxi through the tunnel. Charlie was a cockney by birth but he'd spent time in New York.

And Charlie was probably the most highly paid chauffeur in London. Paid to keep his mouth shut. He had developed a terrible memory for who he drove and where he drove them to. He needed the big money. Charlie had a liking for the girls: high-class Sloane Rangers. And diamonds were a *man's* best friend when it came to making it with the opposite sex.

Behind the closed glass screen of the limousine, separating driver from passenger, Galvone opened his executive case. Disguised as toilet equipment all the apparatus was there – the listening device and several sophisticated miniaturized bugs. Before Carver had left Helsinki Galvone had secreted a tiny bug inside Carver's case.

'495 Greenway Gardens, here we come,' he said to himself.

Evelyn was feeling very lonely when the doorbell rang. She was also wary. She opened the front door on the chain and her eyes widened. Half expecting to see the hideous little creep, Grimwood, with his partner, Steve, the smartly dressed good-looking man standing there was a surprise.

'Yes?' she said.

'My name's Adam Carver. Here's my card.' He passed his embossed visiting card through the gap. 'I remember passing you in the corridor at the INCUBUS building in Helsinki. You were wearing a blue gaberdine suit and a white blouse with a pussy bow at the neck.'

Evelyn rather liked that. She liked his appearance, his manner. And he was a senior vice president. But she was still wary.

'You've come to persuade me to accept the pension, haven't you?'

'No. Look at the card again. I'm on the banking side. I heard you'd left and I had business over here.' He smiled. 'I expect you'll think it was a colossal cheek, but I called the Norwich HQ to get your address.'

'Are you alone?' She peered through the gap.

Carver opened his unbuttoned raincoat and smiled again. It was a pleasant smile. 'Look, no one here but me. No one hidden inside my mac.'

She returned his smile, took off the chain, asked him to come inside. Leading him into the living room, she indicated the armchair for him to sit in. Carver nodded, walked to the window.

'This is a spacious bay,' he said from the far side of the couch. 'Pity it stares out at a row of other houses.'

'That's London.'

Carver stood holding his executive case. He had paid off the taxi, had given the driver a generous extra to drop his suitcase at the Hilton in Park Lane. He frowned as he gazed down the road to where a black limo was parked.

'Could we talk in your kitchen?' he suggested, turning back to her. 'Somewhere we can have running water while we chat?'

Her reaction was as though he'd hit her in the face, then she recovered, left the room and walked into the kitchen at the end of the hall. Turning on a tap, she confronted him.

'Not again, for God's sake.'

He said nothing, perched his executive case on a working surface, opened it, searched it swiftly. He found the bug behind the rear lining, held it up, placed it in the sink, reduced the water pressure to a steady flow and eased the bug underneath it.

'There's a limousine parked down the road,' he told her. 'I think there's a certain individual inside with listening apparatus. If it's who I think it is I'd like to go out there and knock his teeth down his throat. That thing under the tap is a bug . . .'

'I know. I've used them myself . . .'

She stopped speaking and cursed her impetuosity. Carver lifted an eyebrow, said, 'I see. I wondered how you caught on so quickly to the trick of running water which will blot out all our conversation. And that bug must have been inserted in my case before I left Helsinki – without my knowledge.'

'Would you like some coffee and then we could talk?'

That was her desperate need: to have someone she could talk to. Carver said he'd love a cup and carefully chose a stool to perch on well away from the chairs round the table. In that way he wouldn't be too close to her.

He was experiencing a mixture of emotions. Fury at the trick played on him. But above all ironic amusement at how things had worked out. Because he'd found – and shown her – the bug, he'd gained Evelyn's confidence in nothing flat.

In the rear seat of the limousine Galvone was fiddling with his listening apparatus. All he could get was atmospherics, a gushing sound like running water.

He swore foully to himself, then wondered. Was it possible? The Charmer had a great reputation with women, something he secretly envied. But he'd only been inside the place a few minutes. Was it possible Carver was already screwing Evelyn in the bathroom? Maybe later he'd get the information he was after during pillow talk. It was the way Galvone's mind worked.

'. . . so,' Evelyn continued, 'while these two creeps, Grimwood and his pal Steve were here, Bob Newman, the foreign correspondent, arrived. To cut a long story short, he threw them out of the house. Then they came back later in their Volkswagen – which is when Bob found the bug they'd attached to the back of the TV set.'

'And you say this Steve character had a gun?' Carver asked.

He was still perched on the stool while Evelyn sat on the far side of the kitchen table. Don't crowd her, he reminded himself.

'Yes, a Walther something or other. Bob took it away from him and kept it. Later Bob left.' She drank more coffee, put her cup down on the table, looked Carver in the eye. 'I took his advice,' she lied. 'As soon as he'd gone that was when I called the police. They have someone watching this house. Will you excuse me a moment?'

She went back down the hall into the living room, walked into the bay, pulled back one of the net curtains.

To her right, four houses down the street, a black limousine was parked. She dropped the curtain, returned to the kitchen and sat in her chair.

'I have to signal the police at regular intervals that I'm OK,' she continued lying.

Evelyn liked Carver, but he was INCUBUS. After her recent experience she was taking no chances. His next question made her glad she had bluffed him.

'What about that pension document? Did you sign it? Did you agree to accept their terms?'

'Not bloody likely. You think I should accept?' she asked, gazing at him innocently.

'I can't advise you on a thing like that. You must make up your own mind. It's your life.'

She drank more coffee to conceal her expression. Had that been another threat. Subtly phrased, but still a threat? She looked straight at him again.

'Just why have you come to see me, Mr Carver?'

'Adam. I thought we'd agreed that.' He put down his own cup, stood up. 'I came because I liked what I saw when you passed me in the corridor back in Helsinki. Would you have dinner with me? Maybe tonight?'

'Not tonight, Adam. Let me think about it.'

'I'll have to be going. I'm staying at the Hilton. Maybe I'll call you from there.' He took out a notebook, wrote something on it, tore off the top sheet, put it on the table. 'That's the hotel number. Just in case for some reason you want to call me . . .'

She phoned for a taxi which arrived in a few minutes. At the door he saw out of the corner of his eye the black limousine was still there.

Once the cab had left Wandsworth behind it ran into heavy traffic. Carver, his executive case on his knees, the bug inside it, thought over what he'd learned from Evelyn Lennox.

The gun bothered him. Since joining INCUBUS it was the first time he'd come across men who carried guns – outside the States. And he still didn't know any details of Evelyn's job with INCUBUS. She had evaded every probing question on that subject.

As the traffic ground to a halt he glanced round and then behind him. Two vehicles back the black limo was in sight. Impossible to see who the passenger in the rear seat was. Eventually the traffic moved on, crossing the Thames bridge.

When Carver alighted outside the Hilton in Park Lane the limo drove past at speed. Again he found it impossible to identify the passenger.

7

In Lapland the cavalcade of snow buggies bumped and rocked their way through the night over rough terrain. In the moonlight Ion Manescu, sitting in the lead vehicle, peered through his snow goggles at the rolling wilderness. The ground they travelled over was studded with boulders buried in snow-covered moss. In places vehicles which had preceded them along the track had exposed the sterile moss.

Moving in a north-easterly direction towards the Soviet border, they were approaching the shore of an ice-bound lake. Manescu checked his watch. 1 a.m. He glanced at the bearded driver of his vehicle.

'How much further?' he asked in English.

'We are there.'

The bleak landscape would have depressed most

63

people, but Manescu was used to the winters in Romania. As the driver spoke they crested a low ridge. Below Manescu saw a complex of concrete buildings and a circular tower block surrounded by a high wire fence.

Double gates opened automatically and the cavalcade moved inside the perimeter. Driving slowly, Manescu's vehicle entered a huge cavernous opening where a steel door had risen, again automatically. Inside the cavern fluorescent lights threw a weird glow as the vehicle descended a ramp deep into the earth.

The underground complex had been built in summer, the construction teams working in three shifts round the clock. Manescu had noticed a network of aerials, wires and dishes mounted on the roof. They reminded him of a Distant Early Warning System.

'What is this place officially?' he asked as the buggy turned a corner into a vast garage. Manescu estimated they must by now be three levels below the surface of the earth.

'The most advanced Meteorological Institute in the world. And an Observatory. Here they study climatic changes – and the heavens.'

'And that is its only purpose?' Manescu was puzzled.

'What other purpose could it have?'

The snow buggy pulled up alongside a closed elevator door. The driver switched off his engine as another buggy entered the garage.

'This is where you get off,' the driver continued. 'Don't forget your bag. Go to the elevator and press the button marked minus two. I don't know which section is housed at that level . . .'

Manescu was met by a uniformed guard when the doors opened. The guard, who bore no insignia identifying the Institute, escorted Manescu to a large cell-like room with no window. The moment the elevator doors had opened at garage level a wave of welcome warmth had met the Romanian. His room was equally well heated.

Fifteen minutes later he was escorted by the same guard to a huge theatre-like room on the same floor. Rows of hard-backed tip-up seats occupied the room which sloped towards a high platform. To one side was a large white screen, to the other a wall of milky glass.

'You sit in the front row,' the guard informed Manescu as other members who had travelled in the cavalcade began to filter into the large room. No one was offered a seat in the front row except Manescu.

The room was dimly lit by indirect illumination. The guards distributed glasses of mineral water to the occupants of the seats and withdrew. A minute later a picture was flashed on the screen. Manescu stared. It showed Eastern Europe like a smashed jigsaw, all frontiers zigzagged. Then a distorted voice began speaking, his silhouette vaguely seen behind the milky glass. Something wrong with the glass – like a mirror in an amusement hall which contorted the viewer – made it impossible to guess his real appearance.

'All of you seated here tonight are engaged in a great crusade,' the voice began. Manescu thought he detected the twang of an American accent. Which told him nothing. Half of the people in Europe spoke English with that accent. The voice continued.

'A crusade to bring back order, stability and discipline to the world. Eastern Europe – the Balkan states, Czechoslovakia, Hungary, Poland, Bulgaria and Romania – is in a state of chaos and turmoil and turbulence. That political amateur, Gorbachev, talks of a European homeland from the Atlantic to the Urals. Our vision is much greater. The chance is there to create a Western homeland from the Pacific coast of the United States to the Urals. But that homeland must be controlled and organized from New York . . .'

The hypnotic voice paused. Behind the opaque glass screen Franklin D. Hauser mopped his sweating forehead. The heating was turned up high to dull his audience's senses, to make them more receptive to what he was saying.

'Every individual here tonight has a key part to play in this great plan. You have special skills and experience which will help us to achieve our objective. Others will follow you to this training ground, but you will form the leadership. We are creating the most effective secret police the world has ever seen. You will be allocated certain countries to operate inside. And you will be paid huge sums to complete this work. Those of you who wish will one day be provided with new identities and luxurious homes to live in. Inside the United States . . .'

The voice paused again. Manescu leaned forward, tried to get some impression of the shape behind the glass. Impossible. He was impressed by what he'd heard so far, but how was all this going to come about? As though there had been thought transference, the voice continued.

'How is all this to be achieved? By money. Billions of dollars are at our disposal. The broken states I have named are in a condition of near ruin. Secretly we shall buy controlling interests in their strategic industries. This means we must control the governments of these states. By bribery – all men are corruptible – and by removing permanently any so-called idealists who stand in our way. You have had experience in that form of action. Now I come to the main task of all.'

The voice vibrated with power and confidence. The unknown man was a first-rate orator – Manescu recognized that. He sensed a wave of excitement among the people behind him as the audience kept silent, hanging on every word.

'The major task is to take over Russia,' the voice

66

thundered. 'A difficult task, you think? No! Gorbachev has no idea of what he is doing, of the forces he has unleashed – forces we will harness and control. He has announced that private enterprise will be allowed to flourish. *We* will provide that enterprise. The American way. Corruption has been the way of life for years with certain powerful people. If necessary, to win our campaign we will rekindle that familiar flame. We already have agents inside the Soviet Union reporting back to us. That empire is crumbling. We must create a fresh one to take its place, as a counter to one billion Chinese, and we shall control the new Russian state. We may well create an independent Ukraine – the movement exists, the UTS, based in Munich, Germany. With the huge funds we shall place at its disposal the next problem Gorbachev will face is the collapse of his empire – and we will pick up the pieces . . .'

A fresh pause. Manescu had the impression the apparition behind the opaque glass wall was drinking from an absurdly shaped vessel. And behind him he had heard gasps as the voice outlined the plan for Russia.

'But,' the eerie voice continued, 'to ensure the success of this plan I must be sure all of you are fit to carry it out. Which is why you are here. Buried beneath the Arctic snows, you will be subjected to a series of ordeals, tests. This will show whether you have the stamina and braïns to perform your tasks. Do not expect a comfortable time. But remember . . .' The voice dropped. 'Moscow is the ultimate objective, and the rewards of those who lead this gigantic campaign will be enormous. Good-night . . .'

Someone started clapping. Manescu wondered whether it was one of the guards, but if so it wasn't necessary. Behind him there was a crescendo of applause, and before it could stop the guards were ushering the members of that sinister audience to their rooms.

Escorted to his own room, Manescu looked at the

67

guard and pointed to the changes which had taken place in his absence. Two litre bottles of mineral water had been placed on a small wooden table with a hard-backed chair. Also on the table was a large notebook and several biro pens.

'What are those for?'

'From now on,' the guard informed him, 'you will be confined to this room and no one will enter it for forty-eight hours. You have toilet facilities, a bed to sleep on. The light will be left on for the whole time. The notepad is for you to write down any ideas which might aid the crusade the Conductor outlined.'

'The Conductor?'

'The man who delivered the speech.' The guard paused by the door. 'This will be kept locked. No food will be provided. And please give me your wristwatch.'

'Why?' asked Manescu, guessing the answer as he unfastened the watch and handed it over.

'So you will have no way of knowing how much time has passed, whether it is night or day, even which day it is. The other visitors are living under the same conditions.'

Without another word the guard closed the steel door with a clang and Manescu heard the key turn in the lock. The ex-Director of the Romanian *Securitate* smiled to himself as he recalled a passage from the speech. *This will show whether you have the stamina and the brains . . .*

In another cell-like room further along the corridor Irina Serov, once the only woman colonel in the Soviet KGB, now jobless since being thrown out in a Gorbachev purge, slid a comb tucked inside her tights into her hand and worked on her hair.

The guard allocated to her had removed all her make-up kit from her handbag, a subtle attempt at demoralization. She stood five feet six tall in her high-heeled shoes, her long hair was dark, and she was the kind of thirty-five-year-old woman men turned to look at when she passed them in the street. She had long shapely legs and had been known in Moscow by her nickname, 'The Smooch'. During her tour of duty in England she had killed two men without any risk of being apprehended.

She wrenched the cap off one of the two mineral bottles, took a brief sip. The water must be made to last. She could go two days without sleep and was amused by the test she was undergoing.

She sat at the table, picked up one of the pens, and began work. At the top of the first sheet she wrote the subject of her first notes. *Intimidation.*

Muffled in furs, Franklin D. Hauser left the complex in a snow buggy which drove him to a helipad a kilometre away. He had no desire to linger any longer in this white Arctic hell.

A construction company controlled by Hauser had built the Institute complex. The finance had been provided by one of his banks in co-operation with French and German organizations to give the place an international reputation. But neither of his partners had the remotest idea of the existence of Levels Two and Three.

With a sense of relief he climbed aboard the waiting Sikorsky, equipped with skis, which would fly him back to Helsinki. He peered out of the window as the machine rose into the now-moonless night.

'Well,' he said to himself, 'I've started the action. Now I must keep the momentum of the operation going.'

8

Newman timed it so he would arrive back at Greenway Gardens after dark. It was eight in the evening when Evelyn opened the door on the chain, then let him inside. He carried a small bag and she misunderstood the purpose of his visit as they sat in the curtained living room.

'You've decided to stay with me?'

'No. I've decided to get you out of here. I thought about what you told me – your job with the Profiles Division, and what happened later to those two Finn manufacturers. On top of that, the couple of thugs who came here to force you to sign the insurance document, which I've read end to end . . .'

'And there's been another visitor since you left.'

He listened carefully while she recalled the arrival of Adam Carver and her conversation with him. She showed Newman the visiting card she'd kept. He glanced at it, looked at her.

'That does it. The final straw. Why should they send a senior vice president to check out what must be, if you'll pardon the description, a minor cog in such a huge enterprise? The hard men came first, then the softly spoken and sympathetic type. Oldest ploy in the world. And you told him you hadn't signed the agreement.'

'Was that a mistake?' she asked anxiously. 'I'm beginning to feel under siege.'

'Doesn't make any difference. The first two knew that. I think this Adam Carver will try to charm you into signing. If you refuse again, what next? There have already been two murders.'

'Now you're frightening me.'

Which was Newman's deliberate intent. Instead he pressed harder while she was in a fraught mood. 'Since I left you I managed to trace another ex-employee of INCU-BUS. Don't ask me how. Lives in another part of London. I visited him and he closed up like a clam. Wouldn't even give me a hint about what his job had been. He was edgy. Wanted to get rid of me fast.'

'Why do you think he was like that?'

'He'd obviously signed the document, agreed to receive a big fat pension – and keep his mouth shut. He was frightened when I mentioned Fraternity & Equality Insurance, showed me the door. Something pretty devilish is going on. Which is why you're packing a bag, leaving here tonight.'

'Where for?'

'Didn't you say Sandy had a place at Southwold in Suffolk? I never actually visited her there. We used to meet a lot here in town, go out for a meal.'

'The cottage isn't in Southwold,' she said slowly. Newman could tell she was thinking over his suggestion. 'Sandy always said Southwold,' she continued. 'More people know where that is. But the cottage is at a place called Walberswick. She had a Southwold phone number. Who's ever heard of Walberswick?'

'I have. It has a main stem simply called The Street. And nice houses, if I remember rightly. Plus two or three hotels. Very near the coast. You drive to the end of The Street, bear left and drive to the car park. Over to the right is rough dune land, a big area before you top a ridge of shingle. And Bingo! The sea.'

Evelyn smiled, something she rarely did in Newman's experience of her, brief though it might be.

'I can see you know Walberswick . . .'

'It's well off the beaten track,' he continued. 'I'll drive you up there tonight. You have a key to her cottage?'

71

'Yes. You think I'll be safer there?'

'Sure of it. Get packing . . .'

At ten o'clock at night The Street was a deserted tree-lined tunnel illuminated by the headlights of Newman's Mercedes 280E. There were lights in some of the beautiful houses on either side but all of them were upstairs. People went to bed early in Walberswick.

'Slow down,' said Evelyn, seated beside him. 'We're close to the cottage.'

'We'll come back to it. I want to call in at one of those hotels to check something. Here's a nice looking place. Leave the heaters on. Back in a minute . . .'

Before she could reply he had jumped out of the car to walk up the drive to the hotel. The wind hit him the moment he left the vehicle, a ferocious gust off the nearby sea which nearly lifted him off his feet. A storm was brewing up.

'Can you give me a double room for a couple of nights?' he asked the ancient receptionist. 'I'm on my own but I like space. My case is at a friend's house down The Street. I will pay you in advance,' he ended, hauling out his wallet.

He signed the register with a false name and address. *P. Ashbourne, 17 Lever Road, Bournemouth.* The precaution probably wasn't necessary, but on the off-chance that more thugs from INCUBUS came sniffing round, they wouldn't know he was in the area. They had shown very thorough organization so far.

'What was all that about?' Evelyn asked as he got behind the wheel.

'Had a private phone call to make,' he lied. 'Back to the cottage.'

'It's called Rose Bower. Drive slowly. You can park in the drive, or even go on round the back.'

The cottage was an attractive picture postcard by the

72

light of the moon shining between scudding clouds. Thatched roof, two storeys, the second had more mullion windows hunched inside the thatch. He drove round the back, switched off the engine, reached for the key she was holding.

'I'll go in first,' he said casually. On his way up the paved path between walls of rose bushes he picked up a piece of old iron pipe with his gloved hand. There was always a weapon available if you used your eyes. He unlocked the old heavily studded front door, pushed it open. Evelyn reached over his shoulder, switched on a light, and gasped.

'Wait here,' Newman ordered.

Beyond the doorway you walked straight into the main sitting room. It was a scene of havoc. Drawers had been pulled out of military chests, left on the floor. Chintz-covered cushions had been ripped open, left lying on the floor, stuffing scattered. A chintz-covered settee had been upended, the lining torn open.

'Oh, my God!' Evelyn whispered. 'They've been here, too.'

'Stay just inside the door while I explore . . .'

He went swiftly through the house, still holding the piece of piping. The break-in had not surprised him too much. Beyond the sitting room, a large area with an old brick fireplace set back in a spacious alcove, piles of cut logs flanking it, a narrow passage led to the kitchen and a small study.

Both rooms had received the same brutal searching treatment. He returned to the passage, ran lightly up the narrow twisting staircase, checked three bedrooms, the bathroom and the toilet. Nothing had been overlooked. He ran downstairs and Evelyn had collapsed into an armchair.

'The bastards!' she said between her teeth. 'Wrecking Sandy's old home.' She looked up. 'You didn't find anyone?'

'Lord, no. They're long gone. Must have happened some time after Buchanan and his sidekick came here.

They found the key in her handbag in the Jag.'

'But there's no sign of forced entry. Or is the back door . . .?'

'Firmly closed and locked. These jokers will be experts with skeleton keys. You wait here. I'm just taking my case to that hotel. I booked a room while I was there.'

'But you could stay here . . .'

'I could,' he agreed. 'But this is Sandy's house. She once lived here. I'd sooner not, if you don't mind. Back in a minute. I'm helping you to clear up. Don't argue. Bolt the front door after me till I get back . . .'

As he dumped his case in the pleasant bedroom, lifted the lid and left it at that, he reflected. He hadn't strictly told Evelyn the truth. He had seen the outside of Rose Bower. Sandy had been redecorating the place, had forbidden him to enter. 'Until it's all finished and ready for you,' she had said with her glowing smile. The moment he'd entered Rose Bower the smell of fresh paint had assailed his nostrils. He had almost broken down. No, he could never spend a night in that cottage. Quite apart from the problem that Evelyn seemed to like him.

When he returned she had cleared a space in the kitchen, had coffee ready. They drank it amid the ruins, not saying anything. Newman put down his large mug.

'It's freezing in here. First thing, I'll get that fire going in the sitting room. I'd sleep there tonight, if I were you.'

He insisted on staying until the cottage was as shipshape as could be managed. At least there was little evidence remaining of the break-in. He said good-night to Evelyn quickly and that he'd be back after breakfast in the morning.

'We could go and explore Minsmere,' she suggested. 'That's a Royal Society for the Protection of Birds Nature Reserve. The migrant widgeons should still be there. I doubt if they've flown north yet in this weather.'

'Good idea. And again, good-night . . .'

'Before you go, Bob.' She ran to the door. 'What do you think they could have been looking for – the people who ransacked her cottage?'

'No idea,' he lied.

The receptionist at the hotel had given him a key to the front door and his mind was a chaotic mixture of emotions and thoughts as he walked past it towards the shore. He was well wrapped up against the weather. Clad in a heavy military-style trench coat, turned up at the collar, he had a waterproof hat rammed down over his forehead. The storm was increasing in fury as he turned left towards the car park, beyond any houses, then made his way to the east on to the scrubby dunes. He had walked along this track with Sandy, arm in arm, and as the wind beat in his face he recalled the weather had been similar.

A five minute rough walk in the moonlight took him to the top of the shingle ridge. As he crested it he flinched. Surf from giant waves crashing a few feet away splashed his face. Braced against the storm as it howled, he promised himself something.

'I'll burn the bastards who did that to Sandy.'

Newman had very little sleep that night. He had lied to Evelyn when he'd denied any idea of what the ransackers were looking for. He was convinced he was holding what they sought in his hand.

A red clothbound diary written in her handwriting. He had known where to look for it when he'd left the bell tower after finding her corpse. Going over to her parked Jaguar, he had opened the driver's door, bent down and felt under the seat. The diary was attached to the underside with sellotape. He'd torn it free, pocketed it, had not mentioned its existence to Buchanan. Suppressing evidence in a murder investigation, they called it.

To hell with them. He was conducting his own

investigation. And, as Tweed had predicted to Paula in a similar context, he expected it would take him months to unravel the affairs of the world-wide octopus, INCUBUS.

He read again some of her notes. *January 12. Bennington, Swindon. Machine tools. James Archer, Managing Director, sole owner of company. Profile completed, submitted to Division, January 31. Takeover bid, February 20. Note: Archer has daughter, Julia. April 5. Manningham Electronics, Thames Valley. Miniaturized microchips. Chairman: Gavin Manningham. Profile completed, submitted May 2. Takeover bid, May 28. Note: Manningham has a mistress . . .*

There were similar entries for six other companies, all in strategic industries, including two small private banks. Newman yawned. God, he was flaked out. He checked the time – 3 a.m. Undressing quickly, he cleaned his teeth and flopped into bed. The last thing he did before he fell fast asleep was to slip Sandy's diary inside his pillow.

Another day, another storm. Tweed stood behind the heavy net curtains masking the windows of his Park Crescent office, watching the trees in distant Regent's Park shuffle and shudder under the wind's onslaught.

'I've collated quite a lot of information from the researchers,' Paula commented sitting at her desk.

'I'm getting there, too,' Monica said, arranging a series of coded fax messages from Europe.

'So what does it amount to?' Tweed asked, returning to his swivel chair behind his own desk.

'You were right,' Paula continued. 'It does look as though some top Communist agents in the security services in various East European countries have vanished into thin air. We can't be sure, of course. It's pure chaos out there, but one man has, I'm sure, got away.'

'Which one?'

'Ion Manescu, evil genius behind the *Securitate*.'

'I'd already decided we have to check on him closely. On the spot. Subject to your report, which you've just given. Guy Dalby is due here any moment. Flying in from Vienna. By now he knows his sector.'

Despite the arrival of *glasnost*, Tweed had kept in place his extensive network across Western Europe. The situation was too fluid, the future too uncertain for any relaxation yet.

After the tragic murder of Harry Masterson in *The Greek Key* crisis, Tweed had shuffled some of his four sector chiefs. Erich Lindemann, German, was still controlling the Scandinavian sector with a forward penetration zone – Northern Russia. Harvey Wilson, promoted swiftly from field agent, had replaced Paula's deceased husband as controller for Germany, Holland and Belgium. Penetration zone: Poland and Czechoslovakia. Reg Finch, another swift promotion, forty years old and very decisive, had taken over Dalby's old sector in the Mediterranean covering France, Spain, Italy, Turkey and Switzerland. Penetration zone: Libya and the Middle East.

There was a knock on the door, Tweed called out come in, and Guy Dalby entered. Based in Vienna, he was controller of the ultrasensitive Balkan sector – covering Austria, Yugoslavia and Greece. He also had the most tricky penetration zone: Hungary, Romania, Bulgaria and the Ukraine.

'Spot of bother?' he enquired jauntily as Tweed indicated he should sit in the chair beside his desk. 'Message had a mildly urgent ring.'

Dalby, dressed in a conventional grey suit, whipped a cow-lick of dark hair over his forehead. Of medium height and build, he had an air of self-confidence which irked Paula, although she recognized his first-rate brain.

'Ion Manescu,' said Tweed, coming straight to the point. 'You'll have heard of him?'

77

'Heard of him?' Dalby laughed, a hollow laugh. 'He was one of the top men we tried to keep a close eye on – when we could. He's a past master at keeping his whereabouts secret, laying false trails. A dangerous, ruthless and cruel character. Personification of evil. He was close to Ceausescu – and at the same time kept Moscow informed. Ceausescu didn't know that, but we did. If he'd been born an American he'd have been high up in the CIA – and still informing Moscow . . .'

'You mean he's pro-Russian?' Tweed interjected.

'Lordy, no!' Dalby was amused again. 'Manescu's only allegiance is to himself. He kept in with the Soviets in case Moscow ever prevailed in Bucharest – plus the extra money he undoubtedly obtained.'

'Where is he now?' Tweed asked quietly.

'He's performed another of his well-known vanishing tricks.' Dalby made a conjuror's gesture. 'Now you see him, now you don't. Rumour hath it he escaped the country when the revolution revolved. Or he may secretly be under guard in Dracula's castle. Perfect place for him.'

Tweed had taken to doodling. On his pad he drew a fearsome vampire face with fangs, then looked up.

'I need to know for certain whether the Romanians do have him. Alternatively, has he escaped; and if so, his destination.'

'You don't want much, do you? I send in a couple of men?'

'I want you to go yourself. I've arranged with a friend who owes me a favour that I'll supply the supervisor for medical equipment being flown to Bucharest. You'll be that supervisor.' He handed Dalby a slip of folded paper. 'Name and phone number. The consignment leaves tonight from Stansted.'

'Who does he think I am?'

'I was just going to tell you. Usual cover. Special

Branch. Checking a new drugs route – in connection with an IRA group. Just hint at it.'

'Don't think I'd say it outright, do you? I'd better move. Report back to you when I get back to Vienna. If I do.' He stood up, waved at Monica, winked at Paula and was gone.

'That man is too clever by half,' Paula commented. 'I don't think he knows he's not my favourite person.'

'He knows,' Tweed told her, 'which is why he winked. To wind you up.'

'Isn't it taking a big chance, sending a man like Dalby inside Romania? With all the information locked inside his head?'

'It would have been unthinkable not so long ago,' Tweed agreed. 'But they'll welcome him with open arms, bringing them medical aid. He'll make sure they do. And on top of everything else he's a brilliant linguist. Now, all we can do is wait for his report and get on with more work.'

'If you say so,' Paula said dubiously.

The trouble was, Tweed was thinking, Paula had a blind spot where Dalby was concerned. Under that flippant attitude he liked to show at Park Crescent was a mind like quicksilver. Also, among other languages, he spoke Romanian – although Tweed doubted he'd let anyone in Bucharest know that.

'The one advantage of that appalling business of the cottage being broken into,' Newman told Evelyn as they drove away from Minsmere Nature Reserve, 'is they're unlikely even to think of looking for you there.'

'Are you sure?' she asked nervously.

'I can't be absolutely sure,' he admitted. 'But look at it from their point of view. Rose Bower belonged to Sandy – with their obsession for recording details about employees they would know that. They've been there to search for something – whatever – they thought she had. Either they found it or they didn't. But they'll have crossed that place off their list.'

'I have enjoyed today,' she said wistfully.

They had spent the time wandering round the Reserve, watching the widgeon ducks and other wildfowl paddling in the lagoon close to the sea. The sky had been an azure dome, the air fresh and unpolluted. They had eaten a packed lunch prepared by Evelyn. Newman had kept the conversation general, fending Evelyn off when she tried to bring it on a more personal basis. He had decided to drive back to London to check the companies register in the City.

'Do you have to go so soon?' Evelyn pleaded as the car rocked over a series of ramps.

'You'll be safe as long as you stay in the Walberswick area. If you want a change, there's a nice pub at Dunwich. You turn right when we hit the road at the end of this track to Minsmere – instead of left, as we shall, to get you back to Walberswick. But don't go near Southwold,' he warned.

Some bizarre quirk led Newman to take a route back to London past the bell tower where Sandy had died. The Coroner's inquest had been held in Southwold the previous day and he had attended with Evelyn.

Chief Inspector Buchanan had given evidence tersely, in a dry tone. Investigations were continuing. He had no lead as yet. The outcome was as expected. 'Murder by person or persons unknown . . .' As he said the words the Coroner stared at Newman, who stared back. As soon as it was over Newman had driven Evelyn away immediately.

It was night when he turned down the A1120, drove

through Yoxford and continued along the winding country road. There was no other traffic and he kept his headlights undimmed. Sweeping over the ploughed fields the beams showed a blanket of frost forming. The night was cold, the air bitter. It suited his mood.

He was approaching the track leading to the bell tower, a dark grim silhouette in the moonlight, when he saw a great glow of light to his right in the distance. Livingstone Manor, the English country residence of Franklin D. Hauser. As he came closer he saw the old Georgian mansion was illuminated with lights in all the windows. Downstairs the windows were masked by curtains but upstairs the curtains were drawn back. He slowed down.

His eyes narrowed as he saw the outline of a helicopter by the side of the mansion. Newman had spent three days at the hotel in Walberswick – mainly to attend the inquest but also to soothe Evelyn as far as he could. On the day of the discovery of Sandy's body he remembered Buchanan had called at Livingstone Manor, had been told Hauser was in Finland. He also recalled there was a heliport near Beccles to the north.

Was Hauser now in residence? He could have flown by private jet to an East Anglian airfield, been driven from there to the heliport, boarded the chopper and flown to the manor. It was just a chance.

He pulled up in front of the high iron grille gates barring the entrance to a drive, saw in his headlights a speakphone set into one of the brick pillars.

'Robert Newman here,' he announced after pressing the button. 'To see Mr Hauser, but only if he's free . . .'

9

Franklin D. Hauser sat in a large Regency chair, wearing evening dress, in the large living room at the front of the house. The windows overlooked the long drive to distant entrance gates. The parkland was laid out with a smooth lawn. Bordering the lawn was a wall of trees with a huge oak at one corner.

'So, tell me,' he said, addressing Adam Carver, 'how did you get on with the Evelyn Lennox twist?'

'I lost her,' Carver told him bluntly, standing by a spacious fireplace with a drink in his hand. Half a tree trunk surrounded with logs crackled and flamed, warming his backside as he stood with one hand lifting the flap of his jacket.

'My, my, that was careless of you. Losing the girl you'd been sent to interview,' sneered Frank Galvone, standing closer to Hauser.

'Now, Frank,' Hauser admonished him amiably. 'Let Adam finish his story. I'm sure he has more to tell than that.'

'I talked to her at her place in Greenway Gardens,' Carver continued, ignoring Frank. 'In a few words, she did not agree to sign the insurance document. And she told me some character called Steve produced a gun when Newman, the foreign correspondent, interrupted their *tête-à-tête*. I didn't know this company hired men with guns.'

'You're Banking,' Frank said quickly. 'Stick with that.'

'Does that mean we employ men with Walthers?' Carver asked, staring at Hauser.

'Of course not.' Hauser was amused at the suggestion. 'I

should add that Frank was talking about America. Security guards at certain plants may well be armed. That's common practice in the States . . .'

He stopped speaking as someone knocked at the door. Galvone called out, 'Come on in,' and the butler appeared with a folded sheet of paper on a silver salver. He held out the salver to Galvone who took the sheet, unfolded it, read the few words on the paper and handed it to Hauser. He dismissed the butler with a jerk of his head.

'Talk of the devil,' he said. 'Newman is outside the gate, asking to see you. I'll tell him to move his ass.'

'Wait a minute.' Hauser's tone was abrupt. He opened a blue folder resting in his lap, glanced through the typed sheets. 'Grimwood reports Newman did arrive and spoilt their act just as they'd got Lennox to agree to sign. And Adam has just confirmed his statement. Always meet the opposition and hear what it has to say. Forewarned is forearmed, as the Brits say. Adam, would you be so kind as to tell Winterton to admit Mr Newman? Thank you.'

Galvone waited until Carver had left the room. 'I think you're making a mistake. You rarely agree to see a newspaper man.'

'Frank, you're an impetuous man. You'll never occupy this chair until you learn to control that impetuosity. You really must study my methods more closely.'

'I know I get it wrong sometimes.' It cost Galvone a lot to say that but he knew he'd blundered. 'But I do get it right most of the time. I think I'll freshen up my drink.'

He poured himself a double Scotch from the antique drinks cabinet. Hauser leaned over, opened a drawer in a desk and slid the Grimwood folder inside. Then, settling himself back in his chair, he lit a cigarette. Galvone hurried to place a crystal ash tray on a small table beside him.

Newman walked into the room followed by Carver. He carried his trench coat over his arm. He'd declined the butler's offer to take his coat: he might want to leave in a hurry. He smiled as he advanced across the room.

'Very good of you to see me, Mr Hauser. Normally I ask for an appointment, but I happened to be passing and saw the lights – and the chopper. I guessed you might just be back from Finland.'

He saw a flicker in the ice-blue eyes behind the pince-nez. Glancing at Galvone he saw something different. The dark eyes were glowing with hostility and the man's whole body had tensed. Hit them the moment you arrive was a favourite tactic of Newman's. Hauser recovered first.

'And very pleasant to meet at last the famous foreign correspondent. I read your international bestseller, *Kruger: The Computer That Failed*. Must have made you a fortune.'

'It did,' Newman agreed. 'Gave me financial independence. But I do a piece now and again. When the subject interests me.'

'I'm forgetting my manners . . .' Hauser introduced Carver and Galvone. 'Both senior vice presidents.' He smiled. 'One day one of them will take over from me. The question is, which one?'

'Well, I think that's your decision.'

'Frank, get Mr Newman a drink. What's your poison? Then you can tell me what you want.'

Newman thanked him, shook his head, sat in the chair Hauser ushered him to with a wave of his large hand. 'I am hoping you'll agree to an interview for *Der Spiegel*. At your convenience,' he added blandly.

'I can afford to give you fifteen minutes now. Then I have guests arriving for dinner. Shoot.'

Newman took out his notebook, glanced at Galvone and Carver. 'I always interview a subject on his – or her – own. It's the only way it works.'

Hauser beamed. 'Adam, Frank, maybe you could find something to occupy your time elsewhere. Preferably something profitable for the company.'

84

Galvone stepped forward, laid a hand on Newman's shoulder. He was surprised at the hard muscle he felt under his strong grip. 'Before we go I'd better check this guy for a piece – or a tape recorder.'

'The uniformed guard in the hall did just that.' Newman looked up at Galvone. 'Frank, kindly remove your hand or I may remove it myself. Painfully.'

'Try it, smart ass . . .'

'Your impetuosity is showing again,' Hauser remarked. 'Do I have to remind you Mr Newman is a guest? An honoured guest?'

As he spoke he pressed a concealed button in the arm of his chair. The door at the end of the room opened swiftly and the butler appeared. Hauser called out as though asking for the tea to be served.

'Winterton, could you confirm the guard gave Mr Newman the normal check before he came in here?'

'Oh, yes. He did, sir.'

'Thank you, Winterton. That will be all.' Hauser looked at Newman. 'My apologies. But success in this world seems to breed envy which, in its turn, can breed hostility. A sad state of affairs, but it is so. Security has to be total or useless.'

Galvone had removed his hand and stepped away several paces. He glared at Newman and then left the room with Carver. Newman stiffened his back against the chair and smiled. 'About your security. The guard on the gate at the entrance to the drive should really have checked me. If an intruder eliminated him with a weapon and managed to get inside this place you'd be in trouble.'

'Thank you. What do you wish to ask me?'

'Why are you extending your activities to Europe and what are your plans?'

'Very modest. Mr Newman. A small investment – for INCUBUS – in certain companies to give us a toehold inside the Common Market. A sideline, you might say.'

85

'Really? Bennington Machine Tools in Swindon. A key firm in a key industry. Manningham Electronics in the Thames valley. A company with the most advanced products in western Europe.'

'Really, Mr Newman,' Hauser waved his cigarette, but again Newman had detected that brief flicker behind the pince-nez. 'I'm Chief Executive and President of a large international organization. I never get buried in the weeds. I concern myself with general policy. You expect me to know all the details of what is happening in a legion of divisions?'

'You have a reputation for being a master of detail. The companies I mentioned are important acquisitions.'

'The names mean nothing to me. You'd haved to consult Adam Carver – or Frank Galvone.'

'One of whom may – or may not – succeed you some day?'

Hauser threw back his large head and chuckled. 'You are so observant. You noticed my little ploy. Keeps them on their toes.'

'You said your investment in Europe is modest. What about Timo Metsola's electronics outfit in Finland – where you've just flown back from? It seems to me you're spreading your net very wide.'

'Again the name means nothing to me.' Hauser's mood had changed. He stubbed out his half-smoked cigarette savagely in the ash tray. 'You'll have to be careful with this article, Mr Newman. Careful you get all your facts right. I operate in the American way. I'd sue you, strip you bare without a second thought.'

'What is your general strategy in the new fluid situation in Europe?' Newman pressed on.

'To provide more employment where I can. I regard INCUBUS as a brotherhood of man. My only role in life is to help my fellow men and women, regardless of race or creed. You may quote me.'

'And regardless of the business methods you use?'

Hauser pressed the button in his chair. 'This interview is becoming tedious, is terminated. I had expected better of you.' His manner was aggressive, his tone hasrsh. 'Have a care in future. Better perhaps that you retire, enjoy the fortune you made from your book.' He stared across the room as Winterton entered. 'Please show Mr Newman out – he is leaving immediately.'

'And thank you for the interview.'

Newman smiled as he stood up, pocketing his notebook and pen. He walked rapidly across the gleaming parquet floor, slipping on his trench coat as he left.

In response to the two presses of the chair button Galvone hurried in to the living room. He knew from the expression on Hauser's face something was wrong. And tobacco ash was spilt down the front of his evening shirt. Galvone pulled out the display handkerchief from his top pocket.

'Excuse me, Chief,' he fawned and used the handkerchief to flick away the ash. 'Something wrong?'

'Robert Newman has just left. He'll be walking down the drive now. He's investigating us, Frank. And he's getting close. I don't like that. I don't like that at all.'

'So I'd better deal with the problem immediately?'

'That's up to you, Frank.' He turned a steely gaze on his subordinate. 'I don't wish to get meshed in the weeds – use your discretion.'

'He's driving a Merc. 280E. The guard biked down the drive and checked it out . . .'

Galvone was half-running from the room as he threw the words over his shoulder, closed the door, ran down the hall and into the night.

*　　*　　*

Just outside the grille gates – which had opened auto-matically at his approach and then closed behind him – Newman was lying on his back under his car. He aimed his pencil flash, checking the underneath of the chassis. It seemed unlikely they would have placed a bomb so close to Livingstone Manor, but it was better to be sure than dead. He hauled himself over the gravel clear of the chassis, stood up, opened the front passenger door, pulled the lever which unlocked the hood.

With the hood open he made a swift examination of the engine. Nothing there either. He took off his trench coat, shivered in the cold, shook the dirt off the coat, put it on again and slipped behind the wheel. Despite the bitter night he lowered his window before starting the motor.

He was driving away from the grounds of Hauser's estate when he heard a different engine sound. The sound of the helicopter's rotors starting up. He pressed his foot down, sped along the country road which was free of other traffic. He drove with his headlights undipped to see the endless curves in good time. Bare hedges like barbed wire showed in the beams.

The chug-chug of the chopper was growing louder, coming up fast behind him. A minute later he saw it flying past well over to his right at a height of about two hun-dred feet. It flew on, red and green lights flashing, then it descended, disappeared.

Newman frowned as he recalled a snatch of conversa-tion with Buchanan during a break in his interrogation at Southwold on the day Sandy's body was discovered. Hauser's name had cropped up and Buchanan had shrug-ged as he put down his mug of foul-tasting coffee.

'I sometimes think these super-rich men like to show they have made it. Hauser not only has a twenty-acre estate at Livingstone Manor. A constable in Yoxford told me he also owns two hundred acres of farmland to the west of his country retreat . . .'

And now, Newman thought, I'm driving west of that estate. So maybe it was somewhere on that land the chopper has put down. He had been driving at high speed when the helicopter flew past him. And they probably know I'm travelling in this car. He reduced speed considerably, dipped his headlights, began to crawl round the bends, his right foot poised over the accelerator.

He travelled like this for some distance, meeting no other traffic. The moonlight shone off the frost settling on the fields and a wave of mist like sea surf was beginning to rise on either side of the road. He turned yet another corner and saw in the distance a rare copse of evergreen trees close to the road. He stopped, switched off the engine and listened.

Had he imagined it? He could have sworn he'd caught the sound of another engine, a weird noise – a clanking, groaning ratchety sound. The silence of a cold windless night was all he heard now. He switched on the engine and drove on.

He had increased his speed to between forty and fifty miles an hour. Suddenly he wanted to get well clear of the area. He was approaching the copse of trees, a dark island by the side of the road. Because of the chopper's flight he was watching closely and he blinked as his eyes located movement. Something huge emerging from behind the copse, heading for the road. And, much louder, a blasting roar, the sinister clanking sound repeated.

He was ten yards from the copse when the origin of the roar appeared. An enormous tractor with giant wheels was driving across his path. He had a split second to decide. He rammed his foot down, the Merc. responded, shot forward like a torpedo. The yellow monster was almost on top of him, two great lights like enormous eyes now switched on. Newman kept his foot down. To his right the tractor loomed over him, the agent of destruction. Newman's Mercedes skimmed past the revolving wheels with inches to spare. In his rear view mirror he saw the solid yellow wall blocking the whole road. He sped on . . .

Behind the wheel of the tractor Frank Galvone swore foully. He had misjudged the speed of his target by no more than a fraction. Cursing again, he began reversing the machine back up the farm track towards the hollow where the helicopter and its pilot waited.

Newman, with the murder of Sandy foremost in his mind, having passed the fatal bell tower within the past two hours, was shaken by the encounter. His normal reaction would have been to swing the car in a U-turn to return and tackle the driver of the tractor. But he had no idea how strong his back-up might be. And he was no longer armed – he had hurled the Walther taken from Steve into the sea at Walberswick, followed by the magazine he'd first extracted.

Five minutes later he saw the lights of a village pub. The Nag's Head. He parked his car among a dozen others, out of sight of the road, and walked inside.

An old pub with beamed ceilings, smoke-blackened, and a log fire crackling and spitting inside a deep alcove. The place was crowded. Mostly locals. Agricultural workers, their trousers fastened to their ankles with bits of string or bicycle clips. He leaned on the stained wooden bar. The landlord was a short round-headed red-faced man.

'Good evening, sir. What can I serve you?'

'A Scotch. And some water, please.'

The landlord placed the glass in front of Newman, pushed a jug of water along the bar, studying him.

'Stranger to these parts?'

'Yes.' Newman paid for the drink. 'I've just inter-viewed a man called Franklin D. Hauser.' He diluted the

Scotch, sipped at his glass. 'I hear he's not too popular round here.'

He was aware of sudden hush among the men on either side of him. A heavily built man in a corduroy jacket edged closer to him on his left. His elbow nudged against Newman's side.

'You just finishin' that drink and then pushin' off, Mister?'

'What's that 'e said?' Another voice, this time on his right. A six foot two giant with black hair and eyebrows joined over the bridge of his large nose. 'You tellin' Jed you don't like Mr 'Auser?'

'I may have another drink, I may not,' Newman replied, looking at Corduroy Jacket.

'Best make it one and then shove it as Dan said.'

The giant, Dan, lifted Newman's glass and held it close to his mouth. He grinned, showing bad teeth. 'Drink up now, there's a good boy.'

'Put that glass down carefully,' Newman said quietly. 'And I should warn you I'm ex-SAS. If I have to defend myself I'll try very hard not to kill you – but with my training. And I didn't say I disliked Hauser. I said I heard he wasn't popular. That was in Yoxford. I wondered why.'

'Yoxford!' Corduroy Jacket laughed sarcastically. 'What do them yokels know.' He spoke across Newman to the giant. 'I'd put that glass down very carefully if I were you. We mistook the gentleman's attitude.'

The glass was placed gently back on the counter in front of Newman. He drank a little more and then asked his question.

'I gather Hauser is well-liked around here. I'm not surprised,' he lied, 'but will someone tell me why he's liked so much?'

'Generous with his money.' The landlord intervened, relieved there wasn't going to be any trouble. 'Give you

91

an example. We had trees down in a storm. Cottages damaged. No insurance. Who comes along and says he'll pay for everything to be put to rights? Mr Franklin D. Hauser.'

'Very generous, as you say.'

'That's not all,' broke in Corduroy Jacket. 'Anyone who gets behind payments with the mortgage round 'ere, all 'e 'as to do is tell the Manor. Mr 'Auser helps out. You travel round these parts, you'll find folk 'ave nothing but good to say about Mr 'Auser.' He leaned closer and Newman detected evidence of many pints of beer on his breath. 'And they'd go a long way to 'elp 'im if ever 'e 'ad a problem.'

'Well I'm glad you told me.' Newman swallowed the rest of his drink. 'Obviously I was badly misinformed in Yoxford. I must be off now.'

As he drove through the night, heading back to London, Newman was anxious to get clear of Hauser's 'province'. The American was clever, he'd give him that.

Posing as a philanthropist, he had distributed largess on a big scale to the locals. This provided him with an army of allies – and potential spies – surrounding a wide area of the Livingstone Manor estate. Newman wondered whether he employed the same method in other parts of the world.

It also occurred to him that this precaution eliminated the likelihood of ever finding a witness who had seen Sandy arriving in her Jaguar at the bell tower close to dawn. The word had probably been passed around already: see no evil, hear no evil. Which led to a fresh thought.

Assuming Sandy had been murdered because of her connection until recently with INCUBUS, the murderer could be one of Hauser's close associates. Hauser had struck him as a man who moved with great caution. No hired killers for a one-time job. Too risky.

My God! he thought. I could have been in the same room with the murderer back at Livingstone Manor. Newman had noticed Adam Carver seemed the athletic type, very fit and strong. On the other hand there was Mr Frank Galvone. His first impression of Galvone had been of a mobster, but Newman had met other reasonably honest Americans holding high positions who had made the same initial impression. The fact that both men had been at Livingstone Manor intrigued him. What was it they said about a murderer returning to the scene of his crime?

All these disconnected thoughts were roaming through his mind as he drove through the middle of the night close to his flat in South Ken. Hardly any other traffic about at 1 a.m.

He was so close to his flat in Beresforde Road that he had reduced his speed to a crawl, searching for a parking place. The huge articulated truck with a separate cab for the driver appeared out of nowhere, moving at high speed, lights undimmed and aiming straight for him. He attempted evading action but it was too late. The monster slammed into the rear of his car. Despite the fact he was wearing his seat belt he was hurled forward. His skull cracked down on the steering wheel.

Forcing his head up he found everything was blurred. He had braked automatically, which was probably a mistake. Through the shimmer he saw the huge octopus eyes of the juggernaut grow dimmer. The vehicle was backing away. It turned a corner and vanished. Then he blacked out.

10

81°F. 27°C.

The heatwave which had started in May was continuing to roast London in June. Tweed was clad in shirt sleeves and a pair of lightweight slacks as he stared out of his office window. It was mid-morning and tourists were trudging under the blazing sun towards Regent's Park.

Monica was sweltering despite the fan revolving on her desk. All it seemed to do was circulate the warm turgid air. Tweed turned quickly as the door opened and Paula arrived. He sensed she was excited.

'Bob's jogging in Hyde Park. Isn't it wonderful? He discharged himself from the hospital. When he's had a bath at his flat he's coming here.'

'A drink to celebrate,' Tweed said. 'Champagne.'

'Not until he's arrived,' Paula replied. She sank into the chair behind her own desk. 'Three ribs broken and concussion. Now he's as strong as an ox. He's been through a lot.'

'It wasn't the ribs that worried me,' Tweed replied, sitting in his swivel chair. 'He was fit, I was sure he would mend. But the concussion was a dicey business.'

'That's what the doctor kept telling us,' Paula recalled. 'And he was very insistent Bob had to stay under his care until the headaches went away. They were murder for him, I could tell.'

'It was that truck driver who was intent on murder,' Monica interjected grimly. 'And, of course, what do the police do? They find the truck abandoned a mile away, that it had been stolen. No sign of the driver.'

The phone rang and Paula grabbed hers first. She spoke briefly, put it down and grinned. 'Bob is here. On his way up.'

Newman came in with a faraway look. Paula was immediately concerned. She jumped up and ran forward, guided him to the armchair.

'The headache's come back?' she said.

'Nope.' He grinned at her. 'Sorry if I was in a brown study. I feel fine. I was remembering some of the facts I built up from the data you brought me. I used the phone a lot while I was in that private room. In Sandy's notebook – the one I'd found in her Jaguar that morning at the bell tower – there was a reference to Dracon. I know what it is now. INCUBUS has a think-tank called Dracon based outside Boston. All the ideas come from there. And Ed Riverton was the vice president running it. He gave me a hint when I interviewed him in Helsinki not long before he also was murdered.'

'So why do you believe he was killed in that fashion?' Tweed enquired.

'Because he got worried about what they were planning – all those cranky academics Hauser employs. The trouble is I've no idea of what they were planning.'

'Doesn't get us much further then,' Tweed observed. 'We do have a lot of data on that banking colossus. Collected while you were on holiday . . .'

'Some holiday, thank you very much . . .'

'Did you know it's the biggest bank in the United States?' Tweed persisted. 'Bigger even than the Bank of America. It has enormous resources, and controlling interests in key outfits all over the Western world.'

'Power.' Newman paused to drink from the mug of coffee Paula had made. Champagne could come later. 'Power,' he repeated. 'That's the driving force behind Hauser. The acquisition of more power than anyone else in the world. I've been contacting some reporter pals.

Building up a jigsaw. Oh, by the way, Chief Inspector Buchanan is on his way here. Hope you don't mind?'

'Why should I mind? But I'd have thought you might,' Tweed commented. 'He's been here twice since you were carted off to hospital. You still seem to be his prime suspect.'

'So, when you're in a corner, take the bull by the horns – in this case the bull being Roy Buchanan. Questions I want to ask him. With your assistance – and Mauno Sarin's. He's still chief of Protection Police in Helsinki, I hope?'

'He is, but I don't see . . .'

'You will.'

The phone rang, was answered this time by Monica. Paula was watching Newman: he looked remarkably fit. And he exuded an aura of physical energy and driving power. All the old bounce was back. Monica cupped her hand over the phone.

'You've got your chance now. Buchanan is downstairs.' She looked at Tweed. 'All right to let him come up?'

'Wheel him in . . .'

Chief Inspector Buchanan walked in wearing the same grey suit followed by the wooden-faced Sergeant Warden. He glanced at the assembled company as though surprised to see so many people. Tweed ushered his guests to chairs, then sat back, leaving the field clear for Newman.

'Chief Inspector, have you got any further with your investigation of the murder of Sandy Riverton?'

'I usually ask the questions.' Buchanan sounded amused. 'As you've raised the point, no. In one way I wouldn't expect to find any witnesses – since what happened took place close to dawn. In another, I would. It's a farming community – agricultural workers rise early.'

'But you tried?' Newman persisted.

'Yes, and met a wall of silence.'

'Which doesn't surprise me . . .' Newman recalled briefly his experience at The Nag's Head a few hours before he ended up in hospital.

'Interesting.' Buchanan paused. 'But that doesn't give me any direct link with Hauser, who probably has nothing to do with the crime.' Another pause. 'Except for the murder of Edward Riverton, her husband – which Tweed has informed me about while you were in hospital.'

Of all those seated in the office only Buchanan seemed impervious to the heat. He crossed his long legs, the picture of relaxation as he studied Newman, his grey eyes half closed. Warden was enjoying himself in the background: it was a new experience to see someone else tackling Buchanan rather than the other way round.

'That took place in Helsinki,' Newman pointed out. 'A long way from Suffolk.'

'True. But when you've handled a number of homicide cases you learn to recognize a pattern. There are similarities between the two murders which, incidentally, I gather took place twenty-four hours apart.'

'What similarities?'

Buchanan settled himself more comfortably. 'Sandra Riverton was killed at a remote place at a remote hour. Mr Tweed knows Finland and tells me Edward Riverton's body was dumped into the icebound harbour in the dark. At a time when no one would be venturing out. The methods also suggest a similar technique, although I may be stretching a point.'

'Stretch it for me,' Newman urged.

'Sandra Riverton was killed by a rope round her *neck*. Edward Riverton was killed by garrotting his *neck*. A vulnerable part of the human anatomy. And a certain way of murdering someone.'

'I still don't see where you're going.'

'I think you do.' A grim smile. 'I said earlier the crimes were committed twenty-four hours apart. That time element intrigues me. Time for the same man to complete his work in Finland, then catch a plane to London and hire a car to take him to Suffolk. Also, I have found Mr Hauser has a Lear jet which flies him across the world plus a Sikorsky helicopter which I saw taking off from the grounds of Livingstone Manor. And there is a heliport south-east of Beccles, just north of the area.'

You have been a busy bee, Newman was thinking. But why are you telling me all this? The answer to his unspoken question came as Buchanan continued.

'Mr Newman, were you thinking of flying to Finland during the near future by any chance?'

'No, I wasn't. Why do you ask?'

'Just letting my mind wander.' He glanced at Tweed who was saying to himself, That's a laugh. You never let your mind wander in your life. 'Just a thought,' Buchanan added.

'But there was something behind the thought,' Newman insisted.

'Well, it might be interesting if someone like you were to nose around INCUBUS headquarters in Helsinki, ask some questions. Of course, you'd have to track down the right person.'

'Ask what questions?'

'Again, I think you know. Was a member of their staff in Helsinki during the night of Edward Riverton's murder? And was that same person *absent* the following day? That is, the same day Riverton was dragged out of the harbour. Someone who flew to Britain, so they were over here at the time of the Sandra Riverton crime.'

'You don't want much, do you?'

'Just a suggestion. Now, if that's all I'd better leave. At the moment I'm up to my neck in the Camden Town murder.' He stood up, refusing Tweed's offer of coffee. At the door he looked back at Newman. 'If you found someone such as I have just described it would let you off the hook.'

'So I'm still your number one suspect?'

'Let's just say, Mr Newman, that in so many murder enquiries the culprit turns out to be the person who discovered the body. Goodbye, Mr Tweed . . .'

On that note he left the room, descended the staircase, handed the identification form to the guard, went outside with Warden to his unmarked parked car. Warden asked the question as he settled himself behind the wheel.

'So you still think it could be Newman?'

'I have an open mind until further evidence comes to light. I certainly left Newman with that impression.'

'What was all that Finland business about, Chief?'

Buchanan smiled drily. 'If Newman is innocent he'll want to clear himself. I asked the Assistant Commissioner to let me go to Helsinki and he refused. Said I must concentrate on the Camden Town case. So maybe Newman can go in my place, do the job for me.'

'You think he can cope?'

'He's ideal for the role. A very experienced foreign correspondent, he'll be highly skilled in interrogating people. It was his profession for so many years – not unlike my own.'

You sly bugger, Warden thought. He was careful not to voice the thought aloud.

'Back to the Yard,' ordered Buchanan.

'So where does dragging Buchanan here leave you?' Tweed asked.

'It tells me I'm still his chief suspect. That was what I was really after. But he gave me more than I'd expected.'

'Which particular aspect?'

'The Finland business,' Paula interjected. 'Bob is going to fly to Finland. I can tell from his expression. And,' she continued firmly, 'I'd like to go with him. Women sometimes see things men miss. Don't forget I've done the bulk of the research on INCUBUS.'

'I'll think about it,' Tweed told her. 'It could be dangerous.'

'We've had this conversation before,' she flared up.

'And it was dangerous when we were in Germany. And on a previous operation it was damned dangerous in Rotterdam. So I'm not to be coddled like a twelve-year-old, thank you very much. 'Or,' she played her trump card, 'have you become old-fashioned? Women can't do a man's job?'

'I said I'll think about it,' Tweed responded, refusing to rise to the bait. 'And we don't know whether Bob is going to Finland yet.'

'I think it's my next port of call,' Newman replied. 'But first I'd like all the dope Paula has dug up on INCUBUS . . .'

He stopped as the phone rang again, Monica answered it, and again cupped her hand over the phone.

'It's an American. A Mr Ward Dexter. He says you're expecting him, that you were informed he would be coming a few months ago. He's waiting for you at Brown's Hotel.'

'Tell him I'll be there within an hour.'

Tweed paced the room, wiping moisture off his forehead as Monica relayed the message. The heat was becoming torrid and under his armpits his shirt was pasted to his body.

He was also recalling that Guy Dalby, sector chief for the Balkans, had earlier reported from Vienna. In Bucharest Dalby had been told by a totally reliable source that Ion Manescu, brutal *Securitate* chief, was alive. 'He escaped to God knows where,' Dalby had stressed. 'But he was very much alive when he vanished . . .'

'Mr Dexter will be waiting for you,' Monica said.

'The tempo is beginning to accelerate,' Tweed commented as he slipped on his linen jacket. 'That sounds like the secret aide sent personally by the US President. Now I'll find out what is really worrying Washington. A separate problem from yours,' he said to Newman.

11

Tweed caught a cab, told the driver to drop him at the Piccadilly entrance to the Burlington Arcade. He strolled up the long arcade, pausing frequently to peer in shop windows at the expensive goodies. He also glanced back the way he had come.

Emerging from the top of the arcade, he turned left and slipped inside Brown's Hotel in Albemarle Street. He walked swiftly to the reception counter midway down a long hall leading to Dover Street. A good hotel to stay at: apart from the excellence of its discreet service it had two exits. Mr Ward Dexter was in Room 144.

Tweed took the elevator the receptionist guided him to, stepped out, walked along the deserted corridor. He rapped three times on the door of Room 144, it was opened a few inches. A man with dark hair and thick eyebrows opened it a few inches.

'Mr Dex—'

Tweed stared as the man opened the door wide. He would be in his early fifties, was tall and well built with a craggy face. Beneath the strong nose was a dark moustache, thin and slicked down, which gave him a Latin look. It was the ice-blue eyes which told Tweed he was right.

'Come in,' the man said impatiently.

The door closed behind Tweed as he scanned the luxuriously furnished double room which overlooked Albemarle Street. He walked to the window and gazed down through the net curtains. Of all the people he had expected from Washington 'Dexter' was the last person.

101

He turned round to gaze at Cord Dillon, Deputy Director of the CIA.

'A rough diamond,' Paula called him. 'The manners of a bull elephant,' was Monica's elegant description.

'You've grown a moustache, I see,' Tweed remarked. 'And what have you done with your hair, for Pete's sake.'

'You recognized me quickly?' Dillon asked aggressively.

'No, I didn't. What have you done to yourself?'

'Grown myself a moustache, used hair colourant on it – as I did on my hair. If you didn't check me out who else will?'

Tweed sat down. The Cord Dillon he had known had a shock of thick brown hair and was clean shaven. The sunken cheeks which emphasized his cheekbones, the thin tight-lipped mouth were the same but they merged with the Latin appearance – further highlighted by the cut of his lightweight suit.

'What are you wearing?' Tweed asked as Dillon poured glasses of Perrier water. 'Thanks, it's a thirsty day.'

'The suit came from Italy. Let's cut the cackle. I'm on my own. When I say that I mean I'm operating without back-up. Even the Director has no idea I'm here.'

'Who does know then?'

'The President.' Dillon padded heavily across the room to sink into a chair next to Tweed. Even his walk was changed: normally he'd moved like a man with springs in his feet.

'Who else?' Tweed asked.

'No one. Just the President. I'm not joking.'

'Why this incredible degree of secrecy?'

'I want to stay alive . . .'

Tweed was stunned. He was talking to one of the toughest, cleverest Americans he had ever encountered. He had never expected to hear Cord Dillon make such a statement. Dillon gave no sign of being frightened, but Tweed sensed he was like a coiled spring.

'Could you elaborate on that a little?' he suggested.

'Sure. But first – so you know I'm *bona fide*, as the Uzbeks say – read this document.'

Tweed was relieved the American had not lost his rare sense of humour. He took out of a thick envelope a sheet of thick paper. The top of the sheet was embossed with the great seal of The President. The authorization was brief and addressed to Tweed. He ran his eyes down the typed message. A passage attracted his attention.

Cord Dillon is travelling as my personal representative with instructions to report back to me about this subject directly and without reference to any intermediaries however highly placed.

Below was the signature of The President. Tweed refolded the sheet, slipped it back inside the envelope and handed it to Dillon.

'Why did you say "I want to say alive"?'

'Because INCUBUS has penetrated the US government at all levels. It has infiltrated the CIA and the FBI. Hauser is a billionaire several times over. We've only rumours to go on but the sums he's paid out are astronomical.'

'Bribes?'

'Yes. He's established a power structure inside the Washington power structure. The President feels himself in a state of siege. We can no longer trust anyone. They might belong to INCUBUS.'

'So why have you come here?' Tweed demanded.

'Because it's in Europe we think we can bring him down with all his works. Franklin D. Hauser. We suspect he's operating illegally. We need absolute proof of that. Rumours say he's co-operating with some strange bedfellows. But who they are we don't know. Goddamnit, Tweed, we don't know a bloody thing!'

'Then we'd better start to find out exactly what he is up to. Especially in Finland.'

'Why would he choose Finland?'

'The perfect neutral base, would be my educated guess. It's a long way north – apparently out of the mainstream of the chaos which is afflicting Eastern Europe. We need a plan of action – to find out what Hauser is doing. He's built a big HQ in Helsinki, has another building in Turku, the second city. And he spends a lot of time in Finland.'

'So we go there, start something, blow his operation wide open.'

Typical of Dillon's tendency to use bull-at-a-gate methods. Not always. Dillon was clever, experienced. But he was under stress – because he was working on his own. Normally he directed a large team. Maybe it also highlighted the difference between the British and the American temperament, Tweed reflected.

'I'd go easy, Cord,' he warned. 'Keep under cover. I can't come yet – but Bob Newman is possibly making the trip there. If he agrees, the two of you could travel in harness.'

'The foreign correspondent? We don't get on. And he's a lone wolf character.'

'What cover are you travelling under?'

Dillon grinned, drank more water. He was calming down under the influence of Tweed's self-controlled personality, his off-hand way of talking.

'Officially I'm attached to the *Washington Post*. As a roving foreign correspondent . . .'

'And if someone checks back?' Tweed asked quickly. 'You've said only the President knows . . .'

'The paper's editor will back me up. He thinks I'm investigating the world drug trade. Which covers my ass.'

'Then it would be ideal for you to travel with Newman. He certainly doesn't dislike you,' Tweed continued, shading the truth. 'But only if he agrees. Wait here a few days, then Newman will contact you, again providing he agrees. If not, I'll contact you myself.'

'I can't sit on my rear for long, hanging round this ancient hotel. It's quite a place, I'll give it that. Service is

104

very good. Must have been built in Georgian times.'

'Not quite.' Tweed suppressed a smile. 'But Agatha Christie used to stay here.'

'You're not going to tell Newman what I've told you?' Dillon demanded.

'I'll have to. Look, Bob Newman has worked with me as you well know. He's fully vetted.'

'OK.' Dillon sounded dubious. 'Don't forget I'm staying here as Ward Dexter. And you won't be saying anything to that ponce of a boss you've got, Howard?'

'Howard isn't included in the magic circle on this one. Sit tight . . .'

Otmoor, north of Oxford, is a bleak lonely wasteland of sour fields with few trees. Newman drove along the narrow road he'd turned on to off the B4027 at no more than thirty miles an hour. Beside him sat Paula, checking her map and acting as navigator. In the rear sat a restless Cord Dillon.

'We're crawling on our bellies,' the American complained. 'You do know where this Archer guy lives now?'

'Yes, we have a general idea, Mr Dillon,' Paula replied tartly. 'Keep a lookout for Begonia Cottage.'

'Begonia! Sounds like a spaghetti joint,' Dillon growled. 'You really think this trip is worth it?'

'If I didn't we wouldn't be here,' Newman told him. 'And it gets you out of London . . .'

'But we were tagged. That silver Chevrolet was following us. Make no mistake about that, brother.'

'And I spotted it the moment we drove off from my flat,' Newman rapped back. 'I told you about my holiday in hospital. That episode shows the opposition knows where I live. I spotted it and lost it at that last roundabout. Whoever was tailing us will never find their way

105

inside Otmoor. And if they do we'll see them coming miles away.'

Which was true, Dillon admitted to himself as he glanced out of the rear window once more. The road – little more than a track with deep ditches on either side – was elevated above the surrounding countryside. No other vehicle was in sight as far as the eye could see.

'Newman,' he persisted, 'you're sure you've got this right – about Bennington Machine Tools being taken over against this Archer's wish by INCUBUS?'

'I'm sure.'

Newman left it at that. He hadn't thought it necessary to recall for Dillon's benefit the tragic death of Sandy, the notebook he'd found secreted under the seat of her Jaguar parked close to the bell tower. The notebook which recorded her interviews with Archer of Bennington, Swindon, and Manningham Electronics in the Thames valley.

Newman slowed down, stopped outside a cottage set well back from the road so Paula could read the name. He had his window down. The heat was overpowering, the sun glared out of a clear blue sky, the inside of the car was like an oven. He wiped his forehead, his hands.

'Holly Place,' Paula said, reading the name board. 'The wrong place.'

'Let's get a hustle on, I'm baking,' snapped Dillon.

'We all are, Mr Dillon,' Paula said amiably as Newman drove on.

In the distance was a large L-shaped residence, also well back off the road. It had a newly thatched roof and was enclosed inside a privet hedge. Newman slowed again and saw the name himself. Begonia Cottage. All the research he had done, using the phone while in hospital, had paid off. Providing the owner was at home. Then he saw the mullion windows were open.

*   *   *

James Archer was a tall man in his sixties, white-haired and clean shaven. He wore horn-rim glasses and had an air of authority. He had reluctantly agreed to let Newman and Paula into his home after some persuasion.

They sat in armchairs in a low-beamed room at the front while Archer perched in a rocking chair. Paula glanced up and saw cobwebs in the corners, a whole network. If there was a woman in the house she was sloppy, and that didn't seem to go with Archer.

'So, you're the foreign correspondent, Mr Newman. What can I do for you?' Archer enquired, rocking gently.

'Over two years ago you sold your company, Bennington Machine Tools, to Columbia High Multi-Machines Inc. – a subsidiary of INCUBUS Inc.'

'I see you've done your homework,' Archer replied after a slight pause.

'May I ask why you sold out?'

'I decided to retire, enjoy life a little more. Columbia offered me the market price.'

'And yet, when I got in touch with some of your business friends in Swindon they all expressed great surprise. They said you'd told them you'd never sell, no matter how much was offered.'

'You *have* done your homework.' The rocking stopped, the chair was suddenly still, as motionless as the man who sat inside it.

'How is your daughter, Julia, these days?'

Archer froze. A shot in the dark but it had struck a target. He stood up slowly, asked if they would like coffee, made his way out of the room when they accepted the offer. Paula stood up, whispered to Newman that she would be back and followed Archer. Newman stood up, stared out of the window. He could just see his Mercedes with Dillon seated in the back. It had been decided three people might overwhelm the man they were calling on.

Paula found Archer in a small kitchen at the rear of the

cottage. He stood with his back to her, watching a percolator. She was wearing a brightly flowered summer dress, high necked and with short sleeves. She leaned on the working surface and peered at him. There were tears in his eyes.

'Mr Newman hasn't come here to upset you,' she said gently.

'What has he come here for then?'

'He's investigating INCUBUS. He thinks there's something very wrong with that mammoth organization, with the methods it uses. He wants to expose it before the whole world, but he needs your help.'

She left it at that, opened a cupboard, found coffee cups, a jug, milk and sugar, and laid a tray. He dabbed at his eyes, blew his nose, then emptied the percolator's contents into the jug.

'No, I'll carry the tray,' Paula insisted.

'It's your dress,' he said. 'My wife had a dress very like it. She'd have been wearing it on a day like this.'

'And now your wife . . .' Paula began as they entered the living room and she placed the tray on the table, then began to fill the cups.

'She's dead.' Archer sat in a hard-backed chair, very erect. 'The stress of the enforced take-over was responsible. I'm certain of that.'

'Enforced?' Newman enquired as he picked up a cup.

'You were very direct. You seem honest. I've nothing more to be frightened of losing. My wife, as I told you, is no longer with us. And my daughter, Julia, is thousands of miles away, in another country which I won't name. She's married someone in that country so her surname is changed. She's safe.'

'What happened about that takeover?' Newman asked quietly. 'And I saw you glance at my car. That man sitting inside is from the *Washington Post*. He also is investigating INCUBUS, as I am.'

108

'I'll tell you the whole horror story. You were right – I had no intention of selling. I told that to the American who came to my office and made the offer. A small brute with dark hair and a face like a gangster. A Mr Moroti. An hour later – after I'd rejected the offer – I get a phone call . . .'

He lifted his cup and swallowed more coffee. Paula refilled the cup as he continued, his voice stronger.

'I get a phone call,' he repeated, 'from someone else. An Englishman with a smooth voice. He says they met Julia when she left her secretarial college in Swindon. That she is in good health at the moment, but health is a precarious commodity . . .'

Archer's expression was grim, his mouth closed tight briefly as it came flooding back to him.

'I can remember his exact words. He went on to say all that was necessary to solve the small domestic problem was to be sensible. Just to accept the business deal.'

'You could have contacted the police,' Newman suggested.

'I was warned against that. The Englishman said all my telephones were tapped with a sophisticated device, that I was being watched. They gave me two days to decide – two days of hell.'

'So no one knows about this until now?'

'No.' Archer snapped his fingers. 'I forgot something very important. A week before Moroti called a girl arrived at my office after making an appointment. She said she was from the American magazine, *Leaders of Mankind*. Wanted to do an article on how I'd built the company from nothing. I know it must sound like an ego trip, but I thought the publicity might help the company with more export orders . . .'

'Could you describe this girl?' Newman asked.

'Yes. Very attractive. In her mid-twenties, I'd guess. She was small, no more than five foot five tall, I'd guess.

109

She had the most beautiful blonde hair. It draped over her back.'

Newman felt sick. He had just described Sandy.

'Go on, please,' he said.

'She asked me a lot of personal questions as well as about my business. My family. I mentioned I had a daughter, Julia. It was only later I suspected this was how they'd obtained their detailed information about me. My routine, where I lived, the fact that Julia was taking this secretarial course.'

'So you never went to the police. You discussed the situation with your wife?'

'We stayed up all night. It was a diabolical dilemma. Should we risk the police? Amelia – my wife – was against it. The point was what they offered valued the company at its market worth. The bastards had done their research.'

'So you sold out to them – and kept quiet.'

'Yes, wouldn't you?'

'Probably. Julia was unharmed when she was returned?'

'Yes. But very frightened. And they'd told her that if she ever talked about her experience I was liable to have a very nasty accident, probably fatal.'

'I see.' Newman looked at Paula. 'I think we ought to leave Mr Archer in peace. Unless you have something to ask.' He looked at Archer. 'I don't intend to mention your name – at least not until we've destroyed INCUBUS.'

Archer jumped up. 'Destroy the bloody bastards root and branch!' He looked at Paula. 'I apologize for my language.'

'I'd have used something stronger,' Paula told him.

12

Peggy Vanderheld stood quivering with fury, silhouetted against the picture window in Hauser's Helsinki office. Behind her the sea glittered as the sun reflected off the waves.

'I'm sure you take my point,' Hauser continued from behind his desk. 'Trust is the first quality I require in those who work close to me.'

'How was I to know the goddamn file was that confidential?' she raged. 'You told me to take the Riverton file down to the vault. I noticed the serial number wasn't right. So,' she drew herself up to her full height, her tight black dress clasping her full figure as though the material was pasted to her, 'so,' she repeated, 'I opened it to check the photograph and saw it *was* Ed Riverton's. That was when you walked in.'

'And what else did you check?' he enquired, his voice soft. 'The biography, maybe?'

'I never saw the goddamn biography. I only saw the first page which, in case you've forgotten the system, shows the subject's photograph, age, length of time spent in the employ of the company, when he – or she – joined us, when he – or she – left us. Unless, of course, they're still with us.'

He ignored the sarcasm, rolled his shirt sleeves higher up his strong, thick arms. Christ, it was hot. He was studying her as he performed this action. He was inclined to believe her: her anger was a natural reaction to his accusation that she had been prying into data which was not her concern.

'It's the heat,' he said eventually and gave her his big smile. 'You know I never could stand humid heat. Who

111

would imagine we'd get this kinda heatwave this far north?'

'You can ask someone else to take the file to the vault.'

'I'm asking you to take it for me – because you always have my full confidence as my personal assistant. And I think the time has come to consider extra reward financially for your loyalty. Thank you, Peggy.'

He watched her leave the room. She would be in a glow of appreciation. Hauser prided himself on his ability to manipulate human beings. He sat thinking about her. Maybe she *had* held her position for long enough. It was his policy never to keep staff below executive level too long – it eliminated the danger of their learning too much. I'll put the skids under her, he decided. Soon . . .

In the elevator Peggy Vanderheld was steaming, and not only with the heat. She knew the signs. He's getting ready to fire me, she thought. So how can I kick the bastard in the balls first?

'Frank, our plans for penetrating Europe and Russia are well under way. I think it's time we increased surveillance on all arrivals into Finland.'

Galvone nodded to Hauser and walked across to the picture window. Heat shimmered in a boiling haze over the sea. He wore a short-sleeved shirt and pale cinnamon slacks. His large feet were shod in trainers. Hauser noticed again that Frank was very physical, could hardly keep still for more than a few minutes.

'We already keep watch on all the air and sea ports,' he reminded his boss. 'And I study the lists of known visitors.'

'That's the point, Frank. We need to be on the look-out for unknown visitors. Use our travel company's film unit. We have reached a sensitive stage in the operation. So get pictures taken of everyone coming in. Then study the films they take.'

'Consider it done.' Galvone sat in a chair, wriggled his feet. 'How are things going in the Soviet Union? A hard nut to crack. They're suspicious of foreigners.'

'It's already cracked.' Hauser was in an expansive mood. 'We have Angel in place, so we don't have to use foreigners, as you called them.'

'Angel? Sounds like a woman. You don't trust women.'

Hauser smiled, waved his cigarette holder. 'Angel is a man, a member of the Politburo in Moscow.'

Frank whistled. 'That must have taken some delicate handling, to get a man at the very top in that secret society.'

'More open now, Frank. This is the era of *glasnost*. And some men at the top in little old Moscow are not sure how it is going to work out in the end. So dollars, especially in a bank account outside Russia, is mighty appealing. Gives a kinda insurance policy for the future.'

'Can I ask who this Angel is?'

'You just did.' Hauser puffed at his cigarette. 'And that was a mistake, Frank. Not like you to poke your big nose into areas that don't concern you. Your area of operation is Europe. I'm dealing personally with Russia. My, my, I am surprised.'

'Sorry, Chief,' Galvone said hastily. 'It just slipped out. I was so stunned you'd managed to pull off such a coup – but I shouldn't have been surprised, remembering how you built up the company from nothing.'

'Which I did . . .'

A dreamy look came over Hauser's large face. He was going back to La Jolla, the small town in California about ten miles north of San Diego on the Pacific coast. The place where he was born. The place where he had founded a small bank. And slowly he had extended his grip. The huge leap forward had taken place in the eighties when he had used junk bonds to enlarge his empire at a fantastic pace – until suddenly it was realized in the States that Hauser controlled the largest private financial institution in the republic.

Hauser, who worked by instinct, unloaded his mountain of junk bonds in the late eighties – and converted it into a mountain of money. He bought politicians at the lowest level – and the highest. Several state governors were tucked away safely in his pocket.

In the corridors of Congress the name 'Hauser' was whispered behind closed doors. What would be his next move, they all wondered. And everyone tried to climb on the bandwagon. INCUBUS was the next decade. INCUBUS was power. But power presided over by a benevolent father figure whose only motive was to do his best for humanity. He had said so. Himself . . .

'Ion Manescu has perfected the new East Expansion Division,' Galvone reported. 'He has sent representatives to Budapest, Bucharest, Prague, Warsaw, Sofia and Berlin. They're already establishing commercial cells in those areas.'

'Reprentatives, commercial cells.' Hauser chuckled. 'I like the terminology – considering their real purpose.'

You would, Galvone thought. You invented the terms yourself. Hauser had a passion for intrigue, for disguising sinister moves by using commercial jargon.

'They all passed the special training course at Kemijärvi,' Galvone continued. 'With special emphasis on tough strong-arm methods.'

'The American way,' Hauser commented approvingly. 'If you're going to compete you remember the game is winners and losers. We're winners. What can stop us – stop us establishing control from the Pacific coast to the Urals – especially with the help of Angel?'

'What can stop us?' Galvone repeated. 'I'll set up the film units on all access points to Finland.'

*   *   *

On Otmoor Archer followed his guests down the garden path to the front gate. Newman sensed he had something he wanted to say and wasn't sure how to put it as he opened the gate for Paula.

Over Otmoor a dirty mist like marsh gas was rising above the depressing fields. The sun was squeezing the last moisture out of the deserted landscape. A heavy silence filled the air and Newman suddenly realized he had heard no birds sing since they entered the area.

'My daughter, Julia,' Archer began, his hand on the gate.

'What about her?' Paula encouraged him with a smile.

'I don't communicate with her. Not by letter or over the phone.'

'I'm sorry to hear that. Don't you get on?'

'Oh, yes, the relationship is very good. She's bright – she was at Bristol University before she went to the secretarial college. She's a graduate.'

'So what's the problem?'

'Fear. As long as they don't know where she is they can't touch me. They wanted me to stand by as a consultant. I refused. That was after I'd sold out and sent Julia to . . . overseas. You won't try and find her, will you, Mr Newman?'

'You have my word. Under no circumstances. And your own name, your company, will also not be mentioned until I've stopped Hauser in his tracks, destroyed him.'

'You really think you can do that?'

'I'm going to have a damned good try.'

It was Paula who had helped Newman with his research during his stay in hospital, who had traced Gavin Manningham, ex-owner of Manningham Electronics in the Thames valley area.

She had travelled to Maidenhead to his old address and the new occupants of his small mansion had no idea where he had gone. Paula had persisted with the wife and had obtained the address of the housekeeper who had looked after Manningham's home. She had invited the housekeeper, a Mrs Parsons, to have dinner at a nearby de luxe hotel. She had soon realized Mrs Parsons had a liking for gin and tonics. After six drinks the housekeeper confided in Paula, gave her the new address.

'Sacked me without even a bonus,' she complained. 'And that after six years' faithful service. I saw his fancy woman by chance one day. Crossing the bridge on to Riverboat Island, she was. Wearing a very expensive new outfit. Not short of a pound when it came to putting clothes on *her* back, I can tell you . . .'

Newman had left Otmoor and was now driving back towards London, guided by Paula to Riverboat Island in the Thames. A weird island, they found as they walked the last half mile – after leaving the Mercedes in a car park with Dillon seated in the rear.

'I don't know why I came,' he snapped just before they left. 'Why can't I come and see this guy for myself?'

'Because I spoke to him on the phone and he sounds a tough customer. Not the type to talk if too many of us arrive like a delegation. He may not talk at all . . .'

In this assumption Newman was wrong. They crossed a wide roadbridge over a backwater of the Thames, the only way of reaching the place. Boats were moored to the main bank, mostly small powerboats with a few dinghies. The Lodge, as Manningham's new home was called, was a large bungalow which had obviously been built within the past couple of years. Manningham, a burly fifty-year-old with an aggressive manner and a paunch, met them as they descended the far side of the bridge. He was carrying an iron bar and his welcome was far from warm.

116

'You're Newman. I recognize you. What the hell is all this about?'

Newman decided the gentle handling of James Archer wouldn't work with this type. The direct approach was called for.

'It's about INCUBUS, the way they grabbed your firm. I am researching a series of articles for *Der Spiegel*. That's the leading German news magazine . . .'

'I know. What's the angle?'

'I'm building up an *exposé* on the methods they use, how they victimize people all over the world. How did they pull it off with you?'

'Come in and I'll show you.' He had been studying Paula's figure. 'Who is your friend?'

'My assistant, Paula.'

'That's a new name for the relationship. Follow me. Don't touch the wire fence – it's electrified.'

'Is that legal?'

'I didn't bother to ask. There are warning notices as you can see . . .'

The interior of The Lodge was like a show house, flashily furnished, expense no object. The living room overlooked a landing stage with a small power cruiser moored. The room had black leather armchairs and couches scattered on a wall-to-wall pink carpet. Silver cups – golfing trophies – crammed the mantelpiece over a huge arched brick fireplace. Framed photographs of Manningham swinging a club decorated the lime green walls. Their host saw Paula gazing at the carpet.

'Phoebe chose that. Great isn't it? Anyone want a drink?'

They both refused and Manningham poured himself a large Scotch as Paula sank carefully into a vast armchair which enclosed her. Manningham perched on a black leather stool by a well-stocked bar with a large mirror behind it. He opened the conversation with a clenched fist gesture.

117

'They're gangsters. Damn Yankee gangsters. Phoebe is up in town, buying more clothes, spending my money, so this is a good time to tell you . . .'

It was the same story as Archer had told but the sinister technique had varied. A Mr Vicenzo, an American, had met Manningham at his office. The description again matched that of Frank Galvone. Vicenzo had offered the market price for Manningham Electronics. Manningham had said he wasn't for sale, but he might consider double the figure offered.

'Who was he representing?'

Newman interjected the question quickly. Manningham was in full flood, downing his drink and pouring himself a fresh one. The answer was Columbia High Multi-Machines Inc. It was the same outfit Archer had told Newman that made the bid for Bennington. Newman's detailed researches in hospital had come up with the fact that this company was a subsidiary of INCUBUS.

Vicenzo had gone away. A few days later an Englishman had spoken to him on the phone, saying an envelope of pictures Manningham might find interesting were on the way by express registered post. That it would make life a lot happier for Manningham if he closed the deal at the price offered.

'I kept some of the photos that came in that envelope. They wanted them all back when I agreed to sell – at their price – but I said I'd spilt coffee on some of them and thrown them away. You have to understand I'm getting a divorce from my wife. We were separated at the time – the woman in the photographs is Phoebe. Two taken outside a flat I'd rented for her.'

Newman examined the five prints, handed them to Paula and lit a cigarette when Manningham told him to go ahead. The prints showed the same woman. Leaving a shop, outside a block of flats. One close-up taken with a zoom lens. The ugly factor about each print was someone had fashioned a rubber stamp showing the crosshairs of a sniperscope rifle. In each case the rubber stamp had been positioned on the prints so it was aimed at Phoebe's back, the centre of her chest. On the close-up the crosshairs stamped her blonde-framed face.

A high-class tart, Paula thought. A brazen expression. She must have spent half an hour making herself up. Paula spent two minutes putting on her face first thing. But clearly Manningham was in love with the girl. She handed him the pictures.

'They scared me. I admit it,' Manningham told them. 'I was frantic that they'd found out about the flat, where she lived. And then those hideous photographs.' He finished his drink.

'Before this Vicenzo came to see you did, by chance, you have any unusual interviews with an American flavour?'

Manningham stared. 'My God! That girl . . .'

Again it was a repeat performance. The girl who had interviewed him for *Leaders of Mankind*. And the description he gave of the girl was a perfect portrait of Sandy. The same formula all over.

They left Riverboat Island a few minutes later, walked over the wide bridge in silence. Paula was the first to speak.

'It's hideous,' she said. 'The technique they use. And Manningham dare not call the police because they convinced him his every move was being monitored. Which makes it even more diabolical because he's a tough nut.'

'Oh, it's diabolical,' Newman agreed grimly. 'But first we must dig deeper, get much closer to INCUBUS. And the answer probably lies in Finland.'

'Helsinki next stop?'

'I think so. But I've decided to press Tweed to let you come with me. You handled Archer well – and two men and a woman travelling together attract less attention.'

'We're going to let Cord Dillon come with us then?'

'Yes. We may need back-up – Dillon isn't a man I like but in a tight corner he's formidable.'

'So we all fly direct to Helsinki?'

'Not direct,' Newman said as they approached the car park. 'We go in by a roundabout route. Via Sweden. Someone may just be waiting for us to arrive.'

The following day Tweed announced his decision to Monica as they sat alone in his office. He was feeling the heat and kept mopping his forehead and hands.

'I'm going to send Marler to Finland to nose around and see if he can find out where the missing men have vanished to. Men like Ziegler of the STASI and Manescu of the *Securitate.*'

'Why Finland?'

'Because I'm getting reports from Europe that a new underground route has been established. It runs from the Balkans and Central Europe to Travemünde, the German port on the Baltic.'

'Where would they go from there?' Monica asked and looked at the wall map of the continent.

'They could catch the ferry to Helsinki. That way they would disappear without trace. In the present state of chaos no one is checking the passengers on that ferry crossing.'

'Shouldn't Newman know about this?'

'Definitely not. We are running two separate investigations. One into INCUBUS and all its activities. That problem is being tackled by Newman, Paula and Dillon. Marler will be searching for these vanishing men . . .' There was a knock on the door. 'Come in.'

Marler was in his early thirties, slim in build, wore an expensively cut sports jacket. Fair-haired, he was clean shaven and had a strong face. Only five feet seven tall, he spoke in a high pitched drawl, a public school accent he often emphasized abroad. Foreigners viewed him as the typical Englishman, a bit of a dandy. It put them off their guard. They would have felt more cautious if they'd known one of his qualifications was that he was the most deadly marksman in Western Europe with a rifle.

'Mornin' to you.' He perched his backside on the edge of Paula's desk, swung his legs. 'I was up till three ack emma memorizing those files you gave me. I've returned all of them to Central Registry. I concentrated on Ziegler and Ion Manescu. He was a big wheel in Bucharest *Securitate*, Mr Manescu. And I got the Engine Room boys in the basement to give me three photocopies of our Romanian friend.'

'Why three?' asked Tweed. 'You'll have to be careful who you mention his name to. He's dangerous.'

'Don't I know it? His track record is a shade beastly – but effective.' He took an envelope from his breast pocket, extracted three photos, laid them on the desk. 'One is the only original picture ever taken of him, the second shows him with a beard as well as his moustache, the third clean shaven. Archie downstairs is quite an artist.'

Monica and Tweed studied the three prints. Monica let out a cat-like hiss.

'It's incredible. He's unrecognizable in the treated pics.'

'Bound to have changed his appearance, would be my guess,' Marler commented and lit a king-size cigarette. 'When I do see him I'll know him – but he won't know me.'

'You should be armed,' Tweed decided. 'Manescu is a killer. The file records he's strangled people with his bare hands in the old days in Bucharest. With the security at airports that creates a problem. Doubtless you'll solve it.'

121

'Consider it solved.' Marler waved an airy hand. 'Is your contact who reported seeing Manescu board the Travemünde ferry for Helsinki reliable?

'Very.'

'You told me about Newman and the tragic death of his girl friend. When was Manescu spotted by that Romanian woman in London?'

'Two days before Sandy Riverton was murdered in Suffolk.'

'Interesting. The file said Manescu spent a year at the Romanian Embassy in London once, that he speaks excellent English. Probably just a coincidence – Manescu's presence in London at that time.'

'The same thought had occurred to me.' Tweed hesitated. 'I haven't told Bob Newman that. He's working on something else. I don't want his mind distracted. He took the death of Sandy very hard.'

'We don't always see eye to eye,' Marler reflected, blowing smoke circles, 'Newman and I. But he's had a tough time, I'll give him that.'

'When can you leave for Helsinki?'

'I've stacked up with Finmarks. I have an open ticket for where I'm flying to first.'

'Where's that?' Monica asked.

'Hamburg in north Germany.'

'That's a funny way to reach Finland.'

'I have my reasons, my dear . . .'

13

The Sikorsky which had flown Hauser from Helsinki to the isolated rendezvous in the Finnish woods stood inside the clearing, its rotors motionless. Hauser walked with Galvone towards the man who stood quite still in the shade of a stand of dense fir trees.

Hauser wore dark glasses, a wide-brimmed straw hat pulled well down over his face. He was carefully not displaying his cigarette holder and wore a floppy khaki drill jacket and baggy trousers of the same material. He was not easy to recognize as Franklin D. Hauser.

'This is Ion Manescu,' Galvone introduced.

'What are my instructions?' Manescu demanded, studying the large man in dark glasses.

'It has been decided to increase the area of surveillance, to widen the ring of protection and observation. We want you to send people to Sweden, to Stockholm. Watch for any arrivals boarding the large ferry ships for Finland.'

'That can be organized within two days,' Manescu replied briskly. 'And I have just the person with me who will be invaluable. Irina Serov.'

'With him?' whispered Hauser. 'He was supposed to meet us by himself. Ask him where this Irina is now.'

Galvone put the question in English. Manescu waved a long slim-fingered hand behind him.

'She is waiting out of sight in the woods. We flew together from Kemijärvi. And we now have fifty agents of different nationalities, all highly trained in the skills taught at the special place.'

'And,' Galvone continued, 'are those agents allocated to treat liberal elements holding positions of influence yet on their way?'

'They are in place already,' Manescu replied, choosing his words carefully.

His lean bony sun-tanned face was relaxed, concealing his high degree of alertness. Instinct told him he was passing some kind of test. He had been careful to answer questions tersely, adding no extra information. But had mention of Kemijärvi been a mistake?

'Ask him when the agents in place will start the anti-liberal operation?' Hauser whispered again.

Galvone put the question to Manescu who stood confidently, hands on his hips, staring at Galvone, never giving a glance in Hauser's direction. He wore a blue check T-shirt, light-coloured slacks. He looked for all the world like a Finn on holiday, which was his intention.

'Today,' Manescu responded, and closed his lips in a tight line which was little more than a gash in the brown hawk-like face.

Hauser turned away, walked slowly back to the waiting Sikorsky. Instead of proceeding at his normal brisk trot, he lumbered up the step-ladder and heaved himself ponderously inside the machine's cabin. There had been too many films taken, shown on TV, of Franklin D. Hauser departing by Lear jet in the States for yet another destination.

At all costs Hauser wished to distance himself from the coming Manescu operation in various ex-Communist European states. When Galvone leapt aboard and seated himself beside his chief Hauser made his unsettling comment before they started up the rotors.

'I'm impressed, Frank. Very impressed with Manescu. He did make one slip, of course – referring to Kemijärvi. But any man is permitted one slip. You think he was telling the truth when the said the anti-liberal operation starts today?'

'It's a sure thing.'

124

Being an American, Hauser referred to all Socialists as liberals. And they wanted to preserve the nationalized industries. You couldn't do business with – take over – an organization unless it was private enterprise. Hauser took off his glasses, substituted the pince-nez.

'So, when the bombs start to go off the Western press will put it down to hard-liner elements still yearning for the days before Gorbachev arrived. And I really was impressed with Manescu, Frank. Maybe one day we'll be able to bring him out of the closet, give him a new identity, promote him to a senior vice president.'

'Why not?' said Frank without enthusiasm, and gave the pilot the order to take off.

'Any idea who the man in the straw hat was?' Manescu asked Irina Serov as he met her as she dropped to the ground from the branch of a tall fir.

'Franklin D. Hauser,' she answered promptly and flourished the monocular glass she had used to study the man in the hat close up. 'I saw him once when I was with the Washington Embassy.'

'You're certain?'

Manescu grasped her firmly by the arm as he asked his question. Her other hand whipped up like a snake, grasped Manescu by the throat. 'You're hurting me. I don't like that.'

Manescu released her and rubbed his throat. She had a grip like an iron clamp. Irina Serov was an ex-colonel in the KGB – the only woman ever to reach that exalted rank. She had fallen foul of the Gorbachev reforms when a new KGB chief was appointed to clean up their act.

One night she had boarded a small fishing vessel moored at a small port near Yalta. With her pistol at his head, the skipper had sailed across the Black Sea to the Turkish coast. As ordered, he had anchored at night off the port of

125

Sinop. Irina had promptly shot him, weighted his body, dumped it overboard.

From Sinop she had made her way to Bucharest via Istanbul when Ceausescu was still in power. Here she had first met Ion Manescu who had taken her under his wing – she was an invaluable conduit as to what was going on in Moscow and sympathetic to the Romanian régime.

When Manescu fled Romania after the collapse of Ceausescu and his evil system he had taken Irina with him. Now he stood facing her inside a remote Finnish forest while she gazed back with eyes like the Arctic ice.

Thirty-five years old, she stood only five feet five and had let her dark hair grow long to change her appearance. She had a natural Slavic beauty, a good figure outlined by her tight high-necked dark green blouse – to merge with the forest – and more than one man had fallen prey to her and regretted it, if he had lived to do so. Her eyes had a greenish tinge and her full mouth was compressed with fury.

'We have to go to Sweden,' he said quietly. 'To check on any strangers coming here by that route. Especially we watch for strangers who are hostile – or might be.'

'Then it's a good job I spent time with the Soviet Embassy in Stockholm before they sent me to Washington. When do we leave?'

He was relieved by her reply. He might have been rather less relieved if he could have read her mind. Irina Serov was disillusioned: she cared no longer for Communism, for Capitalism, for any bloody 'ism'. She had one goal in life: to accumulate a huge fortune in dollars, to leave Europe forever and to spend the rest of her life in luxury in America. The realization that she was working for Hauser was opening new horizons for her, but she'd not had time to work out how she could exploit the knowledge.

'For Stockholm?' Manescu replied. 'Tomorrow.'

*   *   *

In Prague Ladislav Sacher, Minister for Trade and Industry, left Hradcany Castle and walked to his Skoda car parked by the kerb. In his sixties, he had a mane of white hair and a kindly expression. His face was lined after years of 'attention' from the STB, the Czech secret police which had now, thank God, been disbanded.

Sacher was a dedicated socialist who was devoting his considerable influence to blocking the attempts of private firms from the West to establish a dominating position. Especially he was against the Americans with what he called in speeches, 'their Mafia-style methods in business . . .'

Having spent years in prison under the old régime, years that had taken their toll and made him look well over seventy, he got up every morning now, threw open the windows of his apartment, and breathed in 'the good clean air of freedom'.

He carried a stick to aid his ailing right leg which had been broken deliberately by the STB while he was in prison. These days he felt happier than he had at any time in his life. A new era had dawned. A woman walking along the pavement smiled.

'Good morning, Father.'

'Thank you. It really is a wonderful day.'

They all called him 'Father' and he drank in the glowing warmth of the heatwave which comforted his tortured bones. The sun shone out of a clear azure sky. It was good to be alive.

He unlocked his car door, opened it, slid with difficulty behind the wheel, closed the door. A dozen yards away a burly young man, wearing a pale blue shirt, denim trousers and with his goggles adjusted, perched on his moped leant against the kerb. A canvas satchel looped round his neck sagged against his chest.

Sacher turned the ignition key, began to drive slowly away. The man on the moped threw back the flap of his satchel, glanced round, fingered the radio transmitter which would send the signal. He pressed the switch.

The bomb attached beneath the chassis of the Skoda detonated as the signal triggered it off. Sacher's car was lifted into the air by the violence of the explosion, its sides were torn off. Its occupant, the man they called 'Father', was blown into a messy pulp, the corpse unrecognizable, the flesh embedded with pieces of metal.

The man on the moped was already speeding away in the opposite direction. He had no idea that the bomb – with its sophisticated detonating system and the compact radio transmitter – had been smuggled to him by a devious route, via Finland and Germany. Nor that the brain behind the outrage was Ion Manescu. All he was concerned with was the generous fee in Czech crowns now buried under the floorboards of his tiny cottage in the High Tatra mountains.

In Bucharest the sun was not shining. A heavy overcast like a poison gas cloud was stationary over the battered city. The heat was there but in the evening it was humid and sweaty.

Stefan Campeanu, forty years old and a leader of the Peasants' Party, made his way home on foot to his apartment by his usual route, at his normal time. A man of routine, Campeanu had not realized this could be a dangerous habit. It made it easy for an enemy to monitor his movements.

Campeanu was opposed to the National Salvation Front government. Desperate to cling to power, it had agreed to accept help from the US. Campeanu was outspoken in his criticism of the idea that dollars channelled through private corporations should be accepted.

'There are Stalinists at the top of the Front,' he had openly accused. 'We must take no outside help. We must rebuild our shattered homeland ourselves. No to the dollar . . .'

There were still old parts of Bucharest surviving despite the bulldozers of Ceausescu which had torn down the old to build huge concrete cubes. Campeanu walked with his head down, deep in thought as he plunged into a dark narrow back street which was little more than an alley. His feet followed his well-trodden path home.

Half-way along the twisting alley he had to squeeze past a primitive scaffolding – constructed with wooden posts and three storeys high and heavy beams for planks. The structure was held together with ropes binding the beams to the vertical posts. Darkness was falling rapidly as Campeanu eased his way past the narrow gap.

He heard the first ominous creak, looked up. The clumsy structure – the ropes deliberately loosened – was toppling. Campeanu, an athletic man, began to hurry. Then he heard a shout. Ahead of him a shadowy figure stood a dozen yards away, both arms raised, the hands holding what looked like a gun.

Campeanu stopped hurrying, a fatal pause. The scaffolding tumbled down, burying him under a grotesque criss-cross of beams and posts. Silence descended on the alley. When the press photographers took pictures the following morning their pictures of chaos were somehow symbolic of the chaos which was growing worse in Romania.

Two days later Tweed read the *Daily Mail* spread out across his desk. The pictures told the stories. One showed the small boat capsized in the Danube in Hungary outside Budapest. Two leading liberals had drowned. There were rumours the small boat had been hit by a much larger vessel.

The second picture showed what remained of the wrecked car in Prague, the car which had belonged to Ladislav

Sacher. The headline screamed: 'STB ATROCITY!'

The third picture, the last in the double spread, showed the weird spiked mess of scaffolding in the Bucharest alley. It looked like a modern sculpture. The headline was equally sensational. 'LEADING BUCHAREST LIBERAL DIES IN ACCIDENT?'

'It's started,' he said to Monica who had read the paper earlier.

'The strange thing is all four men were killed within hours of each other,' she commented.

'That is the point. One accident. Two could be coincidence. But three – and the Czech liberal was killed by a bomb – is too much. It's part of a plan.'

'You mean terrorists?'

'No. Who ever heard of any fanatical terrorist outfit being able to organize three assassinations in three different countries within the same twenty-four hours?'

'Then . . .'

'It's not terrorists in the normally accepted sense of the breed,' Tweed said grimly. 'This is terror used as a weapon, an instrument of policy.'

'Can you explain that a bit more?'

'It is terror used *pour encourager les autres*, as the French say. To encourage the others – the other liberal and democratic elements in Eastern Europe to keep their heads down. It's cold-blooded murder carefully orchestrated.'

'But who is behind it?'

'I've no idea. Yet. No proof, anyway. We have to start moving faster. And it suggests the driving force – or someone working for him – has a good knowledge of Central and Eastern Europe.'

'Can you back that up – except as a theory?'

Tweed stood up, began pacing round his office, staring at the wall map of Europe.

'Take the Bucharest tragedy. The man who planned all

130

these assassinations knows the right people inside Romania to do his murderous bidding. A scaffolding collapses on this important politician, Campeanu. You'd need someone with a good deal of local knowledge to pull that off.'

'And the killing of Ladislav Sacher in Prague?'

'Again, someone has to know who to hire to do the job – and probably how to smuggle the bomb into the country. The same applies to the so-called accident to two Hungarians who were drowned in the Danube. Both were vocal in their belief that Hungary must pull itself up by its own bootstraps. And to stage that collision someone had contact with the skipper of a larger vessel plying the river.'

'You're reaching,' Monica commented.

'Three in three countries is too much,' he repeated. 'But I haven't worked out yet the full implications of the conspiracy. I also think that we may have to send Harry Butler and Pete Nield as back-up for Newman and Paula later.'

'When are they leaving for Finland?'

'Very soon. But first Bob wants to talk to Evelyn Lennox before they go. He has some obsession she hasn't told him the whole truth.'

'And Marler?'

'Already on his way to Hamburg.'

Hauser also was reading the reports but his newspaper was the *Herald Tribune*. Galvone stood beside him as his chief pushed the newspaper aside.

'Well, they haven't linked up the three incidents. Just a wringing of the hands over the ferment which is developing in Europe.' He lit a cigarette, clenched the holder and sat back with an expression of great satisfaction. 'I didn't think anyone in the West would catch on to our ball game.'

'To scare the shit out of the creeps opposing our offers to modernize their industries.'

'More than that, Frank. Something far more subtle. This campaign Manescu is managing so well has another important purpose – to make the Brits, the Frogs, etc., nervous about investing in those countries. That way we kill off the competition while we scoop the pool ourselves. Then it will be too late. And talking about timing, we have to create a situation so I can fire Peggy Vanderheld.'

'I reckon, Chief, that intimidation of the competition is a brilliant strategy.' Galvone let the fulsome admiration show in his tone. 'You really have worked this one out and we will scoop the pool.'

Hauser patted him on the arm. 'Nothing to it, Frank. It's just the American way.'

14

'Walberswick is a beautiful village,' Paula said as Newman drove slowly down The Street under the arched trees. 'More like a hamlet, actually – but with some wonderful houses and all different and old. I assume Evelyn knows that we are coming?'

It was late evening, close to twilight, but the heat of the day made the atmosphere baking, the air very still. Newman nodded as they passed one dwelling.

'That's Rose Bower. And Evelyn knows *I* am coming but I forgot to mention you'd be with me.'

'Oh, yes?' She eyed him with a roguish smile. 'Do I gather from that that my presence may not be entirely welcome?'

'All I want you to do is to give me your impression of her later. Now I'm letting you have a look at the sea before we call on her. We're a few minutes early . . .'

He turned left when they had passed the hotels, parked the car in the space reserved for vehicles and they climbed out, stretched, stood looking at the view. The wide belt of dune-land with its hummocks and scrubby grass growing out of the sand was deserted at that hour.

A weird isolated structure like a huge cabin reared up close to the harbour entrance. Two storeys high, the walls made of wood, it had a tiled roof and one half had been refurbished. A gull screeched in the distance, dived over the lake-calm deep purple of the North Sea stretching away to a hard straight line, the horizon. In the distance to the north the cluster of toy-like buildings which was Southwold stood a mile away beyond the harbour.

'Evelyn told me she often comes for a walk among the dunes,' Newman remarked. 'When she wants a change she drives south to Minsmere Nature Reserve, a very lonely spot at night.' He checked his watch. 'Time to call on her. While we are there could you excuse yourself, leave me alone with her for a short while. I want to ask her an embarrassing question.'

Paula looked at him wickedly as she settled herself in the front passenger seat. She smoothed her raven black hair with a slim hand.

'I think I can guess what that question might be. And I'm sure she's attractive.'

'You're an imp,' he told her as he turned the ignition key. 'And yes, she is attractive. To some men I'd imagine . . .'

His friendship with Paula had grown steadily. A friendship without complications. As he drove back up The Street he frowned. A man on a motor cycle, a big Honda, had turned round at their approach, parked by the roadside close to Evelyn's cottage. Newman only caught a

133

glimpse of the man in a dark leather jacket but he looked remarkably like Steve, the thug who had accompanied Papa Grimwood on their visit to Greenway Gardens, Wandsworth.

There was a *vr-o-o-m* of engine sound which murdered the silence. The motor cyclist sped off away from Walberswick, was soon a speck which vanished round a bend.

Evelyn, wearing a flowered summer dress belted at her slim waist and clinging tightly to her good figure, led the way into the low-beamed sitting room. It was neat as a new pin and showed no signs of the going-over it had suffered when Newman was last there.

Tugging at her mane of red-gold hair she turned on her heel and looked Paula up and down. Her quick scan took in the pale blue T-shirt, short sleeved, the short pleated skirt, the long shapely legs.

'So you're Bob's . . . *assistant*?' she said with too much inflection.

'His research assistant,' Paula replied with a warm smile, a shade too warm.

Evelyn came close to Newman, dipped her head sideways. He felt compelled to bend forwards and kiss her on the proffered cheek. Which was, of course, for Paula's benefit.

'Lovely to see you, Bob,' Evelyn said again. 'Drinks for anyone?'

They both refused and sat down as Evelyn became the welcoming host. Newman was careful to avoid the couch, to sit in an armchair. Evelyn sat in a Regency chair, carefully crossed her legs, displaying briefly a glimpse of thigh clad in black tights decorated with butterflies.

'Has anything happened to alarm you?' Newman enquired. 'Any strangers in the village? Any motor cyclists visiting the place regularly?'

'No to the first question. No to the second. No to the last one. The bike gangs never come here. Only one very quiet pub and no shop windows to smash in after they've got drunk. Southwold is different. But there was a motor bike went by a few minutes ago. I didn't see the rider.'

'So you feel safe here? No contact with Helsinki since you arrived?'

'Yes, I feel safe.' A brief hesitation. 'And no contact with Helsinki. Not that I'd expect it.'

'Has anyone been fired recently from INCUBUS Oy.? Someone who might harbour a grudge against the company?'

'Not while I was there,' she said, answering now at her normal pace.

'Who employed there would know most about Hauser's day-to-day work, the orders he gives?'

'Well, there's Adam Carver, a VP in charge of banking. Then Frank Galvone often turns up, another VP. Information and Planning is his division, whatever that might be. But if you're thinking of someone who would talk to you, forget both men. Hauser must pay them big money.'

'Anyone else?'

'Not really.' She puckered her shaped eyebrows. 'There is Peggy Vanderheld. A typical New York career woman. But she's about forty and has been with the company ages.'

'What position does she hold?'

'Hauser's PA. He trusts her. That is, as far as he trusts any woman. His wife left him – and I don't blame her – but apparently since then he's gone off women.'

Paula stood up. 'Miss Lennox, do you mind if I pop out and have a look at your front garden before it's too dark? I love wild roses and your path is clustered with them.'

'Take as long as you like. Leave the door with the lock on the latch so you can get back again . . .'

Newman waited until they were alone. Evelyn pulled

135

her chair closer to him. Her wide mouth, emphasized with her scarlet lipstick, parted in a glowing smile. She reached out, took his right hand.

'I feel even safer now you're here.'

He hit her with his direct question. 'Evelyn, were you Ed Riverton's mistress?'

She snatched her hand away. 'What makes you say a bloody awful thing like that?'

He counted on his fingers. 'One, when I was having dinner with you and Ed in Helsinki at his apartment I sensed a certain intimacy between the two of you. Two, when I called Ed's Helsinki apartment to tell him about Sandy *you* took the call, you were there again – in his apartment. Three, you went all out to persuade me to call Sandy to break the news about Ed's murder. More naturally one sister would have gritted her teeth and done the job herself. You do have grit. But if you'd been playing about with your sister's husband you might feel inhibited. Enough?'

'You expect me to admit it?'

'You just did. I don't care about your private life. But I'm trying to track down the man who brutally murdered Sandy, your sister. Did Ed Riverton ever tell you anything confidential about INCUBUS? About his job? What was his job, for God's sake?'

'He was very close-mouthed . . .'

'Come off it, Evelyn. Pillow talk. That's when men let their back hair down. And when I interviewed Ed he was on edge, very nervy. He'd need someone as a safety valve – you fit the bill.'

She played with her lace handkerchief, just as she had done at Greenway Gardens. Newman lit a cigarette, blew smoke rings, watched them float up, collapse against a heavy wooden beam. He kept silent.

'He was in charge of Dracon,' she began. 'That's the think-tank for INCUBUS, based outside Boston. He told me he used to catch the train from Penn Station, New York, get off it at a station called Back Bay where a car would be waiting for him. He'd be driven to Dracon which is a complex of well-guarded buildings off what they used to call Space Highway . . .'

'Yes, I've heard of it. What went on at Dracon?'

'Ed said they were a lot of kooks. Academics from the Ivy League universities, planners who were ex-generals lured from the Pentagon for huge salaries, economists. I remember a name. A Professor Hiram Goldstein. He'd written a book.'

Now we're getting somewhere, Newman thought. 'I read the book,' he said. 'The one by Goldstein. *No More Space.* But what did these freaks *do*?'

'They were producing plans for expansion, Ed said. He didn't like the plan Hauser chose. He didn't say why, didn't give me any idea of the plan. But Goldstein had a lot to do with it. Ed told me he'd had a lot of bitter arguments about this plan with Hauser.'

'When did he tell you this? About the arguments?'

'A week before they . . .' She choked. 'Before they dragged him out of the harbour. Not a human being any more. Just a mulch of flesh frozen solid as a rock.'

'That doesn't sound like your phraseology. Who used those very graphic words?'

'A Finn called Mauno Sarin. Some kind of detective. He called on me at the apartment a few hours before I left for the airport. I told him nothing. There was nothing I had to tell him. But I was frightened. It was one reason why I caught the first flight home. I never want to have anything more to do with INCUBUS. There's something sinister going on up there in Finland.'

It was very dark as Newman drove along the road away from Walberswick on their way back to London. Paula sat

137

by his side, checking the map spread on her lap with a pencil flash.

'What did you think of Evelyn?' he asked.

'Do you want me to be nice or honest?'

'Honest.'

'You'll think me catty, but you asked for it. She's a man-hunter. It's second nature to her to check that she's still attractive to men with every one of them she meets. And she wants you. Maybe permanently. Or hadn't you realized it?'

'She wants a protector. And yes, I think she's decided I fit the role. But after seeing that motor cyclist, she may need a protector. So if you spot a public phone box tell me. Anything else about the seductive Evelyn?'

'She's a liar. Does that sound catty, too?'

'Just tell me why you said that.'

'When you asked her whether anyone from Helsinki had got in touch with her, that's when she lied. I was watching her. She hesitated before she answered that one. Perhaps only another woman would have noticed.'

'I noticed. The problem is if we can ever trap Hauser in a situation that's illegal we'll need every witness we can get. Evelyn could be one of those witnesses.'

'Well,' Paula teased him, 'you could always keep in touch – she's quite a flirt.'

Adam Carver returned on foot to Rose Bower for the second time that evening. On his first excursion he'd seen a Mercedes parked outside so he'd turned back, returned to his hotel room further down The Street.

Evelyn peered through the newly installed spyhole after turning on the porch light, unfastened the two fresh locks and gave her visitor a radiant smile. She invited him in, pulled at her hair, relocked the door and followed him into the living room.

'I've had a visitor since you were here this afternoon,' she informed him. 'The handsome and beguiling Bob Newman. Care for another drink?'

'A double Scotch would go down nicely – providing you'll join me.' Carver gazed with open admiration at her figure. 'And I see you've dressed yourself up for me. You look – terrific. Sexy.'

'Really?'

She was pleased as she poured the drinks. Carver was a good-looking bastard, had nice manners, and she liked his warm smile, his smooth ways. Deliberately she'd omitted the fact that Paula had accompanied Newman. He asked the question as she handed him his drink.

'Newman, the foreign correspondent? I see. And what did he want coming to this back of beyond?'

'I got the impression he came to see me.' They clinked their glasses. 'We're just good friends, Adam.'

How unsubtle can you get, he thought, but he grinned, drank half the Scotch, placed his glass on the paper mat Evelyn had provided. They were sitting close together on the couch. He put an arm round her waist, pulled her close, kissed her full on the mouth. She went limp, kept her eyes closed, her hand round his neck. He wiped lipstick off his mouth with a handkerchief, reminded himself to lose it. Evelyn had an expression like that cat which has swallowed the cream.

'How did you find me out here in this back of beyond?' she asked.

'When you didn't call me back from your place in Wandsworth I checked with headquarters in Norwich – to find out where your sister had lived,' he said casually. 'I thought it was worth a try, so I drove up here, booked myself in at a hotel down the road. Hey presto! I'm on your doorstep this afternoon.'

'You don't give up easily, do you?'

'Not where a girl like you is concerned.' Can't lay it on

139

too thick, flattery with a trowel, he thought. 'Did Newman ask questions about your sister?'

'No!' She was annoyed. 'I told you, he came to see me.'

'Understandable. Exactly what I've done myself. Is it just as nice upstairs?'

She gave him a sideways look. 'You can come and see, if you like.'

Paula spotted a phone box near a crossroads. Newman called Tweed, explained the position quickly and Tweed agreed to send Harry Butler to Walberswick within the hour. Newman gave Tweed the name of the hotel he'd stayed at during his earlier visit, said yes, he was phoning from a call box when Tweed posed the question.

'Should he be armed?' Tweed asked quickly.

'Yes,' Newman advised. He'd remembered the Walther Steve had brandished in Evelyn's Wandsworth house.

Driving on, he told Paula that Harry Butler was on the way, that he'd given a brief description of Evelyn so Butler would recognize her, plus her address. They travelled the rest of the way into London in silence. Newman dropped off Paula at her flat in Putney, then drove back to his own place. As he entered Beresforde Road at three in the morning his eyes were everywhere, remembering the juggernaut which had put him in hospital. Which is why he spotted the stationary police car.

It was parked beyond his flat on the opposite side of the road. Two men in the front in uniform and their radio aerial extended. He went inside the building and was not too surprised when the bell rang as he was making coffee. He went into his narrow lobby, picked up the phone, pressed the button which operated the visual screen. Chief Inspector Buchanan was standing outside the closed front door.

140

'Newman here. I've just got back. It's after three in the morning. What do you want?'

'A brief word with you. Possibly you'll find it helpful.'

'Leave Warden outside, please. I could do without the double act just for once . . .'

He pressed the button which released the lock on the hall door, opened his flat door and said nothing as Buchanan strolled inside. Newman led the way into the large sitting room at the front, gestured towards a couch.

'I'm just making coffee,' he said reluctantly.

'Thank you, but I'm not thirsty.' Buchanan gazed round the room, taking in everything, then spoke again as Newman stepped down out of the galley kitchen with his mug of coffee. 'I'm sorry to disturb you at this hour . . .'

'But your watchers parked in that patrol car radioed in that I'd arrived back. Can we cut this short? I'd like a spot of sleep before dawn breaks.'

'You've not yet left for Helsinki but I have a feeling that you will go there.'

He paused, but Newman was accustomed now to this tactic and said nothing. Carrying his mug of coffee, he sat down on a hard-backed chair by the dining table. He drank some of the hot liquid and felt less weary.

'Just assuming that Hauser is involved in the murder of Sandra Riverton,' Buchanan continued, 'and I emphasize it can only be a vague assumption, there's no hard evidence —'

'Have you even any soft evidence?' Newman snapped.

'Circumstantial, you mean? Well, I've kept coming back to the fact that both murders have certain similarities – as I mentioned to you before. Also they took place within the short time span of twenty-four hours, approximately. Also both victims worked for the same organization.'

'Can we get to the point, please?'

'The point is that if my assumption is right then

141

whoever committed those murders may well be someone close to Hauser.'

'What exactly does that mean?'

'It means that from the little I've been able to learn about Hauser he runs a tight ship. He only allows top people to handle major policy decisions. In short, the murderer would be one of his close associates. So, who is close to Hauser?' Buchanan stood up. 'I thought you might like to bear that in mind. When you visit Finland.'

'Thank you.'

'If you locate the murderer you'll then be in the clear, which you aren't yet.'

'Thank you.'

'Good-night. I can find my own way out.'

'I'd hope so. You are a detective.'

Evelyn was up late the following morning. She looked at the rumpled bed and decided it would have to wait. She felt in a restless mood and after drinking a cup of strong coffee she went for a walk towards the sea.

She wore a white high-necked blouse in preference to one of her low-cut jobs. No point in provoking the locals into talking about her. But her pale blue skirt was short, displaying her elegant legs. She saw the well-built man, in his thirties she judged, for the first time as she strolled across the grassy dunes towards the shingle bank which reared up like a dyke with the beach and the sea beyond.

He wore a shabby blue check shirt, open at the neck, a windcheater, grey slacks and trainer shoes. Round his neck was slung a loop supporting a pair of binoculars. Evelyn veered towards him: she needed the company of a man.

Adam had left her cottage early in the morning. He had said he had to fly back to Helsinki. 'Business, darling. I have to earn my living like the next man, get back to my base . . .'

142

Evelyn thought his departure was a great bore. And in no way was he like the next man. Not after their night together. Had it been a one-night stand? She had no idea. He'd promised to keep in touch, but didn't they always do that?

'Good morning,' she greeted the well-built man. 'Isn't it a fantastic day? Yet another one. The heatwave goes on.'

'Good morning to you.' Harry Butler raised his deer-stalker hat, revealing his thick brown hair. 'Yes, Miss, it's just great.'

'Mind if I walk a little way with you? My sister died just recently and I'm feeling lonely. What are the binoculars for?'

'Watching birds. A hobby of mine.'

'You've come to the right place . . .'

She said nothing more for a while, waiting for him to talk about himself. Butler, clean shaven and with a poker-faced expression, kept silent. Before leaving London he had been briefed by Tweed, who had supplied data on the area obtained from Newman. When the Minsmere Nature Reserve was mentioned Butler immediately decided on his role.

'Bird watcher,' he had told Tweed. 'Perfect cover. A bird watcher can go almost anywhere in the country without arousing any comment . . .'

As they walked up to the shingle bank Butler was thinking Evelyn would be stunned if she knew he had seen Adam Carver leaving Rose Bower just after dawn, that he'd taken several pictures of Carver with his camera equipped with a telescopic lens. What could be more natural than a bird watcher prowling round close to dawn with a camera?

She would have been equally surprised had she known Butler had already explored all round the outside of Rose Bower. Sleeping in his car parked at an isolated spot,

143

Butler had arrived at the hotel Newman had recommended and claimed the room he had reserved the night before by phone.

As they scrambled up the shingle bank he zipped his front half-way up to make sure the hip holster carrying his .38 Special Smith & Wesson revolver was concealed. Standing on the crest of the bank Evelyn appeared to slip, caught hold of Butler's arm, then slipped her arm through his.

Butler was thinking getting to know Evelyn had proved a lot easier than he'd anticipated. Which would help him in his protection role. He'd planned to ask her the way to Minsmere but she'd done the job for him. On the other hand as a man he was wary: he liked to make the first move towards a woman himself. Evelyn showed a shade too much initiative for his liking.

'Isn't the view just too wonderful?' she glowed.

'Great.'

He was eyeing the wooden piles which lined the harbour entrance between which a powerful tide was surging in. His experienced eye had found an ideal way for an intruder to get to Evelyn. They came in by boat after dark, moored to one of the piles, did the job, and were away before anyone even knew they had arrived. Walberswick was by no means the out of the way safe refuge it had seemed.

15

All roads led to Finland.

Tweed received the mysterious call on his scrambler line at ten in the morning. The man at the other end spoke good

English, spoke rapidly. He gave the correct password which the PM had told Tweed during his interview with her months earlier. *Endgame.*

'Could you please fly to Helsinki, Mr Tweed? A room is reserved in your name at the Hotel Hesperia, which we believe you know. Tomorrow please wait at the end of North Harbour near the cathedral at eleven o'clock at night. Alone. We will make contact with you there.'

'And who is this speaking?'

'Lev Frolov . . .' The voice spelt it out. 'You will meet us, Mr Tweed, at the appointed rendezvous? It is very urgent.'

'I'll be there, yes. What is urgent? We're on scrambler . . .'

The line had gone dead. Tweed replaced the receiver slowly and gazed at Monica. He looked thoughtful.

'At long last the Russians have got in touch. Book me on a flight to Helsinki today. Yes, in my own name.'

He repeated the gist of the conversation. Monica listened, looked worried.

'Do you know this Lev Frolov?'

'I've never heard of him. It could be an assumed name. I thought I recognized the voice, but probably I was wrong. It has to be someone very high up because it's the personal representative of the Soviet president – just as Cord Dillon is of the American president. I've never known such tight security.'

'You do realize that this rendezvous could be very dangerous,' she persisted. 'North Harbour is the place where they found the frozen body of Ed Riverton on the ice back in February. Shouldn't you take someone with you?'

'No. The arrangement is I meet my opposite number, whoever he may be, alone.'

'Eleven o'clock at night. Will it still be light in Helsinki then?'

'No. At this time of year they have two hours of darkness – between eleven and one in the morning.'

'I don't like the sound of this at all.'

'I'll be careful. Nice of them to fix me up with a room at the Hesperia,' Tweed commented.

'You sound ironic.'

'Well, it's obvious, isn't it? My hosts, if you can call them that, will have the place under surveillance. And after all this time it suddenly becomes urgent. I wonder why?'

'I still don't like it,' Monica repeated. 'The situation inside Russia is so unstable.'

'Just book my air ticket, there's a good girl. And it isn't as though I'm going to Russia . . .'

Newman, Paula and Cord Dillon caught Flight SK526, departing London Airport at 1100 hours, arriving Stockholm, Arlanda airport, at 1425 hours, local time.

Newman had driven them to Heathrow, leaving his Mercedes in the long-term car park. On their way there Cord Dillon was in an explosive mood. He sat alone in the back as he barked out his questions.

'Can you tell me why the hell we're flying to Stockholm – which is in Sweden if my geography's any good.'

'Your geography is OK,' Newman assured him breezily. 'I decided we'd move in on Scandinavia by a devious route for two reasons. First in case there's surveillance on everyone arriving in Finland. INCUBUS is a huge organization, and from what Evelyn told me it's run like a military outfit – with some high-pressure security systems.'

Paula giggled. 'Which explains the fancy dress you have decked yourself up in?'

'He looks OK,' Dillon growled.

Newman wore a baseball cap. He was clad in a jacket

146

made of a loud check material. His trousers, also a loud check, were tucked inside leather boots, knee length. He was sporting a pair of large dark glasses.

'And the second reason?' Dillon demanded.

'You'll find that out after we arrive. And the heatwave is hitting Scandinavia like it is here. You'll find the drive in from Arlanda gives you time to adjust – it takes three quarters of an hour to get into the city . . .'

Aboard the flight after take-off Paula, sitting in the window seat alongside Newman, glanced back. The two seats behind them were empty and they were at the front of Business Class. As arranged, Cord Dillon was three rows back, apparently travelling on his own.

'That book you had almost finished when I called at your flat last night. What was it? You seemed absorbed.'

'Evelyn put me on to it – something Ed Riverton once told her. About the Dracon think-tank which dreams up ideas for Hauser. They have a Professor Hiram Goldstein on the staff. It was his book I was reading. *No More Space*.'

'What is it about then? Come on. Give.'

'Goldstein has obviously been influenced by a man called Haushofer. He was an expert on so-called geopolitics – global strategies. Hitler approved of Haushofer. Goldstein argues that the United States is hemmed in from any further expansion to the west – because Japan controls the Pacific Basin. He's worked out that the only direction America can expand in is to the east – Europe and Russia. Hence the title – *No More Space*. To the west. Only to the east.'

'Does that tell us anything?'

'It might.'

'Then tell me what. You've obviously been impressed by that book.' She punched him on the arm. 'I like to know what's going on.'

'Then read the book.'

'I will. But tell me what so struck you.'

'Goldstein refers to *Lebensraum*, living space. Hitler, the history books tell us, made a big song and dance about just that. *Lebensraum*. But Hitler meant living space for people. Just an excuse to conquer all and sundry. Goldstein uses it in a different sense. He means space to expand American business. The new objectives – Europe and Russia.'

'Isn't INCUBUS big enough already?'

'Too damned big. But these billionaires can never stop – get enough. They have to look for new worlds to conquer. I need a nap. I'll skip lunch. Watch the view . . .'

There was no cloud bank to obscure the view and some time later Paula stared down on Sweden from thirty-five thousand feet. A patchwork quilt of brown and green fields. Here and there a large dark island which was a forest of evergreens. Then a series of lakes, the water very still and blue under the glare of the sun: like lakes of ice. She checked her watch. Soon they would be approaching Arlanda.

Ion Manescu and Irina Serov travelled to Stockholm overnight aboard one of the large Viking Line ships which ply between Helsinki and the Swedish capital. They disembarked in the early morning at the quay close to the city centre.

The ancient stately buildings of the city of bridges and waterways gleamed in the sunlight, each building a differently muted colour of stone. The twenty-man team which formed the film unit came ashore separately with its equipment and travelled immediately by hired cars to the locations Manescu had specified.

'Well, we've arrived,' Irina commented as they waited for a taxi. 'Do you think we've covered all major entry points?'

'*I* have,' Manescu informed her, stressing who was in charge of the operation. 'One unit goes to Gothenburg Airport on the west coast. Another to the sea crossings from Copenhagen. Another to Bromma Airport just outside Stockholm – a small airfield but someone may try and get clever. And the main unit will be at Arlanda within the hour.'

'That should do the job for us,' Irina replied.

'Just so long as no one from the Soviet Embassy recognizes you. At one time you did work there,' Manescu warned.

Irina stroked her long dark hair brushed to frame her oval face. She wore tight denims which emphasized her long legs, high-heeled shoes which increased her height, a form-fitting windcheater. Yes, Manescu was thinking, you think you look pretty good, and you do. He wouldn't have minded laying her himself, but he never mixed business with pleasure.

'When I was at the Embassy,' Irina told him in her slow deliberate way, 'my hair was cut short, I wore dowdy clothes as ordered by the military attaché. You really think they would recognize me? Because I don't. And you imagine anyone at the Embassy in those days is still there? You have to be joking.'

'You have the instrument on you? Just in case,' Manescu snapped to reassert his authority.

'Concealed in a special pocket inside my windcheater. I do know my job.'

'The instrument' was a specially designed hypodermic perfected in the laboratories of INCUBUS's Pharmaceutical Division. A very slim needle of hardened glass with a pin-point tip, it contained air and was carried in a protective leather sheath. Irina had only to insert the tip into the target's veins, press the plunger, and death would follow in minutes. With no trace of how the victim had died.

149

Manescu watched as the last team came down the gangway and climbed inside a waiting van with their equipment. Along the side of the van were inscribed the words *Commercial Film & Publicity Unit* in Swedish.

'Here's our taxi,' Irina said. 'It's not far to the Hotel Diplomat.'

'Wait a minute.'

Manescu watched the team stowing the film cameras inside at the rear of the vehicle. He stood there until the last man had climbed aboard and the van doors were closed. It was driven off, crossed the bridge on to Gamla Stan, the island crammed with medieval buildings, and headed north.

'Now we know we have Arlanda, the gateway to Stockholm, covered,' he said and stepped into the taxi.

Marler had flown to Hamburg First Class aboard a Lufthansa plane. He preferred Lufthansa or Swissair for European flights: they were the only airlines which provided first-class accommodation. It was not only more comfortable – first class carried far fewer passengers and made it easy for him to study his fellow passengers.

Disembarking at Hamburg Airport, he was certain he had not been followed. The heat hit him as he left the aircraft but Marler was immune to extremes of climate.

Dressed very much as an Englishman of means in his expensive sports jacket, his silk shirt, regimental tie and well-pressed slacks, he collected his single case from the carousel. In his other hand he carried a long hold-all with the handle of a tennis racquet protruding.

A cab took him to the luxurious Four Seasons Hotel and, as requested by phone, his room overlooked the Binnen Alster, the smaller of two lakes in the centre of the great port. After lunch in the dining room he made a phone call, told the man at the other end he had arrived,

150

and slept until late in the evening. So far he had behaved as the impeccable Englishman abroad.

Just after dark he took a taxi to a restaurant in an old converted warehouse on the waterfront overlooking the river Elbe. The restaurant was a de luxe establishment but the district wasn't. It had begun to drizzle heavily as he got out of the cab and paid it off.

A long line of heavy trucks was parked in the middle of the deserted street lined with more warehouses. In the distance girls tried to shelter under the lee of the warehouses. One of them called out but Marler ignored her as he dashed inside.

Hugo Hildebrandt was waiting for him at a table perched on an upper level looking down on the main restaurant. Beyond the lower level Marler could see a tugboat slugging upstream through the misty drizzle.

Hildebrandt, an arms dealer, was dressed like a prosperous businessman. He greeted Marler amiably, said he was paying, handed him the menu. Hildebrandt was slim and tall with a high forehead. In his forties, he stooped as tall men are apt to. They ordered their meal before Hildebrandt – H.H. as he was known in international circles from Hamburg to Iran – raised the subject of business.

'The merchandise you require is available. At a price, of course,' he said in German.

'Of course,' Marler replied in the same language. 'So, how much?'

'It is not damaged goods, it is new . . .'

'Skip the sales talk. How much?'

'Ten thousand deutschmarks . . .'

'You must be joking.'

'I never joke where business is concerned,' Hildebrandt replied calmly, gazing down into the lower restaurant. 'There is Lisa Krenz, the well-known actress.'

'Three thousand,' Marler snapped.

151

'Now that is what I call a joke.' Hildebrandt started eating. 'The bread is very good here,' he remarked. 'When the bread is good the rest of the meal should be edible.'

'Five thousand deutschmarks. That is my final offer.'

Marler crushed his napkin. Pushing back his chair he stood up prior to leaving. Hildebrandt gestured for him to stay.

'Very well. Five thousand. That is under cost, but for you I make the exception. A small loss . . .'

Marler carefully concealed his surprise as he sat down again. He had expected to go up to six thousand. Hildebrandt was obviously short of cash. An hour later the German led the way out of the restaurant. Marler pulled up the collar of his raincoat as they plunged into heavy drizzle and made for the waterfront.

A small sailing vessel with a wheelhouse aft was moored to the quay. Marler saw the skipper inside the wheelhouse and a burly seaman preparing to cast off. He stayed on the quay as Hildebrandt jumped aboard.

'He,' Marler pointed at the seaman, 'does not travel with us. No more bloody argument.'

He only went aboard as the German shrugged, told the seaman he would see him later, and the vessel chugged through the heavy mist-drizzle into midstream. Marler placed his hold-all behind the wheelhouse as Hildebrandt hauled out from under a pile of ropes a package wrapped in polythene. From it he extracted a dismantled Armalite rifle and a sniperscope.

Marler examined the weapon with the aid of a pencil flash. Not renovated, brand new – so no track record. Swiftly he assembled the rifle, attached the telescopic sight, asked for ammo, loaded the weapon. They were passing a distant lighted buoy, the light blurred in the haze, the buoy bobbing up and down. He aimed, squinted through the sight, pulled the trigger. The light went out.

'They said you were pretty good,' Hildebrandt commented, 'but I've never seen shooting like that. Just so long as I'm never the target . . .'

'Cut the flannel. Now, the handgun.'

Hildebrandt burrowed inside the polythene, produced a 9 mm. Walther P38 automatic. He inserted a magazine, handed it to Marler. The Englishman glanced up and down the river: no other vessels were in sight on the murky surface. He checked the weapon, raised it, gripping the butt with both hands, fired at a small piece of driftwood floating down the Elbe, then nodded.

'The five thousand deutschmarks,' Hildebrandt reminded him, his right hand inside his trench coat pocket.

'We do it my way,' Marler said brusquely.

Dismantling the Armalite, he tucked the weapon inside his large hold-all underneath the tennis racquet. The Walther was inserted under the rifle and both were covered with a small travelling rug. He handed the hold-all to Hildebrandt.

'Tell the skipper to pull in at the quay we're approaching by the cab rank. I go ashore, you hand me the hold-all as I give you the envelope. And I want ammo for both weapons. Ten mags. for the Walther. And a hip holster.'

'That will be extra . . .'

'It will not.'

Hildebrandt shrugged again, extracted ammo for both weapons from the polythene roll, handed it over and called out to the skipper to put ashore. Opening his trench coat, he unfastened a hip holster, gave it to Marler. Which meant the weapon it had sheathed was in the arms dealer's right-hand pocket. Marler grinned as he slipped his hand inside the hold-all, came out with the Walther.

'Just a precaution, H. H.'

The exchange took place at the quayside, Marler said

good-night, walked to a cab which was dropping a fare, a heavily made up woman who eyed him hopefully. 'Not tonight, Josephine,' Marler told her and climbed inside the taxi, telling the driver to get moving. Only when he was clear of the quay did he give his destination, the Four Seasons Hotel.

The precaution was useless. Lighting a king-size cigarette, Marler glanced through the rear window, saw the motor cyclist who had been parked near the quay following him. Typical of Hildebrandt: how simple for the motor bike rider to pick them up as they left the restaurant, then cruise along the road parallel to the waterfront, keeping the fishing vessel in sight. It didn't spoil his night's sleep.

The following morning Marler took a cab back to the airport. Carrying his case and hold-all, he avoided the check-in counter, walked inside a washroom. Fortunately it was empty.

He began washing his hands in a basin. The door opened and a burly man wearing denims, a grubby shirt and a black stubble on his heavy jaw came in. Marler recognized him as the seaman he'd turfed off the fishing vessel. Hildebrandt was becoming a bore: he wanted to sell the same weapons again.

'Do anything stupid and I'll slit your gizzard from ear to ear. I'll take that hold-all . . .'

There was a click and the seaman was holding a wide-bladed flick knife. Marler took his hands out of the basin, held up his left hand. With his right he aimed the hair spray canister he'd been holding, pressed the plunger. A jet of hair spray splashed over the seaman's face, into his eyes.

He gurgled, raised his free hand to his eyes, gave a groan of agony. Marler's stiffened right hand chopped down on the wrist, the knife clattered on the floor. Marler dropped the spray, grasped the German by the shoulders, shoved him with great force into an empty cubicle, kept up the momentum. The seaman's skull cracked against the tiled wall at the rear and he sagged at the knees. Marler pressed him down on the seat of the toilet. The seaman crumpled, his head slumping forward into his lap.

Closing the door, Marler picked up his spray, the knife, retracted the blade, slipped both into his pocket. Carrying his case and hold-all, he walked out, dropped the knife into a nearby litter bin, went outside.

He got into the first cab, told the driver to take him to the Hauptbahnhof. At the main station he bought a ticket to Lübeck, was just in time to catch the Copenhagen Express a minute before it moved off. He read Somerset Maugham's *The Painted Veil* as the train sped across the flat fields of north Germany.

Leaving the train at Lübeck, the ancient Hanseatic port on the Baltic, he caught another cab to Travemünde Häfen, terminal for the car ferry to Helsinki. He remembered to make sure the tennis racquet handle was protruding from the hold-all.

At Travemünde he bought a return ticket for the ferry to Helsinki. The heat was ferocious as he boarded the enormous ship. Inside his stateroom cabin he took off his tie, loosened his collar, sat down on the bunk, picked up his book.

No one had even glanced at his luggage. His last thought as he settled into his bunk when the ship was moving was that Hugo Hildebrandt must be very short of cash. Poor chap.

16

Howard, Director of the SIS, arrived back from holiday at his villa in the south of France at just the wrong moment. Tall, plump-faced, his complexion pink, he strode into Park Crescent and met Monica with the Finnair tickets in her hand on her way to Tweed's office. He stopped her on the staircase.

'Someone else off on his hols?' he enquired in his plummy voice. 'Who is desertin' the ship in our hour of need?'

Oh, hell, thought Monica, he's in one of his so-called jokey moods. She paused on the stairs and looked back at her boss. As usual, Howard was faultlessly attired in a new pale grey Chester Barrie suit from Harrods. His shirt was white, starched like armour plating. The scarlet display handkerchief peering out of his breast pocket exactly matched the colour of his tie.

'I've got to deliver these in a rush,' she replied, glancing down at George, the guard, seated at his desk by the closed front door. 'You'll excuse me.'

'What's the great state secret I've stumbled on?' he asked jovially, following her upstairs and into Tweed's office.

'Here are your tickets,' she said, placing them in front of Tweed, frowning over her shoulder.

'Got back a couple of days early,' Howard announced breezily, closing the door behind him. 'The heat in Provence was like the local baker's oven. Off somewhere, are we?'

He sat in the armchair, perched one long leg over the arm and admired his gleaming black shoe. Tweed put the tickets in his pocket, leant back in his chair.

'Something urgent. I have to leave here in five minutes.'

'Good. So we have five whole minutes for you to tell me all about it. Where are you drifting off to?'

'Helsinki.' Tweed stood up, checked his watch, picked up his case.

'Wait.' Howard stood up and Monica frowned. He was going to cause trouble. '*Why* are you going on this trip?'

'A special directive from the PM. I'm sorry, but the lid on this business is screwed down tight. Tighter than I've ever known.'

'I see.' Howard took it with surprising calm. 'I bumped into Pete Nield as I came into the building. He knows Scandinavia. Take him with you. That's an order. It's not safe to have you floating round without back-up.'

'The turbulence is further south.'

'Is it? While I was in France I talked to Pierre Loriot on my way back through Paris. He says some very dangerous characters have gone underground from the Balkans. Professionals. He's heard a tip from a reliable source that they're heading for – Scandinavia.'

'I'm just about to catch a plane . . .'

'I'll not sleep if you don't take Pete Nield. He can travel separately from you on the same plane. I'm not asking about the PM's directive, but I am running this outfit. You know Pete always has a case packed for instant departure and money in God knows how many currencies.'

'He may not be able to get a seat on my flight . . .'

Howard swung on his heels. 'Monica, phone London Airport and book another seat on the same flight. That also is an order.'

Tweed nodded, Monica picked up the phone. Tweed was taken aback by Howard's forceful concern for his safety. He couldn't think of an argument to counter what his chief had said. And he could always lose Nield after they'd arrived. Monica made three calls in rapid succession, then replaced the receiver.

157

'Pete has a seat on the same flight, ticket waiting for him at the airport. He has a room in the same hotel where you're staying. A separate cab will be here in three minutes to get him to the airport on time.'

'Then I'll be off,' Tweed said and looked at Howard. 'Thank you for your support. I'm not sure how long I'll be away.'

'Well,' Howard told him jovially, repeating a remark Tweed had made earlier to Monica, 'it's not as though you're going to Russia . . .'

Tweed peered down through the window of the Finnair machine as it flew over the Baltic in a clear blue sky. They were passing over the incredible Finnish archipelago, the second largest in the world. Twenty-five thousand feet below, a vast labyrinth of islands spread out on the dazzling blue sea, countless islands of various shapes and sizes stretching out from Turku, Finland's second city. Here and there on the open sea he saw a tiny white streak, the wake of some large ship.

He glanced back down the cabin. Two rows behind him Pete Nield was reading a newspaper. Nield was in his early thirties, a slim, neatly dressed man with dark hair and a small trim moustache. He had boarded the aircraft without even a glance in Tweed's direction.

As the plane began its long descent towards Helsinki airport Tweed counted off mentally the strategy he had set in motion. Newman, Cord Dillon and Paula were also heading for Scandinavia to investigate INCUBUS. He'd no doubt Newman would pursue his search with ferocious energy: the murder of Sandra Riverton had filled him with cold rage.

And my own mission is similar – but different – he reminded himself. I also am investigating INCUBUS, but collaborating with an unknown Russian. It's like penetrating a spider's web, he thought.

Then Marler was also on his way, tracking down the dangerous men who had gone missing from the ex-Communist states. And he had a lead: Ion Manescu had been spotted boarding the ferry at Travemünde which sailed regularly – for Helsinki.

Marler, very popular with the girls because of his distant cynical manner, was ingenious and experienced in locating people no one else could find.

It was a double-pronged strategy for two different problems. Penetrating INCUBUS to find out how that colossus operated. And tracing the vanishing ex-secret police criminals. The comparison between INCUBUS and a spider's web came back into Tweed's mind as the plane began to descend more steeply. Who was the spider at the centre of the web? Was it really Hauser?

'It's a problem we must solve. By any method which works.'

Three men sat in Franklin D. Hauser's spacious office at the top of the glass tower outside Helsinki. Hauser stared out of the window at the shimmering heat haze over the sea. Behind him Adam Carver sat in an executive chair while Galvone prowled across the shag carpet.

'What's the present position in Frankfurt?' Carver asked.

'Egon Schmidt owns this private German bank. He won't sell under any circumstances.' Hauser consulted a red file he held in his hand. 'Evelyn Lennox produced the Profile on Egon. He has a son, Dieter. She had dinner with Dieter at the Frankfurter Hof. Dieter is a playboy, has no interest in the bank, would sell tomorrow. Relationships are bad between father and son. But because Egon has no other living relative the bank would pass into Dieter's hands.' He looked up at the two men. 'If anything happened to Egon.'

159

'Then the solution is obvious,' Galvone said in his hoarse voice.

'What solution is that?' Carver asked quietly.

'We can discuss that later,' Hauser interjected. 'But we need that bank to get a foothold in Germany. So many key companies in Germany are controlled by the banks.' He put the file on a table, changed the subject. 'Tell us, Adam, how did you make out with the Evelyn Lennox girl?'

'She's still nervous, won't accept the insurance money.'

'That means the twist could start shooting off her big mouth,' Galvone warned.

'I think she regards me as a friend,' the Englishman remarked. 'So I could always go back to her, try a little more persuasion.'

'And you could always set fire to where she lives.'

'That would be drastic and possibly counter-productive. And there is a complication.'

'That we could do without, that we don't need,' rasped Hauser.

'What complication?' Galvone demanded.

'While I was in London I checked with Steve Abbott, the not very subtle assistant to Papa Grimwood. Steve reckoned he saw Robert Newman, the foreign correspondent, with Evelyn in Walberswick.'

'What the hell is that?' Hauser asked, lighting up a cigarette. 'Gentlemen, you may smoke.'

Carver took a cigar from his case, lit it, puffed at it and watched Galvone through the smoke. 'Walberswick is a small village on the Suffolk coast. Where Sandra Riverton used to live. Now her sister, Evelyn, stays there.'

'We shouldn't leave that dame hanging around,' Galvone protested.

'Now, Frank,' Hauser chided, 'you are always so

160

impulsive. I'm sure Adam has the situation well in hand, will bring it to a successful conclusion.'

'Don't bet on it,' Galvone sneered.

'I never bet on anything – or anyone.' There was a hard edge to Hauser's tone. 'What worries me more than a little is Adam's reference to that nosy foreign correspondent. Newman. I'd like to know where he is now. Check on it, Frank. You stay, Adam. There's something we have to settle without wasting time.'

The machine continued its descent. Flight SK526 was due to arrive on time at Arlanda at 1425 hours. Paula stared out of the window as the arid landscape came up to meet her, a landscape of earth baked bone dry, islands of dense green firs and rocks scattered about, embedded in the earth.

Hardly any sign of human habitation except for the sprawl of airport buildings. Arlanda was growing much larger with each year. Newman opened his eyes, yawned, glanced back at Cord Dillon who already was stirring restlessly.

'He's going to be a problem,' he said to Paula. 'He's action man. Mind you, he's an asset in a tight corner.'

'Why should there be any tight corners? No one can possibly know we're heading for Finland via Sweden.'

'Famous last words. We're landing . . .'

Passport Control and Customs took no notice of them. They walked down steps from a high landing into the main concourse. Dillon, wearing a rumpled grey suit, followed several passengers behind them.

'Must be someone important aboard,' Paula commented as they reached the spacious concourse. 'A film star?'

She waved a hand towards a film unit, four men and a girl with cameras aimed at the incoming crowd, filming

161

the new arrivals. Newman, still wearing his dark glasses, touched the peak of his baseball cap with a mock salute aimed at the unit.

'It certainly can't be us they're interested in,' Paula joked.

The remark startled Newman. As they carried their bags to find the hire car he'd ordered he glanced back. The cameras were still filming the crocodile of passengers trudging down into the concourse. As they emerged into the sunshine the heat hit them like a hammer. Paula slipped on a pair of tinted glasses. The glare was so strong it hurt her eyes. Newman hurried towards a Volvo estate car where a uniformed girl stood holding the keys.

The paperwork took no time at all: the girl seemed anxious to retreat back inside the concourse. Just before they left the kerb Dillon slipped into the rear and Newman drove off, heading along the main highway towards distant Stockholm.

'What caught your eye back there?' Paula asked. 'Just as we walked out of the concourse.'

'That film unit. Why should they be recording everyone who came off the plane?'

'No idea.' Paula fanned herself with a brochure brought off the plane. 'Lord, it's like an oven.'

'You've got the window open.'

'Which is just letting in more boiling air. Anyway, it will be cooler in Finland.'

'And how the devil do we get there?' demanded Dillon. 'Some round the houses route you're taking us on.'

'By ferry tomorrow night. You'll find it a comfortable crossing from Stockholm to Helsinki. Huge car ferries sail the Baltic.'

'I'm a bad sailor,' Dillon complained.

'It will be like gliding over a mirror.'

162

'You could be wrong about that film unit,' Paula suggested. 'There could be a reason for what they were doing.'

'Well, after we get to the Grand Hotel and settle in there's one way to find out. You can come with me if you want to. Unless you're off to that department store, NK.'

'And how are you going to find out?' Paula enquired.

'To hell with that,' Dillon burst out. 'Why are we going to Finland by that route?'

'We need to be armed, that's why. Now leave it alone.'

'You didn't tell me how you're going to find out about that film unit,' Paula reminded Newman.

'You'll find out this afternoon.'

Paula swore inwardly and gazed out of the window. Already her dress was beginning to cling to her and she couldn't wait to have a bath at the Grand Hotel. The broad highway was bordered at intervals with limestone gulches and beyond them she looked out across fields stretching away, vaguely seen through the heat haze. And she couldn't imagine what Newman had in mind for the afternoon.

Marler walked down the gangway after the ferry berthed in North Harbour, Helsinki. He immediately saw the men with cine cameras aimed at the passengers. He hurried, merged with a crowd, avoided the queue of waiting taxis and walked round the harbour front to the Palace Hotel.

'You have a reservation for me,' he told the girl behind the counter, gave her his name, let the porter take his case but said he'd carry his hold-all himself.

His room overlooked the harbour and he glanced out at the blazing sunshine. He was dressed for the heat: a jacket of a linen suit and slacks, an open-necked shirt. He placed the hold-all in a prominent position on a chair, the handle of the tennis racquet protruding. Pulling a hair from his head he inserted it under the zip which was open a few inches.

163

He left his case locked where the porter had put it on a rack. If anyone searched the room they'd be interested in the locked case. The hold-all was too openly displayed to attract attention. Then he left his room, walked along the Esplanade and turned south into the old city. In his breast pocket he carried a copy of the photograph of Ion Manescu.

Tweed looked out of the window in his room at the Hotel Hesperia. It was supposed to have a 'sea view' but he had stayed at this hotel before, a modern curved concrete block. He looked down on a tall metal mobile sculpture which revolved in a wind. The air was still and so was the mobile. Beyond the Mannerheimintie, the highway which led into the city a short distance to the east, he could observe the 'sea'. It looked like a small lake and was an inland arm of the invisible Baltic.

A neat orange and cream tram trundled past on its way into town. Which reminded him he wanted to check out the rendezvous point at North Harbour in daylight. He took the elevator down to the lobby, wondering whether he would encounter Pete Nield who was booked in at the Hesperia. There was no sign of him as Tweed crossed the spacious lobby and glanced up at the digital meter above the door which registered the temperature.

82°F. 28°C. He shrugged, thankful that he was wearing a tropical drill suit, walked into the inferno, felt the sun burning the back of his neck. The tram shelter was only a short distance closer in to the city and a No. 4 tram pulled in as soon as he arrived. He boarded it, paid the driver with a Finnish coin, was given a ticket and remembered to punch it with the time and date in another machine behind the driver.

Helsinki was Granite City. Coming in from the airport his cab had passed enormous outcrops of the stone and

164

the buildings were constructed of the same material. The tram cruised past a museum with a sloping lawn. An immense granite boulder protruded from the trim grass. Granite everywhere. The Finns had to be tough to have created such a capital.

Ten minutes later he was strolling along the tree-lined Esplanade leading to North Harbour. Men and women walked slowly in the heat, wearing the minimum of clothing. Tweed reached the tip of North Harbour as a car passed him. He stood on the edge of the quay. Behind him market stalls were doing good business and the waterfront was alive with activity. It would be very different at eleven at night during the two brief hours of darkness Helsinki experienced at this time of year.

Why here? Why at that late hour? There had been no message from Lev Frolov, whoever he might be, waiting for him at the Hesperia. And Howard would have a fit if he knew of the arrangement he had agreed to. It was at that moment that he noticed the car which had passed him was parked close by.

A slim man agile man wearing a scuba diver's outfit was running down the nearby steps. His face mask was in place but something about his movements seemed familiar as he plunged into the harbour, floated and then vanished under the surface of the lake-calm sea. Tweed then realized who the man was.

Pete Nield was an expert scuba diver. He had followed the tram Tweed had travelled in, doubtless driving a hired car. Tweed turned away, began to walk back to the tram stop. Nield was taking his instruction to protect Tweed very seriously indeed. And now he would know the rendezvous.

It was mid-afternoon in Stockholm. The air was like turgid hot gas. The sun was roasting the Swedish capital as Newman drove at speed in the hired Volvo with Paula beside him. He was moving along a two-lane highway with water to the left and apartment blocks to the right perched up behind green lawn slopes. Dillon had stayed behind at the Grand Hotel, was taking a siesta.

'How far is it to this Bromma airport?' Paula asked. 'And why are we going there?'

'No more than fifteen minutes from the hotel. You'll see why when we arrive.'

The road was traffic-free, the lights green all the way. Later they were driving on to a single-lane road past old wooden houses painted bright green or yellow. The houses were one or two storeys high and fronted with small well-kept gardens.

'What is Bromma?' Paula pressed. 'Why do they need it when they've got Arlanda?'

'Arlanda replaced it years ago. Now Bromma is used for internal flights and by some private planes. It's a convenient place for people who want to slip quietly into Sweden. And here we are . . .'

The sign read BROMMA AIRPORT. The reception building was tiny compared with Arlanda. Only two people were in sight and when Newman parked a short distance away and switched off his engine a foetid silence descended. Paula had the feeling they were way out in the countryside.

'I was right,' Newman said grimly. 'I want you to do something for me. Get out of the car, wander inside, wait for a few minutes and then come out again.'

'That man leaning against the van is holding a cine camera.'

'And the name on the van is the same as on a van parked outside Arlanda. Do your thing.'

Newman, who had thrown his baseball cap into the river outside the Grand, lit a cigarette. Paula stepped out of the car, strolled towards the building. She wore shorts which exposed her long shapely legs and a loose blouse. As she passed the van the man stared at her legs, the girl with him dug her companion savagely in the ribs.

Inside Paula found the reception hall was fairly spacious but there was no one about, no staff at the counter, no sign of another human being. She walked over to a window, stared out at the small airfield fringed with fir forest. There was a single runway with an approach runway leading off it. A Swedair plane was parked at the edge. Nearer to the main runway stood a Lear jet. Inscribed along its fuselage was the name INCUBUS.

17

'We're in trouble, Hauser has forestalled me. I've badly underestimated him. From now on it could be dangerous – very dangerous.'

Newman was grim as he spoke to Paula in the luxurious bar of the Grand Hotel. He sat in a comfortable armchair with Paula in a similar chair drawn close to him. Dillon had said he was hungry when he met them on their return, that he was going to get a meal in the restaurant overlooking the waterfront where the boats brought back tourists from the archipelago.

'You didn't say a word all the way back in the car,' Paula reminded him. 'Explain. I told you what I saw. And that couple with the cine camera took no notice of me, never took any film of me.'

'That was because you hadn't just flown in from somewhere. That's what they were waiting for – anyone coming into Sweden, just as they were at Arlanda, and they took plenty of film there.'

'What do you think was the significance of that INCUBUS Lear jet? It looked to be waiting for someone . . .'

'Or something. Tomorrow I'm going to purchase weapons. And that's another reason I came this route. You can't obtain weapons in Finland.'

'But you can here? Is that what you're saying?'

'Yes. Tomorrow I'm going to the Sergels Torg. That's in the centre of Stockholm, a square where the boys gather, the boys who can sell you almost any kind of automatic weapon or handgun.'

'I'd like a Browning,' she said promptly. 'But how can we smuggle it into Finland?'

'That's the easy part. We're travelling to Helsinki on the night car ferry. There's no real supervision or examination of baggage. And it's easier to slip ashore at the other end unseen from a ship rather than from a plane at the airport. Again, remember Arlanda.'

'Can I come with you to Sergels Torg tomorrow, Bob?'

'I'll think about it. Also we may stay here an extra day. I just hope I'm wrong about all this.'

'You're worried because you brought me,' she accused.

'I never said anything of the sort,' he lied. 'Let's go and get some dinner. Tomorrow is going to be a very busy day.'

The films taken at Gothenburg Airport in western Sweden, the films taken at Malmö, the hydrofoil crossing from Denmark, the films taken at Arlanda – they were all flown to Bromma by helicopter.

At Bromma the same evening they were carried aboard the Lear jet waiting at Bromma. The jet took off at nine in the evening and the machine landed at Helsinki well before the two hours of darkness descended. They were rushed from the airport to the headquarters of INCUBUS Oy. By 10.30 p.m. they were inside the glass tower.

'Nothing like a good film to watch in the evening,' Hauser remarked.

He was settled in a seat in the cinema at Level Two and to his left sat Frank Galvone. To his right Adam Carver sat upright and alert as the next film began running, the one taken at Arlanda.

'Watch this carefully,' Hauser advised. 'See if there's anyone either of you recognize. If so, give a shout, the projectionist will stop the film, and we'll freeze it at that point.'

Galvone was bored, leant back with his elbows on the rear of his seat. He watched as another flight from London disembarked, trailing down into the concourse. The bright light of the day had given exceptional clarity to the picture.

'See anyone yet?' Hauser enquired, waving his cigarette holder.

'Nope,' said Galvone.

'Freeze!' Carver called out. 'Go back a way, run it slowly, wait for me to call you again,' he ordered the projectionist, 'then freeze it instantly when I call out again.'

'Didn't see anything, Adam,' Hauser commented.

Carver said nothing, leaning forward to concentrate as the film was run in slow motion. A girl with raven black hair came down the steps, walked across the concourse. Behind her a man wearing a loud check jacket and a baseball cap followed. He touched the peak of his cap towards the camera in a typical American gesture . . .

'Freeze!' Carver shouted. The film stopped. 'That man in the check jacket. It's Newman, Robert Newman the foreign correspondent.'

169

Hauser frowned, clenched his teeth on the cigarette holder. 'What makes you think that? Looks like a tourist from back home.'

'His movements.' Carver sat back. 'You know I study body language. Remember when Newman came to see you at Livingstone Manor that evening in Suffolk? I had a good opportunity to observe him.'

'What do you think, Frank?' Hauser asked.

'Run the film again from where he comes down those steps,' Carver ordered the projectionist. 'Now, both of you, think back to Livingstone Manor. And watch carefully the way he moves.'

There was tension inside the large cinema occupied by only three men. They were leaning forward, staring with great concentration. Carver had no doubt.

'What do you think, Frank?' Hauser asked again.

'I guess that is Newman,' Galvone said reluctantly.

'No guess about it. Adam has a sharp eye. His movements, his gestures identify him positively for me. The cunning bastard, arriving like an American.'

'So what action do we take?' Galvone enquired.

'Oh, the answer to that is obvious. Newman is becoming a dangerous nuisance. First, he visits Evelyn Lennox just as Papa Grimwood is on the verge of concluding the insurance deal. He balls us up on that. Second, he was tracked to the vicinity of where that ex-owner of Bennington Machine Tools lives, whatever his name was. Wherever it was.'

'James Archer. Otmoor,' said Carver.

'Whatever. Earlier, he calls on me at Livingstone Manor. Then he visits that tavern afterwards and asks about me. A good job we have friendly folk in Suffolk. Third, he's turned up now in Stockholm, an hour's flight from here. Frank, send a coded fax to the Swedish office for Manescu. Tell him the situation. The instruction is simple. Find Newman, stop him travelling around.'

'And how do we propose to do that?' Carver asked.

'Leave that problem to Frank. He knows how many beans make five. Get on it, Frank . . .'

Marler had been asked to come back at nine that evening when Mauno Sarin would be available to see him. He had used all his powers of persuasion with Karma, Sarin's deputy, to get an appointment. What had turned the trick was when he revealed he was carrying a letter of introduction 'from a highly regarded friend of Sarin's based in London'.

Karma, a short, stocky dark-haired Finn, looked at Marler across the desk in the office he had taken him to. His English was good and he was obviously the guardian of his chief's valuable time.

'If I could show Mr Sarin this letter . . .'

'Out of the question. The letter is very personal. I must hand it to Sarin myself. But you can show him my card.'

Marler gave Karma the visiting card which carried his name and the firm which was a cover for SIS at Park Crescent, General & Cumbria Assurance. Karma, whose clean-shaven face gave nothing away of what he was thinking, turned over the card.

'There's nothing on the back,' Marler said jauntily. 'It's a visiting card, you know . . .'

Karma had left him alone, returned five minutes later with the news that Mr Sarin could see his visitor at nine that evening. Marler had said thank you for saving his own valuable time and left.

At precisely nine o'clock, still in broad daylight, he had walked back to the headquarters of the Protection Police, a title which concealed their real function: counter-espionage. The headquarters was located in the old city which reminded Marler of Leningrad. The address, Ratakatu 12, was a grimy four-storey stone block on the

171

corner of Ratakatu and Fredrikinkatu. The windows on the ground floor were made of opaque glass and on the upper floors grubby net curtains masked the windows. It was always very quiet in Ratakatu with very few people about.

The heat was overpowering as Marler approached the entrance. Across Fredrikinkatu was a small open space with half a dozen trees, their leaves drooping. Two seagulls perched on a seat, motionless, their wings flopped. Two stone steps led up to the heavy wooden door with a long metal bar attached at a diagonal angle. Marler peeled the front of his shirt off his chest, carried his linen jacket over his arm as he went inside. Karma was waiting for him and escorted Marler to an office on the third floor. Mauno Sarin, seated behind a desk, rose reluctantly to greet his visitor.

'You can leave us, Karma. Now, Mr Marler, what can I do for you? As you'll see, I'm rather busy,' he continued in English and indicated his desk which was piled high with files and documents. 'Please sit down. I understand you have a letter of introduction?'

Without a word Marler handed over the envelope. He waited while Sarin relaxed a little as he sat down again and scanned the letter. The chief of the Protection Police was over six feet tall. In his forties, he had a balding head, a dark fringe beard, was slim and athletic-looking. His personality radiated an air of restless energy and impatience. His shirt sleeves were rolled up above the elbows.

'I thought it might be Tweed,' Sarin commented, handing back the letter. 'What is the problem?'

Marler produced the Manescu photograph, leaned forward and handed it to the Finn over the carnage of paperwork. 'Would you recognize that man?'

'No,' Sarin said promptly. 'Should I?'

'I'd be surprised if you did. Ion Manescu, ex-member of the Romanian *Securitate*.'

'So, he's in prison in Bucharest, along with the rest of his tribe.'

'No. A totally reliable witness saw him boarding the ferry at Travemünde earlier in the year. The ferry which docks here in Helsinki. He escaped from Bucharest. Just as some others have escaped. Including Ziegler, ex-chief of the Leipzig STASI.'

'I see.' Sarin swivelled his chair and stared through the net curtains at the wall of buildings opposite. Then he turned back to face Marler. 'Why are you here?'

'To track down Manescu, find out what he's up to. Tweed is worried. Too many of the villains from security services in ex-Communist states have disappeared. Maybe up here. You think that's impossible?'

'Unlikely.'

'And yet that terrorist attack on the Lockerbie aircraft had origins in – warnings came from – Finland.'

Sarin gazed at Marler, but his brown eyes seemed focused on some distant thought. Marler waited. He could almost hear the wheels whirring inside the Finn's head. He was deciding whether to reveal certain information.

'It's difficult for us,' Sarin eventually began. 'Geographically we are one of the largest countries in Western Europe – with immensely long borders, to say nothing of the Baltic coast. But our population is little more than five million. And we have a tradition of neutrality.'

'I understand all this,' Marler encouraged him quietly. 'I also realize it must be impossible to watch all potential exit – and entry – points.'

'Exactly.' Sarin began playing with a ruler, twisting it in his hands. 'We have had reports of some highly undesirable people slipping into our country over many months. Always by unauthorized routes. A fisherman in the archipelago off Turku saw a motorboat landing two men at night. It's not possible to seal off routes like that. Have you heard of a company called INCUBUS?'

'The biggest bank in the States. Bigger than the Bank of America.'

'Yes, but they control many other companies outside banking, presumably through their bank. They have a big headquarters to the west of the city, a huge glass tower. They also have established other companies here, providing much-needed employment.' Sarin grinned without humour. 'You could say Mr Franklin D. Hauser is a benefactor.'

'You wouldn't by chance have a list of those companies?'

For Marler it was a shot in the dark. He was intrigued by Sarin introducing the name of the mammoth organization into their conversation.

'I just might have . . .'

Sarin burrowed among the mounds of papers. He extracted a sheet, handed it to Marler.

'There is the list. You can keep it, if you like. It is a photocopy of the original.'

Marler glanced down the list, startled by the number of companies, all with Finnish names. Except for one. He looked up at Sarin, who was again gazing into space.

'This Institute for Meteorological and Astronomical Studies at Kemijärvi. Why would a bank be interested in that?'

'A question I often ask myself. Its construction is a weird story. It was financed partly by two other companies, but the major funding was supplied by INCUBUS Oy . . .'

'Which gave them control?'

'Exactly. A number of construction firms were invited to bid for the job, but the lowest tender came from a construction company controlled by INCUBUS. And the curious thing is they imported Sicilian workers to build the complex. As soon as the project was complete they were all sent back to Sicily in specially chartered aircraft.'

'And Sicilians would hardly speak Finnish,' Marler commented.

'They didn't even speak English. The project was very hush-hush, as you say.'

'And this complex is at Kemijärvi, north of the Arctic Circle?'

'No. That is the nearest large town but the Institute is in a remote spot in the wilderness of Lapland.'

'A funny place to build anything.'

'*They* say it is ideal – for studying weather conditions.'

'Why would a huge banking outfit get involved in such a project?'

'Mr Hauser is a philanthropist.' Again Sartin smiled without humour. 'So our government feels rather obliged to treat him as an honoured guest. He also supports the theatre opposite the Marski Hotel. A man of culture, our Mr Hauser.'

'And a man of money. A shipload of it.'

'That also. A billionaire, I gather. The second richest man in the United States. He spends a lot of time here. I often wonder why, especially in winter.' Sarin looked quizzical. 'Perhaps he likes our climate.'

'You've visited this Institute near Kemijärvi?'

Sarin's expression changed, his tone of voice became harsh for the first time. He burst out, as though impulsively. 'I would like to obtain a search warrant to examine it from top to bottom. But it is more than my job is worth to even make such a request. Certainly it would never be granted.'

'What made you mention INCUBUS when actually we were talking about Manescu?'

Another dreamy look. Sarin couched his reply carefully. 'I suppose it was pure coincidence. Not linked at all. But *if*, and this is pure assumption, if ex-members of the *Securitate*, the STASI, the Czechoslovak STB, etc., *were* finding refuge here – and not a single one has been caught – then surely it suggests a large, well-organized and powerful apparatus with plenty of money must be behind the conspiracy. That, I must stress, is only a theory.'

You artful devil, Marler was thinking: the subtle way you're suggesting avenues of investigation to me. He checked his watch, stood up.

'Thank you for giving me so much time – remembering how very busy you said you are.'

'I am always ready to help my good friend, Tweed.'

Sarin stood up and shook hands. He had a grip like an alligator. Marler turned at the door. Sarin had switched on the overhead fluorescent strip. It was still daylight outside but little of it penetrated inside the room. Sarin was gazing hard at his guest.

'You say you couldn't possibly go anywhere near this Institute in Lapland. I suppose the easiest way to get there is to fly via Finnair first to Rovaniemi north of the Arctic Circle,' Marler suggested.

'Yes, that would be the thing to do. You'd have to fix up transport to get you to Kemijärvi from Rovaniemi airport. And, after all, Mr Marler, *you* are a free agent. My regards to Mr Tweed. I wonder where he is now?'

PART TWO

Angel of Moscow

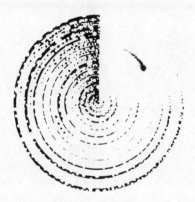

18

It was dark in Helsinki. It was 11.05 p.m. It was two hours before the sun would rise again. It was deserted on the North Harbour waterfront except for one man.

Tweed stood well back from the edge of the silent quay. The only sound was the quiet lapping of water against the harbour wall, a gentle swishing sound. Behind him the market stalls had disappeared, the bustle of daily activity was no more. He stood listening, his hearing acute. In his right hand he held a canister of hair spray, a weapon Marler had once recommended.

He had not heard a word from Lev Frolov, the man who had phoned him when he was in London, the mysterious man who had set up this rendezvous. Out on the black surface of the harbour a large fishing boat was chugging home, its nets hung out to dry. His night vision was keen enough to make out the nets . . .

'Don't move, Mr Tweed, this is a gun. Drop what you are holding in your hand. Now you can move. Walk towards that flight of steps leading down to the landing stage.'

Tweed began walking slowly; the canister hit the cobble stones with a soft thud. It felt very much like the barrel of a gun pressed against his spine. The voice which spoke good English in a clear whisper, began to talk again.

'I am the emissary from Lev Frolov. Now please walk slowly down the steps.'

'Supposing I don't? Supposing I just stand here?'

'I must remind you, this is a gun. The gun is loaded. We

are quite alone and no one will miss you. Not in time. Please be sensible.'

The fishing vessel was very close, its navigation lamps turned on, but somewhere there was another sound, almost muffled by the vessel's engine. A peculiar swishing he could not identify. He walked slowly down the flight of steps, waited at the bottom, watching the incoming fishing vessel which was manoeuvring to berth. A seaman jumped ashore with a rope, looped it round a bollard. Tweed was reassured by the reference to Lev Frolov. That had come through on the scrambler from Moscow. He was not reassured by the gun still pressed against his spine.

The hull of the vessel bumped against the lowest step. So far as Tweed could see there were only two men aboard – the skipper in the aft wheelhouse and a shadowy figure standing at the stern. He was again aware of the silence. The only sounds the water lapping, the vessel creaking.

'Step on board,' the man behind him ordered. 'Please, no tricks.'

Tweed climbed over the gunwale, his captor jumped after him, the vessel's engine increased in power as the seaman ashore unlooped the rope, flung it aboard and walked off up the steps. The fishing vessel moved out into the harbour, headed down the channel for the open Baltic.

The shadowy figure came forward. He wore a smart business suit, was slim in build, tall, clean shaven and had trim black hair. Tweed stared now he could see him better.

'Welcome, Mr Tweed,' the man said, holding out his hand.

'Captain Valentin Rebet,' Tweed responded, shaking hands. 'Several years since we met.'

'I used the name Lev Frolov. It was necessary in the interests of security. And from what you have just said your intelligence sources inside Moscow could be better. I am now General Rebet . . .' He made the statement modestly. 'I have enjoyed rapid promotion under the new

180

régime. Also, I have been transferred from the GRU to the KGB,' he went on in English.

Tweed nodded. He was well aware of all this, but pretended ignorance so Rebet would not know how good his sources were. The Russian was in his late thirties and, as in the old days, had a pleasant smile.

It was at this moment something dramatic occurred – the skipper had his back to them, concentrating on threading his course between the lighted buoys. The man with the gun was also standing with his back to the stern, both hands out of his coat pockets, staring ahead. There was a slithering noise at the stern. Tweed swung round in time to see a man in a wetsuit jump aboard, throw his face mask back and aim his harpoon gun at Rebet.

'No one moves or this man is speared. Throw up your hands, you bastards . . .'

Rebet froze, raised his hands above his head. The man with the gun spun round, saw the harpoon aimed point blank at Rebet, raised his own hands. Tweed spoke quickly.

'It's all right, Nield. For God's sake don't shoot. The natives are friendly.'

'How friendly?' Nield demanded, dripping water and keeping his weapon aimed.

'This is the man I came to meet, Pete.'

'You were supposed to be alone,' Rebet accused with an edge to his voice. 'Who is this?'

'My guardian angel. As you see, he looks after me quite effectively. And you never warned me on the phone that I'd be hijacked. I don't appreciate a gun in my back.'

'It was not loaded.' Rebet spoke to his subordinate in Russian, which Tweed, who spoke the language fluently, understood. 'Take out your gun carefully with two fingers, hand it to Mr Tweed, Andrei.'

Tweed warned Nield not to worry. Andrei inserted a couple of fingers, extracted the gun, holding it by the butt, handed it to Tweed. He examined the Makarov. No magazine. He smiled at Nield.

'He's right. The damned thing wasn't loaded.' He looked at Rebet. 'What happened to my old adversary, General Lysenko?' Again he knew the answer.

'Our president has no time for old Bolsheviks,' Rebet replied. 'He was retired on his pension and spends his days chopping wood outside his tiny house near Odessa. Now can your protector kindly lower his weapon? My arms are aching.'

'When you tell me where we are going.'

Tweed glanced to the west. They had already sailed past the tip of the peninsula which was the end of Helsinki. Soon they'd be heading for the open Baltic and, a bad sailor, he thanked God the sea was so calm.

'I am the contact from Moscow you came to meet,' Rebet said, lowering his voice. 'The president's special emissary. We are very worried about the way the situation is developing. I am taking you to meet someone.'

'Rebet, I asked you where we are going. Tell me or turn this old tub round and take me back to North Harbour.'

'A Soviet corvette is waiting for us outside the limits of Finnish coastal waters. You will be comfortable aboard that ship for our short voyage.'

'To where?'

'Leningrad. Now, may we lower our arms? And your assistant needs dry clothes we can provide at once.'

'It's all right, Pete,' Tweed called out to Nield. 'No need to keep them covered anymore. We're going on a trip to Leningrad.'

The Diplomat Hotel in Stockholm overlooks a stretch of water, as does the Grand. This is yet another arm of the Mälaren, the main waterway which stretches many miles into the interior beyond Stockholm. Irina Serov had a bedroom with a view of the creek which looked like a river. She was sitting in front of the dressing table, brushing her long hair in front of the mirror when she heard the special knock on the door.

'Where the hell have you been, Manescu?' she demanded as the Romanian entered, closed the door, locked it, tossed a travel folder on her bed. 'It's evening,' she raged. 'I've been waiting for hours. What do we do next?'

'You'll have enough to keep you occupied with your special talents from now on,' he told her with a sneer.

He disliked Russians. What Romanian didn't? And especially he disliked Russian women. Above all, he disliked Soviet women who were ex-colonels in the KGB and threw their weight about.

'Well get on with it,' she snapped. 'Why have you taken all this time?'

'I will tell you.' He adopted a lecturing tone. 'First, I visited the INCUBUS headquarters on Sveavägen . . .'

'I was stationed in Stockholm,' she reminded him.

'As I was explaining, I visited headquarters. There was an urgent fax from Helsinki, orders from the top. The target is Robert Newman, the foreign correspondent . . .'

'I heard about him during my London posting.'

'Please keep quiet. Just listen for once. *Newman is here in Stockholm.* He was filmed leaving Arlanda. Following the fax instructions I drove to Bromma Airport. I arrived just as the Lear jet which took our films to Helsinki returned. It brought us – me – photographs of this Newman. We have been ordered at all costs to prevent him reaching Finland.'

'And we know where he is? What route he will take?'

'For God's sake – and mine – stop interrupting. I have already arranged for a team – with one of the photographs – to wait at Arlanda. They have tickets for every flight.

But I have been warned he is devious. I doubt if he will use Arlanda. I think he will use the night ferry.'

'To Helsinki?'

'Possibly. So more men, also with a copy of his photograph, will be waiting at the terminal where the boat leaves for Helsinki. We will be elsewhere.'

'May I possibly ask for the location of elsewhere?'

'We shall be waiting at the Vartan terminal where the car ferry leaves for Turku. I have reserved two staterooms in case we see Newman going aboard. Here is his picture.'

'He's good looking.' Irina preened herself in the mirror. 'I might be able to get next to him with my little hypodermic needle.' She frowned. 'Why Turku and not Helsinki?'

'Because as I told you, this Newman is devious. Helsinki is convinced he's on his way there. But does he fly there direct? No! He flies first to Stockholm. You think he will fly direct – or take the ship direct – to Helsinki? I do not think so. The other exits are covered, but we will watch the night ferry for Turku. Tomorrow also if we must.'

It was dusk as Newman drove alone to Sergels Torg. Very little traffic about. He had refused to allow Paula to join him on his weapons expedition. On the seat beside him rested a small suitcase. It contained two crumpled shirts and nothing else.

His shopping list included a .32 Browning automatic for Paula, a .38 Smith & Wesson Special for himself. Dillon favoured a 9 mm Luger. It was a tall order but Newman knew you could buy a wide range of guns at the infamous Sergels Torg.

Sergels Torg was a spacious square open to the sky but about fifteen feet below the level of the surrounding streets. Newman drove slowly down the wide ramp which led into the square and continued straight across it to the maze-like underground shopping complex. He stopped, leant his elbow on the lowered window, switched off his engine and waited. Within two minutes a man wandered towards him. As he came closer Newman saw he was no more than twenty, brown hair cropped close to his head, dressed in clean denims and a clean shirt.

'You wanted something, Mister?' the youth enquired in English.

'Depends what you're selling. No drugs. Maybe you know a guy who sells guns. Handguns.'

'You'll have to come and see my friend. He's inside the subway. Leave your car here.'

'Anything you say, Tosh.'

Newman closed the window, picked up his case, got out of the Volvo, locked it carefully, followed the youth inside the shopping complex. Here and there youths gathered in twos and threes, smoking, apparently just passing the time. Newman knew better.

His own youth took him along an arcade to where a beggar was slouched on the ground, a cap for krone coins lying in front of him. To one side of the man was a shabby duffel bag which presumably contained most of his worldly possessions, to the other an open suitcase of book matches.

'Tell him what you want,' the youth said.

Newman crouched on his haunches and saw the man was much younger than had appeared at first sight. In his twenties, he had a stubble of beard and alert eyes which watched Newman. In a low voice the Englishman itemized his wants. The beggar nodded, looked carefully round, fumbled inside the duffel bag, brought out a Browning. Newman checked the state of the weapon under cover of the flap of his jacket. The Smith & Wesson appeared next, followed by a Luger. The duffel bag was a secret armoury.

185

There was a brief haggle over the price and ammo for each weapon was extra. Newman extracted a roll of Swedish banknotes from his trouser pocket, counted out the amount. In his other pocket was a second roll of money but he didn't need to reveal that. He quickly slipped the weapons and ammo between his soiled shirts, closed the lid, stood up, dropped a coin into the cap and walked away. The youth stayed, obviously to extract his commission for the sale.

Newman thought it had seemed too easy as he dumped the case on the front passenger seat, climbed inside, closed the door. In his rear view mirror he saw a white car with twin blue lights on the roof and the word POLIS along its side. It turned down the ramp, came straight towards him, flashing its lights on and off. He was going to be checked.

The main exit from the square, the ramp down which he had driven, was blocked by the approaching police car. Thank God I know this area well, Newman thought. I'll just have to risk it. Five years in a Swedish prison didn't appeal to him.

He drove forward into the shopping complex, head-lights full on. As the police car came closer, siren blaring now, he drove in and out among a series of rounded pillars, skimming them by centimetres. The police car followed. Newman drove along a right-hand arm of the complex, praying there wouldn't be pedestrians. The arcade was deserted. A ramp came into view with an overhead sign. GALLERIAN. He was going the right way. The banshee howl of the siren was magnified by the enclosed space. Newman pressed his foot down, roared up the ramp, emerged into the open, turned the wheel. A few moments later he sped past the building which had been the headquarters of Ivar Kruger, the match king in the 1930s. The police car came close again. He swung the wheel, began driving more slowly down a wide cobbled sloping short cut which descended at a steep angle, not meant for vehicles. His wheels bumped over the cobbles. In his rear view mirror he saw the police car turn, speeding down the cobbles.

Inside the car the driver, Bertil, a short plump officer with a flowing moustache, sat beside his sergeant, Otto. The sergeant urged him to move faster. Bertil obliged, hanging on tight to the wheel. The car suddenly slewed sideways, smashed into a wall, wrecked one wheel as the transmission gave way. The car stopped, the engine gave up.

'Did you get the registration number?' Otto demanded.

'No! Did you?'

'You should have got the number. And you're one lousy driver.'

'OK. You take over the wheel . . .'

Out of sight Newman turned on to the Vestra Tradgardsgatan. Three minutes later, all lights in his favour, he parked at the back of the Grand Hotel, took a deep breath.

Newman, carrying his case, knocked on the door of Paula's room overlooking the Strommen. As she let him inside he heard through the open window the siren of a ship returning from the archipelago, the screech of gulls through the open window. The room was still like a furnace.

Paula wore a T-shirt and a white skirt. At a table near the window Cord Dillon sat holding a handful of cards with an unhappy expression. Newman saw a pile of banknotes on Paula's side of the table near her cards, splayed face down. Dillon glared at Newman.

'You might have warned me. I suggested a game of poker and she said she hadn't played for ages. She's already got two hundred dollars of my money over there.'

187

'You can't win them all. I could do with a drink, Paula.'

He sagged into a chair and while she fixed his large Scotch he recalled for them his experience at Sergels Torg and the later chase.

'After this drink I'm returning the Volvo immediately to car hire,' he went on. 'Those cops may think of checking up on every car hire outfit. If they didn't get the number, and I doubt they did, they know the make. Lucky that car hire stays open late at this time of the year.'

'What about the equipment?' Dillon asked, indifferent to Newman's near escape.

'In this case. Hide it while I'm out.' He drank half his Scotch. 'Thanks, Paula. You've got your Browning.' He felt in his pocket, brought out several heavy polythene packets. 'Ammo for your Luger, Cord. And here are spare mags for the Browning . . .'

'When do we leave and by what route?' Paula enquired, after asking him if he was all right.

'Tomorrow night. I managed to reserve three staterooms earlier today. Aboard the car ferry for Turku. Leaves from the Vartan terminal at nine in the evening.'

EGON SCHMIDT, BANKING CHIEF, KILLED IN FRANKFURT
BOMB BLAST. FRESH RED ARMY FACTION OUTRAGE?

Franklin D. Hauser read the headlines in the *Herald Tribune* with interest. The story which followed told how the banker had climbed into his Mercedes parked outside the bank on the highway to the airport. The theory was that when he turned on the ignition the car was blown to pieces.

Hauser laid the paper on his desk with a sense of satisfaction. Now he could instruct Adam Carver to open

188

negotiations with the playboy son, Dieter. Undoubtedly he'd sell out, so INCUBUS now had a foothold in Germany.

He was at his most affable when Peggy Vanderheld, summoned to his office, walked in. With a wave of his cigarette he ushered her to a chair.

'Yes, Mr Hauser.'

She sat with her legs crossed, her notepad on her lap. She was tense. There had been bad signals recently. And she knew from long experience Hauser was at his most deadly when he displayed such amiability.

'How long have you been with us, Peggy?' Hauser began.

'Five years.' As well you know, she thought.

'And how old are you?'

'Thirty-eight.'

She was sitting up very straight now, her dark eyes staring straight at the billionaire. She knew where this was leading, the bastard.

'So with all that experience, with such a prestigious company, it shouldn't be in the least difficult for you to find another very well paid position?'

'Can we cut the preliminaries?' she asked between her teeth.

'If you prefer so. You know it is my policy to inject fresh blood into the organization at regular intervals? I feel now the time has come for you to look elsewhere for more suitable employment. I can well understand that after ten years you must be bored with the job.'

She said nothing. She was studying the newspaper Hauser had been looking at. Peggy had always concealed the fact that she was an expert at reading newspapers and documents upside down.

'So,' Hauser continued when he realized she was not going to react, 'in your own best interests would it not be better if you gave me your resignation? We will, of course, provide an excellent reference, to say nothing of the generous pension rights with Fraternal & Equality.'

'The bottom line is I'm fired,' she threw at him.

'I don't like to put it that way, my dear . . .'

'Then how the bloody hell do you like to put it, for Christ's sake?'

'No need to get emotional about something that happens every day.' Hauser's manner and tone had changed, had become ugly. 'You have three hours to clear your desk and leave.'

'It may take me longer.' She stood up, threw notepad and pencil on his desk. 'But I'll be out of this octopus of a company by the day's end. And it hasn't been nice knowing you.'

She walked out, closed the door quietly behind her. In the elevator she took a deep breath. One thought was running through her head. How can I get back at the smug bastard?

In his office Hauser took several puffs of his cigarette, then lifted one of his three phones, pressed a button.

'Hauser here,' he said when the voice answered. 'I think we may have a problem with Vanderheld. Get up here fast so we can decide how to handle it.'

19

It was going to be another scorching day at ten in the morning. Marler sat in the hired Saab concealed in a copse of firs on the outskirts of Helsinki way beyond the Mannerheimintie. Below him rose the glass tower which was the headquarters of INCUBUS Oy.

He was high enough to see over the wire fence surrounding the huge building. The camera he held at eye level had a zoom lens and he snapped three pictures of a man with dark hair and thick eyebrows wearing an American T-shirt, pale slacks and trainers. The close-up revealed the man's grim expression, his prominent cheekbones. His expression would always be grim, Marler guessed. And he looked like a gangster, but so many Americans did.

The man walked to a red Cadillac, climbed inside, slammed the door so hard Marler heard the *clunk!* a hundred yards away. The uniformed guard operated the automatic gate in the wire, it swung open, closed as the Cadillac vanished in a cloud of dust.

To be driving a Cadillac he had to be a top executive, Marler reasoned. Now he was on record. Earlier he had seen the largest stretched black limousine he'd ever observed turn into the compound and glide smoothly to the entrance. It had tinted glass windows which made it impossible to see who was inside.

The uniformed chauffeur had leapt out, opened the rear door. The unmistakable grandiose figure of Franklin D. Hauser had emerged, spoken briefly to the chauffeur and disappeared inside the glass tower.

Marler had little hope that sooner or later his camera would snap Ion Manescu entering or leaving. But lying in bed the previous night at The Palace, unable to sleep because of the heat, he had recalled his visit to the Protection Police.

He had been particularly intrigued by the way Mauno Sarin had offhandedly pointed a finger at INCUBUS. He had decided it was worth spending a day checking out the HQ of the banking colossus, recording who came, who went.

Half an hour later Hauser reappeared accompanied by a tall slim man carrying two cases. They disappeared inside the rear of the limo and the chauffeur closed the door, ran to his own seat. Inside a minute the immense vehicle was on the move, disappearing in the direction of Helsinki. Mr Hauser was on the move. To foreign parts?

Marler took another small drink of mineral water from the plastic bottle he'd bought. No point in getting dehydrated. Tomorrow, or at the latest the day after, he would fly to Rovaniemi, north of the Arctic Circle. Objective: the mysterious Institute somewhere out in the wilds.

Aboard the Soviet corvette, *Kalinin*, Tweed had travelled up the Baltic to Leningrad with General Rebet and Pete Nield. Again the sea was as calm as a millpond.

For some reason – Rebet said 'engine trouble', which Tweed did not believe – the vessel made slow progress. Consequently they reached the great city and port during the few hours of darkness. Tweed couldn't be sure whether this timing was to ensure he couldn't spy on certain defences on the banks of the River Neva. After all, Rebet had been an officer of the GRU, the military espionage arm of the Red Army, before being transferred to the KGB. Or was it possible his visit was being kept so secret it had seemed wise to land him in the night?

At the dockside a Volga car waited for them. Rebet was apologetic.

'With my present rank it should be a Zil limousine for a guest of your eminence. But a Volga is far less conspicuous . . .'

Which rather confirmed Tweed's second theory. Heavy net curtains were drawn over the windows as he sat in the back with Rebet. Peering out as the car moved fast he could make out very little. The occasional monument rearing in the darkness like a menacing sentinel. Then they arrived at the Hotel Moskwa at the end of the Alexander Nevski Prospekt.

Tweed and Nield were hustled inside the hotel by Rebet and soon they were shown into a spacious two room suite with windows overlooking the Neva. The furnishings were heavy, old fashioned and almost Victorian. Tweed opened a vast wardrobe and found it full of clothes.

'We, of course, have taken your measurements,' Rebet explained, 'so please make use of anything which takes your fancy while we have the pleasure of your company.

'Why evening dress?' Tweed enquired, fingering the suit.

'There is a reception here,' he checked his watch: one in the morning. 'A reception here tonight,' he concluded. 'That will be an important occasion. You will want to keep your eyes open.'

'Open for what?' Tweed demanded and faced Rebet. 'I have been very patient . . .'

'Please give me a few more minutes of that incredible patience.' He turned to the guard who had accompanied them in the Volga. 'Yuri, please show Mr Nield his suite —which is next door to yours,' he added to Tweed.

For the next ten minutes Tweed watched with a sense of foreboding as Rebet examined the suite with a small instrument like a squat torch. He was 'flashing' the accommodation to check for bugs. Here I am, thought Tweed, inside Russia and no one knows I am here. Now even Rebet seems nervous. It was not encouraging.

Tweed perched his backside on a cushion he'd placed on the wide window ledge. As Rebet continued his meticulous search, paying great attention to the chandeliers, he looked out of the window and watched a bridge lift to permit the passage of vessels downriver. Several freighters, a sturdy stubby-nosed tug hauling a barge train.

Nield returned, wearing a navy blue suit instead of the fisherman's clothes he'd been given aboard the fishing

193

vessel which had transferred them to the *Kalinin*.

'They're well organized,' he whispered to Tweed. 'Rebet must have radioed ahead that I was with you. My wardrobe has a selection of clothes in various sizes. This one fitted me best.' He looked at Rebet who was climbing down from a chair under a chandelier at the far end of the huge living room. 'What's up with him? Checking for listening devices? I thought he was a KGB general.'

'Not reassuring, is it.'

Rebet completed his task in the adjoining bedroom and bathroom and returned. He waved both hands in an apologetic gesture.

'I am sorry for the precaution, but we still have hard-liners who try to spy on what we are doing. Nowhere is safe. No one can be fully trusted. Which is why you are here.'

'Why is that?' Tweed demanded with an edge in his tone.

'I am forgetting my duties as host. You would like something to drink? Then, rather than talk now, perhaps you would like some sleep?'

'A vodka for me,' Nield said quickly.

'Yuri . . .' Rebet gave the order in Russian.

'We talk now,' Tweed said. 'I slept on the corvette. I wish to know what this is all about.'

'Treachery.' Rebet perched himself on the arm of a chair, looked at Nield, then at Tweed. 'You know whom I personally represent. You said your companion could be trusted? Can I speak frankly.'

'It would make a nice change,' Tweed said drily.

'I am the personal representative of the President of All the Russias. I report direct to him alone. There are con-spirators everywhere. Under the old régime, which I am so glad has gone, we at least had stability. Now we have the most terrible chaos. We have treachery at the very top.'

194

'What is the very top?' Tweed asked calmly.

'The Politburo.'

Howard walked into Tweed's Regent's Park office and Monica looked up warily. Her loyalty was to Tweed and she regarded Howard, the director, as a man to avoid as far as possible. She waited for him to flop into the armchair, perch one leg over the arm, his normal posture.

'Good morning, Monica,' Howard said quietly. 'Seems quiet with Tweed away. And I'm a very worried man.'

Monica blinked. This was a side to Howard she rarely saw, the sympathetic and – in an emergency – decisive chief. She closed her file.

'Why are you worried, sir?'

'Because we have had no word from Tweed, we have no idea where he is and I'm deeply concerned for his safety. Last night I phoned Mauno Sarin . . .'

Oh, my God! she thought. That's torn it. You've botched up the whole operation. His next words were equally surprising.

'I was very careful what I said to Sarin. I remarked it was a long time since we'd been in touch with him, that it was a long time since he'd seen Tweed.'

'And what did he say?'

'He immediately agreed, asked after Tweed's health, gave me the definite impression he had no idea Tweed was in Helsinki. I find that very worrying. You know who Tweed went to meet? I assumed it was Sarin. It wasn't. Tweed may be in great danger.'

'I'm sure he knows what he's doing.'

As she said the words Monica felt equally perplexed. Sarin was the obvious contact for Tweed to make, even if only as a courtesy gesture. The more she thought about it the more worried she became. Howard was pacing round the office, his brow furrowed. Even though the heat was

195

building up he wore his complete suit. It occurred to Monica she had never seen Howard in shirt sleeves, and then he spoke.

'Whereabouts is Paula at this moment?'

'I'm not sure . . .'

'But you do have a general idea. Of that I'm sure. Tell me.'

Monica hesitated. Normally she would have denied all knowledge of Paula's destination, but her anxiety made her change her mind.

'She's somewhere in Scandinavia. I honestly don't know in which country.

'I checked the visitors' book downstairs. Not so long ago Bob Newman was here. Is Paula with Tweed or with Newman?'

'With Newman. He's making some personal investigation – in connection with the death of his girl friend, Sandy.'

'The murder of Sandra Riverton? So, whatever is going on it's happening in Scandinavia. Tweed needs back-up in addition to Pete Nield. Where is Harry Butler?'

'Protecting Sandra's sister, Evelyn, in Walberswick.'

'This Evelyn – she's been threatened? Attacked?'

'Not so far . . .'

'Then that's it.' Howard was decisive. 'This is an order. Harry Butler must leave for Helsinki at once. No argument. He's worked a lot as a team with Nield. His task is to locate Tweed.'

'A bit of a tall order,' Monica ventured.

'If necessary Harry Butler will visit every hotel in Finland. He's like a bloodhound. Never gives up.' Howard turned at the door before he left. 'And, Monica, if I'm not available and an emergency arises, take a decision yourself. Without referring it to me. I sense the action is in Scandinavia. In my absence, you're in charge . . .'

After he'd gone Monica was stunned for a few minutes.

She had never known Howard hand her such power. Then she sat up straighter, smoothed down her bun of grey hair, stood up to haul Tweed's camp bed out of the cupboard. From now on she would stay in the office twenty-four hours a day. She was no longer nervous – even though she had the strong foreboding that there would be an emergency soon.

It was eight o'clock at night at the Grand Hotel in Stockholm when Newman rapped on Paula's door. She opened it and outside stood Newman and Dillon, holding their bags.

'Are you packed?' Newman asked quickly. 'We're ready to leave for the Vartan ferry terminal to catch the ship for Turku.'

'Of course I'm ready,' she replied as they came into her room and shut the door. 'I've been ready for half an hour. So you've decided definitely we go first to Turku, Finland's second city? Not direct by the ferry to Helsinki?'

'Yes. It's less likely they'll be watching that route. I have your Browning in my bag. They rarely search any luggage but I won't risk you getting caught with a weapon.'

'If you say so. Then what are we waiting for?'

The cab drive to the terminal was uncomfortable. Still daylight, the air was heavy, foetid. Although she had just had a shower, Paula, sitting next to Newman, kept plucking her T-shirt away from her body. The heatwave was getting worse and Stockholm had just endured one of the hottest days of the year.

'If it's a car ferry,' she whispered to Newman, 'why didn't you hire a fresh car?'

Dillon, who sat on her right, heard what she had said and replied, keeping his voice low to avoid the driver overhearing.

'Because Bob is smart. The opposition might think of checking all the car hire outfits. They pass a little money,

197

get the make of car, its registration number. Bob phoned ahead to Turku, made arrangements for a car to be waiting for us there. That's why.'

Paula nodded, glanced at the craggy-faced man who seemed unaffected by the torrid atmosphere. 'Bob.' He had used the name twice, had praised his tactics. Coming from Dillon that was praise indeed. She realized with surprise that the two men were drawing closer together.

The terminal came into sight, still well inside Stockholm. She saw for a few seconds the ship waiting for them. The ferry was huge, a great big five-decker. She'd had no idea such massive vessels plied the Baltic. Then she saw the film unit.

Manescu, dressed in a T-shirt and denims, wearing wraparound tinted glasses with curved lenses, stood a short distance from his camera team. Wandering slowly up and down behind him the dark haired Irina Serov was also casually dressed and her hair was tied in a pony tail. She also sported wrap-around tinted glasses, the standard equipment for directors of a film unit. Her denims were tight, looking as though they were pasted on her long slim legs.

'That man approaching the gangplank is Robert Newman,' she warned Manescu as she passed behind him.

'You're sure.'

'I don't make mistakes.'

She had paused to light a cigarette so she could talk behind her cupped hand. She watched the Englishman moving slowly up the steep entrance.

'Appears to be on his own,' Manescu commented. 'Follow him. You know my cabin number. I've got time to phone Helsinki, get final instructions . . .'

*   *   *

Cord Dillon had boarded the ferry earlier. Paula climbed the gangplank on her own. When Newman went aboard, holding his ticket, he was met by an attractive hostess who escorted him to his stateroom at the bow of the ship on the top deck. It was a comfortable room and there were bottles of mineral water and orange juice on the table.

He uncapped a bottle of mineral water, poured a glassful and swallowed the lot. The air inside the cabin was like an oven. He heard a gentle tapping on the door, put on his jacket, slipped his hand inside to withdraw the .38 Smith & Wesson, unlocked the door. As he'd thought, it was Paula.

'You saw the discothèque as you came on board,' she teased him. 'And you must have heard the music. All those beautiful lint-haired Finnish girls. Just your scene.'

'I might have a look at it later.'

'Where's my Browning? I feel naked without it.'

'You don't look naked. Unfortunately.'

'Are you making a pass at me, Bob?'

'Bet your sweet life I am.' He grinned drolly. 'And here's your Browning, plus some mags.'

She was examining the weapon, checking that it was unloaded, experimenting with the action. She slid it inside her shoulder bag with the mags., one inserted in the butt. Newman's manner changed.

'You saw the film unit on the dock. We've been tagged. At least I have.'

'And you thought we'd elude them by sailing for Turku.'

'Actually, I doubted it. But it makes it more nerve-wracking for Hauser. I'm stalking him, getting closer lap by lap. A little exercise in psychological pressure. He might just panic, make the wrong move. We've no evidence at all yet linking him with Sandy's murder.'

'But you'll get it. I know you when you're in this mood.'

199

Newman grasped her arm to emphasize what he was saying. 'One thing I must warn you about. We could be in great danger – now, aboard this ship which takes all night to reach Turku. Another reason why I didn't bring a car.'

'I'm not with you.'

'Think about it. We drive aboard, we're spotted by that film unit, they get the make and registration of the car. And all night it's sitting there deep in the bowels of the ship. How easy it would be for someone to monkey with it, mess up the braking system. Even attach a bomb. You've seen the paper – that report about Egon Schmidt, the well-known German banker, being blown up.'

'Yes, you passed it to me. I don't get the connection.'

'It's a *bank*. A very important private German bank. INCUBUS is basically a bank. Earlier I read a gossip item that Egon wasn't in the market for selling, but his son, Dieter, would be only too happy to sell out. I'm getting to know these people, how they operate. If anything stands in Hauser's way he removes it.'

'So he may try to remove you?'

'Exactly. That's why you mustn't be seen with me. And the same applies to Dillon, which is why he's staying in his stateroom.' He grinned. 'So if you do decide to have a look at the discothèque you can dance with me once. But only once.'

'Unless I find someone more attractive,' she said impishly. 'I can't see we're in any danger at a discothèque – in full view of a whole mob of rave-up teenagers.'

Manescu had sent off the film unit to Bromma to fly the new film to Helsinki. He had phoned Helsinki, had been told by Galvone that Hauser was travelling, so he made his report on Newman to Galvone.

'I'll take the responsibility for this one myself,' Galvone had decided. 'That reporter is becoming a nuisance. And

200

the best way of dealing with nuisances is to eliminate them. I rely on you to see the nuisance doesn't leave that ship . . .'

Manescu hurried aboard just before they removed the gangplank. He tapped in a special way on the door of Irina's cabin, slid swiftly inside to talk to her. The Russian girl sat in front of a mirror, brushing her cascade of glossy hair.

Manescu explained the situation quickly. Irina nodded, slipped a well-shaped hand down inside her jeans, felt the sheathed hypodermic needle. She began to apply lipstick.

'Maybe I can get him to go to bed with me. Men on the loose, a long way from home, are susceptible.'

'I don't care how, but do it.'

The great ferry had long ago left the terminal, had sailed down the approaches to Stockholm, had entered the open sea and was gliding over its smooth surface. Newman, shirt hanging out over his denims, walked into the disco and stood on the edge of the gyrating crowd, lighting a cigarette.

The amplifiers were bellowing out Sinead O'Connor, a blast of deafening rhythm. The strobe lights flashed on and off, a blinding glare converting dancers' complexions rapidly from red to blue, to yellow, to green and back again. It was a bedlam of sound, lights and the thump-thump of the dancers' feet. And to hell with inhibitions.

Paula, her hair tied in a pony tail, her legs encased in soft-soled knee-length boots, appeared behind Newman. Immediately a tall Finn with his shirt open down the front beckoned her on to the floor. She began gyrating grace-fully, keeping a foot between them. As she danced her eyes were everywhere. She frequently swung round to scan the floor, to watch Newman.

A trim small Finnish girl with lint hair tapped Newman on the arm. He nodded, said, 'OK,' stubbed out his cigarette in an ashtray, joined her on the floor. He realized at once that she was very good and her green eyes were inviting. She came close, spoke very clearly in English above the bombardment on the eardrums.

'Like to take me out to dinner tomorrow night in Turku?' She smiled. 'It's almost tomorrow now. You're English, aren't you?'

'Go to the top of the class, kiss the teacher, I'm the teacher.'

She obliged, eyes glowing, staying close to him. He spread his hands in a regretful gesture.

'I'd love to, but I'm here on business. Tomorrow night I'll be in Tampere . . .'

The music stopped. Couples paused. Some left the floor. A new fast number Newman didn't recognize started playing. The Finnish girl started to come back but was too late. A small slim girl with long black hair and scarlet lipstick had taken her place. Newman studied the Slavic cheekbones as they moved close together. The girl moved her hands a lot, well-shaped hands. Paula, dancing with a short stocky Swede, had moved closer, kept spinning round, her left hand held by the Swede who was a good dancer. Newman's partner placed both hands on her hips, moved her body slowly, a half-smile on her face. Paula was still spinning and the floor was more crowded as new couples took up more space. The girl with long dark hair pushed her right hand deeper inside her denims, her eyes holding Newman's. Her hand emerged in the crush, she reached out to grasp his wrist. Paula suddenly seemed to become a little drunk. Her body hammered against Newman's partner with force. The other girl lost her balance, began to slip. Paula hammered against her harder. The girl fell over. Couples reached out to break her fall as she slid to the floor. Newman saw the small hypodermic drop from her hand, saw Paula's right boot lift, smash down on the hypodermic, crushing it. Then she vanished in the crowd as the dark-haired girl climbed to her feet. Newman jerked her upright, pushed her into the eager arms of a tall Swede, slipped away out of the milling crowd.

'I'll recognize the little bitch again,' Paula said as she slumped on Newman's bed in his stateroom. 'You did say we could be in danger,' she reminded him as she took the glass of water he offered.

'Saved my life, you did,' Newman commented, sagging into a chair. 'What put you on to her? I need my head examining.'

'She kept glancing up at the flashing lights. I realized she was timing the change to a fresh glare, that brief second when you can't see what's going on. That's when she lunged at you with the hypodermic. I wonder what was in it?'

'Nothing for my health, that's for sure. And she's clever. Had I collapsed on the floor everyone would have assumed I was drunk, or was on drugs. She'd have been long gone. We have to be more careful.' He grinned ruefully. '*I* have to be more careful. And they'll be waiting for us when the ship docks at Turku. I suggest a late breakfast and we'll be last off the ferry. It will be daylight, of course.'

'I think I need some sleep now,' Paula decided, sat up, swung her legs over the edge of the bed, stood up, stretched herself. 'I'd better get back to my stateroom, otherwise I'm going to lose my reputation.'

'Would you mind?' he asked, still sitting down.

'What about Dillon?' she asked.

'I arranged we'd meet in the canteen. He'll wait there until we appear. The ferry docks at seven. So, if you insist

203

on going, I'll see you six-thirty in the canteen.'

'I have to think of Tweed.' She looked at him. 'Sometimes a woman takes a lot of time to make up her mind – especially when she knows two very different men.'

'I'll see you safely back to your stateroom. You're right – we need the sleep. God knows what is waiting for us when we set foot in Finland.'

20

Most people who knew Marler would have said he was impatient, wanted quick results. But Marler, when it was necessary, had the patience of Job. Concealed in his car inside the copse of trees above the INCUBUS HQ outside Helsinki, he had spent two days in the broiling heat, taking pictures at long intervals as people entered or left the building.

Back at The Palace Hotel overlooking North Harbour, he sat in front of the phone in his shirt sleeves, his collar open at the neck. He had delivered several films to a twenty-four-hour development shop. He was confident he now had pictures of all the top executives: he had identified them by the expensive cars they drove.

He picked up the phone and dialled Park Crescent. Monica answered his call.

'General and Cumbria Assurance . . .'

'It's Marler, Monica. Anyone I can talk to – and I'm calling from a hotel in Helsinki,' he warned.

'Understood. As to who you can talk to, only me. Believe it or not, our plummy-voiced upper-crust chief has left me in charge.'

Which meant Howard. Marler was surprised. Monica was good, very good, but Howard usually thought there were only two uses for women, one being to stay at home.

'Monica, I need info. Who is where. That sort of thing.'

At the other end of the line Monica hesitated for only a second. She was there to make her own decisions.

'Marler, our immediate sales director is in your area. But we haven't had any contact from him for days – and I'm worried stiff.'

That had to be Tweed. Marler lit a king-size cigarette, gave himself a brief pause to think. 'I'll do some checking,' he told her. 'Any more of the team floating round?'

'Yes, Paula and Bob are travelling together. They're heading your way. No idea by which route.'

Newman's a lone wolf, Marler thought. Although he doesn't sound too lonely this time. Maybe it was the murder of his girl friend which had made him long for company. No, that wasn't right. Paula could only be with Newman with Tweed's sanction. Which meant they were after someone.

'Anyone else?' he enquired.

'Yes. Harry Butler is flying out as an extra representative. He'll be calling me sooner or later.'

'Tell him I'm at The Palace Hotel, to come and see me. And don't worry. Our sales director knows what he's doing.'

Which was the understatement of the year as far as Tweed was concerned. Monica was speaking again.

'He took Pete Nield with him.'

'There you are. Not a thing to get hot and bothered about. Cancel the first part of that remark, Monica. It's bloody hot here. May call you again . . .'

Monica is clever, he thought as he put down the phone. Anyone listening in to that conversation would assume we were a commercial organization after business. So, the clans were gathering. He opened his door, hung the *Do*

205

Not Disturb notice on the handle, closed and locked the door.

Rummaging in his hold-all he brought out the Armalite rifle, began cleaning the weapon. It helped him to concentrate. And the hair he had laid over the zip had not been moved – no one had searched his room in his absence. The problem was which route would Newman come in by?

The airport? Marler didn't think so. Too obvious. And Newman was a devious bastard. By ferry from Travemünde – the route he'd used? He didn't think so. By car ferry from Sweden? That was the most likely, so he'd meet the ship arriving tomorrow. And Harry Butler? Marler out-ranked Butler but secretly called him The Beaver: Butler was a man who had immense stamina, who kept on working away at his appointed task until he'd done the job. A definite asset.

Marler decided he'd delay his flight to Rovaniemi, to explore this strange Meteorological Institute Sarin had pointed him to. Developments could be about to take place in Helsinki. The one thing which puzzled him was Tweed's whereabouts.

It was early evening in the Hotel Moskwa in Leningrad when Tweed, irked at the passing of time, forced the issue with General Rebet. They were sitting round a large table piled high with food and drink in Tweed's suite. Near a wall sat Pete Nield, keeping a wary eye on the slim Rebet who talked a lot with hand gestures.

'You spoke of treachery in the Politburo,' Tweed began, 'and then you veered off on a different subject. Rebet, I want to know why you brought me here, I want to know now, or I want to be flown back to Helsinki within the next hour.'

'Surely our hospitality has been . . .'

'It has been overwhelming.' Tweed, who had refused any sort of alcoholic drink, sipped his Russian tea. 'But I didn't come here for a holiday. Answer my question.'

'We are holding a large reception in this hotel to which you are invited.' Rebet checked his watch. 'I will escort you to it within the next thirty minutes.'

'Answer my question.'

'I have just done so. That is why you are here – to attend this reception *incognito* . . .'

'*Why?*' Tweed had raised his voice. 'I know that Russians take hours, weeks, even months to get to the point. I am the wrong man to treat in that way. Make arrangements now for me to fly back to Helsinki where you hijacked me. That I will not forget.'

'We know there is a high-level go-between – traitor, if you like – in the Politburo who is secretly co-operating with the military-industrial complex in America to help them dominate the Soviet Union. They see this as a unique opportunity to infiltrate my country, to reduce it to a commercial satellite of the United States. Because chaos has broken loose here. You understand me so far?'

'Yes, but I find the idea fanciful. Continue. Where does the traitor in the Politburo come in?'

'We cannot trace his identity. What I am going to tell you now is top secret. We infiltrated an agent inside Dracon, the huge think-tank located outside Boston. He reported an agent at the highest level was co-operating with the conspiracy. That he went by the code name Angel. We have narrowed down the suspects to three members of the Politburo. Marshal Dimitri Zaikov, Minister of Defence. Anatoli Dikoyan, an Armenian and Minister for Foreign Trade. Viktor Kazbek, a Georgian, Minister of Communications. One of these three men is collaborating with the Americans.'

'I fail to see how he could do that,' Tweed snapped.

'We know that Angel has close links with the Mafia . . .'

'The American Mafia? Come off it, Rebet.'

'No, my apologies, I referred to the Soviet Mafia. The underground movement which is so well organized, I fear. The men who are black marketeers, officials who have been bribed with large sums, even members of my own KGB. Angel has woven a web throughout the Soviet Union and these are the people the Americans are using.'

'Surely you can penetrate this movement?'

'We have tried to do so, of course. Agents have been infiltrated into this highly secret organization – and have been found dead. Murdered in a back alley in Moscow, here in Leningrad, in Kiev and so on. We have no inkling who Angel is – but he will be at the reception. All three men I have named will be at this reception. Maybe if you mingle with them you will see something with your fresh eye we have missed.'

'I think it highly unlikely.'

'Our President himself has asked you to try. We are running out of time.'

'I'll do what I can, but I promise nothing.' Tweed looked at Rebet. 'You must be desperate to call on me,' he said with a dry smile.

'We are desperate . . .'

Rebet continued talking as they descended a large staircase of stone. Below, guests in evening dress mingled, many of the women bare shouldered. Tweed could hear the clink of glasses, a babble of voices as Rebet instructed him while Nield followed behind them.

'You can spend most of your time observing. I will be by your side. If I introduce you it will be as Mr Gubenko, our commercial attaché at the London Embassy. You speak Russian well but that role will explain any trace of English accent that is detected.'

'I don't feel like Gubenko.'

'You look like him!'

It was the first joke Rebet had cracked since they arrived. As they edged their way into the vast hall Tweed looked up at the great chandeliers glittering high above his head. It was still daylight outside. To one side of the hall there was a buffet almost sagging under the mountains of food, the immense array of bottles. No sign of a food shortage here.

'That distinguished man with greying hair and pink cheeks is the British Ambassador,' Rebet whispered.

'Keep me well away from him, for God's sake . . .'

Then for a split second Tweed froze. In the centre of the hall a large party was gathered round a tall well-built man who wore pince-nez and flourished a cigarette holder. Franklin D. Hauser.

Tweed had a glazed look, seemed half asleep as Rebet escorted him slowly round the crowded room. But the apparently sleepy eyes never left Hauser or his companion. Marshal Zaikov was a short burly man who frequently made some humorous remark and Hauser would throw his head back and roar with laughter. In full dress uniform, Zaikov was clean shaven with a bull-like jaw and never stopped waving a clenched fist. Drawing closer, Tweed was surprised to hear Hauser speaking fluent Russian. The intensive research had not revealed this ability.

As the evening progressed Hauser began to circulate. Tweed sipped at his vodka as a great bear-like man with a black beard and a mane of black hair approached Hauser. They moved into a corner to avoid the crush. The bear-like man hugged Hauser, kissed him on both cheeks, then began to gesticulate. The man was a dynamo of energy, even more so than the American.

'The Georgian?' Tweed whispered.

'Yes, that is Viktor Kazbek, Minister of Communications. A man who likes women, plenty of women.' Rebet shrugged. 'But then he is a Georgian. They have great appetites for food, drink, all the good things in life.'

Tweed nodded, refused a waiter's attempt to freshen up his glass. Hew watched as the Georgian constantly touched Hauser to emphasize a point. Very little sign of inhibition there. Tweed stood quite still for a quarter of an hour while the two men conversed non-stop. Hauser certainly had a way of getting on with other nationalities.

'You would like to talk to someone? Maybe a beautiful woman?' Rebet suggested.

Tweed shook his head, raised his glass to his lips, held it there without even sipping. The Georgian had made way for a very different type of personality. A small slim man, faultlessly dressed, his dark hair brushed carefully back from his high forehead, sporting a trim moustache, was shaking hands with Hauser who had moved away from the corner.

'The Armenian?' whispered Tweed.

'Yes. Right again. Anatoli Dikoyan, Minister for Foreign Trade. He travels a lot in the West, trying to fix up barter deals. We are in a bad way here.'

'His background?' Tweed asked abruptly.

As Rebet gave him a pen portrait Tweed watched the Armenian, who, because of his small stature, had to look up at Hauser as he spoke non-stop to the American. His slim hands gestured frequently to emphasize a point. A clever man, Tweed decided, as Rebet spoke.

'Dikoyan is a brilliant politician. He has adapted himself to every change of régime. He was one of the first to admire the extraordinary man who would ultimately become our new President. He is fluent in four languages, one of them English. He has a genius for always staying in the background so no one can ever point the finger and say he was one of the Old Guard . . .'

The crush of people was beginning to move towards double doors which had been opened into the next salon. Rebet nodded towards the shifting mass.

'There will now be a banquet. You are invited. I hope you'll agree to attend?'

'Of course. I want to watch all three men. Do you know when Hauser leaves Russia?'

'After the banquet he flies straight back to Helsinki. He is not a man who stays here long.'

'And I have already seen him talking to the man you call Angel,' Tweed whispered.

'You mean you have identified him?'

Rebet could not conceal his astonishment. Tweed smiled, shook his head.

'After the banquet I may know. Especially as Hauser is leaving immediately it ends.'

'You are being very mysterious, my friend. One other problem is troubling us. A number of the key figures in the old security apparatus in various countries have disappeared. Including some of our own. This is highly confidential, Comrade.' Rebet had lowered his voice so Tweed only just caught what he said. 'A woman from my new organization, a colonel, too, Irina Serov, has vanished. We think she crossed the border into Finland – but that is a guess.'

'And the other key figures?'

They talked as they drifted towards the banqueting salon in the wake of the excited alcoholic crowd.

'One name we have heard several times is Ion Manescu, a tartar in the Romanian *Securitate*. There are names from the German STASI, which has been dissolved. My agents can find no trace of where these people are vanishing to.'

'But any strong evidence that they are going anywhere?'

'The numbers.' Rebet chuckled without humour. 'One

211

might have fallen down a hole in the ground. Also two. But it would need a very big hole to swallow up those who have performed this disappearing act. With all the troubles we have with so many of our republics it is worrying. Now, I must keep quiet . . .'

As in the old days the banquet went on for hours. Tweed was careful to sip at the variety of drinks put before him, asking frequently for more mineral water. And all the time he sat next to Rebet and ate small portions, his eyes kept glancing towards Hauser who had the place of honour to the right of the head of the table. Their official host was Marshal Dimitri Zaikov who occupied the end seat, ate huge quantities, drank litres of alcohol and told jokes.

Half-way down the opposite side of the table and close to Tweed sat the huge jovial figure of Viktor Kazbek. Constantly proposing toasts, he drank a great deal less than he appeared to. His dark eyes swept the guests, caught Tweed's, paused. Then Kazbek raised his glass and Tweed followed suit, nodding to the dynamic Georgian, sipping, looking away.

The diminutive figure of Dikoyan was paying great attention to an attractive woman who sat facing him. Tweed watched while the Armenian entertained his friend. As the banquet ended guests stood up, began chatting in groups. Hauser, Tweed noted, hurried from the salon escorted by guards, presumably on his way to the airport. Rebet, who had stood up with Tweed, seemed to read his mind.

'The motorcade is waiting for Hauser. He never hangs around for longer than he need. He'll be in the air within an hour.'

Dikoyan appeared at Tweed's side, was introduced by Rebet, and smiled cordially.

'I know London well,' he began in his quick way of speaking in English. 'I remember well catching the train from Charing Cross for a weekend in Bournemouth, Britain's Yalta nestling by the sea. A beautiful place.'

'Except that you must have travelled from Waterloo.'

'Of course!' Dikoyan threw up his hands in apology. 'So many stations in London . . .'

After a few minutes' lively conversation he disappeared in the crowd. Tweed glanced at Rebet.

'I thought he was devious. That reference to Charing Cross was a trap – to see if I really had been attached to the Soviet Embassy there . . .'

He broke off as the huge bulk of Viktor Kazbek loomed over him. Again Rebet made the same introduction in Russian. Kazbek stared at Tweed, asked Rebet to repeat the name.

'Igor Gubenko, commercial attaché to London,' Rebet replied.

'I am so pleased to meet you at our little party. Mr . . . Gubenko? Have I got the name right now?'

'Yes, you have.' Tweed stared straight back up at the glowing dark eyes of the bearded Georgian. 'You enjoy being Minister of Communications?' he enquired.

Kazbek threw back his maned head and roared with laughter. 'I enjoy it? Who on God's earth enjoys being a Politburo member these days, except the boss, maybe.' He tapped the side of his hooked nose with a large forefinger. 'Now I am being wicked. You quote me, Mr . . . Gubenko, and I get the sack. Now I am in your power!'

Another roar of laughter, his thick mane shook, he slapped Tweed on the back, grinned, exposing gold teeth and turned to kiss the hand of a fat woman.

Rebet drifted towards the exit and Tweed followed slowly, turning his head to survey the room. Nearby stood Marshal Zaikov, a motionless stocky figure with a face like Siberia. He was watching them and for a moment

213

Tweed felt sure he was going to come over to talk to them. Then the soldier seemed to change his mind. His eyes caught Tweed's for a fleeting moment and he moved in the opposite direction.

Rebet waited until he had escorted Tweed and Nield, who had sat a few places away, to their rooms before he asked Tweed the question.

'That's it. Hauser has gone. I believe you wish to return in the morning. You will be flown to Helsinki.' He paused. 'Have you any inkling as to which of the three men is Angel?'

Tweed said good-night to Nield, opened his door, turned and gazed at Rebet. The Russian had asked the question casually but Tweed sensed his anxiety. He shook his head.

'I am sorry but I really have no idea,' he lied. 'But thank you for the hospitality. It was worth a try.'

Had he told the truth, had Rebet asked him the reason for his identification, he would have replied, 'It was the absence of something I observed . . .'

21

Newman, Paula and Dillon were the last three passengers to disembark from the Silja Line ferry at Turku. After a late breakfast aboard they had assembled in Newman's stateroom and the argument had broken out.

'We're going ashore together,' Newman announced. 'With no attempt at concealment.'

'That's crazy,' Dillon had growled. 'After all the trouble we've taken to slip into Finland unseen.'

'I'm inclined to agree with Cord,' Paula had commented.

214

Newman had been firm, even aggressive. 'Listen, we tried and what happened? My invisible man act was a flop. They have the whole area cordoned, all entry points watched. You think it will be different here at Turku? Well, it won't be. So I'm changing the strategy. Let them see us – and we'll see them. I'm not picking up the hired BMW until early in the evening. Then we drive like hell along Highway E3 from here to Helsinki.'

'I still don't get it,' Dillon rasped. 'I don't agree with it . . .'

'Either come with us or make your own way there,' Newman told him brutally. 'Your choice. But remember, we now have guns. We can protect ourselves. And three is a formidable group if we come under attack during the drive.'

'And what, may I ask,' Dillon persisted, 'do we do during the day while we wait for evening? Give them a good chance to spot us, lay plans for an ambush? Stroll round Turku openly? Maybe have lunch at a hotel? More public exposure?'

'Exactly that,' Newman told him. 'Now it's time we went ashore. I know Turku. We'll dump our bags at the station, then take a look at old Turku. That's a collection of old wooden houses showing Finland as it was a hundred years ago. Relax, always in the open. That's what we're going to do. On second thoughts I'll hire a second car – which we won't use. It's psychological warfare – to throw them off balance.'

'What the hell does that mean?'

'That the one tactic which confuses the opposition is the unexpected.'

Irina Serov, wearing white shorts, a white blouse, a pair of tinted glasses, a wide-brimmed straw hat which concealed her hair, bare legged and shod in trainers, watched

215

as Newman walked out of the car hire firm. She slipped inside quickly as the girl behind the counter was completing a form, read it upside down.

'Can I help you?' the receptionist asked, looking up.

'I'd like a brochure showing the cars available and prices, please . . .'

Once she was outside in the steaming heat she looked round for a convenient doorway. Further along the street Manescu, also clad in casual clothes and wearing a straw hat, followed Newman as he joined Paula and Dillon.

Irina slipped inside the doorway alcove, felt inside her capacious shoulder bag, brought out a miniature walkie-talkie. Extending the aerial, she contacted INCUBUS Oy. in Turku.

'Joanna Star speaking. The subject has hired another white Volvo station wagon. Registration number . . . He has not driven the car away, so presumably he is still attending the convention. Over and out . . .'

Paula spoke casually as Newman joined them. 'You do realize you were being watched?'

'Girl in a straw hat and tinted glasses. Could be the one who tried to kill me last night at the disco – except that she's taller.'

'She's wearing trainers with specially elevated heels,' Paula informed him. 'And the little darling moves in the same way. She followed you into the car hire place.'

'Great. She'll have checked and report we're travelling in the wrong kind of car.' He looked at Dillon. 'Don't look back – we're now being followed by a man slouching along in a straw hat.'

They were strolling along together in the middle of Turku. The buildings were a mix of new and old, mostly three or four storeys high, so they were not shielded from the sun. The traffic in Turku was quieter than in Stockholm: they could even cross the street almost

216

whenever they wanted. Newman nodded, glanced back and led the way to a bar on the far side.

'Time for a drink. Whatever else you have, order some mineral water and drink the lot. We must guard against dehydration. And it will be fun to see what Straw Hat does.'

'I don't like this cat-and-mouse game,' Dillon said as they sat at a window table. He waited until the waitress had taken their order. 'I'd like to shove Straw Hat into one of those alleyways, squeeze his throat until he talks, then make him unconscious.'

'And give away the fact that we know what's going on?' Newman grinned, shook his head. 'We're playing innocents. We think we've shaken them off. That way they'll make a mistake.'

'I don't think INCUBUS makes many mistakes,' Paula observed when the waitress had delivered their order. She sipped her orange juice through a straw. 'Do you think it was such a good idea leaving our weapons in the cases we deposited in the station lockers?'

'Oh, definitely.' Newman was in a good humour. 'That way we can't get caught by the police. Whoever is running the surveillance operation on us might just get the idea of giving the police an anonymous tip. They catch the three of us with guns and that's it. The Finns don't like strange people in town tooled up with guns.'

Dillon grunted. 'And I've got sand in my shoes – or whatever that stuff was we walked through prowling round those old cabins.'

Newman stiffened, then relaxed. He gazed out of the window across the street at the men's outfitters shop where Straw Hat was taking his time examining the merchandise. But his expression had frozen and only Paula realized what had happened. Dillon's reference to sand. It had shot back into Newman's mind his girl friend, Sandy, and he was reliving the nightmare dawn in Suffolk when he'd discovered her hanging by her neck in the bell tower.

Earlier his mind had been concentrated on outwitting their pursuers, which had driven the horror into the background. Now he sat with his jaw muscles clenched tight and a blank look in his eyes. Paula knew that look, had seen it only once or twice before. Newman was feeling like murder.

Franklin D. Hauser's Lear executive jet had flown him back from Leningrad and landed him at Helsinki airport. The waiting bullet-proof limo drove him straight to INCUBUS Oy. HQ. He hurried out of the car into the building, in a rush as always.

Concealed inside his car in the copse overlooking the HQ Marler snapped off three shots with his camera, recorded in his notebook the time. Early that morning he had met the Silja Line car ferry from Stockholm, had checked each passenger off the ship. No sign of Newman: he had guessed wrong. Was the reporter coming at all? he asked himself.

On the top floor Galvone was waiting for his chief. Seeing his expression, he began talking at once as Hauser settled himself behind his desk. No small talk: get to it.

'Newman has arrived in Finland.'

Hauser's expression froze. He reminded Galvone of one of the great faces of four American Presidents carved out of the stone cliff at the summit of the Black Hills in South Dakota.

'Here in Helsinki?' he demanded, his voice harsh.

'Not that bad . . .'

'How bad? Get to it.'

'Newman is in Turku. Arrived on the ferry from Stockholm this morning. Manescu and Serov have the situation in hand. Newman has hired a Volvo, is expected to drive

218

here soon. He has people with him. A man. A girl.'

'Why didn't they do the job on the ferry?'

'Serov tried. She just got unlucky.'

The door to Hauser's penthouse office opened and Adam Carver strolled in. It was early evening but the Englishman looked fresh as paint, ready to start a new day.

'We're in conference,' Hauser snapped.

'I just got in from Germany. Egon Schmidt's bank is ours. I persuaded the surviving son, Dieter, to sign a preliminary agreement. There'll be more paperwork but the bank is yours. You have your foot in the German door.'

'Good.' Hauser was pleased but impatient. 'You'll be tired. Go and freshen up. Then stay in your office. I want to see you later.'

He waited until he was alone with Galvone. Leaning back in his chair he stared at his subordinate.

'Frank, this is an order. Finish him off. No way must he reach Helsinki . . .'

Inside a café opposite the car hire firm Irina, the last customer, sat making her second cup of coffee last out. A waitress came to her table, said they'd soon be closing. Irina told her she was waiting for a friend she expected any minute. She passed the waitress a banknote, a generous tip.

Five minutes later she saw a BMW drive out with Newman at the wheel, the girl beside him, the second man in the back. She extracted her pocket walkie-talkie from her shoulder bag, extended the aerial after checking the waitress had disappeared. 'Joanna Star here. The subject is driving out of town. Not the Volvo I reported earlier. He's changed cars. Now in a cream BMW. Registration . . . Over and out.'

Manescu walked into the café as she finished her coffee and prepared to leave. She told him what she had reported to INCUBUS Oy. HQ in Turku.

'It's all arranged,' Manescu assured her as they walked into the street. 'Orders from the very top. They'll die on Route E3.'

'You've been this way before,' Paula said as they left behind the outskirts of Turku. 'How far to Helsinki?'

'Exactly a hundred and fifty-eight kilometres. Take us about a couple of hours.'

'Where are we staying in Helsinki?' Dillon demanded from the rear.

'Decide when we get there,' Newman said tersely. 'Not the Hesperia if we can avoid it. I've stayed there before. Just leave it to me, there's a good chap, Cord.'

Paula glanced at Newman. Ever since Dillon had made the remark which had reminded the Englishman of Sandy, Newman's manner had been polite, his mood grim. They were speeding along Route E3, a two-lane highway each way. Very little traffic as behind them the sun sank into lower orbit. Paula checked the dashboard.

'What are the speed limits in Finland?'

'Sometimes 80 kph, sometimes 100. Further along there's a special stretch called The Highway. There you can ram your foot down a bit. 120 kph.'

Again he was terse. Hands on the wheel relaxed, Paula noted. Newman was a superb driver but she sensed the tension inside him. Was it because they were approaching their objective – Helsinki? That Newman couldn't wait until he confronted Hauser? Newman's thoughts were really miles away. He was recalling what Chief Inspector Roy Buchanan had said. The points he had made.

Try and discover which top executive was in Helsinki when Ed Riverton had been garrotted, his body dragged

220

off the ice in North Harbour. Try and pinpoint an executive who had been *absent* from Finland when Sandy was murdered at the belltower in Suffolk. Hope that the same man fitted both situations.

Paula looked out of the window as they drove through countryside. Stands of great firs, the sky luminous with that pearl-like and crystal-clear light you only saw in Finland. The firs reared up like silhouettes, their edges sharp-cut against the sky. Dream-like land . . .

'We're moving on to The Highway,' Newman commented.

Paula was aware they were racing much faster, again checked the dashboard. 120 kph. 75 mph. The BMW glided along, adding to the dream-like atmosphere. This is pure heaven, Paula thought.

'There's a huge truck coming up behind us,' Dillon warned. 'I saw a name splashed along the side as it came round a curve. INCUBUS Oy.'

'A juggernaut,' Newman replied calmly. 'And I have seen it. Moving up on us like an express train . . .'

Paula twisted in her seat, strained against her belt to see the vehicle. It was enormous. It had a separate cab for the driver attached to the mammoth load behind it. They were now separated from all traffic coming in the opposite direction by a high shrub-covered bank. She looked at Newman, saw his lips were pressed tightly together.

'Trouble?' she asked quietly and reached inside her shoulder bag, her right hand gripping the butt of her Browning.

'Could be.'

Newman's tone had become laconic. He glanced in his rear-view mirror, then grinned at Paula. The juggernaut was bearing down on them like a battleship, far exceeding the speed limit even for The Highway. Behind the driver's cab the immense load swayed ominously and slowly from side to side. Then with a burst of speed the juggernaut overtook them on the left, was driving alongside them, looming over Newman like a mountain. He dipped his head briefly, caught a glimpse of the driver on the far side. A stocky man hunched over his wheel, wearing a peaked cap, dark glasses. The vehicle began to move closer, the driver turning his wheel inches at a time.

Paula hauled out her Browning, leaned forward. Newman had his window lowered all the way to counter the hot foetid air of evening. Paula dipped her own head, raised the gun barrel.

'Put that thing away! Newman snapped. 'You want us arrested for murder?'

'So,' Dillon called out from his seat, 'we're going to be the meat in the sandwich . . .'

'Thanks for the vote of confidence,' Newman rapped back.

There was still about one foot between the two speeding vehicles. The gap was closing second by second. To their right, on Paula's side, ran an endless steel barrier, closing off the inner lane from a slope descending to a wall of firs. She saw it all in a blur – the canvas covering of the juggernaut moving towards them, the highway ahead with not a vehicle in sight. She had obeyed Newman, thrusting the Browning back inside her shoulder bag, her right hand moist and slippery on the butt. Every muscle in her body seemed to scream with tension, the tension of waiting for the impact as the juggernaut smashed into them, hurled them against the steel barrier, the sparks flying as metal collided with metal, the awful moment when she felt the barrier give way, the BMW begin to turn turtle . . .

Newman again dipped his head briefly, saw the driver inside the cab change his grip on the wheel prior to swinging it in a large arc to his right. Nineteen drivers out of twenty would have tried to race ahead, ramming their foot down, but Newman was the twentieth man. He had heard the deep-throated boom-boom of the juggernaut's souped up engine. No chance of out-racing it. He did the dangerous unexpected thing. He reduced speed as rapidly as he dared, waited for the skid – and there was no skid. The driver in the cab had swung his wheel, was cutting across Newman's bow to crush him against the steel barrier. Newman took his second lethal risk. He rammed on the brake. The BMW came to a shuddering halt. Paula glanced back at Dillon. The American had braced himself with his left hand against the back of her seat. His right hand held his Luger, muzzle pointed towards the left. The driver of the juggernaut had turned his massive load inwards, knowing the collision with the BMW would cushion him. But the BMW had vanished. He saw the steel barrier fly towards him, felt the vehicle crash against the barrier, heard a wrenching sound as the barrier gave way, tried desperately to turn his wheel. Too late.

Newman, rubbing his aching right arm inside the stationary BMW, watched as the juggernaut destroyed the barrier, began to topple sideways, turn over as it rolled down the slope. It hit the wall of firs like a cannon firing, three firs tilted sideways, there was a brief moment of silence when the only sound was the ticking over of the BMW's engine, then the motionless juggernaut burst into flames, cremating the driver as the flames soared up in a gigantic torch consuming the tilted firs.

Newman glanced in his rear-view mirror. No traffic coming up. He drove on, pressing his foot down until the speedometer reached 120 kph. With one hand he lit a cigarette: the only sign of any reaction to what had occurred. Paula knew he normally never smoked when driving. She relaxed her grip on the Browning, took a deep breath, wiped her hands on a handkerchief, looked back at Dillon.

The American's craggy face showed no indication of what they had just experienced. He winked at Paula.

'I'll be ready for a drink, I guess, when we reach

Helsinki,' he remarked. 'I wonder what happens when we get there.'

'We need a lucky break,' was Newman's only reply.

22

Peggy Vanderheld had cleared her desk, had left INCU-BUS Oy.'s HQ forever. She had taken a taxi to her apartment overlooking the sea, which she still thought looked more like a lake.

She sat by the window, drinking a dry martini, still seething over the way Hauser had treated her. Her apartment was in a block near the end of tram stop No. 4 coming out from the city. It was located only a short walk from the Hotel Kalastajatorppa up the hill, a weird complex of buildings which some Finnish architect had designed so it looked as though it grew out of the granite it stood on. Maybe she would go there for dinner.

No, she decided, I have a ticket to the theatre opposite the Marski in town. I want to be among a lot of people. She sat gazing down at the scrubbing platform, a wooden structure projecting into the sea at two levels. Wooden rails surrounded it.

Peggy had often watched Finnish women working on that platform in the morning, dipping their carpets in the sea water, then scrubbing them clean on wooden tables. It was incredibly hard work and yet many of the women who used it were middle class. The thought had just passed through her mind when the bell rang.

'Hell! Who's come to bother me when I want to do a Garbo?'

She operated the speakphone, asked who it was.

'Peggy, it's Adam Carver. I'd really appreciate it if I could have a word with you. I know you must be raging at what they did.'

'OK. Come up. If you must . . .'

She pressed the button which released the lock on the door to the main lobby. Checking her appearance in a wall mirror, she had the door open when Carver, looking very smart in a cream silk suit, entered.

'You'd better sit down, I suppose.'

She was damned if she was going to offer him a drink. But she recognized she had mixed feelings towards Carver. Certainly he was a handsome brute, but she mistrusted his British charm. He gave her what she supposed was his winning smile and sat in an armchair. She chose a hard-backed chair and crossed her shapely legs.

'Well, what is it?' she demanded.

'Don't be like that. I thought we got on pretty well when you were with the company.'

'Everyone has their illusions.'

'I don't necessarily agree with everything Hauser does, you know.' He gazed at her. 'You really have the most superb figure, if I may say so.'

'You just did. Who am I to argue with a vice president?'

'This is getting us nowhere . . .' He smiled again.

'So goddamnit, let's get somewhere. Let's get to the point of why you came here.'

'INCUBUS is willing to offer you a very generous pension.'

'Which I'll take because it's owing to me. Nice to be referred to like an old horse put out to grass.'

'Peggy! Please! I didn't imply anything like that. You're still a young woman. With your track record you could get any job you want. And I didn't get the chance to explain – INCUBUS is offering you double the pension you're expecting.'

Her eyes narrowed. She stroked her dark hair. 'And what is the catch, Buster?'

'A good question. Nothing more than your signing the usual agreement which forbids revealing any information picked up while you were in the company's employ. No talking about it. No newspaper interviews. No writing your memoirs for a big fat advance from New York.'

She stood up. 'You know something. You just gave me a great idea. Glad you called, Adam. And now, if you'll excuse me, I have a ticket for the theatre and I have to change.'

He stood up slowly. 'But what about what I just said? I'd like a reaction before I go.'

'Just like that? You have to be joking.' She opened the door. 'I'll give it some thought. May take some time. Nice knowing you . . .'

Carver left the apartment block and walked slowly up the street to where he'd parked his car. He rubbed his freshly shaven chin. Was he losing his touch? He'd felt sure he could twist her round his little finger.

He climbed behind the wheel, sat staring at the deserted street. A No. 4 tram appeared in the distance, trundled to its terminus a hundred yards away. Carver picked up his mobile phone, dialled Hauser's private number.

'Adam here, sir. The problem is unresolved. Difficult to foretell how the subject will react . . .'

'You're saying negative?' Hauser rasped.

'Up to a point. At the moment . . .'

'You're saying negative,' Hauser repeated. 'Get back here fast. I want a full report.'

Newman had decided against the Kalastajatorppa. Too many painful memories. He had stayed there years before when his wife had been murdered in Estonia. He could do

226

without that on top of Sandy's death. Not the Hesperia: he had stayed there before. Which left three hotels – the Marski, the Intercontinental and The Palace. He chose the latter.

Waiting in the lobby for Paula and Dillon – Newman was an expert at swift unpacking – he found arriving back in Helsinki he was reliving earlier experiences. He needed a drink. Wandering into the bar the first person he saw sitting by himself at a corner table was Marler.

'Large Scotch, please,' Newman ordered at the bar.

He carried his glass as he strolled round as though unsure where to settle. As he reached Marler's table he appeared to stumble, spilling some of his drink on the table top. He took out a handkerchief, talking as he mopped up the liquid.

'Sorry to mess up your table. Not like me to be clumsy, but I'm bushed. Just got in after long drive.'

Marler waved a hand. 'Be my guest. Take the weight off your feet . . .'

To an onlooker it appeared to be a chance meeting between two strangers, Englishmen who were glad to encounter a fellow-countryman. Newman sat down, blew out his cheeks in a gesture of relief.

'Thanks.' He lifted his glass. 'Cheers!' He lowered his voice as he placed the glass on the table. 'The INCUBUS octopus lot have just tried to kill me twice.'

Marler grinned. 'They must be amateurs. If I'd been hired by them you wouldn't be there drinking Scotch.'

'I love egomaniacs,' Newman responded. 'And don't be surprised when Paula and Cord Dillon walk in. We're travelling together.'

'Dillon? The deputy director of the CIA. Care to enlighten me.'

'Can't. Not about Dillon. Tweed's orders. Sorry. But I can tell you why I'm here . . .'

He gave Marler a concise account of his investigation of

227

INCUBUS, including his interviews with the two Englishmen who had been forced into selling out to the corporation against their will. Briefly, he described the two attempts on his life, told Marler how he had obtained weapons. Marler stroked his fair hair, said nothing while Newman explained, then extracted from his jacket pocket an envelope.

'Care to see my holiday snaps, chum? Taken in secrecy from a point overlooking INCUBUS's HQ west of the city. No idea who is who, but I didn't see the man I was looking for.'

Newman looked at the glossy prints, identified certain people as he handed each print back.

'That's Adam Carver. English. Met him when I called on Hauser at his Suffolk home, Livingstone Manor. Not a mile from where I found Sandy hanging by her neck. He's a vice president. And this one is Hauser, which you probably know from seeing his picture in the papers. This thug is Frank Galvone, another vice president. These two I don't know. Now, this handsome-looking brunette . . .'

He stopped speaking as Paula entered the bar with Dillon.

'Don't stare, Cord,' Paula warned, 'Newman's in the far corner. And somehow he's met up with Marler of all people. I think we had better stay away.'

'Suits me, honey. Don't too much like either of them. Even if they are two tough pros. Let's have a drink together, get our nerves back into shape.'

It was the first hint Paula had that Dillon, always outwardly calm and unruffled, had been affected by the terror on The Highway. She accepted his offer gratefully and they took their drinks to a table well away from where the two Englishmen sat.

Newman nodded to Marler. 'Paula is smart. They're

228

pretending they don't know us. Which probably suits you. Now, you were about to say something.'

'I've identified that handsome-looking brunette. She's American, was Hauser's highly confidential personal assistant, until he gave the lady her marching orders, which she doesn't like one little bit. Peggy Vanderheld. I even know where she lives in Helsinki.'

'How the devil did you work that one?'

'Charm, old boy. I followed one of the Finnish secretaries home in my car one evening. I thought she might just be my type. She stopped at the Marski bar for a drink. I went in after her. We got on fine over a few drinks. She thinks I'll soon bed her. I'm not sure I need go that far. Want the details?'

'Of course I do. Stop being tantalizing. Give me the lot.'

'The Finn girl told me Peggy Vanderheld knows more about INCUBUS operations than any other employee below the rank of vice president. She also told me Vanderheld is blazing with hatred about the way Hauser kicked her out. She's still in Helsinki. I even managed to wheedle Vanderheld's address out of my girl friend.' Marler took out a small pad, scribbled on it. 'Here it is, if you think it'll be of any use. You know Helsinki pretty well, don't you?'

'Yes.'

'Then the easiest way to reach her apartment block is to catch a No. 4 tram. Go to the end of the line, get off, walk down towards the sea and it's the last block on the right. I got that out of the girl friend, too.'

'Thanks, Marler. This could be the break I've been hoping for. I suppose you'd laugh in my face if I asked you what brings you out here?'

'No. I'm tracking some dangerous ex-secret police types – thrown out of a job when Communism collapsed in the Balkans and East Germany. One is Ion Manescu . . .'

'The Romanian. I've heard of that bastard. Expert in a

nice line of torture among other talents. Why look here?'

Marler told him about the sighting of Manescu boarding the Travemünde ferry reported to Tweed, the ferry sailing for Helsinki. About his interview with Mauno Sarin, Chief of the Protection Police, who had deviously pointed him towards INCUBUS.

'So that's why you were watching their HQ?' Newman remarked.

'It was a long shot and it didn't come off. Here is the only picture ever taken of Manescu.'

Newman studied the photograph, frowned, gazed round the bar to where Paula and Dillon were engaged in deep conversation. Then he studied the print again and finally looked up at Marler.

'I can't be sure. I'm probably wrong . . .' He hesitated.

'Go on,' pressed Marler.

'While we were hanging around in Turku waiting for evening before I drove here we were followed. I was sitting inside a café with Paula. This character I called Straw Hat was pretending to examine the clothes in a men's outfitters on the other side of the street. It was very hot and for a few seconds he took off his hat to mop his forehead. It was bloody hot, as it is here. I caught a glimpse of his face and it looked damned like this photo. But without a moustache.'

'He could have shaved that off,' Marler said quickly. 'How can you be sure he was working for INCUBUS?'

'Because, as I told you, it was an INCUBUS juggernaut which tried to turn us into mashed potato on Route E3. That links Straw Hat direct to INCUBUS.'

'Of course.' Marler went to the bar, ordered fresh drinks, came back and sat down again. 'It's strange,' he continued, 'but before I saw Sarin I'd have said we were working on two separate operations. Now I wonder. Where do you think Ion Manescu will turn up next?'

'If it was him, here in Helsinki.' Newman stood up,

folded the sheet of paper with the address on it, put it in his wallet. 'This information about Manescu should go to Tweed.'

'He's disappeared,' Marler said quietly. 'I called Monica and she said he'd come here. I checked every hotel two days ago. No trace.'

'Check them over again,' Newman advised.

'Where are you going? I'm staying at this hotel, incidentally.'

'I was about to ask you that. Where am I going? To talk to Peggy Vanderheld.'

The theatre opposite the Marski was a modern circular edifice, its walls covered with creeper. Peggy Vanderheld, wearing a chestnut-coloured suit, left the theatre and walked to the No. 4 tram stop. A large brown Buick moved from the kerb, crawled slowly after her.

She boarded the tram and looked out of the window as it moved out of town. She was on the right-hand side and watched people strolling in the green park, the huge granite boulders rearing up out of the earth. Behind the tram the brown Buick drifted in its wake.

She couldn't make up her mind what to do about Hauser. While watching the performance her mind had been free of problems. Now they all kept flooding back. A double pension? That was a load of money for life – if she kept her mouth shut. Screw that, she thought, I want to kick Hauser in the balls. That mistaken remark Carver had made about not writing her memoirs for a big fat advance from New York had opened up new horizons.

The tram left the city behind, entered a wooded suburban area. She was the only passenger to leave the tram at the end of the line. With her mind in a whirl she didn't notice the Buick which had parked a dozen yards up the road. Nor did she see the cream BMW parked beyond the stationary tram near the sea.

Inside it Newman sat behind the wheel, all the windows open in an attempt to counter the torrid heat of late evening. He recognized Vanderheld at once from the photo Marler had shown him. Earlier he had pressed the button for her apartment outside the locked front door. No answer.

He sat quite still as she entered the block. He had noticed the brown Buick, a big job, which had followed the tram and then parked. No one alighted from the vehicle. Beyond the amber-tinted windscreen he saw the silhouette of a chauffeur wearing a peaked cap and dark glasses.

He waited a few minutes, closed the windows, got out, locked the car and walked up the steps to the entrance. Once again he pressed the bell on the speakphone alongside the card with *Vanderheld* inscribed in neat script.

'Who the hell is it now?' a feminine voice with an American accent demanded.

'Robert Newman, foreign correspondent. I'd much appreciate ten minutes of your time. It concerns an investigation I'm making.'

A pause. Newman carefully said nothing more.

'An investigation into what?' Vanderheld demanded.

'Something too serious for me to discuss standing in the open.'

'Ten minutes. Not a second more.'

A buzzer sounded. Newman pushed the door open into the lobby, heard it close automatically behind him as he ran up the staircase. She was standing in the doorway of her apartment, ready to slam the door in his face. Instead she stood aside and he walked in to a modern apartment, comfortably furnished without clutter. A place for everything and everything in its place. The home of a professional businesswoman. He perched on the arm of the chair she ushered him to.

About five feet nine, Newman estimated, a slim figure clad in a lightweight brown suit. Sheer black tights, high-heeled shoes and a mass of coiffured black hair. Good bone structure, a full mouth, bright red lipstick. Early forties and a handsome woman. She stripped off her jacket, exposing well-formed breasts, placed it carefully over the back of a chair.

'I recognize you from pictures I've seen in the papers a few years back. You've worn well.'

'Thank you . . .'

'An investigation into what?'

She stood gazing down at him from a distance of six feet, her hands on her hips. There was a challenging note in her tone. She lit a cigarette, remained standing, one arm beneath her breasts, the other holding the cigarette.

'An investigation into INCUBUS.' He took a quick decision, began telling her about the murder of Sandy, the proximity of Livingstone Manor, the murder of Ed Riverton, his interviews with the two English businessmen forced to sell out.

'Why come to me?' she asked. 'What is there in it for me?'

'Your chance to get back at Hauser. I blast his operation wide open in *Der Spiegel*. But I need information. Hard facts.'

'I'll think about it. Where can I reach you?'

'I'm staying at The Palace.'

'And why, may I ask, Mr Newman, are you doing all this? I recall you wrote that huge international bestseller, *Kruger: The Computer That Failed*. That must have made you financially independent for life.'

'It did.'

'So why? You don't need to work as a foreign correspondent any more. *Why?*'

233

'I told you,' he reminded her. 'Because of Sandy. I think Hauser is linked to her murder. If he is, I'm going to bring him down.'

'I see.' She stubbed out her cigarette while Newman watched her. He rather liked Peggy Vanderheld. She was attractive, had brains and guts. 'Come back and meet me here tomorrow night at the same time,' she decided. 'I'm going out to the theatre again. I want to sleep on all this.'

He stood up. 'Sleep well . . .'

Newman settled himself behind the wheel of the BMW. The brown Buick was still parked further up the street. As he cruised past it slowly he glanced at the driver. The chauffeur was slumped in front of the wheel, peaked cap dipped over his head. He appeared to be asleep.

Newman had a good look at the vehicle. It was a very large American job: a LeSabre estate wagon. A four-door car, it had brown wood bodywork below the tinted windows, sleeping space in the rear and a chrome rack on the roof.

As Newman drove on through the late evening, still in daylight, the main stem of Mannerheimintie traffic-free, the air crystal clear, into the city and past the Marski Hotel, the heat so intense his shirt was pasted to his back, he wondered about Tweed. Where could he be at this moment?

23

Tweed sat with Nield in the basement restaurant beyond the bar area in the Marski. They had flown in from Leningrad and Tweed had chosen the Marski because he'd never stayed there before.

'Nice to get back to familiar food, Pete,' he remarked as he tucked in to fried chicken and saffron rice. 'Finnish cooking is marvellous.'

'And that salad we started with was quite something. It fascinated me watching the girl mix it so skilfully . . .'

They occupied a curtained banquette at the far end of the restaurant so they were able to talk openly. Nield was relieved to be back in Finland but Tweed seemed more interested in his meal. Occasionally he would stop to look at three postcards – on the back of each he had written a name. Kazbek. Zaikov. Dikoyan. It helped him to sift his thoughts by having the names in front of him.

'Which one?' asked Nield.

'Difficult to be sure . . .'

Tweed looked up as a well-built, clean-shaven man in his thirties, wearing an open-necked white shirt and grey slacks stopped at their table and looked back at Tweed. Harry Butler. Nield goggled at the appearance of his old partner. Tweed shifted his plate and glass further along the banquette and merely invited his subordinate to join them.

'What brings you up here, Harry?' he enquired.

'Howard was worried about you – really worried. He ordered me off the job of protecting Evelyn Lennox in Walberswick and sent me here in case you needed reinforcements. And Monica is out of her mind with anxiety about what's happening to you.'

'Not any more. I made a brief call to her as soon as we got back to Helsinki. We've been abroad.'

'You're abroad now,' Butler pointed out in his impassive way.

'There's abroad and abroad.' Tweed smiled. 'Pete would agree with me, but don't ask him questions. How did you find me?'

'By checking every hotel in Helsinki daily since I arrived. I said you were a business associate and I wasn't sure of the date of your arrival.'

'Very diplomatic. And I'm glad you're here – although I'm not happy about Evelyn being left unguarded. But your presence is welcome. I have a feeling that when the crisis breaks it will explode here. We may need every man we can get.'

'Then you'll be glad to hear Marler is based at The Palace. Monica called me at the Hesperia and told me where to contact him.'

'That's a big plus,' Tweed commented as though the information that Marler was in Finland was news to him.

'And that's not all,' Butler continued in his placid manner. 'Marler told me Bob Newman and Paula came in recently. They're also staying at The Palace. What they are here for I don't know.'

Tweed nodded. He realized Butler had been careful not to ask why. Butler was reliable: he knew that at times Tweed operated several groups independently on a cell system similar to that used by the Russians. One cell might have a different task from another. Only Tweed decided the moment when battle had to be joined, when his forces must be merged into one big spearhead group to attack the target.

'No coffee for me tonight,' he decided. 'I need the sleep. Harry, stay at the Hesperia so I can call you the moment an emergency arises.'

'You're expecting one soon?' Nield asked.

'Once Hauser discovers the opposition is on his doorstep – that's when the balloon goes up.'

The following day Peggy Vanderheld phoned Newman at The Palace. She had slept badly the previous night, her mind churning over her problems. She was still unsure whether to blow the whistle on Hauser to Newman.

'I'd like you to delay calling on me at where we met yesterday,' she said crisply. 'I find my theatre ticket is for tomorrow night,' she lied. 'So I'm going out of town to see a friend. Maybe I'll see you tomorrow night. Don't do anything until I call you.'

'Anything the lady wants . . .'

Newman put down the phone in his room and frowned. No point in pushing a woman – you had to let her take her time, make up her mind one way or the other. And he and Paula had an appointment to see Tweed at the Marski late in the afternoon. The sooner Tweed knew about the two murderous attempts on his life the better. And what could go wrong during a twenty-four-hour delay?

The weather changed in late afternoon. The azure dome of sky vanished. The sun no longer shone. A heavy overcast hung over Helsinki and the murky sky looked like grey smoke. The atmosphere became horribly humid, pressing down on the city like an iron lid.

Peggy Vanderheld had heard the weather forecast and when she left the theatre again in late evening she was prepared for the heavy drizzle which had begun to fall. Over her brown suit she wore a cream raincoat bought at Stockmann's, the leading Helsinki department store. Wrapped round her dark hair she was protected with a highly coloured scarf she had also purchased at Stockmann's.

She was walking towards the tram stop when she noticed several yards ahead another woman of similar build who also wore a raincoat exactly like hers. Well, Stockmann's must sell a lot of them. What surprised her was the woman also had exactly the same scarf wrapped over her head. Peggy *had* thought the scarf was exclusive when she chose it. At the time it had been the only one on the counter. Presumably all the others had already been grabbed earlier. I suppose she's also wearing the brown suit I got from Stockmann's, she thought ruefully.

The woman in front of her was boarding a No. 4 tram. Peggy ran to catch it: they came only infrequently. Out of breath, she jumped aboard, purchased a ticket from the driver, slid it inside the slot machine which stamped the time and sat down.

The woman dressed so like her was sitting five seats in front of her. Peggy was so absorbed in thinking about Newman she never noticed the brown Buick which had been cruising behind the tram. As it approached the last stop but one she never saw the Buick suddenly speed up, overtake the tram, driving on to a point near the last tram stop.

Peggy glanced out, realized it had stopped raining, decided she needed a little exercise. Unusually, she left the tram at the last but one stop. Vaguely she was aware that the other woman dressed so like herself was still aboard.

Her long legs carried her swiftly along the tree-lined sidewalk. The air was fresher now, the goddamned humidity had evaporated. Earlier it had been like moving through treacle. As she turned into her apartment block entrance she was vaguely conscious her 'twin' was walking down to the shore near the scrubbing station. No one else about.

She took a quick shower, smoked one last cigarette, fell into bed and seconds after her head hit the pillow she was asleep. The sound of police cars woke her at seven the following morning.

Curious, she pulled back the curtains of the window overlooking the sea. She stared at another glorious sunny day in amazement. Clustered round the scrubbing board platform area was a cordon of police cars. A crowd of early risers, some men carrying briefcases stood close to the cars. Dressing quickly, she went downstairs and walked to see what all the fuss was about.

More police cars were arriving, uniformed men jumping out, trying to form a barrier to hold back the crowd. Peggy walked slowly forward. A lint-haired girl clad in denims and a windcheater open at the front was scribbling in a notebook. Peggy stood beside her.

'What is going on? Why are you making notes?'

'You live in that apartment block?' the girl asked, pushing her glasses further up her nose. 'I thought I saw you come out of it.'

'Yes, I'm a resident. I have an apartment . . .'

'Did you hear anything unusual in the night? Or maybe in the evening late on?'

'Why? Who are you?'

'I'm a reporter on the newspaper *Iltalehti*. A woman has been murdered on the scrubbing platform. She was garrotted.' The girl drew a finger swiftly across her throat. 'Then, from what I can gather, the back of her skull was bashed in.' She looked round. 'Oh, God, here comes the TV crew.'

Peggy glanced over her shoulder. A white van had pulled up a few yards up the hill, well clear of the police cordon. The rear doors opened, men carried out a wooden platform with two steps leading up to its top. A man with a mobile TV camera jumped up the steps, aimed the camera over the heads of the crowd, took pictures, jumped down as a man in a linen suit and a hard-faced woman began talking to him.

Peggy strolled over to the van, climbed up the steps and had a perfect view of the scrubbing platform. Police photographers were taking pictures. On the lower level of the scrubbing platform sprawled the lifeless body of a woman, face down. Peggy gazed at the horror, hypnotized. She was looking at *herself*.

It was the woman in the cream raincoat like her own. Round her head was the highly coloured scarf, again like her own. But the garish colours seemed stronger in the brilliant sunlight. The scarf was soaked in blood. As if in a nightmare Peggy recalled how the woman had got off at the last tram stop, the one she always got off at. Except that last evening she had left the tram one stop earlier. She saw the woman walking down the street towards the sea . . .

She felt faint, almost toppled off the perch. Before anyone saw her she forced her stiff legs to go down the steps. She walked slowly up the hill, went through the entrance to her apartment block in a daze.

She sat inside her living room for half an hour, smoking cigarettes. Then she picked up the phone after consulting the directory.

'Palace Hotel,' a man's voice said.

'I want to speak to Mr Robert Newman who is staying with you . . .'

'Newman here. Who is this?'

'Peggy Vanderheld. Newman, could you come and see me at my apartment tomorrow evening? Same time as you called before.'

'I'll be there.'

24

'So you bungled the job,' Hauser shouted at Galvone. 'You let Newman reach Helsinki alive despite my specific order. Frank, it's not good enough. I'm beginning to worry about you.'

The two men sat inside Hauser's office. Beyond the picture window the sea was dark and hostile, large waves rolling in to the shore. Galvone sat opposite his chief with the desk between them. Hauser tilted his jaw, clenched his teeth on his cigarette holder.

'We don't know Newman has come to Helsinki,' Galvone ventured. 'OK. He was on Route E3 driving in this direction from Turku . . .'

'So where the hell else would he go? And Manescu isn't the hot shot he was bummed up to be.'

'You could talk with him. He's in the building . . .'

Hauser erupted. 'Here! Are you mad? There must never be any direct link someone could trace between people like Manescu and INCUBUS . . .'

'I had to take a quick decision,' Galvone said defensively. 'Manescu was worried about the truck fiasco when it tried to run down Newman . . .'

'Well at least the schmuck of a driver is dead,' Hauser said savagely.

'True. No danger of him talking. As I was trying to explain, Manescu drove here to report to me because he was worried. It was a complete surprise to me when he turned up here. No need to worry, I've put him in a locked room at Level Five . . .'

'Then get him out of it. Now! Drive him to the airport. Get the chopper to airlift him back into the jungle where I met him. You've bought a summer house in the woods and he can simmer there until we need him again. Ziegler is out there too?'

'Yes. I bought three summer homes in the same area. Very remote. The others are there – including the two Czechs, who were STB men, three more *Securitate* and Irina Serov.'

'Serov was with Manescu. How come she went into the woods while Manescu blunders in here!'

'Well . . .' Galvone had hoped this question wouldn't be asked. 'Irina has a mind of her own. She *was* a colonel in the KGB. She decided she should vanish . . .'

'So!' Hauser exploded. 'She has more savvy than Manescu – more than you. It looks to me as though maybe we ought to put Irina in charge of the whole operation. Yes, I like the idea.'

'Manescu won't like it,' Galvone warned.

Hauser, shirt sleeves rolled up above the elbows, exposing his powerful arms, leaned forward. He spoke with the cigarette in his mouth, a sure sign of his wrath.

'Frank, who cares a shit what Manescu likes? What he likes is the big money I'm paying him. For that he takes orders and likes *them*.'

'He did organize those bombings in Prague, Bucharest and . . .'

'Frank! We don't talk about things like that. Now go down to Level Five and get Manescu to hell out of my HQ. You can manage that?'

'I'm going now . . .'

Alone in his office, Hauser took out of a drawer a copy of the Finnish newspaper, *Iltalehti*. Splashed over the front page was a huge photograph of the woman lying on the scrubbing platform. Hauser had had the text translated and the typed English version was inside the newspaper.

242

He read the first few words of the article again, his face grim.

Anna Jarva, secretary who worked with a well-known Finnish firm of timber merchants, was found murdered . . .

Anna Jarva! The wrong woman had been killed. So his own ex-personal assistant, Peggy Vanderheld, was still walking around alive. And with all those company secrets locked up inside her clever skull. What made it worse was that Carver had reported she didn't seem interested in the double pension he had offered her. That was what had triggered off Hauser's decision that something should be done about Vanderheld. Something permanent.

Galvone unlocked the door at Level Five and walked into a luxuriously furnished room with a bathroom leading off. Manescu was sprawled on a couch, reading an American comic paper. The bony-faced Romanian looked up at his visitor and went on reading the comic.

Galvone padded over to him slowly, reached down, took away the comic. Manescu, his face tanned from the sun, wore a check shirt, slacks and special shoes with concealed metal tips in the toes. Strapped under his left trouser leg was a sheath with a knife: he was right-handed and the sheath was attached to the inner side of his leg.

'Time to return to the backwoods,' Galvone told him.

'What about Newman?'

'We can work something else out later. At the moment you must leave this building unseen. Collect your satchel and follow me . . .'

At the exit to the building Galvone ordered Manescu to stay inside. He strolled out and the glare of the sun blinded him. He shielded his eyes, looked carefully round. No one in sight. The car park was almost empty. His red Cadillac was parked next to Hauser's stretched black limo and there were a couple of other cars. He ran back into the vast entrance hall.

'Come out now. Follow me to the Cadillac, get in the front passenger seat as soon as I unlock. Make with the feet.'

Inside the Saab parked in the copse of firs above INCU-BUS's HQ, Marler was drinking out of his plastic bottle of mineral water when he saw below the man emerge. It was the last day Marler was going to keep up his surveillance. The interior of the Saab was like a furnace but Marler was tireless. He reached for the camera with the zoom lens, aimed it, lowered it.

'I already have you in my photo album, Mr Frank Galvone,' he said to himself.

He was relaxing when he suddenly sat up straight. Something odd about the way Galvone was staring round. Marler reached for his camera again. Galvone disappeared inside, came out again almost at once as Marler aimed his camera. But his time he was not alone.

'My God!' Marler said to himself. 'At the last moment, on stage Mr Ion Manescu . . .'

Manescu was also blinded by the sun's glare. He stopped to haul dark glasses out of his pocket, perch them on his nose. During the time it took him to do this Marler snapped off six shots. And there behind Manescu's head was the company sign, INCUBUS Oy.

Galvone walked back, grabbed Manescu by the arm, hurried him to the Cadillac. There was a brief pause while he unlocked the car, then Manescu disappeared inside the front and Galvone ran round, jumped in behind the wheel, slammed the door and fired the engine.

Seconds later he was driving at speed past the gate the guard had opened, skidding round on to the road and roaring off out of sight in the direction of the city.

'Terrible driving,' Marler commented to himself. 'And

about time I left. That camera shop will have to work fast producing these new prints.'

Hauser was in a mood of cold fury when Galvone returned from seeing Manescu aboard the helicopter. Outside it was still daylight. Galvone had prior warning of Hauser's state of mind when he saw the number of cigarette butts crushed out in the crystal ash tray.

'Manescu is a world away from Helsinki,' he reported.

'Goddamnit! That was a real balls-up on Route E3, Frank. You even used an INCUBUS juggernaut – which Newman must have seen. That ties us in to the attempt on his life.'

'Manescu organized that. But you can't blame him either. Had he hired a truck he'd have had to show identification and you wouldn't have wanted that. Even if he'd used one of the Turku staff to do the hiring they'd have had to provide identification. That would have been dangerous.'

Hauser lit a fresh cigarette, regarded Galvone through the smoke. It had always been the same right back from the early days when he'd sweated to accumulate the money to bid for a tiny bank in La Jolla in California. If you wanted a job done properly, you had to do it yourself.

Now his organization was so vast he had to rely on executives to carry out his instructions. And even though he handed out the biggest pay cheques of any company in the world they were still second rate. He sat back, forced himself to relax. He'd faced plenty of crises before and come through triumphantly. This one would be no different. Now he was thinking calmly and fast.

'The first thing to do is to locate Newman. Put as many men on the job as necessary. Check every hotel. And I do mean *every* hotel. We have his photo. Run off a whole load of copies. He may be staying under another name. Use money to get receptionists to talk, show them his picture. I

245

want Helsinki turned over. Don't you interrupt me, Frank. Manescu gave you descriptions of the girl and the man who came off the Turku ferry with him? Good. Tell the bastards who go out to use their eyes for once. I wish to God I could do the job myself. Frank, why are you still sitting there? Get on it. Now!'

The phone rang as Galvone left the office. Hauser picked it up, asked his operator who the devil it was now at this hour? 'A Mr Robert Newman, sir . . .'

At The Palace Hotel Newman was perched on the edge of his bed. In shirt sleeves, the windows wide open, he mopped his forehead with one hand while gripping the phone with the other. His tone was harsh.

'That you, Hauser?'

'Franklin D. Hauser speaking.'

'Let's cut out the bullshit, shall we? I'm at The Palace. I think it's time we met again, talked. Tomorrow suit you?'

'Certainly, Mr Newman. What time would you suggest? At your convenience, of course.'

'Noon. At your headquarters. Is that OK?'

'I shall look forward to renewing our acquaintance. Could you give me some hint as to what we'll be discussing?'

'Information I've dug up about your operations. Noon tomorrow. Good-night, Hauser.'

In his office Hauser put down the phone, then called his operator and told her to intercept Galvone before he could leave the building. A few minutes later his vice president hurried into his office, then stopped. Hauser was gazing out of the window. It was the first time Galvone had ever seen his chief look stunned.

In his room at the Marski, Tweed listened while Newman gave him a terse account of his experiences since leaving

246

London. On a nearby couch sat Paula, chin cupped in her hand, listening. Cord Dillon occupied a chair against the wall where he could watch his three companions.

Newman checked his watch as he concluded his account. 'I'll have to leave in a minute. An appointment with Vanderheld.' He grinned. 'Oh, by the way, I borrowed Harry Butler. He's parked outside Peggy Vanderheld's apartment block. I don't want her doing a disappearing act.'

'I think this meeting with Hauser is impetuous, too early in the game,' Tweed informed him.

'Don't agree.' Newman's expression changed, became stubborn. 'His minions tried to kill me twice, as I've told you. And,' he looked at the couch, 'the second time Paula and Cord would have died. So Hauser is a billionaire. So what? I think I threw him off balance. He's had the initiative so far – tracking me across Europe. Time I confronted him.'

'You have absolutely no evidence to link him with any misdemeanour, let alone assassination attempts,' Tweed persisted. 'What we need is hard evidence. You're going in with not one damn thing to hit him with.'

'I've made the appointment.' Newman stood up. 'And it was an INCUBUS juggernaut which tried to mow us down.'

'Which they will already have reported as stolen. If I could I'd take you off this operation, Bob. You're too personally involved – with the appalling murder of Sandy driving you on.'

'You can't take me off anything,' Newman snapped. 'I don't belong to you – or your organization.'

'Cool it, Bob,' Paula said quietly. 'Tweed is only thinking of your safety.'

'Safety first?' Newman rapped back.

'From where I sit Tweed is right,' Dillon interjected with unexpected support. 'You have to time these operations. You're charging about like a mad bull.'

'OK. So that's what I'm doing.' As he turned to leave Newman spoke to Paula.

'Sorry I snapped at you. I realize you're concerned.'

'And next time,' Tweed told him, leaning forward, 'kindly ask my permission before you hijack Butler.' He paused. 'Even so, I think you got that right. Vanderheld may just prove to be the weak link in Hauser's chain.'

'Newman is in town,' Hauser told Adam Carver as they sat next to each other on a couch in the penthouse office. 'I was just about to have every hotel checked to see if he was here when what the hell do you think happens?'

'No idea.'

Adam Carver was wary. He sensed Hauser was in a rage and he'd always trodden carefully on these rare occasions. You never could be sure which way the American would jump in a crisis situation.

'The bastard actually phones me here, suggests he comes to see me tomorrow. He even tells me he's staying at The Palace.'

'No reason why he shouldn't,' Carver responded smoothly. 'He'd guess you'd check his whereabouts so he tells you . . .'

'He's got a lot of gall.' Hauser quietened down. 'You're a Brit. What's your impression of Newman? You had a chance to assess him that night he dropped in on us at Livingstone Manor.'

Carver lit a cigarette with his strong, well-shaped hands. He gave his answer a bit of thought.

'Very experienced in grilling people. A lone wolf. Used to operating on his own – his days as a foreign correspondent, a top one, would teach him that. He knows his way around. A determined and resourceful opponent.'

'Sound as though you admire the crud,' Hauser grumbled.

'I'm simply saying he's a man it would be a great mistake

to underestimate.' Carver was cool as ice while Hauser stood up and prowled restlessly round the huge room. 'Another point,' he continued, 'it would also be a great mistake to alienate him. He carries a lot of clout with the media.'

'Maybe.'

Carver kept quiet. He had answered the question without frills. He was wearing a pale grey silk suit and he uncrossed his legs and adjusted the crease. He had half a dozen silk suits. The trouble was they creased easily and cost him a fortune at the cleaners. But they impressed women and Adam Carver was a great ladies' man. He had mistresses in London, Brussels and Frankfurt.

'Time to go over on to the offensive,' Hauser decided. 'Pussy-footing isn't my style. So this is what we do next . . .'

25

It was late evening, the light that glorious clarity you only found in Finland glowing over the fir-fringed sea, as Newman got off Tram No. 4 at the last stop. Parked on the far side of the road was the hired BMW, opposite the apartment block where Vanderheld lived.

Butler sat behind the wheel with the window down. His hand was tapping a tattoo on the window ledge. For a brief moment as Newman glanced across the road he gave the thumbs up sign. Peggy Vanderheld was safe.

She answered the speakphone immediately, released the front door, and again was waiting for him in the doorway to her apartment. He smiled, walked inside and she closed and locked the door. She was wearing a form-fitting black dress which outlined her figure provocatively. The garment was strapless and her beautifully shaped shoulders were bare, the colour of ivory. Newman was never sure what kept the damned things up. Watch it, he warned himself. This time his reception was quite different.

'Do sit down, Mr Newman. What would you like to drink? Tea, coffee, or something stronger – maybe that would be a nice idea?'

She waved an arm towards a large cocktail cabinet which was now open, exposing a huge array of drinks, including just about every known liqueur as far as Newman could see.

'A strong Scotch wouldn't go amiss. I've had a somewhat trying day.'

'I think I'll join you. Straight up? Fine . . .'

As she poured the drinks he glanced round the room. On the occasional table close to the couch she had ushered him to lay a copy of *Iltalehti*. The newspaper was spread out exposing the front page with the huge photograph of Anna Jarva sprawled on the scrubbing platform. Peggy followed his eyes as she sat beside him, handed him his glass.

'That should have been me,' she said and clinked his glass.

Newman had noticed that when she was pouring the drinks her hand had trembled, tinkling the bottle against a glass. He studied her as he sipped his drink. She looked good, make-up skilfully applied, but he thought he detected dark circles under her eyes.

'What did you mean when you said that?' he enquired.

'That murdered woman is wearing clothes just like I wore on my way back from the theatre . . .'

Speaking rapidly, her voice slightly high-pitched, she described in detail her journey from the moment she left the theatre, ending with the moment when she had stumbled down the steps from the TV platform after seeing the body. Newman listened in silence, his eyes holding hers, registering every minute of her macabre journey.

'I see,' he said eventually. 'And you're convinced . . .'

'For Christ's sake!' she blazed. 'Isn't it obvious? Hauser sent a hired assassin to kill me. Because I know too much about his crooked operation.'

'Crooked? Now do you really mean that?'

He let the scepticism show in his voice deliberately and the ploy worked. She swung round on the couch until she was almost touching him, her dark eyes glaring.

'I worked for INCUBUS for ten years, five as Hauser's personal assistant. I ought to know how they run that outfit. Hauser divides the world into winners and losers. OK. A lot of people do that but it depends on the methods you use. He'll use any method on God's earth to get something he's after – and a few maybe God never heard of. I could see he was going to kick me out weeks before it happened. He was too nice to me. So I gradually built up a dossier of items of his more shady operations. I took photocopies of documents – so after I'd gone he wouldn't realize I had those records. Including a highly secret file on some creep called Popescu . . .'

'Who did you say?'

'Popescu. Damned stupid name. Comes from somewhere in the Balkans. Is it important?'

'Might be. Anything might be.' Newman kept his tone casual. 'Popescu. Sounds Romanian.'

'It is. He came from Bucharest.'

'I'm surprised that Hauser, a man I've heard plays his moves close to his chest, let you in on so many sensitive topics.'

'He didn't. I overheard things. And he's normally careful but he has an advanced electronic intercom he sometimes forgets to switch off. I made tapes of some of his confidential conversations.'

'Where is –' He nearly said Manescu. 'Popescu now?'

'No bloody idea. I do know he travelled some route planned by one of his executives . . .'

'Which one?'

'That I don't know. As I was saying, Popescu came in aboard a ferry from Germany direct to Finland. And he wasn't the only one who used that route.'

'Where are those tapes you mentioned, that dossier? Here in your apartment?'

'God no! INCUBUS have turned over more people's apartments to search for something than I've had hot breakfasts. I've stored them in a deposit vault in a Helsinki bank. Not the bank I normally use. I could take you there, hand them to you. The material will sink Hauser. What do I get for it? I could make a lot of money writing a book and selling it in New York.'

'Except you'd never live to complete the book. The vital thing now for you to do is to vanish. I'll think of somewhere if you'll trust me.'

'I have an option?'

Newman indicated the newspaper picture. 'What do you think?'

'I suppose you're right. You propose I go into hiding?'

'Yes. With protection.'

She stood up, went over to the window, looked out, came back and sat close to Newman. He lit a fresh cigarette for her and saw her hand tremble. She took a deep drag.

'I have news for you. I'm being watched at this moment. A guy in a white BMW on the other side of the street.'

'That's my protection for you. The chap's a pro. His name is Harry Butler, in case for some reason he calls on you.'

252

'My!' She leaned closer to him and he caught a faint whiff of perfume. 'You do look after a woman. I'd like to show my appreciation for that . . .'

'Then perhaps you can answer a tricky question.' Newman had recalled what Chief Inspector Buchanan had said to him back in England. 'I don't suppose you brought any appointments diaries with you and put them in that safety deposit.'

Peggy studied the end of her cigarette. 'As a matter of fact I did. Not that it was really necessary. I'm blessed with an encyclopaedic memory for dates. I can reel them off for months back.'

'Let me test you. I'm trying to identify an executive at the INCUBUS HQ here who was absent on two dates. On *both* dates, I stress. Although you probably don't know about the movements of Popescu . . .'

'I do. I read his file before I photocopied it. Shoot.'

'One date is the day an executive was here in Helsinki – I put it badly a moment ago – I stress was *here* on the night when Ed Riverton was murdered . . .'

'That I recall. And the other one?'

'It was a date close to that one . . .' He gave her the date when Sandy was murdered in the Suffolk bell tower, trying to keep his tone offhand. Then he waited while Peggy stared into the distance. He could almost hear the wheels revolving inside her mind.

'Let me get this straight,' she said after awhile. 'You want someone who, as far as I know, was present the night Ed Riverton was garrotted and thrown into North Harbour. You also want the same person who was *absent* from Helsinki, maybe abroad, on the date you specified?'

'That's exactly what I'm after.'

'Tell you later. After I'm sure of the protection.'

*   *   *

Newman was late up the following morning, was finishing his breakfast in The Palace dining room at 9.30 a.m. when Marler joined him.

'Losing your grip, old boy?' Marler greeted him. 'I had my breakfast at seven and I've done a day's work already.'

'Bully for you,' Newman responded without enthusiasm.

'I've got some additions to my photo album in my room. Care to see them? When you've eventually finished, of course.'

'Of course.'

Reluctantly, Newman admitted to himself that Marler looked very chipper. He wore a well-cut tropical drill suit, an open-necked shirt, a pale red silk cravat. His complexion was tanned. He vibrated energy as he lit a cigarette.

'You were damned late in last night, Newman,' he commented. 'I checked in at midnight and your key was still with the concierge. Still no excuse for spending half your life in bed. Oh,' he continued breezily, 'Tweed phoned me. He's nearly going spare – couldn't contact Harry Butler.'

'I know where he is. I'll call in at the Marski and give him the good news.' He finished his coffee. 'Let's look at your new pics. Probably all out of focus, as usual. You're a lousy photographer.'

Which wasn't true: Marler was as expert with a camera as he was with a sniperscope rifle. But the two men had never really liked each other and frequently exchanged insults – just to show nothing had changed.

In Marler's room Newman waited while Marler lifted up the false bottom of his suitcase, revealing a secret compartment. He took out an envelope, produced the three photos of Manescu which had been treated in the Engine Room in the basement of Park Crescent.

'I've seen these before,' Newman complained. 'Manescu as he was in Bucharest with a moustache, then minus the 'tache and finally with a beard. What's the point?'

'I took these late yesterday evening looking down on INCUBUS's headquarters.'

He produced six more prints and watched Newman's reaction. Newman stared at them, noted the INCUBUS Oy. sign behind the head of the man Marler had snapped. He looked up.

'This links Ion Manescu directly with Hauser's mob.'

'And Mauno Sarin did point me in the right direction when I visited the Protection Police at Ratakatu. Frankly, I didn't think he was right – and those pics were taken just before I gave up.'

'You didn't by any chance photograph any of their cars?'

'As a matter of fact, chum, I did just that. Mainly to fill in time. Got a shade boring sitting in my Saab hour after hour.'

Marler dived into his envelope again, produced more prints. Newman examined each colour shot. He came to the last one and whistled softly, then held up the print.

'This one of a big brown Buick. That was in the car park?'

'On only one occasion while I was spying on them. A chap in a chauffeur's uniform drove it away. Didn't bother to snap a minion. Seemed pointless.'

'Pity. But you've done marvels.' He looked at Marler. 'I have to visit Tweed at the Marski now. Can I borrow these pics of Manescu – the lot? Plus the one of the brown Buick?'

'Be my guest. Just let me have them back, there's a good chap. My regards to Tweed. Thank the Lord he's surfaced – I somehow found the time to check a few hotels trying to locate him. I'll drop round to see him later. Gentlemen first.'

*   *   *

Tweed stood staring out of the window of his room at the traffic while Newman brought him up to date on recent developments, concentrating on his interview with Peggy Vanderheld and the arrangements he'd made for her safety. Paula sat perched on the edge of the bed, taking it all in.

'Now don't blow your top,' Newman continued. 'I decided we had to move quickly to protect Vanderheld. Butler has taken her aboard a flight to Stockholm. From Arlanda he'll drive her in a hired car to a cottage on the island of Örno in the Swedish archipelago. From what she told me, as you'll have gathered, she's in great danger, and she's a key witness. Harry flies back to Helsinki this evening, so he'll be here if you need him. No time to contact you.'

Tweed swung round. 'You did the right thing. But how did you obtain use of this cottage on Örno?'

'I know the people who own it, a Swedish couple. They have a luxury apartment in the centre of Stockholm. I phoned them and they said I could use the place as long as I liked. Butler will call on them for the key, then drive Peggy via the ferry to the island.'

Cord Dillon had been sitting on a hard-backed chair tilted against a corner of the wall. He made his first comment.

'I guess Newman has done very well. He's secured a potential witness. And he moved fast – hiding Vanderheld away after one attempt on her life was smart.'

'A *potential* witness,' Tweed repeated with a hint of scepticism. 'What about the dossier she spoke of, the diaries, the tapes? Where are they now?'

'Still in the safety deposit in some bank here in Helsinki.'

'Which one?'

'No idea. She wouldn't tell me. But this arrived for me at The Palace this morning by special courier.' Newman produced a key. 'The trouble is I have no idea which bank she used – and, as you know, safety deposit keys are anonymous. Peggy said that was her insurance policy – that we'd continue to guard her while we didn't know where the evidence was.'

Dillon sighed. 'That's one smart cookie.'

'Have you by any chance a copy of her signature?' Tweed enquired.

Newman shook his head. 'No, I thought of that. After she'd told me just before Butler flew her to Sweden. She had told me this key would be delivered today. I asked her to sign a statement that she was travelling with Butler of her own free will. She refused.'

'As I told you,' Dillon repeated, 'one smart cookie. The fun will come when we transport her to the States. Hauser has things pretty well tied up there. We don't know who we can trust. She'll have to be guarded every moment before she testifies in court against Hauser.'

'If she ever does,' Tweed warned him. 'We've got to move in another direction. We need more.'

'Isn't it lucky we have more?' Newman replied. He took out Marler's photographs. 'Manescu has surfaced . . .'

Again Tweed listened in silence as Newman explained how Marler had obtained the pictures. Tweed polished his glasses on a corner of his handkerchief, standing quite still, then walked over and examined the prints with Dillon at his side.

'My congratulations to Marler,' he said eventually. 'These tell *us* that Manescu – and probably Ziegler and the rest of the ex-secret police thugs from various countries – has been recruited by Hauser. So, it's a step forward in our information. But I doubt that these photographs would stand up in court. In Britain.'

'Or in the States,' Dillon said. 'A good attorney could argue they were fakes. And what do they prove? That one

257

man wanted in Romania made a brief appearance at INCUBUS headquarters. Hauser could say that the man gave another name, that he applied for a job with their security apparatus and was turned down. I could kill the case myself.'

Newman stood up. 'Marler is coming over to see you,' he told Tweed. 'Meantime, I have an appointment to keep – with Mr Franklin D. Hauser.'

Paula jumped up. 'I'm coming with you, Bob. I may notice something you'd miss.' She gave him a big smile. 'The well-known feminine instinct. And my powers of observation aren't bad either. Give me five minutes to change and I'll be with you.'

'I don't like the idea,' Tweed said quickly but she had unlocked the door and left the room.

'She may be right,' Newman argued. 'And nothing deadly will happen to us at INCUBUS's headquarters. I'll drop a remark that the police know where we've gone.'

'Still don't like it,' growled Tweed.

He stood gazing out of the window, hands clasped behind his back until Paula returned in less than five minutes. She wore a form-fitting, knee-length printed linen dress with a floral design. Sleeveless, it exposed her shapely arms and round her waist was a leather belt. The ensemble was completed with flesh-coloured tights and gold high-heeled shoes.

'Lady, you look pretty damn sexy,' Dillon commented.

'Thank you, sir.' She curtsyed.

'Both of you, have a care,' Tweed warned.

When they had left he paced backwards and forwards. Dillon sat down in the hard-backed chair in the corner, tilted it.

'You know,' he remarked, 'that bluff Newman is pulling about the police knowing they're there may not work. Hauser does have all his marbles.'

'I agree. I've been thinking about just that.' Tweed went to the phone. 'Which is why I'm calling Mauno Sarin. He's rather fond of Paula.'

26

A high-speed elevator shot Newman and Paula up to the penthouse floor. When the doors opened a woman remarkably like Peggy Vanderheld in poise and manner waited for them in a business suit. Crisp, competent, controlled, the main difference was her blonde hair.

'Mr Hauser is ready to see you now, Mr Newman.' She looked at Paula. 'We were expecting you to come alone.'

'Paula Grey, my assistant. She travels with me most places.'

'I see.'

The woman eyed Paula up and down briefly and her look conveyed a world of understanding. She led them into a vast office with a huge picture window overlooking the sea. The glass doors were open and beyond was a large balcony. Hauser was sitting behind his desk, dressed in a pale blue suit. Adam Carver stood close to the balcony and his eyes lit up as he saw Paula.

'Welcome to INCUBUS, Mr Newman.' Hauser stood up, walked swiftly round his desk, held out his hand. In his left hand he held his cigarette holder; his trademark, Newman thought. 'This is the second time we have had the pleasure of meeting. I trust life has treated you well since last we met?'

'This is my assistant, Paula Grey.'

'And from my point of view it was worth Mr Newman

sparing his valuable time to come and see me so I could meet you, my dear. Come and sit with me on the couch. What would you like to drink?'

'Mineral water, please,' said Paula.

She was aware that the other man by the balcony was studying her with frank interest and pleasure. She disliked his method of scrutiny intensely, felt almost naked under his gaze.

'A double Scotch for me,' said Newman, choosing a high-backed chair facing the couch.

'I'm forgetting my manners,' Hauser went on in the same affable tone. 'This is Adam Carver, one of your countrymen – and Vice President of Banking Operations.'

'Hello,' said Paula and left it at that.

Carver held on to her hand a little too warmly for her liking but she smiled as though enjoying herself. Carver then fetched the drinks as Hauser adjusted his pince-nez higher up the bridge of his strong nose. Since they had entered he had been the soul of amiability, as though meeting Newman again was one of the most pleasurable moments of his life. He stretched an arm along the top of the couch behind Paula who sat between the two men when Carver joined them on the couch.

'To answer your question,' Newman said, holding his glass, 'it has been hazardous in the extreme.'

'What has?' The beaming smile slipped for a fraction of a second.

'You asked if life had treated me well since last we met.'

'Oh, that.' Hauser sipped his martini. 'Hazardous? I'm sorry to hear that. The life of a foreign correspondent, I suppose?'

'A little more than usual. Including surveillance of our movements non-stop. Plus an attempt to kill me aboard the ferry to Turku. To say nothing of nearly being crushed

260

to death by a juggernaut on Route E3. Little things like that.'

'My, my. This sounds dreadful.' Hauser assumed his statesman's expression. 'It does sound as though you've provoked a determined enemy, Mr Newman.'

Adam Carver leaned forward, after watching Paula's crossed legs. 'Maybe you should seek some kind of protection, Mr Newman. Yours sounds a dangerous occupation.'

'Oh, I can look after myself.' Newman stared at Hauser. 'To give you one example, I told the police I was visiting your headquarters. They like to know where I am after what happened.'

'Really? You surprise me. I'd have said this was one place where you could feel perfectly safe.' He beamed at Paula. 'You feel quite safe, I hope, my dear?'

'Depends what you mean by safe,' she responded, gazing sideways at Carver.

Adam Carver took her by the arm. 'I think maybe Mr Newman has business to talk over with Mr Hauser. Come and look at the view from the balcony. It's especially spectacular on a day like this . . .'

She allowed herself to be guided on to the balcony which was wide and stretched beyond the window opening. Carver led her to a swing seat at the far end, still holding her arm with one hand while he grasped his drink with the other. Paula glanced over the rail before she sat down. The sheer drop was like a precipice, brought on a feeling of vertigo.

'Sit down, please. A lot of people find this height a trifle awesome.'

'Or awful?' she suggested sweetly as he sat beside her.

'You have a way with words. I like your dress. Perfect for a day like this.' He took hold of her left hand. 'Really you're dream-like.

She withdrew her hand, smiled. 'That belongs to me.'

261

'Very good.' He grinned. 'I know this may sound a bit fast. But would you like to have dinner with me tonight? I admit I'm overstepping the mark but I'm appalled that this may be my only chance.'

'I'll think about it.' She sipped her drink. 'I've thought about it. Collect me from the lobby of the Hesperia. Seven o'clock. Tonight.'

'Great . . .'

Inside the office Newman had refused Hauser's offer to join him on the couch, staying in the high-backed chair. He was inwardly experiencing a sensation of cold fury. Meeting Hauser again brought back to him their last interview way back at Livingstone Manor, the image of Sandy in the bell tower hanging from her extended neck, her eyes and tongue protruding.

'You might like to know I've talked to the ex-owners of Bennington Machine Tools and Manningham Electronics – both of them forced by illegal methods to sell out to your organization,' he said brutally.

There was a brief flicker in the cold blue eyes. Hauser then raised a hand to his forehead as though trying to recall something. He smiled broadly, waved his hand in a dismissive gesture.

'Neither name means anything to me.' He leaned forward and smiled again. 'You must realize that with a company as large as mine I delegate many small deals to my executives . . .'

'I didn't say they were small companies. Why did you make that assumption?' he demanded aggressively.

'Can't say I too much like your tone, your attitude. And I think you ought to be careful of throwing around that word "illegal". I have an army of attorneys. They could ruin you tomorrow.'

'They could try. But the publicity could be damaging to your whited sepulchre reputation.' Newman sipped a little of his drink. 'It might even ruin you tomorrow. I

262

don't think you yet control the world's media.'

'Mind if I take off my jacket?' Hauser beamed again. 'It really is a very hot day. Ah, that's better. Now let's get down to the bottom line. Let me give you a few words of advice, Mr Newman. I get the impression you're thinking of going up against what is a global organization, an international world-wide power structure . . .'

'*Power*. That's the key word, isn't it? Money no longer means much to you – you're so loaded you think you've got the Midas touch. What you get your kicks out of now is the acquisition of more and more power. At anybody's expense. No holds barred . . .'

'Business is a jungle,' Hauser interjected, his facial muscles tensed.

'Oh, I know that. The whole of life is. But in moderate degree. You're bringing the jungle into the whole of Europe. At least I'm damned sure that's your plan. You're Public Enemy Number One, Hauser. Men and women are just counters to be moved on your huge chessboard, to be thrown away when they're no longer any use.'

'Women?' Hauser's tone was contemptuous. 'Marriage is a trap women lay for men. OK. So one time a hundred years back they were subservient to men – for centuries they were. So to protect themselves they developed all kinds of devious techniques to influence and control men. Understandable – that way they survived. What's the situation now? We have Women's Lib triumphant. Equality and all that crap. But still they use their devious techniques, exploit their feminine charms.' He folded his arms covered with light-coloured hair. 'But not with me they don't. No, sir.'

Newman half closed his eyes. He had hit a nerve. Maybe it was the billionaire's experience with his ex-wife? But he also spotted Hauser was guiding him away from the main point at issue.

'Not only power,' Newman continued in full flood. He was facing the man he was convinced was responsible for Sandy's brutal murder. 'Money, too, is your god. You can't get enough of it. Now you've taken over Egon Schmidt's private bank in Frankfurt. The *late* Egon Schmidt . . .'

Again he saw the hostile flicker as Hauser gazed straight back at him. The temperature in the room was rising rapidly, and it wasn't only the sun's heat.

'I'm beginning to think you could become a minor nuisance,' Hauser commented, stubbing out a cigarette, inserting a fresh one in his holder, lighting it. 'You're naïve, Newman. No idea what you're up against. I could squash you like a fly.'

'You could try,' Newman agreed. 'Seems to be a sensitive subject – the Schmidt bank. The first step in moving on to take over Germany?'

Hauser flushed with fury. He leaned back against the couch, tilted his jaw, making a supreme effort to regain self-control. He smiled, made a gesture towards the balcony with his left hand.

'I trust you have Paula Grey's best interests at heart? I have noticed it's a long way down off that balcony.'

Newman froze for a couple of seconds. Hauser was attempting to provoke him, but the implied threat infuriated Newman. He stood up, walked out on to the balcony. Paula was perched on the swing seat while Carver leaned towards her.

'Paula,' Newman called out, 'I think we've exhausted our welcome.'

She jumped up and Carver followed her. They hadn't reached the entrance when the door to Hauser's office burst open. Mauno Sarin, tall, athletic in his stride, walked in while behind him on his heels came Karma, his assistant, his right hand in his pocket. Newman felt sure he was gripping a handgun.

'What the hell is the meaning of this? Who are you?' Hauser demanded. 'You can't storm into my office like this . . .'

'I just did. Protection Police.' Sarin flipped open a folder. 'I have a warrant for the arrest of Robert Newman.'

Sarin said nothing until he was driving his Saab back into the city. Beside him sat Newman while Paula occupied one of the rear seats. Sarin drove fast, just inside the speed limit. He frequently glanced in his rear-view mirror.

'Well, no one is following us.' He glanced at Newman. 'I must say you have a habit of walking into the lion's den.'

'What about the warrant for my arrest? On what charge. And how come you turned up when you did?'

'No warrant. No charge. Just an excuse to get you out of that place. Tweed called me, said he was worried, could I help out?'

'You arrived very quickly,' Paula said to the small stocky Karma who sat beside her.

'Mauno was driving,' Karma replied with the ghost of a smile.

'What the devil did you hope to accomplish? Taking such a risk?' Sarin demanded.

'Exactly what I did accomplish. I rattled Hauser's cage – he was fit to explode when you arrived. If I'd had a few minutes more he was so worked up by what I said he might have let something slip.'

'Gratitude!' Sarin drove with one hand, fingered his fringe beard with the other. 'I tell the most blatant lies and I get a kick in the rear.' His tone was mocking.

'I'm grateful,' Newman told him. 'Frankly, it was getting a little ugly. The swine had just threatened Paula.'

265

'Then maybe we could swear out a complaint against Hauser which would give me the chance to question him about some of his operations.'

'I'm afraid not. He's clever. He phrased the threat by implication. He has an iron nerve even in a rage. He was trying to provoke me. I hit him pretty hard verbally – it may cause him to make a blunder. Object of the exercise. I was pretty convincing for a certain reason . . .'

Briefly, he told Sarin about the February dawn in Suffolk when he had discovered Sandy hanging in the bell tower. Sarin listened as they started down the Mannerheimintie, his expression blank.

'So,' Newman concluded, 'history can repeat itself in the most macabre way. The last time I was here I was hunting down the killer of my wife Alexis – and you'll well recall our trip across the Baltic to Estonia. Now I'm determined to identify the murderer of Sandy and I find myself in the same part of the world. Finland.'

'Very curious, and nothing personal, but we could do without your presence. It always brings trouble.' Sarin's voice changed. 'I'm very sorry to hear about your girl friend's death. I gather that's what is driving the motor on this visit. Do you mind if we call in at the Marski? I said I would let Tweed know when you and Paula were safe.'

He swung across the road suddenly in front of an advancing tram and Paula closed her eyes in horror. When he parked outside the Marski Newman let out his breath. Now they *were* safe. From Mauno's driving.

'Thank you for looking after Paula and Bob,' Tweed said to Sarin after the Finn had told his story.

Earlier they had heard from Newman an account of his meeting with Hauser. Sarin had listened with great attention and Paula noticed he was staring into space as though taking a decision. Dillon sat in his usual place on a chair in the corner. He had been introduced to Sarin as Ward Dexter, a commercial attaché on his way to join the American Embassy in Helsinki. He disguised his position cleverly, remarking to Sarin:

'London told me to contact Mr Tweed so I could get the lowdown on the situation here. Of course our interests do not always coincide. INCUBUS is a major force in the US and I have to adopt a neutral stance in these matters. A question of diplomacy, Mr Sarin.'

'I understand,' Sarin looked at Tweed. 'My own position is very similar to Mr Dexter's. A neutral stance. May I suggest that if you have the spare time you may find a visit to the remarkable Meteorological Institute complex near Kemijärvi interesting? I must go now.'

Karma opened the door for him. Sarin paused and turned, before leaving, to make one more remark.

'I would appreciate it, Tweed, if you would keep me informed of any further developments in case I can assist you.'

Tweed showed his anger as soon as the two Finns had left the room and Pete Nield, who had remained silent, had locked the door. He glared at Newman.

'That was a very dangerous and foolish tactic – to stir up Hauser in the way you did. God knows what might have happened if Sarin hadn't arrived.'

'What might have happened is Hauser would have blown his cool and told me something,' he snapped back. 'Give me a little credit for not mentioning Ion Manescu, the fact that we have photographic evidence that Romanian *Securitate* was inside the INCUBUS building. And God knows why you didn't show those pictures to Sarin. He's trying to get something on Hauser, something his government simply can't ignore.' Furious, he wiped sweat off his forehead before going on. 'And I gave no hint that we're holding Vanderheld, that she has information which could rock INCUBUS to its evil foundations.'

'That is what she says,' retorted Tweed. 'Has it occurred to you she could be bluffing? To get the protection you've provided her with? She thinks one attempt was made on her life . . .'

'No *thinks* about it,' Newman retorted. 'Her story links up with the picture in the paper. She actually showed me the outfit she was wearing. It fits the description given in that news report.'

Tweed was still glaring. 'She could have gone to Stockmann's and bought that outfit ready to show you. She had time to do just that . . .'

'Another thing you're forgetting,' Newman threw at him, 'is the brown Buick I saw parked outside her apartment – which links up with the picture Marler took. Same registration number as the car I saw parked outside her place. What more do you want? Hauser's head on a platter? And another item you missed. You should have shown Sarin the picture of that car and I'd have made a statement to what I saw.'

'What more do I want? Tweed repeated quietly. 'Some hard evidence.'

'Cool it, Newman,' Dillon advised. 'Tweed is right. Showing those pictures to Sarin would have bought us nothing. It's not Sarin's fault – he is in hock to his government – this country has to tread carefully. Russia is in turmoil. They can do without a breach with Washington.'

'The trouble, Bob,' Tweed explained in the same controlled tone, 'is that your motive is revenge. Naturally your only thought is to track down the man who murdered Sandy. That is blinding you to the bigger issue. Investigating INCUBUS. That has top priority.'

'Not with me any more!'

Newman stood up, wrenched on his jacket, ready to walk out. He caught Paula's eye.

'Bob,' she said, 'can I come over and see you and Marler at The Palace. I have something to tell you, something you'd like to know.'

'OK. Be my guest.' He paused before Nield unlocked the door for him. 'Paula, you're welcome. Even for a drink . . .'

There was silence as Newman left, a silence which continued for several minutes. Paula stood up and stared out of the window, her arms crossed. She was appalled. She had never witnessed such a blazing row between Tweed and Newman. She glanced over her shoulder. Tweed was cleaning his glasses, watching her with a quizzical expression.

'Thought I got it all wrong, didn't you?'

She walked slowly towards him, her eyes half closed. 'What are you up to? I know that expression. You're up to something. My Lord! You were putting on an act. You weren't losing your temper at all. Give. Now, please.'

Tweed glanced round the room at Dillon and Nield. He put on his glasses, settled back in his chair. He's giving himself time to decide something, Paula thought, still standing as she gazed down at him.

'You wound him up,' she accused.

'Yes, I did,' Tweed admitted. 'Let's face it. Newman is already wound up like a coiled spring, bent on revenge. Nothing is going to change that, stop him. To bring down Hauser is not going to be easy.'

'So why do we want to bring him down?' Paula prodded.

'Because *we* know he's using the ex-secret police who have been vanishing off the face of the earth. Marler's pictures of Manescu prove that to me. And it won't be only the *Securitate*. It will be the STASI, the STB from Czechoslovakia and God knows who else. If he's using them in Finland it's only a matter of time before he infiltrates them into Britain. So we have to stop him.

269

Because INCUBUS doesn't stop at murder – the horrible death of Ed Riverton shows that. He knew about Dracon, the think-tank outside Boston. He probably knew all about the plan – Hauser's plan to control a lot of the world. And one of the murders took place in Britain – Sandra Riverton. No one, nothing is safe while Hauser is operating.'

'But why use Bob Newman?'

'I'm not using him. He undertook the job himself. And don't forget he – together with yourself – have dug up more information than I have so far. It was Newman who visited the old owners of Bennington Machine Tools and Manningham Electronics in Britain – and got them to talk. It was Newman who deliberately provoked the attempts on his life – to smoke out the opposition. The three of you – Newman, yourself and Marler have provided me with pointers as to what Hauser is up to. And this,' Tweed said grimly, 'is now a duel between myself and Franklin D. Hauser.'

'With Bob in the front line?'

'Yes. I've launched him as a missile – a torpedo, if you like – against INCUBUS. Because he's getting results – and can look after himself. Are you satisfied?'

'You're wily, you're devious,' she said, crossing her ankles, her arms, staring at him.

'You know any other way of fighting a man like Hauser? And something interesting has happened. I started out with two quite separate investigations, as I thought. One, Newman and Cord here investigating INCUBUS's activities. Two, Marler on the trail of the vanishing secret police. Now both investigations have merged.'

He stopped speaking as someone tapped in a certain way on the door. Tweed nodded to Nield who unlocked the door. Marler walked in.

'On the dot, as always,' he said jauntily, 'for our meeting.'

'We need more data on INCUBUS,' Tweed said immediately. 'So how do we go about getting it?'

'I do a recce,' Marler said, perching on the arm of a chair Paula was sitting in. 'I fly to Rovaniemi north of the Arctic Circle, spy out the ground a bit. If that Meteorological Institute looks as peculiar as Sarin suspects, then maybe we organize a strike force to go up there, turn the place over.'

'The problem,' Tweed pointed out, 'is to work out how a group of people can move around in the wilderness without arousing suspicion.'

'Haven't worked that one out yet.' Marler stood up. 'First thing is the recce. I'm good at playing the Invisible Man.'

'Nothing like knowing you can pull off anything,' growled Dillon. 'You could end up in a box the way these people operate. I was inside that car when the juggernaut came at us.'

'Have faith, dear boy,' Marler assured him. He turned to Tweed. 'I'll fly up there in a jiffy, if that's OK.'

'Best to fly up in a plane,' Paula teased him.

'I agree,' Tweed decided. 'But be cautious . . .'

'I'd like to go with him,' Paula chimed in. 'No argument, if you please. That is, if Marler is happy.'

'Welcome aboard,' said Marler.

The phone rang as Tweed was about to protest. He picked it up. The voice at the other end did not identify itself but Tweed recognized the distinctive tone of General Valentin Rebet.

'I need to see you urgently. There has been a development you should know about. I can meet you at a rendezvous in the Finnish archipelago . . .'

'No!' Tweed's tone was abrupt. 'In Helsinki or not at all.'

'Would you consider Turku? Please. I do not wish to be seen.'

'Yes.'

'There is a colony of old wooden houses, a creation of Turku a hundred years ago . . .'

'I know it.'

'By the entrance to the colony at, say, twelve midday tomorrow?'

'First I must know something of what this is about,' Tweed demanded.

'Take my word for it. You will want to hear my news.'

'I agree to the meeting.'

'Thank you so much. It is a crisis situation.'

Tweed put down the phone. Paula was watching him closely. 'I asked you if I could go with Marler. That phone call. Was it trouble?'

'No. And you can go.' He looked at Dillon. 'Cord, you wanted to contact your embassy. Now might be a good time. Paula, why don't you go to lunch with Marler, plan your trip?'

Tweed waited until he was alone, locked the door and noticed Newman had left his pack of cigarettes. He took one, lit it, one of his rare cigarettes. He had felt the need to be alone, to sort out his thoughts.

Everything was happening at once. Nield sat silent by the wall sensing his chief's mood. Yes, everything was moving faster. Manescu had been located, was employed by INCUBUS. Had he any connection with the newspaper reports of bombs going off in various countries? All the victims were key liberal statesmen who might have stood in Hauser's way.

On top of that Newman had spirited away a vital witness to a safe refuge. Peggy Vanderheld. Butler was due back any time now. Newman was on the rampage, must have rattled Hauser's cage. That would, Tweed had no doubt, trigger off a violent reaction.

Then there was this mysterious Institute located in the Arctic Circle. How the devil could they transport a strike force up there if it came to that? Tweed stubbed out his half-smoked cigarette. Of course! Newman had by chance given him the solution. He picked up the phone to contact Monica. They would need certain equipment.

But, as he dialled, Tweed couldn't get out of his mind what Rebet had said. Am I right about the identity of Angel, he asked himself once more. And Rebet's last words were unsettling.

'It is a crisis situation.'

27

'Frank, I want you to fly to the Meteorological Institute and double up the security.'

Hauser was restless, exuding an aura of impatient energy as he prowled in his shirt sleeves round his office. His subordinate, sprawled in a chair, legs stretched out, ran a hand through his thick black unruly hair.

'Security is very tight now,' he ventured. 'What's on your mind?'

'What ought to be on yours. Goddamnit, you know what happened. Do I have to work out everything myself? Yes, I do. Always have had to. Get your bloody legs out of my way. I'll spell it out like I would for a child of ten,' he raged.

'I'm listening . . .'

'Then keep your trap shut and do just that, you crud. Listen! OK?'

Galvone stiffened. Crud? Did he really have to take all these insults his chief hurled at him? Then he remembered the money he was being paid. Yes, he did. He listened, his dark eyes narrowed as he responded tersely.

'OK.'

'I'd just asked you to launch a big tracking operation for Newman. Next development? Newman has the gall to arrive here, to tell me he's digging up dirt I thought was buried. He's very active, that nosy Brit. His next objective may well be a visit to the Institute. If he gets into the wrong area we're in trouble, big trouble. So, to hell with the security you've installed. You get up there fast in the jet. You do what I tell you. You double the security.'

'I'm on my way . . .'

'Keep your butt in that seat until I say you can go. I've just had an idea. Something's been bothering me, my instinct has never been wrong before. We're missing something. Newman has all his marbles, but he's a newspaperman. I think behind him there's another brain directing this operation against me. Before you fly north organize a dragnet – check all the hotels in this little town. The men you instruct are looking for new arrivals during the past week. Brits or Americans.'

'I'll get it moving. Anything else?'

'Yes. The campaign to take over Europe to the Urals. We're mounting a vast bombing operation to create more chaos – then we move in on certain areas we haven't touched yet. I want Irina Serov, Manescu and Ziegler flown out of the forest to Turku. They stay in hotels. You provide their papers. I want them there tomorrow. So any opposition has to be neutralized. Meantime I'll walk down another avenue.'

'Which one is that, if I may ask?'

Galvone stood up. Hauser, despite the heat – there were damp patches under his armpits – was in full flood, at his most dynamic. Lusting for action.

'You just did ask.' Hauser was still prowling like a panther. 'Adam Carver has fixed dinner tonight with that twist who came with Newman. Paula Grey. So Adam can

274

get her drunk, bed her, pump her. Maybe that way we'll hit on the mastermind behind this investigation into the corporation. Make with the feet, Frank. I think I'm homing in on the real enemy.'

Tweed lunched with Paula and Dillon at the Marski restaurant in the basement. They occupied a banquette at the end of the restaurant and Tweed, who ate quickly, had finished his plate of fried chicken coated with sesame seeds and saffron rice. Harry Butler, who had just returned from Sweden, sat in an outer seat facing Tweed.

'Peggy Vanderheld is holed up in that cottage on the island of Örno in the Swedish archipelago,' he reported. 'We may see her back here. She's restless, an energetic lady and didn't like being left on her own.' Butler's normally poker-faced expression showed a hint of embarrasment. 'She seems to have taken a fancy to me. I don't believe that,' he went on hastily. 'I think she just wants male protection next to her.'

'It would be very dangerous if she did come back,' Tweed mused.

'I did my best to get the idea out of her head,' Butler told him. 'But I thought we needed an insurance policy, so I let her know she could find me at the Hesperia. If she flies back I'm sure she'll come straight to me.'

'Did the best you could,' Tweed assured him. He looked at the others. 'I've been trying to put myself in Hauser's place after that confrontation he had with Newman. I think we've got to keep on the move, leave the Marski today.'

'And go where?' asked Dillon, pausing between mouthfuls.

'To the Hesperia, where Butler's staying. But we register under false names. All three of us.' He opened the briefcase he'd brought with him, slipped an envelope across the table to the American. 'There's your new passport, not that they check much here. You're now British.'

Dillon took out the passport below the level of the table, flipped it open to the page with his name and a photograph opposite. He grunted.

'Lawrence Dawlish. Sounds like a faggot. And I know I've an ugly mug, but this is ridiculous.'

'It's the kind of picture which could fit almost any clean-shaven man. And they never look at it, as I said. Here is yours, Paula. Your real photo. As you know, we have a selection at Park Crescent. I brought several in case of need. I've another for myself. I'm Martin Baker. We move after lunch. Just a precaution . . . It could save our lives.'

Tweed caught a train to Turku the following morning for his meeting with General Rebet. Pete Nield came with him after an argument which Nield won. Tweed used the railway because it was easier to slip unobserved out of Helsinki as opposed to using the airport.

The main station was close to the centre of Helsinki. Its façade had a weird 1930s look and Tweed assumed it must have escaped the destruction of World War II. He timed it so they arrived at the colony of old houses in Turku a few minutes before the noon rendezvous with the Russian.

To kill time he wandered among the old wooden houses with Nield, trudging up the sloping cobbled streets between the wooden cabins. No traffic was permitted inside and it was oddly quiet and deserted. The weather had changed again and dark storm clouds like an invading army were rolling in over Finland's second city. Inside the colony Tweed had the sensation of being miles away from the twentieth century.

At noon they had wandered back to the entrance and a taxi, the word spelt *taxsi*, pulled up. General Rebet stepped out by himself, wearing a dark overcoat and a peaked cap. As he paid off the driver, Tweed thought he looked more like a Finn. What the devil had he flown here from Leningrad for?

Newman was concealed inside the same copse overlooking INCUBUS Oy. HQ which Marler had used. He had asked Marler to draw him a map of the layout of the area and Marler, without asking what Newman was up to, had obliged. Arriving at 8 a.m., it was an hour before Newman saw what he had been hoping for.

A large stretched black Mercedes limo was driven close to the entrance to the building. A uniformed chauffeur jumped out of the vehicle, opened the rear door and immediately Hauser emerged with another figure. Through the lenses of the binoculars he had borrowed from Marler, Newman focused and identified Hauser positively. He had recognized the American from his walk but his garb puzzled Newman. Normally dressed in an expensive business suit, Hauser was clad in a rumpled windcheater, baggy denim trousers and a peaked cap pulled down over a pair of dark glasses. No pince-nez? He looked like a seaman.

'What's going down?' Dillon asked, seated in the rear of the BMW.

'Hauser going places . . .'

'And the guy with him?'

'Adam Carver. Hardly the fashion plate this morning. He's wearing denims, a scruffy windcheater like his boss. There they go . . .'

The automatic gate in the wire fence was opening, the limo was driving through the exit, turning towards the city. Cord Dillon grunted. From the Hesperia he had called Newman at The Palace when Tweed said he'd be absent, maybe for the day.

'What are you doing today?' Dillon had asked. 'I'm redundant. Can I help?'

Newman had decided that maybe some back-up wouldn't do any harm. And Dillon was as involved in breaking INCUBUS as he was. He'd told the American to be with him in fifteen minutes or he'd be gone.

Now as the limo disappeared from view Newman started up the BMW, let it glide down the spiral road which emerged on to the highway nearer the city and beyond INCUBUS. Within two minutes he had picked up the limo which was moving just inside the speed limit.

Dillon felt under his armpit where his Luger rested inside the shoulder holster. It was safer carrying the weapon on his person rather than leaving it in his room back at the Hesperia. He was glad he'd taken the precaution when Newman strapped on his own holster containing his Smith & Wesson just before they'd left The Palace.

'Expecting trouble?' he asked as Newman drove on.

'Aren't you? After what happened on The Highway?'

'So what's your plan of operation?' Dillon demanded.

'Stick to Hauser like glue. I stirred him up yesterday. I think sooner or later he'll react. That's how he got where he has. On top of the world.'

'Owns half the States, the bastard,' Dillon growled. 'That we don't like. They say he has a third of the Senate in his pocketbook. What's the problem?'

Newman had sworn half under his breath as he swung the car off the highway into Helsinki and followed the limo away from the centre of the city. They were driving with parkland on either side: wooded ground with grassy hills over which pathways wound out of sight. Newman nodded to his right.

'In a moment you'll see a really crazy old house with turrets. Like something out of Disneyland and very old. One of the houses which Russian Tsarist generals used as summer residences a hundred years ago when Finland was a principality of Russia.'

278

Dillon stared out of the window. Beyond some trees a weird house painted white was perched up on a knoll, four storeys high with elaborate balconies and circular turret towers at the corners.

'And that,' Newman told him, 'is Hauser's town house. How he managed to buy a national monument is probably quite a story.'

'Passed money to the right bureaucrats?'

'That wouldn't work in Finland. My guess is he's built so many plants here, provided so much employment, the government are naturally sympathetic to him. Same technique as I found he employed in Suffolk back in England for miles round his home there, Livingstone Manor. Play the philanthropist, recruit an army of spies and allies. Yes, I think there is a problem coming up within the next half hour.'

'Which is?'

They were well clear of the city, were driving along a highway which passed between gulches of granite outcrops. It almost reminded Dillon of the Wild West. Here and there an isolated house, a small lake in front of a cliff wall. Granite again, of course. Granite City. In the distance the black limo was moving round a long curve.

'The problem,' Newman informed Dillon, 'is that we're on the way to the airport. The locals call it Seusta. Looks as though Hauser is flying off somewhere. This car can't take to the air.'

'We board his flight.'

'I don't think so. My bet is he'll use the Lear jet. And it looks like some secret meeting. Hence the mess of clothes Hauser and Carver are wearing. To avoid recognition . . .'

'Checkmate. You were right,' Dillon commented as Newman parked the BMW.

They had arrived at the airport, the black limo had

dropped Hauser and Carver who hurried inside the building. Newman jumped out with Dillon, slid a press card from his wallet, tucked it under the windscreen wiper. It might work.

Inside the small airport building – small by comparison with Heathrow or Frankfurt – he walked rapidly after Hauser and Carver who ignored the normal departure route. From a window he watched the two men hustling over towards a Lear jet which was being refuelled.

'Checkmate,' Dillon repeated. 'Shit.'

'There may be a way . . .'

Newman walked back to a door marked *Security* in Finnish and Swedish. The latter language he could understand. Knocking on the door, he opened it, walked inside, closed it, leaving Dillon outside. He flashed his press card.

'Liaison with Protection Police,' he said to the uniformed officer who looked up from behind a counter. 'I need the flight plan for that Lear jet out there. Call Mauno Sarin at Ratakatu if you want to. We need to follow that jet.'

'Then we'd better not waste time making phone calls. The flight plan is for Turku. A scheduled flight takes off for the same place in fifteen minutes. You'd better hurry.'

'Thanks a lot. Sarin will be grateful . . .'

They bought tickets, caught the scheduled flight with minutes to spare. Newman thanked God there was no known terrorist problem in Finland – so no security apparatus to detect the guns they were carrying. The door was closed as they sat down, the motors hummed into high pitch and they were off, moving down the runway.

'And when we get to Turku?' Dillon whispered as the machine lifted into the dazzling clear blue sky.

'We just hope this beats the jet. If it does we can pick up where Hauser is going, track him to his destination.'

*   *   *

'Adam, this goddamn outfit I'm wearing reminds me of those days when I worked as a longshoreman on the San Francisco waterfront,' Hauser remarked as the jet left the ground.

'You've come a long way since then.'

'Yes, it's been one helluva journey and it's not over yet. Want a drink?'

'Just mineral water,' Carver replied. He liked to keep his mind clear. 'What is this meeting we're attending? And I should be back in Helsinki this evening. I have a date with Paula Grey. Of course,' he added quickly, 'if necessary I can stand her up. She'll be that much more eager when I make a new date.'

'Don't do that, boy. You could extract valuable data from that dame. You'll be back in Helsinki late this afternoon.'

Hauser sipped at his bourbon. The interior of the jet was luxurious. They sat side by side in leather armchairs. In front of Hauser by the bulkhead was a fully stocked cocktail cabinet with a door which opened and closed at the press of a button. In front of Carver was a telephone linked to a sophisticated communications system using a satellite. With this phone Hauser could call any of his companies spread out across the world and the conversation would be scrambled and automatically decoded at the other end. The jet was a flying HQ of INCUBUS.

'This meeting,' Hauser began, 'is top secret.' He paused, sipped more bourbon. 'I brought you along in case we have to discuss prices, even negotiate a final deal. I do doubt the latter, the people we're dealing with think time is a weapon to wear down the impatient. So I'm offering them a deal they can't refuse.'

'Do I sit in on it with you?'

'I think not. These are very security-minded people. So security minded even the people back home where they've come from don't know they're in Turku.'

'So nothing recorded, I assume?'

'You assume right, boy.'

'How do we organize liaison with each other, if necessary?'

'I'll leave them in one room, come through to check with you in another.'

'Can you be a little more specific?' Carver pressed. 'It helps if I know in advance what's going on. I'll be quicker with answers for you.'

Hauser paused again. 'You might as well know. It's a Soviet trade delegation – interested in my forming private companies inside Russia. We hold fifty-one per cent of the equity – which gives us control, as usual. It's all new to them so I have to lead them by the hand.'

'You must have worked to pull off a deal like that,' Carver remarked, encouraging more revelations.

'It's a long upward haul. Those peasants are living in the last century. I once had dinner with a top bureaucrat. He'd lived in the West, was decently dressed. When the soup came he scooped it up, shovelled it in his mouth.' Hauser demonstrated, dipping his head, working his elbow. 'Peasants,' he repeated. 'And the three men I'm flying to meet are top people. Time we civilized them.'

'Where in Turku is this meeting taking place then?'

'The last place you'd expect to find three top Russians. In the two cabins we bought in that colony of old houses . . .'

28

After buying a ticket, General Rebet entered the compound of old houses, shook hands with Tweed, with Nield.

'I suggest we stroll round this strange place,' he said after checking his watch.

Nield dropped back behind the two men. His right hand rested inside his jacket close to the Browning automatic tucked inside his belt. He had borrowed the weapon from Paula.

'Crisis was the word you used,' Tweed said, coming straight to the point. 'What's happening? Why are we here?'

'To witness a meeting between Franklin D. Hauser and three members of the Politburo. Kazbek, Marshal Zaikov and Dikoyan. And I still don't know which one is Angel, the traitor.'

'But you hope to find out this time?'

Rebet shrugged as they walked up a cobbled ramp-like street with cabins on either side. 'My informants – who are risking their lives – found out the meeting would take place here, who was coming.'

'How are these three men travelling? Presumably they don't want the Finns to know. Certainly Marshal Zaikov's presence would cause a furore with the Finnish government.'

'That's the intriguing part. Their mode of travel. Two of them – and I don't know which two – are flying in by Aeroflot to Turku airport. Their cover is the trade exhibition opening in Turku today. They're travelling in a separate compartment aboard the aircraft. Also aboard is a low-level trade delegation visiting the fair. The two Politburo men will go straight to a car which will drive them here.'

'And the third man?'

'Whose identity I also don't know. He's flown to Tallinn in Estonia across the Gulf of Finland. From there he's travelling by fast power cruiser to one of the islands in the archipelago. There he transfers to a fishing vessel for the short voyage to Turku.'

'A complex route. Sounds like Angel.'

'I agree. The problem will be to identify which of the three arrives here on his own.'

Tweed stopped alongside Rebet. They had almost reached the summit of their climb. A rope, waist high, barred their way. A man dressed in working clothes held up his hand. He spoke in English.

'Work proceeding repairing the street. You can't come any further this route today.'

A dozen paces behind the two men Nield took a firm grip on the Browning. He had noticed the bulge under the shoulder of the workman's clothes. Did Finnish workers normally carry handguns?

Tweed nodded, gazed beyond the rope. Two large wooden cabins stood close together with only a tiny alley separating them. Behind heavy net curtains all the main curtains were closed. And despite the storm clouds gathering it was broad daylight. The two men turned back.

'We've found the meeting place,' Rebet whispered.

'I think so. But when?'

Rebet checked his watch. 'They are due here in fifteen minutes from now.'

The Finnair machine made a smooth landing on the Turku runway. A mobile staircase was brought out. As Newman descended with Dillon following he glanced up

284

at the sky. A Lear jet was coming in to land. They had beaten Hauser to it by minutes.

'I'm staying here,' Newman said as they entered the reception hall. 'You go outside and grab a cab. Give the driver a large tip. Tell him you're waiting for another passenger . . .'

Newman walked back to a window overlooking the airfield. As the jet landed, slowed to a halt, a black limo drove out to meet it. Hauser seemed to favour black cars. He used his binoculars, focused them on the rear of the Mercedes, memorized the registration number, walked quickly outside to where Dillon stood by a cab.

'They're leaving any moment, Cord. Get in.'

Inside the cab Newman gave precise instructions to the cab driver, including the registration number. Casually he mentioned they were reporters, that they were interested in the two passengers in the limo, that they were checking out a story.

'I understand,' the driver replied and drove off, then stopped.

As the limo passed them he followed without making it obvious, keeping a reasonable distance behind the vehicle. After they had travelled a short distance the driver spoke over his shoulder.

'They look like they are heading for the settlement of old houses. Maybe you have heard about them?'

'We have heard about them,' Newman said as the cab slowed.

Tweed and Rebet had positioned themselves inside one of the cabins open to the public close to a window. It was dark inside the room, the furniture was heavy and ancient in keeping with the turn of the century. The guardian of the cabin, deciding they were harmless, had left them alone.

'Here, I think, comes Hauser,' Newman said.

Carver jumped out of the vehicle the moment it stopped, bought two tickets and walked into the colony with Hauser. The two men walked straight to the cobbled avenue leading up to where repair work was supposed to be taking place. Rebet checked his watch again.

'This operation is being carried out with great precision. My three are due any moment now.'

Pete Nield, who stood behind Tweed, stared out of the window as a taxi pulled up. He stiffened as the door opened and gently nudged Tweed in the back without letting Rebet see his signal. Tweed kept his expression blank as he watched Newman and Dillon pay off their driver, buy tickets and enter the compound.

Inwardly he was fuming. What on earth did Newman think he was doing? How could he have turned up here at this sensitive moment? Swearing to himself, he preserved his blank look as the two men walked swiftly to the cabin facing the building Tweed watched from. They both kept out of sight and Newman peered round the corner. Tweed guessed he was observing the progress of Hauser and Carver up the hill towards the meeting point.

'Those two visitors seem to be taking a great interest in Hauser,' Rebet remarked.

'Probably INCUBUS guards,' Tweed suggested. 'Hauser doesn't travel many places without protection.'

'I suppose you're right,' Rebet responded dubiously. 'And now we have another taxi coming . . .'

Newman had heard it too. He grabbed Dillon by the arm and they slipped inside the open door of the cabin before the cab reached the entrance. They're doing what we are, Tweed said to himself: observing from under cover.

The cab stopped and three men stepped out, one of them paying the driver. Dressed in lightweight raincoats, they all wore caps. Tweed stared as they entered the colony. *Three* men. Marshal Zaikov, Viktor Kazbek,

Anatoli Dikoyan, still managing to look neat and trim in a shabby raincoat and a cap.

'Damn!'

Rebet slammed one clenched fist into the palm of his other hand. 'All three turned up together. Now I have no idea which is our target.'

'Someone played it clever,' Tweed suggested. 'Came ashore from that fishing vessel very early, then waited in a taxi at a prearranged rendezvous until the other two arrived and then joined them to come here. The only thing wrong with that theory is how would he explain his devious route to the other two?'

'I can tell you that at least. There's unrest in Estonia, as you know. One Politburo member was going there to check out the situation secretly. That reason would satisfy the other two, neither of whom are Angel. The trouble is, I don't know which one went to Tallinn.'

Nield had tactfully moved to another window to give Tweed and Rebet privacy. Now he called out softly.

'Two more taxis arriving.'

The three Soviet Politburo men had disappeared up the same avenue which Hauser and Carver had walked up. Marshal Zaikov had marched straight up on his own, followed by Dikoyan and Kazbek who walked side by side, Tweed noted.

Seven men piled out of the two taxis. Several had bottles protruding from their pockets and a couple did a little dance on the pavement while the drivers were being paid off. Rebet leaned closer to the window, his mouth tight.

'My God! Those are Soviet KGB guards disguised as seamen. I recognize some of them. They're protecting those three men – I thought it was odd the way they turned up alone. They'll all be armed.'

Tweed was disturbed. Newman and Dillon were still hidden in the cabin opposite. And he had earlier seen Newman pull down his jacket. Tweed knew that gesture: it was to ensure the gun he was carrying was concealed. This was an explosive situation.

'They're being clever,' Rebet commented bitterly as the seven men bought tickets and rollicked into the compound. They were giving a perfect imitation of a group of seamen who were not drunk but were enjoying a brief period of leave ashore. Several put their arms round each other as they plodded up the avenue which the three Politburo men had walked up.

'That really checkmates us,' Rebet said.

'Not necessarily,' replied Tweed. 'Do you know whether Angel will return by the same route he came in by?'

'Piecing together the bits of data from my informants, yes. He has to. Officially he flew to Tallinn. So he must fly back to Moscow from Tallinn.'

'Using exactly the same route?' Tweed persisted. 'First the fishing vessel, then transferring to the power cruiser to reach Tallinn?'

'The same. In reverse.'

'Then let me have a word with my associate.'

Tweed walked across to the window where Nield stood watching the outside world. He lowered his voice as he gave the instruction.

'Pete, you saw those three arrive shortly after Newman and Dillon? Good. Now this will be difficult, but it's also vital if you can work it. I want you to leave here, look for some transport to follow the taxi which takes those three men away from here. One of them will somehow detach himself inconspicuously from the others who will go to the airport. I want you to stick to that third man like a leech. He will leave Turku aboard a fishing vessel to rendezvous with a big power cruiser somewhere in the archipelago. Understood so far?'

'Quite clear.'

'If you can, I want you to follow him out to sea as long

as possible. As well as transport, buy a camera. I need you to bring back photos of that third man.'

'Got it.' The formidable mission was taken in his stride by Nield. 'Only one objection – I'm here to protect you. I can't be in two places at once.'

'Newman and Dillon are in that cabin over there. They can take your place.'

'Then I'm on my way . . .'

'You have enough money?'

'Plenty. For what I need.'

Tweed watched the slim agile figure of Nield walking swiftly towards the entrance. It was obvious he had already worked out how he was going to handle the difficult and dangerous job Tweed had given him.

Tweed strolled by himself across to the cabin opposite. Out of the corner of his eye he saw the distant summit of the avenue he'd climbed with Rebet. Three of the so-called seamen were leaning up against the walls of cabins just below the roped-off area. That left four: they would be guarding the other sides of the two cabins. He would have given a lot to know what was going on inside. The door of the cabin opposite was opened, Newman beckoned him inside, closed the door. Dillon was standing by a window, the Luger held by his side.

'May I enquire what the devil you are doing here?' Tweed enquired.

Newman, making no apologies, told him how they had followed Hauser from his HQ in Helsinki. Tweed listened, sat down and nodded.

'I suppose I can't blame you . . .'

'I should hope not,' Newman rapped back. 'Our job is to detect what Hauser is planning. Who were those peculiar characters who arrived recently?'

'Emissaries,' Tweed replied enigmatically.

'Your friend across the way is in trouble, maybe big trouble,' Dillon called out. 'He peered out when you left the cabin, must have been seen. A couple of those thugs have just gone inside . . .'

'He must be protected. At all costs,' Tweed ordered.

Newman and Dillon ran past him, opened the door, walked slowly across. Newman glanced up the avenue, saw the other men in the distance were talking, their backs to him. He pushed open the cabin door slowly, his .38 Smith & Wesson in his hand. Dillon followed, the Luger still by his side.

The atmosphere inside the cabin was heavy with the humidity which had descended on Turku. Rebet stood against a wall, facing the two men, his hands raised as Newman and Dillon entered silently. Both men facing Rebet held Makarov pistols aimed at Rebet. His voice was firm as he spoke.

'Starkov, I'm ordering you and your companion to put away those guns . . .'

He had spoken in English, seeing Newman and Dillon entering the cabin. In response both men took firmer grips on their pistols, aimed them point blank at Rebet.

'I wouldn't if I were you . . .' Newman began.

The first man spun round, his Makarov aiming at Newman. A shot rang out. The Russian was falling when his companion, who had turned round when Newman spoke, waved his pistol towards Dillon. A second shot rang out and he sagged to the plank floor beside his colleague.

Rebet ran forward, bent down, checked the neck pulses of both men. He shook his head as he straightened up.

'They are both dead,' he told Newman. 'I have to thank both of you for saving my life. But we must leave here quickly.'

Newman picked up one of the Makarovs, shoved the muzzle into a leather cushion on a couch, pulled the trigger. He did the same with the second Makarov, turned over the cushion to hide the bullet holes, pressed a pistol into the right hand of each Russian, took a bottle from the pocket of one man, spilt vodka over the mouths of the corpses, left the bottle on a table. Had the other guards heard the shots? A plane had flown overhead at that moment. Rebet stood still, watching Newman with interest.

'Now let's be careful getting back to the other cabin,' Newman warned the two men.

He opened the door, peered up the avenue. Some kind of argument seemed to be going on at the far end of the avenue, men gesticulating, their backs turned. He beckoned to his companions, ran over to the other cabin. Tweed opened the door, let the three men inside, closed the door quietly.

'What happened? Where are the two guards?'

'Dead . . .'

Newman explained tersely what had taken place. Rebet made his comment when Newman had finished.

'He saved my life – both of them did. And it was a brilliant trick to make it look as though they'd shot each other. It might work when they're found.'

'Which could be any time now. We have to get away from here,' Tweed said decisively. 'If we can unseen. Immediately . . .'

'What's happened to Pete Nield?' Dillon asked.

'He can look after himself. I said we must get well clear. Now!'

Newman led the way. He checked to make sure the guards were still absorbed and saw two of them strolling slowly down the avenue towards him. They must be wondering where their comrades were. He waved towards Tweed who was watching from the doorway which faced the exit. The four men hurried out of the colony and Tweed ran towards a taxi parked further up the street. The four men jumped inside, Tweed told the cab driver to take them to the Akateeminen Bookshop, the first place which came into his head in the centre of Turku. As the cab moved off he glanced through the rear window. No sign of any guards as the taxi turned a corner.

'We're safe,' he whispered to Rebet. 'As Wellington said at Waterloo, it was a damned near run thing.'

'But we are still no closer to identifying Angel,' Rebet whispered back.

'We may be soon.'

As he said the words Tweed was worried about Pete Nield and the task he had given him. It could be a great deal more dangerous than he had anticipated.

29

Pete Nield returned to the colony of cabins fully equipped. He was riding a powerful Honda motorcycle he had bought second hand. His suit jacket was neatly folded away in the rear carrier and he wore a leather jacket, a Martian-like helmet with outsize goggles. Pulling up at the kerb a short distance from the compound entrance, he lit a cigarette.

He had spent a lot of money but fortunately Tweed insisted his agents carried a generous supply of the local currency when abroad and Nield had been loaded with *markkaa*. After purchasing the Honda he had sped to the port area. The skipper of a small fast fishing vessel had taken little persuading to make his craft ready for immediate departure when he saw the size of the fee Nield was offering.

'Half now, half when we've completed the job,' Nield had insisted.

Paula's Browning automatic was shoved down his belt

inside his jacket. It was a damned hot day for a leather jacket, he thought as he smoked his cigarette, but he had to look the part of a courier. He had also purchased a Japanese camera with a zoom lens, now tucked away in the front carrier.

All I can do is sweat and wait, he thought as he wiped moisture from his forehead.

The humidity was building up. Black clouds sealed off the sky but heat still radiated up from the street. Nield was accustomed to waiting: it occupied half his time on a job. He had just stubbed out the cigarette when he saw three men hurry inside a taxi they must have phoned for.

A great bear of a man with a mane of black hair and a beard of the same colour. A much smaller slimmer man who moved quickly and gracefully. A stocky heavily built man who marched with a military tread. The cab drove off. Nield pressed the starter button, followed.

Had he been there to witness it, Tweed would have admired the military precision of the departure. Shortly after Nield had left two more cabs arrived. Seven men occupied the vehicles. Four men entered the first cab, two carrying one of their number who sagged and appeared drunk. Three more occupied the second cab and again one man, also smelling of vodka, was carried inside. The two cabs then took off along the same route as the first cab.

Several minutes later a black limo driven by a chauffeur pulled in at the kerb. Hauser appeared at the foot of the avenue with Carver. Hauser had heard of the discovery of the two corpses and looked warily around before diving into the rear of the limo, followed by Carver. As the taxi left the kerbside Hauser gave an instruction to the driver and turned to Carver.

'Adam. I'm dropping you at the railroad depot. Take a

293

train back to Helsinki for your dinner with the Grey woman. I have work to do at headquarters here. I'll fly back by the jet later . . .'

Pete Nield stared through his goggles as the cab ahead slid to a halt in a quiet part of town on the outskirts of Turku. He slowed, moved into the kerb, fiddled in his satchel hung across his chest as though checking a delivery.

In front of the cab he'd followed another cab was parked. He watched as the door of the cab with the three men inside was opened. A van masked his view for vital seconds and then he saw a blurred figure disappearing inside the cab parked in front.

He whistled under his breath. A switch. Which one to track now? The humidity was fogging his brain. Of course! Tweed had said follow the third man, the one who detaches himself from the other two. How the hell had Tweed foreseen this manoeuvre?

He started away from the kerb as the first taxi drove off. He checked again in his wing mirror. The same two cabs he had observed behind him earlier were still following. It was a great relief when he checked a minute later and the two cabs were no longer there. They had to be something to do with the cab he'd left behind.

Several minutes later he smelt salt in the air and a waterfront came into sight. The cab in front moved slowly along a quay. Everywhere loomed a forest of masts, swaying slowly. A strong breeze was blowing. Nield eased his machine down the quay, saw the cab stop alongside a large fishing vessel, cruised to a stop beside his own smaller craft. The wheelhouse was aft and the tough, wizen-faced skipper inside waved to Nield.

The Englishman nodded in response, swung his leg off the saddle, took hold of the Honda and heaved it aboard the vessel. Jumping after it, he hauled a sheet of canvas to conceal the machine. Taking off his helmet, he tucked that underneath the canvas. Next he stripped off the leather jacket, shoved that out of sight. Burrowing under the canvas he opened the rear carrier, extracted his folded jacket, slipped that on. It was surprisingly chilly on the waterfront. Then he hauled out his camera from the front carrier and placed it carefully under the canvas for easy access. Nield was noted for his meticulous attention to detail.

He jumped back off the heaving vessel on to the quayside and fingered his trim moustache as he watched the silhouette of the passenger from the cab disappear aboard the fishing vessel. The skipper of his own craft, who spoke English and had told Nield his name was Savola, had already started up his engine, which chug-chugged gently.

A few minutes later Nield thanked his lucky stars he had taken precautions, had completely changed his appearance – two more cabs appeared after the first one had driven past him back to the city. They cruised past him and stopped by the vessel where the third man had gone aboard. They looked like the same two cabs he had seen in his wing mirror to Nield.

Lighting a cigarette, his back to the wind, he watched as seven men emerged and went aboard. Two appeared to be blind drunk. They were carried aboard. Nield pursed his lips. The third man must be important to be escorted by so many guards. He frowned as two guards reappeared on the quayside to stretch their legs. They had lost their loping seamen's walk, were moving up and down, erect and brisk. His skipper, Savola, joined him on the quay.

'That big fishing job further up this quay is the one I want you to follow,' Nield told him.

Savola, a short heavy-set individual with broad shoulders and a wide mouth under an aggressive nose, reminded Nield of old films he'd seen on TV of Edward

G. Robinson. He smoked a curved pipe which was hardly ever alight. He grunted, looked up the quay, took out some matches and lit one, passing it over the pipe bowl.

'That's the *Alskär*. We're a community, we all know each other. Skipper of the *Alskär* told me he was hired by the Soviets – some oceanographic team carrying out research. So they say. Spying more likely.'

'Does he know about me?' Nield asked, deliberately phrasing the question positively.

'How could he? I didn't know that was the ship I had to follow until now. And the fee you paid gives you complete secrecy. What you asked for you get.'

'You can keep up with the *Alskär*?'

Nield looked at Savola's much smaller vessel, the *Skäret*. It was a midget compared with the Russians' ship.

Savola puffed at his pipe. 'I can race him to the Kattegat if I have to. That engine you can hear is powerful. And my *Skäret* had a complete overhaul two months ago. Skipper of the *Alskär* is mean about maintenance.' He knocked out the dottle from his pipe, crushed it under his huge boot. 'And maybe we'd better get aboard. *Alskär*'s engine has just started up.' He unlooped the ropes from the bollards.

Nield followed the skipper into the cramped wheelhouse. It gave him a better view of the target vessel. I hope they don't mind their pictures being taken, he thought as the *Skäret* nosed its way away from the quay, heading out for the archipelago and the open sea.

It was the twenty-first century. After dropping off Carver at Turku railway station Hauser was driven to INCUBUS's HQ in Turku. Another cylindrical building, the walls constructed of opaque blue glass, it towered twenty storeys high. The largest building in Turku.

Hauser sat in the weird interrogation room on the top

floor. Seated at a table which supported a console, he faced a one-way window. He could see into each of the three rooms behind the long sheet of glass. The occupant of each soundproofed room could not see him.

By operating switches on the console he could communicate with each person sitting in the three separate rooms, one at a time. Hauser had a microphone suspended at mouth level, as had the three people he could see so clearly.

In the right-hand room sat Helmut Ziegler, ex-STASI chief in what had been East Germany. In the centre room, erect in her chair, was seated Irina Serov. Ion Manescu sat inside the third room. Hauser was addressing Irina Serov.

'My name is Morrow. I am your boss. Would you be prepared to go back underground inside the Soviet Union, Irina?'

'Such a trip would have to be most carefully planned.'

'It would be. You haven't answered my question.'

'First, tell me what my task would be. Then I will answer you.'

Gutsy bitch, Hauser thought. He pushed the pince-nez further up his nose. Yes, he had been right to choose her as chief of the subversive operations.

'Explosives have been smuggled inside the Soviet Union. I want these used to disrupt Russian rail traffic. To bring more chaos so they need help and technical advice desperately. On my terms. You would choose the strategic points to place the explosives. You would choose the people to plant them. Your answer, please.'

'I think it would be possible. There is growing unrest in almost every republic. The chaos would provide perfect opportunities to use the explosives, to create more chaos. I suggest we concentrate on the Trans-Siberian Railway and all rail routes out of Moscow, which is the hub of the system. One question, Mr Morrow. Through which zone do we smuggle the explosives into Russia?'

Hauser hesitated. Irina had impressed him. She sat so confidently, clad in a tight-fitting blouse and a short skirt revealing her excellent figure. She's every man's woman, he was thinking.

'The explosives dump is already established,' he told her. 'Here in Finland. We moved it from Lapland in the north across the Soviet border.'

'A perfect choice.'

'But before you take charge of that operation there is something else I want you to do here in Finland. A seduction job. I'll come back to you in a minute.'

Hauser switched off the communication with her room, switched on the right-hand room. Ziegler was short in stature, heavy in build. In his forties, clean shaven, his fair hair was trimmed *en brosse*. He had thick eyebrows which almost met in a bar above a pug nose, a tight mean mouth and an aggressive brutal jaw. He stirred restlessly in his chair until Hauser gave him his instructions.

The organization of unrest, mob demonstrations, bomb attacks, all inside Germany. The trouble had to be laid at the door of a revived terrorist group, the Red Army Faction. More than that, Ziegler had to contact the UTS, the Free Ukraine movement based in Munich. If it appeared the Ukraine, the second most important republic in the Soviet Union, might break loose the Soviet president would have his hands full, would not notice Hauser's penetration of his country.

Hauser switched to the bony-faced Ion Manescu. His orders were brief.

'You have to keep the Balkans cauldron bubbling. Targets – Budapest, Sofia and Bucharest. Set those places on fire . . .'

His instructions to Manescu completed, he turned again to Irina who still sat erect, staring at the mirror facing her as though she could see the man who was

298

talking, the man who called himself Morrow, the man whom she was convinced – despite the distortion of his voice – was Franklin D. Hauser.

'Irina,' Hauser began, 'we shall shortly identify the mastermind behind the opposition to us operating in Finland. When we do I want you to meet him as a woman who escaped from Moldavia, the area Stalin grabbed off Romania at the end of the Second World War. I'm sure you have the personality, the equipment physically, to get him to talk . . .'

She's as sexy as the devil, he thought when he'd finished. He blanked out the console. The job was done. All hell was about to erupt across Europe and Russia.

It was fortunate Pete Nield was a good sailor. The *Skäret* had travelled far from the mainland, was threading its way through the archipelago in heavy seas. The fishing vessel pitched and tossed as large waves swept towards it, climbing a surf-topped crest, plunging down into the next trough.

Holding on to a rail alongside Savola who gripped his wheel, Nield was fascinated by the archipelago. A labyrinth of channels, they weaved a course between countless islands of varying sizes. Some were large with a few wooden one-storey houses, their walls painted bright red. What must it be like living in such solitude, Nield wondered. Others were mere giant brown boulders, whale-backed with waves crashing over them. They rounded the point of one large island and the *Alskär* again came into sight.

Savola was showing great skill in navigation, sailing up a channel which took him out of view of the Soviet-hired vessel, emerging later to bring the target into view once more. As the *Skäret* swayed Nield steadied himself against the rear of the wheelhouse, the binoculars he had bought in Turku pressed to his eyes. Guards jumped close in his lenses. In his mind's eye Nield had a clear recollection of the three men who had arrived by themselves at the Turku colony. Not one of them had appeared so far. And how the hell am I going to take pictures with this tub bobbing like a cork, he wondered. Assuming the third man ever did show.

'Could we get a little closer?' he asked.

'Yes,' Savola replied. 'But if we do they may know we are following them. So far we are just a fishing vessel heading for the best hunting grounds. You have seen other ships so why should they think about us? But if we get closer . . .'

'Will the skipper of the *Alskär* betray us to the Russians?'

'No.' Savola spoke with his teeth clenched on his curved pipe. 'He is paid to transport the so-called oceanographic team. He has no interest in making trouble for me. We all have to live together, to fish another day.'

'Then get closer . . .'

They were leaving the archipelago behind, were approaching the open sea of the Baltic. Islands were becoming fewer and fewer, and none were inhabited. In the far distance the horizon was a hard line as black as ink where a solid mass of clouds assembled overhead. Green rollers continued to surge towards the *Skäret*, sunlight had broken through. But leaving behind the archipelago, Nield realized, meant a greater chance of exposure to the Russians. No other vessels were now in view except the *Alskär*. And they were closing fast on their quarry.

Oddly enough, as they sailed into open sea its surface became calmer. Nield took hold of his camera. He slid back the door of the wheelhouse. Savola glanced at him.

'Be careful. They are Russkies.'

'I'll be all right . . .'

The wind had dropped as Nield leaned against the side

300

of the wheelhouse, aimed his camera. A guard's head jumped into the viewer. The guard had binoculars trained on the *Skäret*. He lowered them and there was a sudden flurry of activity aboard the larger vessel. More guards appeared. Nield held his ground.

'Watch out!' shouted Savola, who had slid open the door.

His keen eyes had seen one of the guards holding a rifle, the muzzle aimed at the *Skäret*. Nield had also spotted the weapon. He remained where he was, peering through the camera. The *Alskär* was sailing now with very little motion, which would help the marksman. Savola swung his wheel over, altering course abruptly. Above the sound of the engine there was the sound of a clatter, like pebbles hitting the gunwale. Bullets. The sudden change of course had saved Nield.

Through the viewer, Nield saw a different figure appear on the desk of the *Alskär*. The third man, his features clear and sharp. Nield continued taking shots as Savola weaved from side to side, as the rifleman continued firing. More clatter, again like pebbles hitting the hull.

'Bastards!' shouted Savola.

Nield bent down, picked up something from the deck, hauled the door open, rushed inside the wheelhouse, slammed the door shut, gripping his camera.

'Job done!' he called out to Savola. 'We can go back . . .'

'If we survive.'

Another rifleman had appeared. The third man was pointing at the *Skäret*. Nield grinned. 'Got you, you thug.' The *Skäret* was swinging through a hundred and eighty degrees fast. As it headed back towards the archipelago Nield was staring through the rear window. The riflemen were still firing, Savola was weaving again. Nield saw the calm water near their wake disturbed by projectiles hitting the sea. He opened his left hand, showed what he had picked up from the deck.

'Rubber bullets. Of course if one had hit me in the eye or the throat that would have been it.'

'We go home?' Savola suggested.

'We go home,' Nield agreed.

30

'Don't punish yourself, Bob,' said Paula. 'Poring over that diary of Sandy's you found in her Jag in Suffolk isn't going to tell you anything more. You must know it off by heart now.'

Newman was sitting in a chair in his room at The Palace while Paula curled up like a cat on his bed. It was hot and humid, felt like a storm was coming. 28°C. the forecast had predicted. That was 82°F. Newman, clad in an open-necked shirt and slacks, looked at his hands. They were covered in moisture. He wiped them on the back of his slacks, went on checking through the diary. He came to two pages stuck together. He'd missed them before.

Using his fingernails, he prised the pages apart, stared at the entry.

Porvoo. That's how he said it was spelt when I told him I'd overheard a reference to the word. He said it was some place in Sweden. I don't believe him. He tells lies . . .

'God! And I missed it,' he said aloud.

'Missed what?' enquired Paula, jerking upright.

'This entry. The two pages were gummed together – like they sometimes are in a diary. I suppose I was still so stunned at the time I didn't spot two pages were missing.'

'Give!' commanded Paula. 'And explain.'

He handed her the diary open at the pages, stood up and drank some more mineral water. He paced round the room and it was like walking through treacle.

'The handwriting is Sandy's,' he went on. 'I wonder who the *he* was she refers to. And whoever it was she was too right. He is a liar.'

'Sorry. Am I being thick?'

'It's not a big place so, like most people, you've probably never heard of it. But Porvoo is *not* in Sweden – so why did someone think it necessary to lie about where it is?'

'And where is it? Stop being tantalizing.'

'It's an ancient port no more than forty to fifty miles from here. East of Helsinki along the continuation of Highway E3. I think I'm going to look at that place. I'll see if Marler is in.'

'Can I come too?' she asked as he picked up the phone.

Marler tapped on the door a few minutes later. Newman felt rumpled and creased with the heat: as usual, Marler looked fresh as paint in his tropical drill suit.

'I was having a siesta,' he announced. 'Bored with having to wait for Tweed to get back from wherever he's pushed off to. Said would I wait till we had more data before I flew to Rovaniemi. I didn't agree – the way to collect data is to move around, but Tweed is Tweed. How's the most beautiful girl in the world?' he asked Paula.

'Not in a mood for phoney flattery. Too hot . . .'

'Marler,' Newman interjected impatiently, 'when you visited Mauno Sarin he showed you a list of Hauser's companies in Finland. Was one of them in Porvoo?'

'No,' said Marler promptly. 'Why?'

Newman explained about the diary. He handed it to Marler who glanced at the entry, raised his eyebrows, gave back the diary.

303

'Not much to go on,' he commented.

'I'm going to check it out,' Newman said stubbornly, slipping into his shoes.

Opening a drawer, he carefully removed neatly folded shirts, took out the shoulder holster, strapped it on, sheathed the Smith & Wesson, put on his jacket, checked his appearance in the mirror. Marler raised his eyebrows at Paula. She was standing up, hands on her hips.

'I said can I come too, Bob?'

'I suppose so. Marler, you're invited. You helped me locate that copse above INCUBUS's HQ.'

'I can't imagine why. I must have been bowled over with an excess of generosity. Where is Tweed, by the by? Anyone know?'

Newman kept his expression blank. After the confrontation with the two Soviet guards earlier in the day he had flown back from Turku. Partly because he was worried about Paula. Tweed had stayed on in Turku. Anxious about Nield, he had taken a cab to the waterfront. Dillon had insisted on staying with him.

'You need protection,' he said. 'I have a gun, and now Nield is away somewhere you'd be on your own . . .'

'As far as I know he's safe. Outside Helsinki for the moment,' Newman replied. 'Are you or are you not coming with me to Porvoo?' He had collected the BMW which was still parked at the airport on his return.

'Might as well.' Marler sounded dubious. 'Can't really see the point – all on the basis of a note in a diary. And INCUBUS, as I told you, doesn't have a company there. Still, you need someone to look after you.'

'You can get me back here by seven?' Paula queried. 'I've my date with Adam Carver. Of course you can,' she went on, determined not to be left behind. 'And probably nothing will happen at all while we're there . . .'

*   *   *

With Paula beside him and Marler in the back, Newman drove across the bridge over the river into Porvoo. Glancing downriver towards the sea he saw a collection of single-storey wooden cabins perched at the edge of the water. Each cabin had a wooden landing platform projecting over the river, several with old boats moored to them. The whole atmosphere of Porvoo was so different from Turku's colony of old wooden houses which had an artificial air.

'I like this place,' said Paula. 'It's really old and small. It reeks of what Finland must have been like one hundred years ago.'

Newman parked the BMW, locked it up as Paula and Marler stood looking round. The sun was glaring out of an azure sky in the late afternoon. On the north side of the town old cobbled streets climbed steeply between more wooden houses, many with walls painted rust red and dark roofs. Crocodiles of tourists were trudging wearily up towards the top.

'Where do we start?' Paula asked briskly.

'The waterfront,' Newman replied.

'Why, old boy?' asked Marler.

'I'm not sure why. Instinct. And not so much of the "old boy". Now, let's get moving.'

He led the way across the main road and they walked down a cobbled road behind rows of cabin-like houses which he'd seen crossing the bridge. Narrow cobbled streets, little more than alleys, led down between the houses to where the river flowed. Newman walked purposefully on. Paula had to hurry to catch up with him while Marler trailed behind, smoking one of his king-size.

Paula glanced at Newman as she trotted alongside him. He looked grim. She looped an arm through his.

'Slow down. You look like murder. It's rereading that diary, isn't it?'

'I feel like murder.'

'Do you really think there's any point in poking around here? Nothing I can see will help us.'

'So we ask questions. That used to be my job. I'm still good at it. Let's start now. Here.'

A grizzle-faced fisherman was sitting on a wooden stool, tending his nets. He looked up as Newman stopped in front of him, holding several banknotes between his fingers.

'You speak English?'

'Some.'

'I have been asked by INCUBUS to write a history of their activities. You know what they do in Porvoo?'

The fisherman's hands stopped working his nets briefly, then he resumed work after glancing at the banknotes. He took a little while before replying.

'I have never heard of this company. I don't know anything.'

Newman walked on closer to the waterfront. Paula waited until they were out of earshot of the fisherman before she asked her question.

'You think we're getting anywhere?'

'Yes. He was lying. Didn't you notice? He referred to "this company". I never told him INCUBUS was a company. So why should he lie? I think we've stumbled on something. Let's try this chap.'

He stopped by the side of a fisherman caulking his rowing boat. The same question. The same quick glance at the money, at Newman. The same expression of ignorance. Newman walked on, Paula by his side, Marler still trailing the rear.

They walked quite a distance, parallel to the river, and the landscape became wilder, less inhabited. Still some way from the sea, Newman had questioned three other fishermen. Always the same negative result, always the sensation something was being concealed. Where had he experienced this before? God! Suffolk. In the area round

306

Livingstone Manor. Newman felt the long hand of Franklin D. Hauser reaching out to Porvoo.

It was then that Paula's sharp ears caught the sound of an engine approaching slowly behind them. Then another sound. Someone whistling, a steady persistent whistle. Marler. She glanced over her shoulder. Behind Marler a motor cyclist was cruising slowly, bumping over the rough ground, the rider dressed like a fisherman. Marler cupped his hand in front of his stomach, beckoned for her to join him, a gesture invisible to the motor cyclist. She told Newman she'd join him in a minute, that she ought to have a word with Marler.

'What is it?' she asked, strolling beside Marler.

'Chap on the motor cycle behind us. He's been shadowing us for the past ten minutes, watching the two of you.'

'You don't think he could be an INCUBUS thug?' she asked, alarmed.

'No idea. Let's see how things develop. No other fisher-men in sight.'

As he spoke the motor cyclist rode slowly past them. When he reached Newman he stopped the machine, jumped off and began to push it alongside Newman. He would be in his thirties, Newman estimated. A fresh-faced man with thick dark hair and a five o'clock shadow round his firm chin.

'You've been asking questions, I understand,' he said.

'Have I? So what?'

'You've been asking the wrong people.'

'So I gather.'

Newman was careful not to show any eagerness. He continued walking, the motor cyclist continued pushing the motor bike beside him. There was silence for a couple of minutes.

'Ask me the questions,' the fisherman suggested.

Newman repeated the question he'd put to the other

fishermen. His companion remained silent. Newman produced the banknotes and held them in view. The reaction was unexpected.

'I don't want your money. How do I know who you are? You could be an agent of Hauser's.'

'True. Sensible of you to be so careful.' Newman produced his press card, handed it to the man. The fisherman stopped, screwed up his alert eyes. Newman realized he had never seen the form of identification before. He took a chance.

'I'm Robert Newman, a foreign correspondent. I'm investigating INCUBUS Oy. I think there's something wrong with that corporation.'

'There is.' The fisherman handed back the card. 'I fished for INCUBUS until a few months ago. Here you fish for INCUBUS or have a bad time. They threatened me, told me not to fish for them anymore.'

'Go on. I'm interested.'

'Out there,' he waved a hand towards the sea, 'they have a huge factory ship for processing frozen fish. The *New York*. It is the most advanced factory ship in the world. We supply the fish, take them well out to sea to the factory ship. It cleans, guts, freezes and packs them. They even have the refrigerator trucks on board . The *New York* is like a giant car ferry. They have constructed a large ramp on the coast by a road. Every now and again the *New York* comes inshore – the water is very deep where the ramp is – and trucks drive ashore and on to their destinations for delivery.'

'Sounds like a legitimate operation. Legal,' said Newman.

'Something funny is going on. The *New York* always lands its trucks after dark. No one is permitted near that ramp when the *New York* is unloading. That is one reason I was told I had lost my job. I watched the unloading and the guards caught me.'

308

'Guards?'

'Men with rifles. And no one is allowed near the factory ship after they have delivered the fish. I was curious and sailed close after I'd unloaded my catch. Aboard they have more guards with rifles. I was seen. They opened fire but I got away. The trouble is someone must have had binoculars. They identified my vessel. That factory ship is used for something more than freezing fish.'

'Information should be rewarded,' Newman said producing the banknotes again.

'I said I didn't want your money,' the fisherman said vehemently. 'I want to hit back at Hauser. And there is something else which puzzles me. I have a cousin in Kemijärvi. That is north of the Arctic Circle, on the way to the Meteorological Institute and the Soviet border.'

'What else is there then?' Newman prodded as the man hesitated.

'I was staying with my cousin and saw an INCUBUS refrigerated truck passing through east on Route 82. Who out there would want all that frozen fish?'

'I have no idea. It does sound strange.'

'You might be able to check one of their trucks if you go back quickly to Porvoo. An INCUBUS truck broke down. It was repaired but when I came through Porvoo an hour or so ago I saw the driver in a café having lunch. You might catch up that truck in your BMW.'

'Any idea which route it follows?' Newman produced a map and the fisherman traced a route. 'Through Lahti and then north along E4?' Newman remarked. 'How do you know that?'

'Because one night I followed a truck on my motor cycle. You will have to move fast before he leaves Porvoo. If he has gone – the truck was parked just round the corner where you left your BMW – you might catch up with him.'

'Thanks. Thanks very much.' Newman turned to join

Paula and Marler who had stayed behind as Paula pretended to examine some wild flowers. 'And take care of yourself – these are tough people.'

With Newman at the wheel they were driving through wild forested country and Paula gazed, fascinated, at the lonely wilderness of dense fir trees going on forever as Newman sped along a superbly surfaced road. Through a gap in the trees she caught a glimpse of an idyllic lake, a sheet of pure blue water with not a sign of human habitation. Finland just went on and on, a haven of peace and beauty with pollution unknown.

They had rushed back to Porvoo, found the truck had gone, had jumped inside the BMW and now they were following the route the fisherman had described. Paula sat with the map on her lap and was acting as navigator next to Newman. Marler sat in the back, making discouraging remarks.

'You know,' he began again, 'I can't see we're going to find anything – just supposin' we ever find the truck. I think this trip is a bit loony.'

'Thanks for the vote of confidence,' snapped Newman.

'Any time, old chap. Any time.'

Paula glanced at Newman. His expression was still grim and he stared ahead as they rounded a long curve hemmed in by the walls of forest. No other traffic in either direction. Pure bliss, Paula was thinking. Where else in the world could you find such dream-like country to drive through all by yourself . . .

Her musings were interrupted without warning. The curve had ended and a straight stretch of highway sprawled into the distance. A half-mile ahead was a large truck. As the gap closed she saw it was a large refrigerated truck. Across the rear of the vehicle was the logo. INCUBUS.

'Well, I'll be damned.' Marler leaned forward. 'Take back all I said. Never thought we'd catch the blighter.'

'The next decision is how do we handle it,' Newman commented.

'Pull in by the side of the road, if you please,' Marler requested.

Newman, wondering what he had in mind, pulled up, switched off the engine. Paula, her window down, was stunned by the silence of the forest which she could *hear*. This was paradise.

'Now, listen to me,' Marler went on. 'I'll tackle the driver . No argument. The INCUBUS lot have photographs of you both. God knows how many with those film units you told us about at Arlanda and the Stockholm ferry terminal. They have no pics of me at all. So we change places. I drive and you two occupy the back. When we get close both of you go into a clinch. They'll have circulated the photographs they took of you. And those trucks have large wing mirrors. OK?'

They were outside the car, changing position, when Paula looked at Marler. His expression was businesslike.

'You don't have a weapon to defend yourself,' she pointed out.

'But you're wrong there, my dear.'

Marler hoisted up his left trouser leg. A leather sheath was strapped to the inner side of his slim leg. He hauled out a large knife with a vicious-looking blade, then shoved it back into the sheath.

'Finnish hunting knife,' he told her. 'Available at all good hardware stores in Helsinki. You must have noticed.' He looked into the far distance along the ruler-straight road. 'Nothing coming. Let's get cracking . . .'

Glancing in his rear-view mirror, he saw the road was deserted behind them and drove off. As he got closer to the truck he realized it was trundling along at a steady but unexciting pace. He stared through the windscreen.

311

'They have a load of aerials above the cab. Perhaps they are in touch with Mars.'

In the rear Newman had gone into a clinch with Paula. He whispered, 'Might as well make this convincing,' and pressed his mouth to hers. In his mirror Marler observed their faces were hidden. He accelerated, pulled alongside the large truck, saw to this surprise there was only the driver. No guard beside him. Perhaps it was a clever display of innocence? But what were they guilty of?

Marler began tooting his horn. On. Off. On . . . The driver, short and stocky, stared at him. Marler grinned, gestured over his shoulder, then waved to the side of the road, continuing his nerve-wracking barrage of horn tooting. The driver shrugged, slowed, pulled in to the side, stopped.

Marler stopped just short of the cab, nipped out of the car. He was standing by the cab, looking up as the driver opened the door. He grinned again.

'I say, do you speak English? Jolly good. Thought I ought to warn you. Your bally registration plate is hanging off the rear. End up in the road any second. A patrol car might get excited. You know what they're like. Anything to fill up their little notebooks . . .'

As he was speaking the driver lowered himself on to the footplate, down on to the road. Marler hauled out his hair spray canister with his left hand, pressed the button and spray squirted into the driver's eyes. He yelped, lifted both hands to his eyes.

'Jesus Chr —'

He never completed the expletive because Marler's clenched right fist rammed up into his jaw. The impact knocked him backwards and Marler grabbed him under the armpits as he sagged unconscious. Newman and Paula had dived out of the BMW and ran up to him.

'He's got a whole load of communications gimmicks inside,' Marler warned as he heaved the man back inside the cab. 'Including a microphone and some gimmicks I haven't seen. Stay there a sec.'

Climbing into the cab he searched the pockets of the inert body. He found the bunch of keys in a jacket pocket, held them up.

'Bingo! Now let's see which one unlocks the doors at the back . . .'

He had to try four keys before the lock turned. Reaching up to the handle, he swung the right-hand door open and hauled himself inside. The door had the appearance of a safe vault and icy air met him as Newman followed. Paula stayed outside to warn them if other traffic appeared.

Marler swung up the steel catch on what appeared to be a large consignment of frozen fish, stared down inside with the aid of a pencil flash. He let out his breath between his teeth. He scooped up a handful of grey plastic dough and moulded it, his teeth chattering with the intense cold. Paula opened the second door from the outside. She peered inside.

'You'll freeze to death in there,' she warned. 'The air flowing out feels like the Arctic.'

'It's better with that other door open,' Newman called out. 'And we can see what we're doing.'

He had opened another metal container and stared at the contents. He looked up as Marler brushed past him, jumped out of the truck, ran to the BMW, came back with a cleaning cloth. Newman bent lower over the open container and froze.

'Marler, come here.'

'What is it?'

Marler had been wrapping his cravat round a large ball of the grey dough. He came to Newman and gazed down inside the container. Newman straightened up.

'Unless I'm very much mistaken those are sticks of gelignite. And they're sweating. You took a course of explosives at the training house Amersham in the Chilterns.'

'That's jelly,' Marler said tersely. 'Let's get clear of this truck. It's a ticking time bomb . . .'

'Maybe we should check a few more cases?'

'And maybe we should not. My guess is they all contain explosive. Let's hoof it.'

'What have you got there?' Newman asked.

Marler was stuffing his cravat inside his jacket pocket and jumped into the road. He gestured for Newman to get a move on.

'Semtex, the plastic explosive, is my guess. Luckily it is harmless without a detonator and all the gadgets.'

Marler fetched more cleaning cloths from the BMW, twisted them into skeins as he stood by the cab. 'Give me a bit of help,' he said to Newman. 'We have to immobilize the driver in case he regains consciousness while we're gone.' Climbing inside the cab he checked the pulse of the slumped figure. 'Good pulse rate. He's just out cold for a little longer.'

Newman turned the driver over, held his hands behind his back while Marler tied his wrists together with the makeshift ropes. They then tied together his ankles. Newman looked at the dashboard which was more like a console. He picked up the microphone, smashed it against the floor and they both jumped to the ground, closing the cab door.

Paula appeared from the rear of the truck. She ran to them and spoke quickly.

'I've closed the doors at the back. I heard what you said.'

'Better lock them,' said Marler.

He ran to the rear of the vehicle. Paula took her map out of the BMW and marked it with a cross.

'Mauno Sarin,' Newman said as Marler returned, holding aloft the bunch of keys. 'We have to contact him fast.'

'There was a phone box about ten miles back the way we came,' said Paula.

'Don't get into the car,' Marler warned. 'I want both of you to run a hundred yards up the highway, get as far away as you can before I start up the car. It's just possible the engine vibrations might send this lot sky high. No, don't argue, Newman. Get Paula out of the way. *Now* for God's sake . . .'

Gasping for breath – running in the heat was strenuous – Newman and Paula stopped further up the highway and waited. As the sun beat down on them the tension built up. Newman wished he'd insisted on taking over the wheel. Marler sat behind the wheel alongside the front of the truck. Paula clenched her hands into fists as they waited for the sound of the engine starting up.

What the hell was Marler waiting for? Newman wondered. He reached for Paula's right hand. She unclenched her fist, entwined her fingers with Newman's, gripping him tight. The silence which had seemed so wonderful now pressed down on her like a menace. She prayed it would be all right, prayed with all her might.

Behind the wheel Marler had a fresh unlit cigarette between his lips. He glanced up at the truck. Within the next few seconds he would either be alive or a mess of debris scattered over the countryside. No point in hanging about. Newman was right: they had to contact Sarin.

Paula and Newman stood close together like statues. She was trembling. The silence was broken with the sound of Marler turning on the ignition. It sounded like a thunderclap to Paula. God! The truck was exploding . . .

The BMW slid smoothly away from the truck, drove slowly towards them. Marler executed a U-turn and pulled up alongside them. They jumped into the car, Paula grabbing the front passenger seat, picking up her map. With the unlit cigarette still in his mouth Marler drove slowly back, glided past the stationary truck, continued slowly for a couple of hundred yards and then rammed his foot down.

31

Newman and Marler called on Mauno Sarin at Ratakatu at nine the same evening, as previously arranged when Newman had phoned him from the isolated box on the highway. Sarin was standing behind his desk, nodded to Marler, came round his desk to shake hands with Newman.

'I hope your visit this time is different from a few years ago when we travelled to Estonia together.'

'As I told you earlier, there are grim similarities,' Newman replied and left it at that. 'What's the news about that INCUBUS refrigerated truck?' he asked as he sat in the chair Sarin had ushered him to.

'You would like coffee?'

Sarin looked at Newman, at Marler, who was also seated in a hard-backed chair. There were no frills, little comfort, in the austere Mauno Sarin's office. Both men shook their heads. Sarin settled himself behind his desk, began twiddling a pencil between his fingers.

'I responded to your call immediately,' Sarin began. 'I despatched six patrol cars, each with two armed men. When you handed the phone to Paula Grey she described the location perfectly. The patrol cars arrived,' he glanced at a typed sheet on his desk, 'thirty-five minutes after I received your call. They found an INCUBUS truck. The driver was asleep in his cab, said the extreme heat had affected him.'

Newman frowned, leaned forward. 'Yes. What about the explosives? Go on.'

Sarin waved the pencil like a schoolmaster. 'The patrol car men checked every container in the truck. Frozen fish in every one. No sign of explosives . . .'

'I don't believe it,' Marler interjected.

'You have to believe it. So there is no hard evidence to back up your story.'

'Oh, yes, there is,' Marler snapped. He took out the folded cravat, exposed the ball of dough-like substance, handed it to the Finn. 'I took that myself out of one of the containers. Newman was there, can vouch for what I say. Semtex.'

Sarin stared at the grey ball, pursed his lips. He pressed a button under his desk. A short dark-haired Finn appeared after knocking on the door.

'Karma, take this material downstairs to our explosives expert. Ask him if he can identify it. At once, please.'

Newman waited until they were alone before he asked his question.

'Did the patrol car people describe the driver?'

Again Sarin glanced at the typed sheet. 'Yes, they did. A tall lean-faced man with a moustache. In his fifties.'

'They switched drivers,' Marler protested. 'Ours was short, stocky, in his early thirties.'

'They switched trucks too,' Newman intervened. 'How the devil did they do it so fast? How did they know?' He recalled the interior of the truck's cab. 'I should have thought of it. The dashboard has a complex console system. I smashed the microphone, as I told you. But with a consignment of high explosives they'd have a sophisticated system of keeping an eye on the truck without being obvious, without having a car with guards behind it. What do you think, Marler?'

'Only explanation for their vanishing trick. Quite possibly they had OK signals sent at five-minutes intervals by the driver. There was a load of communication equipment on top of the cab. They're clever. When they suspected something was wrong they sent out another truck, probably with two drivers and several guards. One of the fresh drivers then drove off the explosives truck while the other one parked where we'd left the first one. He pretended to be asleep when the patrol cars arrived. Do you believe us?' he asked Sarin.

'Just a minute,' Newman broke in. 'We left the keys to unlock the rear doors inside that phone box, as we said we would when we phoned you. Did anyone pick them up?'

'Yes. A patrol car picked them up.' Sarin opened a drawer, showed them a bunch of keys. 'Every key was used to try and open the rear doors. None of them fitted.'

'Of course they didn't,' Marler told him.

'And,' Sarin went on, 'there are no markings on these keys to link them with INCUBUS.'

'I'd noticed that,' Marler responded. 'Mind if I light a cigarette?'

'If you must.'

'Do you believe us?'

'What is there to believe?'

There was a knock on the door. Karma entered with his normal lack of any expression. He waited.

'Well?' demanded Sarin testily. 'Any news?'

'Yes. It is Semtex. No doubt about it.'

'Thank you, Karma. That will be all.'

Newman seized his opportunity. 'Also a reliable source told me he'd seen an INCUBUS truck driving through Kemijärvi in the Arctic Circle. It drove on east towards the Meteorological Institute you told Marler about. How much frozen fish do they consume there? And can't your Coastguard people go aboard that factory ship I mentioned on the phone?'

'No. It operates well outside Finnish coastal waters.'

'Then we won't take up any more of your valuable time.'

'And can I take that?' Marler asked, also standing up, reaching out a hand towards the Semtex Karma had left on the desk.

'No, you cannot.'

They left behind a very worried and frustrated Mauno Sarin.

'Why did you try and get hold of that Semtex?' Newman asked as he drove the BMW away from Ratakatu.

'Oh, you never know when it might come in useful. And I do know how to construct a detonator and a timer. Any hardware shop in Helsinki has the equipment – household – I can convert.'

'Except you haven't any Semtex.'

'Shame on you. You weren't very observant when we were out on that highway examining the truck.'

Marler opened the glove compartment. Inside was a cleaning cloth wrapped round what looked like a brick. He peeled away a portion of the cloth, showed Newman its contents. A brick-shaped quantity of grey dough-like material.

'Semtex. Enough to cause quite a devastating blow-up. And I wonder how the fair Paula is enjoying her dinner date?'

Paula wore an exuberant orange print dress decorated with white sunflowers. She had carefully chosen a long-sleeved dress with a high necked collar so that no part of her anatomy was bare for Carver's roving hand to touch.

'I know a marvellously romantic place out of town,' he had said when he met her in the lobby of the Hesperia.

'I've brought my Cadillac so we can get there in no time. You'll love the restaurant, the view over the sea.'

'Thank you.' She had given him her best smile. 'But I've already booked a table in your name at my favourite restaurant. The Palace. And that overlooks the harbour.'

'I see.' For a few seconds he couldn't conceal his annoyance, then he rallied. 'Sounds great. The Palace it is. Let's move. Have a drink in the bar first to warm us up. Although, looking at you, I'm warmed up already . . .'

Carver was wearing an off-white silk suit and a white tie. She thought he looked like a paint salesman but carefully refrained from saying so. Over the dinner table he openly admired her with his eyes but she pretended not to notice his close attention. She waited until they were eating the main course before she broached the subject.

'We have a mutual friend. Evelyn Lennox. I understand you went to see her at her cottage in Walberswick.'

He paused briefly before replying. 'I did know her but only briefly.'

'Really?' She sipped her Chablis. 'She told me you also visited her at her place in Wandsworth. That's in London.'

'I know it is.' He had snapped out the words. 'I mean I did see her there as well. It was a business relationship.'

'I didn't gather that from her. You chased after her up to Suffolk when she didn't visit you in London. Those are her words, not mine.'

She smiled again. Sipping her wine she thought his dark eyes grew even darker, more penetrating. He thinks he can hypnotize a woman, she thought, enjoying herself.

'I think maybe she embroidered things a bit,' he suggested.

'Maybe.' She didn't sound convinced. 'Of course she had a lot to upset her. First the murder of her brother-in-law, Ed Riverton.' She gazed out of the window. 'Weird

320

to think they dragged his body out of that harbour last February.'

'The conversation seems to have taken a macabre turn. I took you out to enjoy yourself.'

'Oh, don't worry. I'm having the time of my life. Then almost at the same time her sister, Sandra Riverton, was found murdered as well. Which way round was it? Did Ed die first or was it Sandra?'

'I'm sure I have no idea. Has anyone? But you're right. Evelyn was, naturally, rather thrown by those grisly incidents. I tried to comfort her.'

'Really? Good for you. But I thought you said it was a business relationship.'

'Well, it was. But she was in a bit of a state. Had to confide in someone, I suppose.'

She hit him again. 'That surprises me. Evelyn isn't the confiding sort of girl. And I wouldn't have thought you were her type. I could be wrong, of course.'

The smooth man of the world was floundering under Paula's onslaught. He wiped his mouth with a napkin, eyed her warily, took a large drink of wine, refilled her glass, then his own.

'Maybe after dinner we could go for a drive outside Helsinki,' he suggested. He glanced at her. Had she had enough to drink yet to mellow? Some of the girls these days had heads like rocks. 'The scenery is superb and it would give us a breath of fresh air.'

'Except the air outside is like the inside of a hot oven.'

She withdrew her hand from the table as he reached out to take hold of it, picked up her fork and smiled.

'This is an excellent dinner. Do you often take girls out? Probably not. Your job must take up most of your time. So I don't imagine you're used to feminine company.'

He didn't like that either, she could see. The image of an experienced Casanova was slipping fast. He started eating quickly, furious, and made no reply as she chattered on, breaking off briefly to drink half her refilled glass of the Chablis.

'Adam, what do you actually do at INCUBUS? Buried in paper work most of the time? Is it boring?'

'No, it isn't.' He put down his knife and fork, wishing he hadn't replied with such vehemence. She was dangling him on a string, damn her. 'I'm Vice President of Banking Ops. I handle very large sums of money, sums you've probably never even dreamt of.'

'So you were involved in the takeover of Egon Schmidt's bank in Frankfurt. I read about it in the paper.'

'That was a straightforward business deal.'

'Was it?' She twirled her glass, watching him over the rim. 'The father, Egon, was determined not to sell out. Then he goes and gets killed when his car blows up. Which leaves the way open for you to make a deal with son Dieter, who was always willing to sell. That bomb must have smoothed the way for you, Adam.'

'The Red Army Faction terrorists killed him. One of those coincidences which happens in business.'

'But the Red Army Faction lot denied they'd had anything to do with it.'

'They would, wouldn't they?'

He refilled her glass, ordered a fresh bottle. How the hell had the conversation taken this twist? Setting out to seduce Paula, he had been coaxed into talking too much about INCUBUS. As she drank more, he waited and then threw at her the vital question.

'We've been talking too much about me. It's you I'm interested in. Who do you work for? Who is your boss? Difficult to work for, is he?'

'I work for an insurance company.' She looked straight at Carver. 'Ed Riverton had a life policy with us. I'm here to find out what happened to him. The policy could be null and void under certain conditions.'

322

'And you're the boss of the outfit?'

'Heavens no. Martin Sheffield is,' she said, making up the first name which came into her head. 'And he's a peach to work for.'

'He's with you now? Here in Helsinki?'

'Half the time I never know where he is. He's a regular will-o'-the-wisp. No, I don't think I'll have a dessert or coffee. I think I'd like to go back to my hotel.'

'The Hesperia? I'll drive you there.' He called for the bill, produced a credit card, dealt with the paperwork. She waited until he had finished.

'Thank you for the offer, Adam. Sorry to break up a lovely evening. I've enjoyed every minute of it. But I'm tired. And I've got a headache coming on. Must be the heat. And I'll go back in a taxi. Don't push me.'

No way was she going to climb back inside his bloody Cadillac. As they stood outside waiting for a taxi in the humid air of late evening Carver struggled to control his frustration.

'At least I can see you again,' he began confidently. 'I'll give you a buzz at the Hesperia. Next time we can go anywhere you choose.'

'Maybe. Thank you again for a superb meal.'

She dived inside the taxi before he could kiss her on the cheek. She didn't wave to him as the cab moved off. Settling herself, she smiled. Newman wasn't the only one who could stir up the pot.

Sitting behind the wheel of his parked Cadillac Carver hammered his fist against the dashboard. The bitch! But with a bit of luck he could get back at her, teach her a lesson she'd never forget.

32

Hauser had flown back from Turku in the evening, had climbed into the waiting limo at Helsinki Airport. The chauffeur drove the bullet-proof Mercedes to Hauser's town house, the weird turreted edifice Newman had pointed out to Cord Dillon when they had followed Hauser to the airport.

Inside the house, after a shower and a change of clothes, Hauser had climbed to the turret room he had converted into a combined office and living room. He poured himself a slug of bourbon, was sipping it when the phone rang. Adam Carver had arrived, wanted to see him.

'Then tell him to drag his ass up here . . .'

The room was eight-sided and Hauser stood looking out of a window at the deserted park while Carver reported on his dinner with Paula Grey. He would like to have edited the version of their conversation over dinner but he knew that Hauser had an uncanny knack of sensing when a man was leaving something out.

He was also annoyed that as he began talking Frank Galvone came into the tower. Hauser told him to sit, to listen, to help himself to a drink if that would help him keep his trap shut. Hauser was not in the best of moods.

Irina Serov had flown back with Hauser but, for security reasons, she had waited half an hour after Hauser left the Lear jet. She had then taken a taxi to a company apartment near where Peggy Vanderheld had lived.

Hauser had ordered Manescu and Ziegler to travel to Helsinki by train. Each had been given a different address in apartments at Setula near the airport. Hauser was assembling his forces.

Carver continued his report while Galvone poured himself a drink, then leaned against a wall, holding the glass in fingers covered with black hair. He watched Carver with a cynical expression.

'Sounds like you boobed it,' he commented when Carver had finished speaking.

Hauser rounded on him viciously. 'Frank, I thought I asked you to keep the trap shut. How are things up at the Institute? You're just back from the Arctic Circle?'

'Flew in an hour ago, Chief.' He smiled with satisfaction. 'Security has been doubled. Really tightened up. I had to kick a few people in the crotch to waken them up. They're awake now. Anyone who tries to snoop around will end up as duck soup.'

'Take that grin off your ugly mug. No security is one hundred per cent. How many times have I to repeat it? Listen. Both of you. We have another problem. Locating the opposition. And there is one – look at how we saved that truck out of Porvoo. I told you about that, Frank, when you called me from the airport. Adam, I'll explain that incident later. Due entirely to my persistence we may have identified the opposition. Including the top man.'

Hauser walked across to a Turkish table inlaid with marble chips of various colours. It was eight-sided, to match the design of the turret. Hauser had an obsessively precise mind. He picked up a sheaf of typed sheets.

'I have here a list of Brits and Americans who arrived at hotels in Helsinki during the past week.'

'How on earth did you get hold of their names?' Carver asked in a tone of admiration.

'Adam, why do you always want to know how we operate even when it's something outside your sphere?

Hell, it was easy. I sent a team round the hotels with plenty of money. We've been careful to see we have friends planted in the major and medium establishments. I checked through this list while I was changing. Something came out of your abortive conversation with Paula Grey. She said her boss was Martin Sheffield. OK?'

'OK.'

'But it's not OK. No one of that name is registered at the Hesperia.' He looked at Galvone. 'Now Adam said when he asked Grey the name of her boss she said Martin Sheffield. She's staying at the Hesperia – but she's just moved there from the Marski. And at the same time a Martin *Baker* moved in at the Hesperia. A Brit. You know, Adam, when you spring a question like you did, the person who wants to disguise a name often uses the same Christian name and alters the surname. Now Adam,' he said sarcastically, 'you've just had an exhausting evening so push off to bed.'

He waited until he was alone with Galvone. Inserting a cigarette into his holder he lit it.

'Frank, that Grey woman knows too much. Some of the things she asked Adam about were too sensitive for my liking – the Schmidt bank takeover, for example. We have to find out more of what she knows.'

'Sure. How do we go about it?'

'We kidnap her, using Adam as bait, you schmuck.'

'You didn't mention the idea in front of Carver.'

'No, I didn't, did I? Think my memory is going? He won't even know the part he's playing. I sensed he's taken a fancy to Paula Grey. Now push off yourself . . .'

Hauser smiled to himself as the door closed. He was skilled at the game: never let the right hand know what the left hand is doing. And vice versa.

He took out a small box from a drawer, extracted a circular filter instrument, screwed it on to his phone. Manufactured in one of his laboratories outside Boston, it

326

distorted the voice. He dialled the number of the apartment where Irina Serov was staying. When she answered he used her code name.

'Sonia, this is Morrow speaking. Name of the subject you contact is Martin Baker. Got it? Staying at the Hesperia. Get next to him tomorrow. He could be the top man causing me a little trouble., Do your stuff. All the way if necessary . . .'

Tweed arrived back from Turku late with Nield and Dillon. It was ten o'clock when he arrived at the Hesperia. He'd had nothing to eat for hours but he was tireless. Before ordering from room service he made a number of calls.

Two were to rooms in the hotel – to Paula and Harry Butler. Then two more, this time outside calls to The Palace to Newman and Marler asking them to come and see him at once. He looked at Dillon as the American came out of his bathroom, drying his face with a towel.

'Nield will be here in a minute. The others are coming in from The Palace. Time we had a full-scale conference.'

'I'd like something to eat. You seem to exist on mineral water. I'm going to my room for a fresh shirt. Be back soon. Don't forget the food.'

Tweed paced round the room when he was alone, hands clasped behind his back. Nield was the first to arrive.

'Couldn't talk to you on the train. Wasn't sure Dillon was in on the third man business.'

'Tell me . . .'

Tweed continued pacing as Nield talked about his experience aboard the *Skäret*. When he said he could describe the third man Tweed made a dismissive gesture.

'You say you can get the photos developed at a shop which prints and develops in a few hours in the morning. Wait until you show me the pictures . . .'

He broke off as Paula came in. 'That was quite an

327

evening I had with that Carver. He's too clever by half . . .'

Again Tweed listened while she relayed to him the conversation in detail. He frowned when she had finished.

'You took a chance, raising some of those issues.'

'Oh, I lied like a trooper. Especially about Evelyn Lennox being a friend of mine. As you've probably guessed, I recalled what Bob had told me about Wandsworth and his trip to Walberswick. As to taking a chance, I thought the plan was to stir up INCUBUS, unsettle Hauser.'

'You did a good job,' Tweed decided.

He broke off as Harry Butler arrived. He glanced at his old sparring partner, Nield. 'On your hols? Lazing in the sun while I do some real work?'

'You wouldn't have enjoyed being with me this afternoon,' Nield retorted.

Butler sat down, looked at Tweed. 'Since I was left behind like a spare wheel I decided to poke around. I hired a Saab, drove out to the airport. Turned out to be a hub of action. Spent the whole day there, a very long day.'

'Do you think you were seen?' Tweed enquired. 'I was counting on there being four people INCUBUS doesn't know exist. You, Nield, Marler, myself.'

'Shortly after I arrived,' Butler reported in his matter-of-fact way, 'I saw an airport official in a pale blue uniform throw his cap into the back of his car, then go back inside for something. I was wearing a blue jacket, the nearest I had to their uniform. I pinched the cap, walked inside the concourse. The owner came out, never noticed his cap was gone, drove off. All day long people thought I was an airport official. Merging into the background you call it.'

'Clever,' Tweed commented. 'What did you see?'

'Hauser and Carver arriving in a whacking great limo. Recognized them from Marler's photos. Then Newman and Dillon arrive. Hauser and Carver board a Lear jet, take off. Newman and Dillon catch the flight to Turku . . .'

'I never saw you,' interjected Newman who had arrived with Marler.

'You weren't supposed to. Can I get on? Then that brown Buick LeSabre, turns up. Six tough-looking thugs jump out, board two Sikorsky choppers, take off, head north.'

'Reinforcements for the Meteorological Institute,' Tweed suggested.

'No idea. But we know now they have two helicopters on the payroll. I then hang around for hours, moving about so I'm not conspicuous. This evening the Lear jet arrives back. The black limo is waiting for Hauser when he walks rapidly from the jet. For a big man he can move. I notice the retractable staircase you leave the jet by is still in place. I decide to follow Hauser. The limo drives him to a house out of Disneyland. I can locate it for you on a map . . .'

'We know where it is,' Newman told him. 'But now we know where Hauser is. Sorry.'

Butler had a large audience as he made his terse report. Paula, perched on the end of the bed, listened attentively. Newman sat astride a chair, watching him. Marler was leaning against a wall, twiddling a cigarette between his fingers. Nield stood with his arms folded. Tweed also was standing, his eyes fixed on Butler, registering every detail.

'Because of that staircase still left in place, I drive back to the airport. I'm lucky. I arrive just in time to see a woman leaving the jet. The brown Buick is back. She gets into it and I follow it into Helsinki, then – sorry about this – I lose her.'

'Description, please,' requested Tweed.

'Difficult. She's wearing those big tinted goggle glasses, a scarf wrapped round her head. She's slim,

329

medium height. I wondered about that last bit – she walks as though she's wearing elevated heels.'

'So she could be small?' suggested Tweed.

'Could be. By then I reckon I've seen all I'm going to at the airport. So I drive to the railway station.'

My God, Paula thought, he never stops. No wonder they nickname him The Beaver.

'I've left my cap on a counter at the airport,' Butler explained. 'I take off my jacket and hang around that station. I see you, Tweed, get off a train with Dillon. Then I see someone else I recognize from the photograph get off the same train after you two have gone. Manescu. And with him is a tough-looking thickset character with a brutal jaw. Looks Teutonic. Then, Bingo! The brown Buick turns up and they jump inside it. I follow the Buick to a place called Setula near the airport, fairly near anyway. Manescu slips away into an apartment block. The Buick drives off with our Teutonic friend and I've lost him.' He drank mineral water from a glass Paula had put by his side. 'That's it.'

'That is indeed a lot.' Marler whistled with admiration.

'The brown Buick,' Tweed said. 'Who was driving it?'

'Uniformed chauffeur each time. He gets around.'

Tweed sighed audibly. Paula looked at him and saw he was still fresh and alert.

'Why the sigh?'

'The precision of it all,' Tweed commented. 'Hauser is a top-flight organizer. I suppose that's how he got to the top of the world.' He looked at Butler. 'Those six men you saw board the two helicopters. Any idea of nationality?'

'Mittel-European. Slav types. Could be Czechs, Romanians, Bulgars. Who can tell the difference?'

'The vanishing men,' Tweed said half to himself.

'Isn't it about time we planned what we're all going to

do next?' drawled Marler. 'We have to stop waiting sometime.'

'We move when the moment is right,' Tweed told him. 'And I said we needed more data. Today we have accumulated more than I ever dreamed was possible. Newman and Marler with Paula discovered Hauser is transporting huge amounts of high explosives north. Maybe to somewhere near the Institute.'

'Maybe to the Institute itself,' Newman suggested. 'It was Hauser's construction outfit which built the place.'

'Butler,' Tweed continued, 'has provided data about where a number of key people are, that they've come in to Helsinki. Harry, are you sure you saw Manescu get off that train? Was it a positive identification?'

'Positive. He wore a beret and a scarf wrapped round the lower part of his face. In this heat! The scarf slipped for a moment and I saw him full face. I've studied the only photo of Manescu taken you showed me. That is until Marler snapped him leaving INCUBUS's HQ. I studied that pic of him without his moustache. Manescu got off that train, is now at Setula. A half-hour's drive from where I'm sitting.'

'Not good news,' Tweed commented. 'Hauser is assembling his forces.'

'Let's not forget,' Newman intervened, 'one of the main objectives. At least as far as I'm concerned. Who murdered Sandy back in Suffolk? Find the killer, make him talk and we have Hauser over a barrel.'

'I agree. Everything is linked together now. The murder of Sandy, the murder last February of Ed Riverton, and the botched attempt to kill Peggy Vanderheld. On top of the murders we have the explosives. On top of that we've the newspaper reports of three assassinations in Prague, Budapest and Bucharest. And Manescu's presence merges the two original investigations – one into INCUBUS, the other into tracing the whereabouts of the professional villains who escaped from the *Securitate*, etc. INCUBUS almost certainly has been recruiting them.'

'So,' Marler said impatiently, 'it's time I made my recce of that mysterious Institute. And I've found out how I can do just that?'

'How?' demanded Tweed.

'This morning I was up early, went to the Akateeminen Bookshop to buy some maps of Lapland. I overheard a couple of women talking about a tourist excursion tomorrow to the Institute. They leave by coach from the Intercontinental next door. Mostly English, I gathered. They're a few places short. I propose to join that tour. Coach takes the party to the airport mid-morning. Perfect cover.'

'I'll think about it. Let you know in the morning.'

'I'd like to have a positive answer now.'

'In the morning.'

Tweed answered automatically. Watching him, Paula realized his mind was far away. He was on the verge of taking a major decision. Tweed straightened up.

'Everyone had better get some sleep. Tomorrow I may move all of us into the same hotel. I think the time has come to mass our forces. I feel Hauser breathing down my neck. So off you go.'

'What do you mean?' asked Dillon, who had been quiet up to now. 'Breathing down your neck?'

'This sudden influx of some dangerous characters into Helsinki. I think Newman achieved his purpose when he went to see Hauser at his HQ. He disturbed him. Now Paula has rattled Carver, who will undoubtedly report back to his boss. Hauser is preparing something nasty for us. Off to bed . . .'

Paula stayed perched on the bed until she was alone with him. He looked at her, wondering what she had on her mind.

'If Marler goes to the Institute with that tourist party

I'd like to go with him. Don't argue again. A couple, a man and a woman are less noticeable.'

'I'll let you know in the morning. Now, I want to think.'

Left to himself, Tweed paced slowly round his room. It had been a long active day but he still felt fresh. He was sorting out the data, the fresh pieces of the jigsaw which he had found out during the day. Newman was right: a lot hinged on identifying the murderer of Sandy and Ed Riverton. The same man, Tweed was sure.

When he eventually went to bed his thoughts still wouldn't leave him alone. He had a strong instinct he'd taken the decision to marshal his forces too late. Hauser was going to strike savagely.

33

The next morning Irina Serov arrived very early at the Hesperia. She had bleached her hair blonde, wore four-inch high-heeled shoes, had piled her hair up, applied mascara to make her eyes look larger and had light green-tinted glasses perched on the bridge of her Roman nose.

She waited until a male receptionist was free, approached the counter with her prepared story. The receptionist gazed at her with interest. She wore a tight-fitting sleeveless blouse which hugged her figure and a pleated mini-skirt. He had seen her legs as she entered.

'I wondered if you could help me?' In her slim hand she held two banknotes. 'I'm trying to get a job with a Martin Baker who is staying here. But I don't know what he looks like.'

'I do,' the receptionist said quickly. 'He's probably

having breakfast on the first floor. I called his room a few minutes ago and there was no reply.'

'I haven't had breakfast,' she said in a husky voice, staring at him. 'If you could possibly see your way to pointing him out to me . . .'

The receptionist accompanied her up to the first floor. In the elevator she hugged her shoulder bag closer, checked to see the flap was unbuttoned. The receptionist pointed out the guest to her, refused the tip.

'Maybe we could have a drink together?' he suggested. 'I go off duty at six.'

'So I'll be here at six. Thank you so much . . .'

The dining room had long tables which could seat eight of the guests. People sat where there was a place. The dining room was fairly full but the seat next to Martin Baker was vacant. She collected bread and jam from the buffet, stood behind the empty chair.

'Do you mind if I sit here? There aren't many free places.'

Tweed looked up, pulled out the chair for her, she sat down.

As he piled butter and jam on a piece of roll Tweed's mind was elsewhere. He was thinking of General Valentin Rebet who had parted from him in Turku. He suspected the Russian was still in Finland: Rebet had made a point of asking Tweed if he was staying on in Helsinki.

'I'm Sonia Drayton. I arrived last night from Turku.'

Tweed noticed her superb legs. Because she was sitting the skirt had slid further up. With mock modesty she pulled at the hem. She had seen his glance.

'Martin Baker,' he replied. 'What were you doing in Turku?' It was something to say. His mind was still miles away.

'I worked for a corporation called INCUBUS. I left them. They are losing staff. A Peggy Vanderheld left

334

their Helsinki office at about the same time.'

'What kind of a corporation is that? I've heard of them somewhere.'

Tweed drank coffee, had shown no reaction except mild interest. Inwardly he had woken up, focused on where he was, on his attractive breakfast companion. She spoke in a soft appealing voice with a trace of accent.

She seemed to read his mind. 'You may have noticed I have a faint accent. It's Austrian. My father was English, my mother came from Vienna.'

'What made you leave this corporation? INCUBUS, did you say?'

'Yes. It is the world's largest bank. American. Bigger than anything in Japan, which gives some idea of its size. Actually I was sacked. So was Peggy Vanderheld. Now they want me to sign a pensions agreement. A generous one. I can't make up my mind whether to do that.'

'Why not?'

'You look like a businessman. I need someone neutral I can talk it over with. Is there somewhere quiet we could talk after breakfast?'

Marler had risen early at The Palace, had eaten breakfast, returned to his room. Now, while Paula watched, he held his Finnish hunting knife by the tip of the blade. On the far side of the room he'd placed a block of wood on the carpet. He had picked up the block from the grass verge the previous day when Newman was using the isolated phone box to call Mauno Sarin. He threw the knife from shoulder height. The tip hammered into a small circle he had drawn with a pen on the block.

'Bull's-eye!' called out Paula. 'Where did you learn to throw a knife?'

'In Arizona. A member of an Indian tribe taught me. They use knives to carve wooden sculptures for tourists.'

He retrieved the knife as Paula unlocked the door in response to a rapping tattoo. Newman walked in. He wore a peaked check cap and tinted glasses. Paula relocked the door as Marler retrieved the knife, slid it inside the sheath strapped to his leg, hid the block of wood inside a wardrobe.

'When do we leave to join the party at the Intercontinental?' he asked.

Earlier Paula had arrived with a message Tweed had preferred not to pass over the phone. He had agreed they should explore the Institute. His condition was that Paula could only go if Newman as well as Marler travelled with her.

'We take a cab to the Intercontinental now,' Marler said. 'Are you carrying that Smith & Wesson?'

'Nice to know it doesn't show.'

'And I got my Browning back from Nield,' said Paula. 'I have it in my shoulder bag. You're expecting fireworks?'

'With INCUBUS you never know. And they'll have trouble recognizing you.'

Paula had taken a leaf out of Irina Serov's book after listening to Butler's description of her. She wore a scarf round her head concealing her raven black hair and a pair of tinted glasses. Everyone was wearing them to shield their eyes against the glare of the sun. Marler had insisted they both disguise themselves, pointing out that he was the only one present INCUBUS had no idea existed. He checked his watch.

'Let's get moving . . .'

With the other tourists, mostly middle-aged English with a few young Finns, an hour and a half later they were airborne aboard scheduled Finnair Flight AY 424 which took off at 12.05 p.m. Newman and Paula sat alongside each other while Marler sat behind them in the window seat.

It was a smooth flight over a vast flat landscape with fir forests and ice-blue lakes scattered about like some crazy jigsaw puzzle. They had one stopover at Oulu near the coast of the Gulf of Bothnia then flew on to Rovaniemi.

Landing at the small airfield amid a wilderness of scrub and rocks they appeared to be miles from the town. It was at this remote airfield after a fifty-minute flight that the tourist party was transferred to a Fokker Friendship aircraft, a smaller machine powered by props.

After the aircraft had taken off, heading east, the courier, a lint-haired Finnish girl dressed in a smart grey suit, took over. 'Call me Irene,' she said in English as she walked down the central aisle. 'We are now flying towards the Soviet border over Lapland . . .'

Paula peered down out of the window, checked her map. They were flying over Route 80 which led to Kemijärvi, the town where the Porvoo fisherman had seen an INCUBUS refrigerated truck driving on east towards the border. She glanced behind and Marler appeared to be asleep. His half-closed eyes missed nothing below as he tilted his head sideways.

Paula looked down a little later, saw a large lake with wispy forest clinging to its granite sides plunging into the still water. The courier was talking.

'We are now passing Kemijärvi to the north. As you will realize the plane is descending. An airstrip has been constructed by INCUBUS Inc., the large philanthropic corporation which was largely instrumental in creating the Institute you are visiting . . .'

Marler glanced round. All the passengers looked pukka. He slipped a small Voigtlander camera out of his pocket as the plane glided down. A complex of modern buildings built of concrete spread out below. In the centre was a tall circular building which reminded him of the INCUBUS HQ in Helsinki. He took several shots

337

while the courier's back was turned. She swung round, came up to him.

'Excuse me, sir. Are you taking pictures? That is forbidden by INCUBUS. It is only by courtesy of the corporation that we are permitted to use the airstrip.'

Marler grinned. 'No pics. I've forgotten to insert the film.' He slipped the camera into his pocket.

'That's all right then, sir. It is the regulation . . .'

The machine dipped as a concrete runway came up to meet it. Newman glanced at Paula. He had an awful premonition he should not have allowed her to come.

Irina had been invited up to his room at the Hesperia by Tweed. He had checked the lobby, found it was crowded with a party of French tourists. As they stepped out of the elevator he clapped a hand to his forehead.

'Miss Drayton . . .'

'Sonia, please.'

'Sonia, do you mind sitting on that couch for a moment? They said there was a message for me at reception before I went to breakfast. I'll be back in a minute . . .'

Irina sat on the couch in the large corridor, relieved to be on her own for a short time. She had received a body-blow shock. While serving with the Soviet Embassy in London six years before, General Lysenko of the GRU had come briefly on a secret visit. From a window in a safe house near Regent's Park he had suddenly called out to her to join him. He had pointed down into the street. 'That man running to that waiting taxi. You see him clearly? Good. Remember that face. He is Tweed, Deputy Director of the SIS . . .'

That had been in the last days of the Cold War – when Lysenko was Tweed's chief adversary. And Irina had just been promoted to the rank of colonel in the KGB. Now, only half an hour ago she had sat down next to Martin Baker, and only when he turned to face her had she recognized him as Tweed.

Irina was thinking fast. She had discovered the identity of the top man behind the opposition to INCUBUS. A much more dangerous man than she – or Hauser – had ever anticipated. Extreme measures were called for.

The elevator doors opened and Tweed emerged, smiling. He led the way to his large room, unlocked the door, ushered her inside and to a chair facing the window. He sat in a separate chair, his back to the strong light.

'Now, what did you want to talk to me about? I can give you half an hour. I have an important business appointment then, I'm afraid,' he said affably.

'The document I have to sign to obtain this generous pension contains certain conditions. For life. If I break the conditions clauses I forfeit the pension.'

'What are these conditions?'

'That I never tell anyone about my work – or anything I learned while in INCUBUS's employ.'

'Could be a precaution against industrial espionage,' he suggested, gazing at the wall.

'But some of the things I had to do were awful.' She hesitated. 'I had to seduce certain businessmen INCU-BUS wished to influence. It was blackmail. That is a crime.'

'It most certainly is,' Tweed agreed.

'And yet the pension is very generous. And I can take any other job I wish to without forfeiting the rights.'

'Why did you come to Helsinki from Turku?' he asked suddenly, watching her.

'To be interviewed for a job with an entirely different type of firm. I go to see them later today.'

'Have you evidence of these criminal activities?'

She hesitated again. 'Yes. Photocopies of certain letters which incriminate INCUBUS. I left them where I'm

339

staying. I could bring them to you tonight at six o'clock. If that would be convenient.' She smiled and looked innocent and pathetic. 'I'm sorry to bother you, but you seem so kind.'

'Then I'd better see these photocopies before I can advise you what to do.'

'Thank you. I wonder if I could use your bathroom?'

'Of course. Through that door . . .'

As he walked to the window he heard her lock the door. Inside she looked swiftly round. A full bottle of indigestion mixture unopened on the glass shelf above the basin. Next to it a glass contained a tube of toothpaste tilted at an angle. The toothbrush was in another glass.

Tweed had struck her as a man meticulous about personal hygiene. So far he had not cleaned his teeth after his breakfast. Opening her capacious shoulder bag, she took out a small oxygen mask with a five-minute duration. She placed it over her face, slipped the strap over the back of her head to hold it.

Next she took out from a special pocket a small cylinder with a screw top. Inside was a hypodermic containing potassium cyanide in solution. INCUBUS seemed to be able to supply anything; she had no idea the device had been produced in a laboratory outside Boston.

Through the goggles she saw her sinister image in the mirror over the basin. She studied the angle of the tube of toothpaste tilted in the glass, lifted it out, unscrewed the top, placed it on the edge of the basin. Unscrewing the top of the cyanide container, she extracted the hypodermic, inserted the slim needle inside the toothpaste tube, pressed the plunger. Withdrawing the needle, she quickly screwed on the cap of the toothpaste tube tight and placed it back inside the glass at the same angle.

Carefully she slid the hypodermic back inside its protective tube, screwed the top on, slipped it back inside her shoulder bag. She went quickly to the window, opened it silently and wide, still wearing the mask. Despite handling the cyanide so carefully she had been warned of fumes being released.

She left the window open while she flushed the lavatory. Turning on the cold tap, she washed her hands, leaving the tap running while she dried her hands. She removed the mask standing near the open window, tucked it away inside the shoulder bag, closed and buttoned up the flap. Only then did she close the window quietly, turn off the tap, unlock the door and walk out.

'See you tonight then at six,' Tweed said, standing by the window. 'Good luck with your job interview. What firm is it?'

'Akateeminen Bookstore,' she said swiftly.

'On the selling side?' he asked, walking forward to open the door.

'No. Admin. For one of the directors. Thank you so much for your time . . .'

Tweed closed the door, stood for a moment. He could taste the remnants of his breakfast. He hadn't cleaned his teeth. He walked into the bathroom.

He stood quite still, looking round, his eyes slowly checking everything. Nothing seemed to have been moved, tampered with. He frowned, puzzled. He made a quick search to see if anything had been left behind. Nothing. He turned on the cold tap, picked up the tube of toothpaste to unscrew the cap.

Harry Butler sat at the wheel of the BMW Newman had driven to the Hesperia while Marler and Paula had taken a taxi to the Intercontinental Hotel next door. Tweed's instructions given on the phone to his room during the few minutes he had absented himself from Sonia Drayton had been explicit.

'A woman in her thirties will leave the hotel in half an

hour or so. Bleached blonde hair, shoulder length, wearing a tight-fitting pale green sleeveless blouse, a cream pleated mini-skirt. Good figure. Oh, her hair is piled on top of her head at the moment. She might drop it before she leaves. She may or may not wear green-tinted glasses. Clear, Harry?'

'There can only be one like that. Height? Weight?'

'Medium height at first glance, but she has four-inch heels. Slim build. Follow her. Don't lose her. Need to know where she goes. Leave it to you . . .'

Butler removed his jacket. It was early yet but the heat was building up. It was going to be another hot day. He watched gaggles of tourists crawling out of the hotel exit. Some stopped to talk, appeared to argue. Shall we go on that long trip in heat like this?

His target walked out ten minutes after Tweed had called him from the phone in the lobby. She walked with a confident strut which just stopped short of a call girl's posture. She's pleased with herself about something, Butler said to himself.

She climbed into the next taxi to disgorge more guests with luggage. Butler switched on his engine, watched the cab head along the Mannerheimintie away from the city. As he drove Butler tried to put his finger on what it was about the girl he found familiar. No good. Forget it – and it would come back to him.

Two things gave him her identity. The apartment block near the end of tramline No. 4 where she was dropped at. And the strut had gone. Nothing marks a person more than their movements. This was the girl who'd left the jet the previous day, Hauser's jet.

Tweed turned the screw cap on his toothpaste tube. The first turn. He paused, frowned. He recalled that when Sonia Drayton had used his bathroom he had heard the tap running until a moment before she emerged. And yet she had dry hands. More sinister, Tweed never screwed the cap of his toothpaste tube tight. It had a tendency to stick so he always left it a trifle loose. Now the cap had been screwed down tight. And the glass holding the tube was slightly moved, exposing the circular mark it had imprinted on the shelf.

He screwed the cap on tight, placed the tube carefully back inside the glass. He looked at the full bottle of indigestion mixture. It did not appeared to have been tampered with. He left the bathroom.

Picking up the phone he dialled Mauno Sarin's private number. The Finn answered immediately.

'You'll recognize my voice, I expect,' Tweed began.

'Yes? A problem.'

'Could your forensic people check certain items from my bathroom? I suspect either poison or explosive – I suggest the items are handled with care.'

'Karma, since you know him, will be on his way over as soon as this call is completed.'

'Tell him to ask for Martin Baker. I'll wait in until he arrives . . .'

34

The Meteorological Institute complex loomed over the airstrip. The tourists disembarked via a mobile staircase. Paula, Newman and Marler lingered behind the crocodile and formed its tail. Irene, the courier, explained in a lecturer's tone as they filed past her towards the entrance:

'I'll have to describe what is going on in most of the

different departments. Nearly all the staff are on holiday.'

'But not all of them,' whispered to Newman. 'Look up at the roof.'

'I saw. I saw him.'

A man standing on the flat roof of the five-storey building was peering over a wall, examining the tourists with a pair of binoculars. As they entered the building each tourist was handed a pass with a clip to attach it to themselves by a sour-faced male receptionist.

'We are going to see the Planetarium first,' Irene called out. 'Not a correct name really. It shows various satellites orbiting above the Arctic Circle. . . .'

They walked into a vast chamber which was almost dark and had a huge domed roof. The courier switched on the tape recorder which began to identify the satellites in English, German and French. The tourists stood huddled together, staring up as their eyes became accustomed to the gloom.

'Satellite Astra is now appearing,' intoned the echoing voice.

An object like a spiked football appeared, was tracked by a spotlight as it moved slowly in an arc just above the rim of the dome. Marler left the group, began wandering round the chamber, looking up frequently as though seeking a better view. He came to a heavy steel door with a handle inset into the circular wall. He tested the handle. It refused to budge.

As the voice droned on he was joined by Newman and Paula as they strolled round the perimeter of the chamber. It was surprisingly cool and Paula guessed it was air conditioned. Hauser had spent a fortune on this showbiz monstrosity. Standing with his back to the wall, Marler tried the handle of a second door. Locked tight. He strolled further round the chamber. Everyone else, including the courier, was staring upwards as the constellations began to twinkle in the roof of the dome. Followed by Paula and Newman, Marler strolled a few yards further. Again he stopped, his back to an inset plate of metal, wide, stretching above head height with a razor-thin split in the centre. No handle. Only a slot waist high. For a computer card. He slipped his credit card from his wallet, inserted it inside the slot, began to fiddle it at various angles. Sometimes it worked.

Paula checked the group of tourists. All heads craned upwards as another satellite came into view. The recorded voice droned on. The tourists were becoming hypnotized by the unending spectacle way above their heads. There were forty of them. With a bit of luck no one would miss three people if they could find some way to explore other parts of the complex. She heard a faint whirring noise, the movement of well-oiled machinery.

'You've opened it,' whispered Newman. 'Let's risk it. Quick.' He turned to Paula. 'You wait here . . .'

Marler stepped inside the large cage-like elevator which had appeared behind the open doors. Newman slipped inside, Paula followed. Marler's eyes whipped down the control panel. Level Four was at the bottom. He pressed the button. The doors slid closed. The elevator began to descend.

Marler looked up, checked the ceiling, the walls of the elevator for spy cameras. Nothing. The elevator continued its descent. Paula slipped her hand inside her shoulder bag, gripped her Browning automatic. Newman withdrew his Smith & Wesson from its holster, held the gun by his side. The elevator stopped, the doors opened.

Marler peered out. He was gazing along a curving corridor, the walls of grey metal, the floor coated with ribbed rubber, which would muffle their footfalls. Which way? To the left or right?

To his left he saw the corridor appeared to end with a windowless door. In the other direction it disappeared round a curve. To the right, he decided. He motioned his companions to stay inside the elevator a moment longer. Stepping into the corridor he saw there was a control panel in the corridor's wall. He beckoned for them to come out. When they all stood in the corridor he pressed the button for Level One. The doors closed and the elevator began its return journey to the so-called Planetarium.

'Then if someone comes along they won't wonder why the elevator is down here,' he whispered to Newman.

'Agreed. Don't let's hang about.'

Marler began walking down the wide corridor slowly, looking everywhere. He looked up, stopped, moved close to the wall and gestured to Newman and Paula to do the same. He pressed himself against the wall, waited for them to reach him. He pointed upwards further down the corridor.

'Surveillance camera. The lens hasn't a wide enough angle to take in the whole width of the corridor.'

Newman knew Marler was an expert on surveillance equipment. They moved forward. Paula slithered forward along the surface of the wall, couldn't take her eyes off the lens which looked like a gun. When she had passed it she glanced at the wall. Dust free. The eerie nerve-wracking silence was broken only by a faint humming sound. Air was being extracted from the corridor; fresh air was being fed in. A noise which reminded her of a visit to Sizewell nuclear power station in Suffolk, south of Walberswick. Which in return reminded her of Newman's description of the horrific murder of Sandy. Could there be any connection between that atrocity and this weird complex in Finland?

Marler stopped again and his companions froze. He was staring at the wall a few feet ahead of where he stood. Newman moved close to him. Marler turned round, gesturing as he whispered.

346

'Electronic beam across the corridor. Waist high. Break that and a flaming alarm system is activated. We have to crawl under it.'

Dropping to his knees, he edged his way forward, keeping his back low. Newman followed, standing up again beside Marler. Paula took a deep breath, shortened the strap of her shoulder bag, slung it against her chest. Crawling forward she watched the innocuous-looking glass button embedded in the wall. It reminded her of an evil eye. She forced her body lower, reached the two men, stood up, gasping with tension.

'We'll have to watch our step for those things from now on,' Marler warned.

The corridor continued its endless curve. Marler guessed they were moving round the perimeter of the tall circular building he had seen from the air as the Fokker came in to land. At widely spaced intervals there were closed doors in the opposite wall, windowless doors. He hoped to God no one would walk out from one of them.

Bringing up the rear, Paula was beginning to suffer from claustrophobia. Level Four. They were buried deep inside the Arctic earth. Entombed. She had a sudden overwhelming urge to scream. She put a hand over her mouth, swallowed rapidly several times. Marler stopped again, held up his hand. What the hell was it now? she wondered.

'Devilish clever security system,' Marler whispered calmly. 'Another electronic beam – at ankle height.'

He pointed downwards. He glanced over his shoulder, grinned at Paula when he saw her face. Gave her a mock salute.

'Watch me,' he warned.

He walked forward, then raised one leg high, like a soldier goose-stepping. He moved his other leg in the same way, stood looking back. Newman imitated his movements. Paula looked down, saw another of those

347

evil glass eyes inches above floor level. Her legs aching with tension, she lifted them over, one by one. Marler clapped a hand on her arm, gripped it.

'Good girl. Keep it up. Not much longer now.'

He walked forward again, sliding along the wall as he spotted another surveillance camera positioned above the centre of the corridor. Paula slithered along the wall with her arms. Her hands were moist. Frequently she glanced back. She had lengthened the strap of her shoulder bag. Wiping her right hand on her backside, she slipped it inside the bag, gripped the Browning. Newman paused, looked back at her.

'I presume you're keeping a sharp lookout behind you?'

'For Christ's sake!' she blazed in a low hiss. 'I've been checking every ten seconds.'

'OK.'

Paula was surprised. Normally she would have expected it would be Newman who realized she was petrified. But it had been Marler who had understood. Then she remembered Sandy. Newman's mind had become one-track. Could she blame him for that?

For Paula their journey round the corridor was becoming a nightmare. She had a vision of their walking round it forever. With no way out. Then she grasped what was disorientating her. The continuous movement in a vast circle, the horrific thought that they would find themselves arriving some day at the elevator which had brought them down into this hell.

She frowned. The flat surface of the corridor was no longer moving on the level, it was climbing, climbing like one of those inclined walks at London's Heathrow Airport on the way to the final departure lounge. The incline increased. They negotiated yet another waist-high beam by crawling under it. The upward slant of the corridor continued.

Marler paused, again held up his hand. Another beam? No. Now he was pointing ahead. The corridor ended. Two doors, closed and with safety bars, masked what lay beyond. Marler bent down, dropped to his knees. Paula was puzzled. He was staring at something on the rubberized floor under one of the overhead fluorescent lights embedded in the curved ceiling. And that's another thing that's driving me crazy, Paula thought. Everything curved. No straight surfaces.

Marler reached out a tentative hand, scraped his fingers over a darkish patch, sniffed at it. He stood up, walked back to Newman who stood back to the wall, revolver by his side. Marler showed Newman the fingers of his right hand.

'Wheel marks. A large vehicle. A smell of petrol. They bring trucks into this corridor. A wide gauge tyre.' He looked up. 'A very large truck could pass under the roof, could edge its way down the corridor – it's wide enough. I kept wondering why they needed all this space.'

'Then let's see what's beyond those doors.'

'If we can open them . . .'

Oh, God, no! Paula thought and clenched her teeth.

Newman gripped the Smith & Wesson in both hands as Marler gently eased up the safety bar of the right-hand door. He pushed at the heavy weight slowly. The gap widened. Newman, with Paula peering over his shoulder, gazed through the gap.

'It's the biggest garage in the world,' Newman commented, keeping his voice low.

They were looking into an immense underground garage with squat support pillars running away into the distance, row upon row. Parked on the concrete was a huge assembly of INCUBUS trucks, like an endless series of convoys preparing for an invasion. The INCUBUS Oy.

349

logo stood out clear under the powerful overhead fluorescents. A large number of trucks in two separate rows had strange lettering on their sides.

'What's written on those trucks?' Paula hissed.

'It's Cyrillic,' said Marler. 'Russian.' He understood the language. 'The words say State Transport.'

'What's going on here?' Newman wondered.

Marler had his head poked through the gap, his head tilted to one side. He listened for several minutes, put a finger to his lips so no one would talk.

'I don't think there's anyone about,' he said eventually. 'Let's explore, see what they're up to . . .'

For Paula it was an enormous relief to emerge from the confines of that horror movie corridor into the spacious cavern. No windows to the outside world: they were still below ground. A long way below. Maybe still at Level Four.

She followed Newman and Marler, holding on to her Browning. The two men kept to the left-hand wall of the garage, walking down a passage between the garage wall and a long line of trucks. There was a smell now of oil mixed with petrol. The lack of anyone else about was uncanny, but still Paula welcomed the space.

Half-way down the garage Marler paused. He pointed to the huge grille doors of a giant elevator large enough to take one of the trucks. All of the vehicles were refrigerated, Paula observed.

Newman tapped Marler on the shoulder, then moved sideways between two trucks across to the first row with the trucks carrying Russian lettering on their sides. He had spotted one truck with the rear doors open. Marler shrugged, moved off further down the garage past one of the squat pillars. Paula followed Newman.

He approached the truck cautiously, peered into the back. Empty of any guards. He crept along its side to look inside the cab. Empty. He walked back to Paula who had stayed at the rear.

'Let's take a look inside,' he said. 'See what merchandise we have this time.'

Paula jumped aboard and Newman followed. Both rear doors were wide open and there was plenty of light. She lifted the hasp of a long metal container, raised the lid, gazed inside. Taking a spare scarf from her shoulder bag, she emulated Marler's earlier treatment of the same grey and dough-like substance. Scooping up large handfuls of the material which reminded her of plasticine, she wrapped a considerable quantity inside her scarf, put the scarf back inside her bag.

'What are you up to?' Newman asked.

He had moved over to look inside the container after opening a larger box. He almost laughed when he saw what she had discovered, although there was nothing amusing about the substance.

'More Semtex,' he commented. 'God! They must have obtained it by the ton.'

'Evidence,' Paula said, taking out a large handkerchief.

She scooped up a much smaller amount and wrapped it inside her handkerchief. Then she stuffed this into the shoulder bag. She straightened up, caught his wry smile.

'What's so funny?'

'Come and look – and remember that truck north of Porvoo. You've taken Marler's place. A repeat performance for me.'

She stared down into the large box he had opened. Now she could recognize some of the deadly toys so-called civilized man produced. The sticks were neatly stacked in rows.

'Gelignite,' said Newman. 'Let's get out of here . . .'

The guard appeared from nowhere as they jumped from the truck. A lean bony faced man with high cheekbones who might have been Manescu. Except he wasn't. Another of the Romanian *Securitate* who had disappeared from Bucharest, Newman thought grimly. His Smith &

Wesson was inside the shoulder holster. The guard held a Colt .445, gripped in both hands, aimed point blank at them. The end of the muzzle looked like the mouth of a cannon. Newman knew that with one bullet the weapon could carve a great hole out of its target, hurl the victim back like a hammerblow. The Romanian spoke in broken English.

'Raise hands high. Sit on truck. Drop to ground.'

Paula and Newman did exactly what they had been told. The guard was standing about twelve feet away from them, too far away for Newman to risk a grab for the weapon. Paula cursed inwardly that the Browning was nestling inside her shoulder bag. They straightened up, raised their hands again. It was horribly silent in the huge cavern.

'Now you walk slowly to wall,' the gun muzzle waved towards the inner wall of the garage, 'and you face the wall.'

Paula walked slowly close to Newman. His proximity was a source of comfort to her. They were going to die – she had no doubt of that. The guard spoke again as they stood facing the rough concrete.

'The man faces me . . . slowly. The girl faces wall.'

Newman turned slowly through a hundred and eighty degrees. The guard braced himself, feet wider apart, took a firmer grip on the Colt with both hands. He squinted along the sight, the muzzle aimed at the centre of Newman's chest. He grinned, showing bad teeth.

'After shooting you I make love to the girl before I shoot her. Do not move!'

Newman had stiffened at the hideous threat. Something shiny, catching the overhead lights, flashing through the air, plunged into the guard's back. Marler had appeared from behind a pillar. The guard grunted, had a look of sheer disbelief. He dropped the Colt and half-turned round, staggering. Newman saw the knife protruding from his back, inches of the blade penetrating the target. The guard's hand flopped by his side. He swayed for a moment, then toppled backwards, hit the concrete floor with a heavy thud, driving the knife deep into his body. He lay still as Marler ran forward lightly on his feet.

Paula, sweat streaming down her back, turned round. Marler was bending over the guard. He checked the neck pulse, glanced up, his tone offhand.

'Dead as doornail. Newman, get me one of those cloths out of the truck. Thanks. Paula, you'd better not watch this.'

She was wiping her moist hands, mainly to conceal the fact that they were trembling. She gripped them tightly together. She forced herself to watch: if she couldn't stand this she wasn't up to her job.

Marler stood up, crouched down again, wrapped the cloth round the section of the blade still exposed. He took a deep breath, heaved with all his strength at the handle. It was hard work: withdrawing a knife from a body. The blade emerged slowly, Covered with blood, then jerked free. Standing up. Marler used the cloth to clean the blade, walked to the truck, shoved the soiled cloth beneath other cloths, pulled up his trouser leg, slipped the knife back inside the sheath. He brushed concrete dust off his trouser leg where it had brushed against the pillar he had concealed himself behind. His manner suggested it was all in a day's work.

'Let's get out of this place,' he said briskly. 'That truck elevator is our best bet. Must lead to the outside world.' He looked at Newman. 'First give me a hand with this scum.'

Between them they half dragged, half lifted the guard. Carrying him to the truck Newman and Paula had explored, they shoved the corpse well under the chassis. Marler brushed off his hands, straightened his jacket,

353

then stood quite still. The huge elevator was moving up, out of sight.

'Someone coming down,' Marler commented. 'We'd better get ready to prepare a reception committee . . .'

Paula, standing in front of the elevator shaft, about six feet back, had insisted on acting as bait. Vehemently she had pointed out that whoever was coming down would be thrown off balance to see a woman waiting. Reluctantly, Newman agreed.

The tension again rose as there was a loaded pause. The elevator was stationary at some upper level. For Paula it seemed hours before anything happened. She stood with her hand holding the Browning inside her shoulder bag.

The whirring noise began again. It seemed an age as it slowly descended. Paula guessed it had climbed to the top level. The outside world, she hoped. Expecting to see a large truck she was startled when the elevator appeared, came to rest. Beyond the grille gates stood a short thin-faced man wearing denims and a jacket. He reacted swiftly. A gun seemed to jump into his hand. A Mauser aimed at her stomach. He used his free left hand to open the gates, stepped out, rapping out the command in English.

'Take your hand from that bag slowly. If it is not empty you lose your belly.'

She carefully withdrew her hand, releasing her grip on the Browning. His face had the same racial appearance as the guard Marler had eliminated. High and prominent cheekbones. He took another step closer to her.

The muzzle of Newman's Smith & Wesson hammered down with great force on the side of his head, with such force the barrel bounced off the split skull. He sagged forward and Paula jumped sideways as he sprawled on the concrete. Newman checked his pulse, shook his head at Marler.

354

They dragged the body under another nearby truck after Marler had extracted spare magazines for the weapon from the guard's jacket pocket. He then picked up the Mauser, checked the gun, shoved it inside his belt behind his jacket.

'Now for the nasty part,' Newman remarked. 'Going up in that elevator and seeing what's waiting for us at the top.'

Paula glanced at him with curiosity. At one time he would have been upset by the grim episodes they had just experienced. They had all noticed a change in his character since his traumatic secret journey into East Germany in the days of the Cold War. His reaction had become *Now for the nasty part.*

Inside the elevator Marler briefly studied the control panel. From the top downwards there were three buttons and then a key at the bottom.

'Intriguing,' he said. 'Buttons for Levels One, Two, Three. A key to operate the elevator down to Level Four. I think I'll take that when we reach the top. No point in leaving behind evidence that someone went down to the garage – and it might come in useful later.'

He pressed the button for Level One. As the elevator began its ponderous climb Paula experienced tension again. What new danger might be waiting for them at Level One? She forced herself to ask the question which had puzzled her.

'How on earth do those monster trucks reach Level Four?'

'Found the exit,' Marler replied, staring at the grille gate. 'I reached the end of the garage. There's a huge tunnel curving out of sight. The floor climbed steeply. Solid doors at these levels.'

Beyond the grille they could see, as they passed each level, solid steel doors. The place was like a fortress. The elevator slowed even more, stopped at Level One. An

355

agonizing pause for Paula. Then the doors slid back with the grille. Marler's right hand was inside his jacket, gripping the Mauser. Newman had slipped the Smith & Wesson out of its holster, thrusting the gun inside his belt under his jacket. Paula blinked as the harsh glare of Arctic sunlight hit her. They had arrived at ground level.

Beyond the elevator was a concrete-floored compound with a massive building on the other side. No windows. Like a vast blockhouse. Marler peered out, looking both ways. He beckoned them to follow after pocketing the key for Level Four. Marler had lost all sense of direction: they could go either way. He pointed to a cavernous opening in the blockhouse.

'See that opening? That's where the trucks drive out and in to reach Level Four.'

'I thought they couldn't just use the elevator,' Paula said. 'It would take forever to send down the number of vehicles down there. So why do they need the elevator when they have the tunnel?'

'My guess,' suggested Newman, 'would be an emergency exit and entrance in case a truck with explosive blows up in the tunnel and blocks it. Mr Hauser is nothing if not efficient. And we move to the right. This curved wall is the outside of the same building where we walked forever along that corridor. With luck we may arrive back at the airstrip one day.'

'Good thinking,' commented Marler.

At his urging they kept close to the wall: Marler had remembered the guards on the roof they had seen disembarking from the aircraft. At intervals there were porthole windows at shoulder height. Marler ducked to creep beneath them and his two companions followed his example. Compared with the cool interior it was like an inferno in the open air. The sun beat down on them mercilessly. They passed a long narrow alleyway carved out of the building: inside were huge metal waste bins.

They had moved a few yards further on when Marler held up his arm.

'Someone's coming. A lot of people. Back to that alley. Fast!'

Paula ran back with Newman at her heels, dived inside the alley. She ran deep inside the narrow space, hid herself behind one of the bins. Newman and Marler concealed themselves behind bins closer to the entrance. Marler watched the end of the alley from behind his bin.

A team of guards appeared – all of these in uniform – strolled past the end of the alley. Not one glanced into the alley. Bloody woodentops, thought Marler, and thank God for that. When the last man had passed he crept to the exit, followed them part way round the wall. He returned quickly to the alley.

'All clear. There were twenty of them. Heavy security on this complex. They all had holstered handguns. Curious for a so-called Meteorological Institute. They went into the vehicle elevator. Chap in front was holding a key.'

'They were heading down for Level Four then,' said Newman. 'We were lucky. They must all go to lunch together, leaving behind just a couple of men.'

'And they'll wonder where they are. They'll look for the two missing men,' Paula interjected. 'Do you think we'll get out of this place alive?'

'Let's keep moving,' Newman told her.

They were following the curving wall when they started to pass the first door they had come to. It opened suddenly. Marler reached for the Mauser. A large woman wearing a wide-brimmed straw hat and a wild orange dress which enveloped her like a tent walked out. Of uncertain age, she beamed at Marler, who recognized her as one of the tourists.

'I'm Mrs Fairweather,' she gushed. 'An appropriate name for this climate, don't you think? You've got fed up with the endless walking too, I expect. And those awful tape-recorded voices blaring at you non-stop. It's all simply too much. I told Irene I must get some fresh air. She tried to make me stay but I insisted. George, my husband, says that when I insist the world had better take notice.'

'I'm sure he's right, dear lady,' Marler agreed, smiling.

'I expect you know we continue following this wall to the right. Irene told me three times as though I was some kind of village idiot. *To the right!* Like someone blaring at you through a megaphone. You're sure you want to leave now, she kept asking. She showed me the passage leading to that door. Once you're outside you can't get back, she went on at me. The door automatically locks so you can't change your mind . . .'

They followed the wall as Mrs Fairweather gushed on and Marler smiled agreeably. He had shoved the Mauser back out of sight just in time. Behind them Newman and Paula kept silent. Mrs Fairweather talked enough for four people.

'Of course,' she gushed on, 'the Planetarium was interesting. I expect you were as surprised as I was when Mr Talking Machine revealed the satellites were weather satellites near the end. We'd all thought they were Soviet spies in orbit. The others are getting fed up and want to come back. We spent too long in the Geological Research Department. That was when it got boring. A crashing bore. And no refreshment. Irene said there would be refreshments on the flight back to Rovaniemi. Oh, look, there is our plane . . .'

The airstrip had appeared. The mobile staircase was still in place. Marler followed Mrs Fairweather up the steps, sat down beside her. He could think of no more excellent cover.

Paula checked her watch as she settled in a window seat with Newman two rows behind Marler. She checked her watch again. Newman knew what she was worrying about. Sooner or later the twenty-man strong team of guards would find their dead comrades. That was when the plane would be stopped from taking off.

Five minutes later the crocodile of tourists appeared, marching determinedly to the plane, hurrying aboard to take their seats. Irene looked depressed. Mrs Fairweather whispered in a voice which half the aircraft could hear.

'You see! I started the revolt. I knew they were all as fed up as I was.'

'You're a tonic,' Marler lied cheerfully.

Paula stared out of the window at the entrance to the complex. She felt certain guards would appear at the last moment. The mobile staircase was moved away, the pilot started his engines, the props began spinning. Paula was still watching the entrance. She stiffened. Three uniformed figures were running towards the plane, windmilling their arms, mouths open as though shouting some orders.

'Whatever they want it is too late. We are *leaving*!' Irene shouted.

Paula heard the slam of the passenger door. The Fokker moved forward, gathered speed down the runway, took off into a cloudless sky. Within thirty seconds the Institute was a toy complex far below as the machine headed back for Rovaniemi.

'You know, Mrs Fairweather,' drawled Marler, 'I'm most grateful you cut short the tour. It was boring. It was *dead* boring.'

35

'You are saying there has been an intrusion at the Institute, Frank?'

Hauser's voice was dangerously calm. He sat behind his desk in the turret tower of his strange home which he used when he was working out his next strategic manoeuvre. Beyond the French windows perched a balcony with an elaborately decorated grille railing. Galvone was striding backwards and forwards nervously, hands in his trouser pockets.

'News just came through over the phone,' he reported. 'Two guards were killed in the garage at Level Four . . .'

'Go on,' Hauser said in an ominous tone. 'Don't feed me it piece by piece.'

'A quantity of Semtex has disappeared from one container aboard a truck. They think the intruders joined a tourist party visiting the Institute.'

'And you had just been up there to double the security. Or so you told me. What went wrong? Do I have to lean on you?'

'Listen, Chief.' Galvone spread his hands in a pleading gesture. 'I left orders all guard teams were to take meals in shifts, to leave half a team on duty. The garage team had lunch together, presumably so they could talk to each other, play cards. They left only the two men behind – the men who were killed. Strictly against my instructions.'

'If you say so, Frank. Stop walking about. Park the butt, for Chrissakes, while I think.'

Hauser lit a cigarette. He was seated in his shirt sleeves:

at six in the evening the heat was ferocious but Hauser had learned to live with extremes of climate. He was thinking about Irina Serov. She had shaken him in the morning when she'd told him that a man called Tweed, Deputy Director of the Brits' Secret Service, was staying at the Hesperia. He had located the mastermind – who by now should be dead. Hauser wasn't sure Irina had done the right thing. How would the British Prime Minister react to the news?

He had another anxiety. Including the raid on the truck north of Porvoo, two lots of explosive had disappeared. Hauser had no doubt now it was the same opposition who'd grabbed more explosives from the Institute. Evidence – which maybe they'd show to the Finnish Government. Most men faced with the situation would retreat. That wasn't Hauser's way. Under pressure you attacked.

'Frank, we're in a crisis situation. Operation Urals has already started. Look . . .'

He pushed a copy of the *Herald Tribune* across the desk and waited while Galvone read it. It was a major headline.

TRANS-SIBERIAN RAILWAY SABOTAGED.
EXPLOSION BLOWS TRAIN.

Galvone read the text. Over a hundred people were feared dead. 'Extremists and Terrorists' were blamed by the Soviet authorities. As Galvone read on Hauser stared out of the window. Irina Serov would never make such a mistake. She'd have arranged detonation after the train had passed. The sooner he sent her back inside Russia to take charge the better. The first consignment of explosives had been smuggled over the border too early.

'What do we do now?' Galvone asked.

'We go ahead with Operation Urals. This time under the guidance of someone who knows what they're doing. What happened at the Institute today means we must transport all the explosives across the frontier into Russia fast.

You're in charge. And you're going to be busy, Frank.'

'That's OK, Chief. What else?'

Galvone was relieved Hauser had switched away from the fiasco at the Institute, didn't want him to return to the subject.

'A contingency plan to move our centre of operations out of Helsinki to the HQ in Stockholm. At twelve hours' notice. All the secret files, the key staff. I'm trying to calm down the Finnish government by offering them three million dollars to build a super icebreaker. But they're so goddamn sensitive about their neutrality they may not play along. The main thrust now is to get Operation Urals moving. A woman will be in charge of the team, a Sonia Drayton. Now, why's your backside still in that chair? And send Adam Carver up pronto . . .'

Alone, Hauser checked over in his mind the different elements of the jigsaw he was juggling. The late Mr Tweed obviously had a team with him in Helsinki, the team which had caused trouble at Porvoo, now up in the Arctic Circle. He needed an execution team. He'd hold back Irina Serov to control the team. It would comprise Manescu and Ziegler, men who wouldn't hesitate to organize permanent accidents for the opposition. In a tight corner, *accelerate*.

Tweed had had a busy day. Monica had phoned from London giving him details of the flight bringing in the equipment he had requested. Butler had driven Tweed and Nield in the BMW to the airport.

Tweed had escorted the equipment through Customs, signing the release as Martin Baker. The boxes had been loaded inside the BMW. They had then driven to a warehouse behind North Harbour Tweed had rented. He helped them to carry the boxes inside.

'Should I ask what this stuff is?' Nield had queried.

'It's equipment for a film unit. Newman gave me the idea

362

when he described how they had been tracked and recorded at Arlanda and the ferry terminal from Stockholm to Turku. By film units.'

'I still don't see,' Nield persisted.

'I couldn't see how we could explore that Meteorological Institute in the Arctic Circle. When I heard from Newman that fisherman at Porvoo had seen a truck pass through Kemijärvi heading east towards the Institute I felt sure it was the base for some operation. Everything depends on what Newman, Marler and Paula tell us when they arrive back.'

'If they arrive back,' Butler said grimly. 'We aren't playing with pussycats.'

'They'll survive. Harry, did you hire that van? Are the posters and pass cards being printed?'

'They are. And the van is at the back of this warehouse. You can't see it because I covered it with a sheet of canvas.'

'Mind if you tell me what you're doing?' asked Nield.

'Butler is getting streamers printed with National Film Unit printed on them in Finnish and Swedish. Two will be attached to the van. While at the airport I arranged to charter a plane if necessary. The passes are for fake identification.'

Butler closed the warehouse doors, attached two padlocks and they climbed back inside the BMW. As they drove away Nield, anxious for action, put his question.

'What next?'

'I'm waiting for Monica to call me. She's researching INCUBUS non-stop through every available source and contact. She might just come up with key data . . .'

At five o'clock during a torrid afternoon Tweed took a call from Mauno Sarin. The Protection Police sounded very serious.

'Could you drop in at Ratakatu at say 6.30 this evening?

Forensic have come up with results I would rather not relay over the phone.'

'I'll be there.'

Five minutes later the phone rang again. It was Newman, calling from Helsinki Airport. He sounded tired, tense.

'Just to let you know we're back. We have information. Top priority. We could be with you in thirty minutes.'

'See that you are. Not only the heat is building up. I have to leave here at six . . .'

He turned to look at Butler and Nield who were were seated in chairs. Nield, always casual, was sprawled, legs stretched out in front of him. Butler sat upright, alert.

'There could be a blonde woman calling here about six – you followed her back to that apartment, Butler. I'm not sure she will appear, but if she does she'll ask for me at reception. Then she'll try and leave. I wanted her grabbed outside and kept on ice. Where, is for you to decide.'

'I'll recognize her,' Butler said. 'I'll describe her to Pete so we both know what she looks like. Maybe we should go down into the lobby now in case she turns up early.'

'Good point,' agreed Tweed. 'She might do just that . . .'

With minutes of their leaving he took another phone call. This time it was a long one from Monica, reporting the results of her research so far. Tweed made a lot of notes. At one stage she repeated what she had just said.

'That house and the power cruiser belonging to Hauser are in the Swedish *western* archipelago. Not the one off Stockholm. It runs off the coast north of Gothenburg nearly up to Norway.'

'I've got it. And the name of the anchorage. Go on . . .'

He had just finished the call, put away his notebook, when Newman and Marler arrived. He checked his watch. Newman said Paula had rushed to her room to have a bath, began his report of their journey to the Arctic. To begin with Tweed sat listening but as the story

364

progressed he stood up, pacing slowly round the room, taking in every word, his expression grave. Marler produced Paula's handkerchief enclosing the substance she had scooped out of the container, but he did not mentioned the scarf containing a much larger quantity. He had deposited that inside the wardrobe in his room before he joined Tweed.

'I'd better take that with me to my appointment,' Tweed said and stuffed the handkerchief with its contents inside his jacket pocket.

He waited as Newman unlocked the door in response to a gentle tapping. Paula walked in, her step brisk, the hint of a smile on her face.

'Guess what? I've got another date with Adam Carver. He said he'd been calling me all day. He's coming over for a drink. I'm to meet him outside the Intercontinental at six this evening.'

'Is that a good idea?' queried Tweed.

She punched him playfully on the arm. 'I haven't fallen for that cardboard matinée idol, if that's what you were thinking. If anything, it appears to be the other way round.'

'Why go?' Tweed persisted.

'All part of your campaign to throw INCUBUS off balance. And I might coax him into letting something slip.'

'Just be careful.'

Tweed checked his watch again. 'I congratulate all three of you on your Arctic Circle trip. You may have brought back just what is needed to stir the Finnish Government into taking action against Hauser. But everyone must be careful. I'm beginning to get inside Hauser's head – his reaction to the events at the Institute may be violent.'

*　　*　　*

Tweed sat silent as he faced Mauno Sarin across his desk at Ratakatu. The Finn reminded him of a studious tonsured monk with his balding head, his fringe beard. Sarin was in a serious mood.

'It is fortunate you didn't clean your teeth early this morning. Forensic have reported your tube of toothpaste is laced with a lethal quantity of potassium cyanide.' He smiled with humour. 'Their precise way of expressing themselves. Cyanide is lethal. The indigestion mixture is harmless.' He perched his elbows on the desk, clasped his strong hands together. 'Now who could have tampered with that tube?'

'A Sonia Drayton,' Tweed said promptly. 'I can give you her address.'

He explained tersely his encounter at the breakfast table with the bleached blonde, told Sarin that she had alleged she was an ex-employee of INCUBUS. He omitted that she had also said she would return to the Hesperia at six.

'INCUBUS again,' commented Sarin.

'You will repeat that remark after I tell you about the visit Marler and Newman made to the Meteorological Institute today . . .'

Tweed omitted any reference to Paula – who was on his conscience because of her journey into mortal danger. Sarin listened, his brown eyes fixed on Tweed. At the end of his report Tweed produced the handkerchief containing the substance Paula had collected. Sarin pressed a button, Karma appeared.

'Have that checked immediately. I suspect our explosives expert will be familiar with it by now. An answer quickly, please . . .'

Karma was back in less than five minutes. He laid the handkerchief with its contents on Sarin's desk.

'Semtex. A positive analysis. You don't need me for the moment? Thank you.'

Sarin poked at the dough-like substance with a long finger. 'As you predicted. INCUBUS again.'

'Surely it's time you went after Hauser,' Tweed demanded acidly. 'How much more evidence do you need?'

'There is a problem. Hauser this afternoon offered the government three million dollars to build a giant ice-breaker. They are considering the offer. Please!' He held up a hand as Tweed began to protest. 'The trouble is an individual can choose his neighbours, a country can't. I would like, myself, to deport Mr Hauser . . .'

'How much more evidence do you need?'

'Let me finish. It is a strange coincidence that Hauser has made this offer so soon after your associates discover explosives in two different areas directly connected with INCUBUS. I think he is a good poker player.'

'Explain that.'

'My government is indebted to Hauser for the employment he has supplied us with. We can't simply throw back his offer in his face. But we have a highly unstable Soviet Union on our doorstep. They might not like our accepting such a massive sum outright from Washington. So it is stalemate for the moment.'

'I said how much more evidence do you need?'

'I personally am extremely worried about your discovery of this Semtex. Not once, but twice. But are you prepared to put Mr Marler in open court, stating his profession, to tell his story? Bearing in mind who you are, and that Marler is a member of your Service?'

'No, of course not. But . . .'

'Then we have no evidence yet we can use. Newman alone is not enough. We need *two* witnesses, one to confirm the other's story.'

'Then we'd all better go home.'

'Were there any casualties during this secret examination of the Institute complex?'

367

'No,' lied Tweed promptly.

'I would be glad if you would continue your enquiries but if necessary I will deny ever saying that.'

'Thank you for all your support,' Tweed said savagely as he stood up to leave.

The streets were quiet as he walked back between the old granite office blocks. After his interview with Sarin at least they knew where they were. On their own.

The news that hit him when he returned to the Hesperia made him realize how much on their own they were.

36

Paula found Adam Carver waiting for her in a deserted area near the rear of the International. Newman had tried to accompany her, but she had refused. She was far more likely to extract information from Carver on her own.

'You're looking terrific,' Carver greeted her. 'And I was worrying you wouldn't turn up. Let's make this an evening to remember. Have dinner after a drink.'

'We'll see. After a drink . . .'

She had just replied with the traditional feminine wait and see tactic when she heard a car, burning rubber, coming up behind her. She swung round. A brown Buick jerked to a halt. The doors flew open. Three men wearing stocking masks, holding handguns, jumped out. One man ran to Carver, who looked astounded, told him to face the blank wall, rammed the gun into his back.

At the same time two other men rushed to Paula. One placed the muzzle of his gun against her skull, the second grabbed her arms, forced them behind her back. She felt the steel of handcuffs round her wrists, heard the click of locking.

She looked quickly at Carver. He was staring over his shoulder, the astonishment now replaced by rage. She was hustled into the rear of the large car. Doors slammed. The gunman holding Carver kicked his legs from under him, he sprawled on the concrete as the gunman leapt into the car. The Buick backed, turned, drove out past the Hesperia on to the Mannerheimintie.

The sheer audacity of the attack had taken Paula's breath away. The two men in the back were half-sitting on her, one holding a large hand over her mouth. She stared up at the sinister figure with the stocking mask as the Buick roared off away from the city.

Tweed was hot, sticky, frustrated as he paid off the cab and entered the Hesperia. Newman and Marler were sitting in the lobby. They jumped up as he came in and he wondered why they were waiting for him.

'Something's happened,' Newman said crisply. 'Better we tell you up in your room . . . '

'Well, what is it?' Tweed asked as he locked the door of his bedroom on the inside.

He peeled off his jacket, slung it over the back of a chair, which was uncharacteristic of him. His shirt was pasted to his back. He jerked it out and let it hang outside his trousers. Again uncharacteristic. He flopped in a chair.

'Get on with it. Incidentally we get no help from Mauno Sarin.'

'We've managed quite nicely on our own,' Marler observed.

'Butler phoned,' reported Newman. 'He and Nield grabbed Sonia Drayton. She came in at a quarter to six, headed for reception . . . '

'To check up I was dead.'

Tersely, Tweed told them of the findings of Forensic at Ratakatu. Marler whistled softly when he told them about the potassium cyanide.

'So it's a good job we've got her,' Newman continued, as he sat facing Tweed. 'Butler wrapped it up on the phone but this is it. He put his arm round her and rammed the end of his pipe into her back, told her it was a gun. They took her away in the BMW.'

'Where to?'

'The warehouse where you stored the film equipment down by the waterfront. That's a clever idea – using a film unit to—'

'Never mind about that,' Tweed snapped. 'Was it clever to let her know the location?'

'She doesn't know where she is, what route they took. I gather Nield blindfolded her as soon as they were driving off in the car. They're trying to get her to talk – with a tape recorder at the ready. No rough stuff, of course. But no food. Just mineral water. So far nothing. She's told them nothing.'

'I wonder whether we ought to hand her over to Sarin for attempted murder – of me,' Tweed mused. His mind was flitting about. 'Where is Paula?'

'Getting Adam Carver drunk with her wiles,' Marler said.

'Damn it!' Tweed punched one clenched hand into the palm of the other. 'We need more data. Something to convince Sarin he has to move.'

He's in a rare irritable mood, Newman thought. The phone rang and he picked it up. Tweed reached out for the extension phone by the bedside, lifted the receiver at the same moment. Maybe Sarin had changed his mind. He stiffened as the distorted voice at the other end began speaking.

'I wish to speak to Mr Martin Baker.'

370

'Not available,' snapped Newman. 'I'm his assistant.'

'You are a member of his organization?' queried the bland voice.

Newman scribbled a note on a pad, handed it to Tweed. In spite of the distortion he thought he recognized Hauser from the way he pronounced certain words. He'd had two conversations with the INCUBUS president. Tweed read the note, *Hauser*.

'I told you I am his assistant, his chief deputy,' Newman said into the receiver. 'What is this all about? Who is speaking? I don't take anonymous calls.'

'You will take this one. Your chief's girl is with us. I'll describe how she is dressed . . .' An accurate picture of what Paula had worn followed. Newman nodded to Tweed, confirming the description was accurate as the voice went on. 'I will be holding the girl as a hostage. If there is any further interference in our industrial operations you will, as a first present, receive through the post her right hand. Do you understand?'

Tweed held up a hand to stop Newman replying. He was in a state of greater fury than either Marler or Newman had ever witnessed. He fought for a moment for iron self-control. When he spoke his voice was implacable, the grimness apparent in the way he spoke slowly, with great determination.

'Hauser, this is Martin Baker speaking.'

He paused to let that sink in. There was a long pause at the other end of the line. His statement had thrown the voice off balance. He continued.

'You are quite right. We do have an organization. You have already experienced its power. With the explosives truck north of Porvoo. With the penetration of the so-called Meteorological Institute. I warn you now, Hauser, if the girl is harmed in any way I will hunt you down if I have to follow you across the face of the earth. You will not sleep. You will look over your shoulder everywhere. There will be no place you can hide.'

'Hauser?' The voice sounded as though it was trying to be mocking. 'I have never heard of the name . . .'

'Release the girl immediately. Unharmed,' Tweed ordered. 'You will be hounded out of Finland. I promise you. Our resources are unlimited. We are ruthless professionals.'

'This conversation ceases now. I will give you an hour to think it over. I will then call you again. Just hope the hostage will not be tortured in the meantime . . .'

The line went dead. Tweed replaced the phone with great care. Neither Marler nor Newman had ever seen such an expression on his face. He looked like a hanging judge, staring into the distance, hands clasped lightly together.

'You didn't play our strongest card,' Newman told him. 'We have Sonia Drayton. She attempted to murder you. She'll have information on INCUBUS which Hauser won't want revealed.'

'I'm aware of that.' Tweed's tone was ice cold. 'I am going to hit him with that when he calls back. At the moment he's in a state of shock – because I'm still living. It's strange – I can think like Hauser, subconsciously foresee his next move. And I believe the reverse is also true. We think of kidnapping the Drayton woman – he thinks of kidnapping Paula.'

He was still staring into space when Marler spoke.

'You know when you arrived back we were waiting for you in the lobby. I thought I saw Adam Carver outside. Someone who was the spitting image of the photographs I took of him leaving the INCUBUS HQ. He looked in a bad way, went off towards the Intercontinental. Think I'll go and look for him. He was the man Paula went to meet . . .'

'No! I'll go,' snapped Newman.

He was out of the room before anyone could react.

372

Like Tweed, it was a dreadful blow to him that Paula, of all people, should be in the hands of thugs who didn't hesitate to kill.

Stepping out of the elevator, he moved swiftly outside, crossed the path leading to the International, walked into the hotel and instinctively headed for the bar.

'Martin Baker – Tweed – is still alive,' Hauser told Galvone. 'That I didn't expect. And bloody aggressive too. You're sure the hostage girl is secured?'

He was pacing round the turret tower, beefy arms folded across his chest. Galcone knew he was disturbed: it was not working out as planned. Yet.

'She's secure,' he assured his chief. 'Locked away in an apartment out at Setula near the airport. Three tough guards with her. Orders not to touch her. Yet. What I can't figure out is why you didn't let Adam Carver know he was bait. He may not be pleased when he gets back. I don't care a cuss,' he added, 'but he's a key executive.'

'I didn't let him know because I think he's sweet on the girl,' Hauser lied. 'And not knowing meant he'd act the part better. That guy Baker, Tweed or whatever his goddamned name might be, is a tough bastard.'

'He'll crack. They all do under pressure.'

'You're right, Frank. Next time I call I'll turn the screw a little tighter, make the bastard crawl. We do this the American way.'

Inside the waterfront warehouse Butler put down the phone. Marler had just called, had asked questions, had told him by implication about Paula. Butler was fond of Paula.

Sonia Drayton was tied to a heavy chair they had found with other old furniture stacked at the rear of the building. She was tied at the ankles, one leg to each front leg of the chair. Her arms were bound behind her back, roped to the chair. She wore a blindfold.

Nield had parked the BMW in a corner of the warehouse, was keeping watch through a window smeared with muck and dust. He turned as he heard noises. Butler was removing the gag, holding a cardboard carton of mineral water to her lips. Important she didn't get dehydrated. The interior of the warehouse was like a furnace.

'If I had some food,' Drayton said, 'I might tell you a few things which would interest you.'

'You'll talk, anyway,' growled Butler. 'When your stomach is screaming for food.'

'What's happened? You sound tougher, less human.'

'I feel tougher, less human.'

Butler applied the gag again, tying it a little tighter this time. It was the first occasion for a long time when Irina Serov had felt frightened. When they questioned her earlier she had refused to tell them anything. She had expected them to slap her around, but they had not laid a hand on her. Now she was worried: her captor's manner had changed, he had sounded ugly. Was it retaliation for the death of Tweed? But how could they have identified her?

Butler wandered over to join Nield, peered out of the window. He wished to God he was out there, searching for Paula.

Imprisoned in a strait-jacket, Paula was streaming with sweat. Thrown on to what felt like a couch, her eyes were covered with a coloured handkerchief. She had counted three men; only two had spoken to her, in English, but with a Mittel-European accent. More *Securitate*? Not a reassuring thought. But she had made herself relax – straining against the jacket used up valuable energy.

374

She was surprised she didn't feel in a state of terror. But she was confident Tweed would find a way of rescuing her. One thing puzzled her: that look of total surprise, then fury, on Adam Carver's face. If he had lured her into the ambush his reaction when it took place was odd, very odd.

What the hell is going on? she wondered. Time seemed to have stood still. Not knowing what the time was bothered her more than anything else. She had only asked them the time once.

'Maybe time to die soon, lady,' had been the reply.

Newman found Adam Carver sitting by himself in a corner of the International bar. It was quiet at that hour and Carver was out of sight of the barman. Newman bought himself a glass of champagne, sat down on the banquette next to Carver who was nursing his chin with his right hand.

'Evening, Carver. Have a tiff with Paula?'

'Good God! It's you, Newman. How the devil did you know I was here?'

'Easy. You had a date with her to meet outside. Where is she?'

'She . . . er . . . stood me up.'

'A handsome chap like you?' Newman sipped at his champagne, put the glass down. 'I can't believe it.' His voice hardened. 'I don't believe it.'

'You can get stuff—'

'You can talk,' Newman's right hand grasped Carver's short collar below the throat, twisted it, banging his head back against the wall, 'or I'll throttle you. Talk! Now!'

'Let go . . . can't breathe . . .' The grip relaxed a little. 'She was hijacked . . . Three men in stocking masks. One held a gun on me. Smashed my chin against the concrete wall. Look at my bloody jaw. I'm still dizzy – or you wouldn't find it so easy to push me around.'

Newman looked at Carver's chin. There was a nasty graze along the side of his jaw. He clenched his fist as though about to punch Carver through the wall, then opened his hand, shrugged.

'All right. Talk. How did they take her away? And I like quick answers.'

'In a brown Buick. I didn't know that was going to happen. For your information it was a bloody great shock.'

'So naturally you informed the police? Gave them your description of the Buick? Sounded the alarm?'

'I'm still in a state of shock.' Carver drank more Scotch. 'It all happened so quickly. And I thought it might be dangerous to inform the police . . .'

'Why?'

'They may ask for a ransom. Don't kidnappers make it a condition the police aren't informed? I could have been putting her life at risk. For Christ's sake, Newman, I'm as worried as you are.'

'Believe that, believe the moon is blue.'

Oddly enough Newman found himself reluctantly believing that Carver *was* telling the truth. But at the same time he couldn't rid his mind of a feeling of dislike, distrust, of Carver. He finished his champagne, stood up, left with a blast.

'Well, I can tell you one thing. I'm going to do something drastic. Very drastic.'

Cord Dillon, who had taken a shower, was sitting with Tweed when Newman arrived back. His craggy face was as grim as Tweed's. He had just listened to the latest developments. The American liked Paula and secretly he was pessimistic about her chances.

'I propose we form a strike force,' Newman began.

376

'Nield can look after the Drayton bitch. Butler can come back to join Dillon and myself.'

'A strike force?' queried Dillon. 'Against who, what and where?'

'Hauser's crazy house. We take out Hauser himself. Give me half an hour alone with him and he'll talk. Boy, will he talk.'

'Don't like the idea,' Dillon objected before Tweed could react. 'Hauser will be heavily guarded. Too few of us to launch an assault. It could end in the death of Paula.'

'I agree with Cord,' Tweed said quickly. 'Cool down, Bob. Storming Hauser's citadel is no way to handle this.'

'Then what the hell is the way?'

'Leave it to me. That's an order.' Tweed's manner was cold. 'And you stay here until the phone call from Hauser comes through. I think I can do a deal with him.'

It was strange, Tweed thought as they waited. This was his first confrontation with the enemy. He had no intention of underestimating his opponent, but he had steeled himself to stay calm.

'I don't see how you're going to persuade him to let her go,' Newman snapped. 'And I did find Adam Carver sitting in the bar next door. I twisted his arm verbally. Said he was there when the kidnap took place, that he was rammed up against a wall by a gunman wearing a stocking mask. He does have a badly grazed jaw. The whole episode seemed to come as a great shock to him. You'll think I've lost my marbles but I believed him.'

'Why?' rapped out Dillon.

'Mainly because of where I found him. In a bar close to where they snatched Paula, drinking, in a state of shock. Had he been involved, known what was going to happen, he'd have disappeared long before this.'

'Makes sense,' Dillon agreed reluctantly. 'The guy who organized it could be Frank Galvone. A near-gangster

Hauser recruited from Chicago.' He saw Tweed raise his eyebrows. 'I did do my homework before I crossed the Atlantic . . .'

He stopped speaking as the phone began ringing. Tweed checked his watch. Half an hour after the previous call. Not an hour as Hauser had said. More psychological warfare. He deliberately let the phone ring a number of times before he picked it up.

'Martin Baker speaking.'

'Do you agree to my conditions?' the distorted voice asked. 'Or do you want her right hand delivered by special messenger? She is right-handed. The conditions are you cease all activities against us, withdraw your soldiers back to Britain. OK?'

'No, I don't agree to any of it. And don't interrupt me, Hauser, I have news for you. We are holding Sonia Drayton in a safe place.'

A pause at the other end. 'Who is this Sonia Drayton?'

'You know perfectly well who she is. She tried to murder me. Cyanide. We have the evidence. You'll do exactly as I tell you or Drayton is handed over to the Protection Police. She has already provided damaging information about your organization, information which was tape recorded. I will immediately give her to the police. With the tape. The Finnish government doesn't like people who compromise its neutrality. People who smuggle explosives into their country. People who employ murderesses. It's all on the tape.'

Another longer pause. Tweed guessed Hauser was using another line to call Drayton's apartment.

'I doubt if I'll agree,' the voice resumed. 'What do you propose?'

'Oh, you'll agree. Or face the Finnish government throwing you out of Finland lock, stock and barrel. There is going to be an exchange. Your hostage for mine. Plus the tape.'

'We might consider that arrangement. In a week's time . . .'

'Nothing doing. The exchange takes place before midnight this evening. Or Drayton and the tape go to the police. I'm not negotiating any more. Make up your mind. Now!'

A further pause. 'It will be difficult to bring in our package tonight . . .'

'No, it won't. You're holding her within half an hour's drive of this hotel.' Tweed was gambling on the data Butler had provided when he had followed Manescu and Ziegler from the railway station to Setula, to an apartment block not so far from the airport.

A brief pause this time. Hauser was absorbing the shock of realizing how much information his opponent had.

'After dark then,' he decided. 'Between midnight and two tomorrow morning . . .'

'Absolutely not. It will be dark during those two hours. That is why I said before midnight. My patience is wearing thin.'

'Then we have to agree the location. In the forest outside Helsinki. I'll give you directions . . .'

'Absolutely not.' Tweed's tone was firm, detached. 'The location for the exchange will be the scrubbing board platform at the end of tram stop No. 4. Where you murdered the wrong woman – Anna Jarva instead of Peggy Vanderheld.'

'Don't know what the hell you're talking about. The names mean nothing to me. The location is agreed. There had better not be any police there or your girl . . .'

'No police. Time for the exchange ten o'clock. 2200 hours. And the hostage had better be in perfect shape. I will have a doctor to examine her before the exchange is completed. You can take the same precaution. Now I want to get some dinner. Have you got the arrangement quite clear?'

'I agree the exchange, the details. Go f— yourself.'

The line went dead. Tweed replaced the phone. Marler, who had sat in a corner all this time, motionless as a part of the furniture, spoke.

'How the devil did you get him to agree? And to the location I suggested?'

'Because I realized he's in the middle of launching some major operation. Those explosives you discovered at the Institute. So close to the Soviet border. And this news in the *Herald Tribune*.' He passed the newspaper to Marler. The headline glared at him.

TRANS-SIBERIAN RAILROAD SABOTAGED.
EXPLOSION BLOWS TRAIN.

'That,' Tweed went on, 'links up with the murders of leading moderate statesmen in Prague, Budapest and Bucharest. Now Hauser is starting to destabilize Russia. I have a contact who confirms my view, a contact from inside the USSR. With the Soviet President distracted by more problems the way is clear for Hauser to infiltrate Russia, to gain a commercial stranglehold on their economy.'

'Then you gambled on Hauser being so concerned with this campaign he couldn't afford to risk being thrown out of Finland?' Marler suggested.

'Exactly,' said Tweed.

'Then let's hope to God the exchange is successful,' Newman commented.

'And that reminds me.' Marler jumped up. 'Gentlemen, I have to leave you. I have to make certain preparations which Tweed has agreed. Precautions to protect the exchange.'

37

At 9.45 p.m. a No. 4 tram stopped at the end of the line outside the city. The last two passengers alighted, Butler very close to Sonia Drayton, keeping pace with his prisoner as they walked down the pavement towards the sea and the scrubbing board platform.

'One wrong move,' Butler warned in a harsh voice, 'and it will give me great pleasure to blow a hole right through your middle.'

They walked slowly, like lovers. Butler had his left arm clasped round her waist. His right hand beneath his jacket held the Luger borrowed from Dillon, the muzzle pressed against her side. She had a long silk scarf they had discovered in Paula's room. It was draped over her shoulders, tied at the ends below her thighs. It concealed the fact that her wrists were now bound with cloth in front of her.

Irina was surprised by the viciousness in Butler's voice. He could not forget that this woman had tried to murder Tweed. They were arriving early deliberately – in case INCUBUS men were concealed in Peggy Vanderheld's apartment which overlooked the scrubbing board. It was only one reason why Tweed, after discussion with Marler, had chosen this rendezvous before taking the second call from Hauser. It seemed likely the INCUBUS group would have a key to the Vanderheld apartment – and watching from it they would see there were no police.

'Then you won't get Baker's girl friend back and he'll be lonely in bed at night,' she rapped back lewdly.

'Clean out your filthy mouth.'

Butler rammed the muzzle into her and she grunted with pain, kept silent. Thank God for a clear sky, Butler thought: dusk, let alone night, would not ruin visibility. Marler had said that was important. They walked across the deserted road, stepped on to the wooden planks of the platform, down on to the lower level projecting over the sea.

It was still very hot. Butler could feel the dampness of Drayton's T-shirt. They stood looking out to sea. The only sound was the lapping of the water against the piles supporting the platform. There were still the relics of a red stain on the planks. The blood of Anna Jarva who had died instead of Peggy Vanderheld. Murder had been committed where they stood.

More like a large lake than a sea, the distant shores were fringed with a wall of dark firs. There was an atmosphere of peace only to be found in Finland. No boats on a surface reflecting sunlight like mercury. The only entrance to this huge lagoon-like stretch of water was a channel from the Gulf of Finland which couldn't be seen to the south.

'What do you do if they don't bring her?' asked Irina.

'Hand you to the police. Charge, attempted murder . . .'

Butler was suspicious she was diverting his attention. He tightened his grip on her waist, turned to face the shore, swinging her round with him. The No. 4 tram was a small oblong, its rear growing smaller as it headed back to Helsinki. Maybe they were waiting for that to go away.

'We'll move around a bit,' he said.

He could see no sign of life in the apartment block on the second floor where Vanderheld had lived. To their right a bank of tall reeds rose out of the water, quite still. There was not a breath of moving air. Inland from the reeds was a dense tangle of undergrowth. Butler took her over close to it, glanced inside the tangle, walked her back to the platform. Somewhere a machine was approaching.

Standing on the lower level he watched the helicopter coming into view from the south, coming closer. A

Sikorsky. He had seen Sikorskys at the airport. On the side of the fuselage he saw the INCUBUS logo.

'They could be bringing her in aboard that chopper,' he commented.

'How the hell would I know. It's your party, Buster.'

'Where did you pick up that awful Americanism from?'

'From—' She clamped her mouth shut.

She had been going to say *from Hauser*, Butler thought as he watched the Sikorsky descending, over-flying them, then cruising at low level over the surrounding land area. He grinned without mirth.

'Just checking, your friends.'

'I don't know what you're talking about.'

The chopper had vanished, its engine sound fading in the distance. Butler checked his watch. Two minutes to ten. They were cutting it fine. Then he heard another faint engine sound behind him. He swung her around again, stared out to sea. A large cabin cruiser was crossing the water at high speed, trailing a white wake. Butler looked over his shoulder, stared up the tramline road to where a side road branched off to the right up a hill leading direct to the Hotel Kalastajatorppa. That road was important.

Another No. 4 tram had trundled to the terminal. A single passenger alighted, walked towards the platform. A lean man wearing a cream linen suit, a straw hat and carrying a brown bag. Walking as though he had small stones inside his shoes, he stepped on the platform. A middle-aged man with horn-rim glasses and a reedy voice.

'Are you Mr Butler?'

'Yes.'

'I am Dr Winter. Mr Baker is most persuasive . . .' Butler felt Drayton stiffen. It was the first news she had had that Tweed was definitely alive. 'This is most

383

irregular,' Winter continued. 'I am supposed to examine a hostage, a woman. It is almost unbelievable. A hostage – in Finland.'

'It is,' Butler agreed, 'but it has happened. Put the bag on the platform. You may make the hostage takers nervous. And they may be arriving now with your patient.'

He turned round and the two-deck cabin cruiser was moving more slowly, almost drifting inshore. Near the prow of the vessel stood a girl with raven black hair, very erect, a blindfold across her eyes, her hands behind her back.

'There's Baker's precious tart,' sneered Irina. 'Now . . .'

She broke off, winced, stifled a groan of pain. Butler had again rammed the muzzle into her side. He had felt like pulling the trigger. There were four men on the foredeck, all with scarves pulled up over the lower part of their faces. One stood beside Paula, gripping her right arm, the other three had one hand behind their backs.

The engine of the cruiser was ticking over, the bow no more than fifty yards from the platform. Another man appeared on the upper deck, a loud-hailer held close to his mouth.

'Set Sonia Drayton free. We want to see her wave her hands about. Then she walks to the edge of the platform. When she is there we bring our boat to the platform. We let our prisoner free. She steps ashore as Sonia steps aboard . . .'

'Get stuffed!' Butler shouted back. 'You think I'm falling for that one?'

He had an uneasy feeling the man with the loud-hailer was talking too much, that it was a cover for some premeditated action. He remained where he was, his arm firmly round Drayton's waist.

'I said release her,' Loud-Hailer repeated. 'We are not staying here all evening. This is your last chance to obtain her freedom. Take your arm off her. Are her hands free? Wave to us, Sonia, if you can.'

'Don't move one inch,' Butler whispered.

'You have to do something, Buster,' Irina mocked him.

There was a sudden burst of another engine. Hidden in the reeds aboard a power boat, Marler peered at the cabin cruiser as Newman jumped ashore, Smith & Wesson in his hand. He moved through the dense clumps of undergrowth, crouched low, found what he was searching for, settled on his haunches to wait.

From his vantage point Marler could see the three men with one hand behind their backs were concealing guns. Earlier he had collected the power boat he had hired from a firm at North Harbour. He had also bought from them a chart. Moving at speed, he had left North Harbour, swung round the tip of the peninsula on which Brown Park stood, had steered the boat inside the channel into the arm of the sea overlooked by the Kalastajatorppa, had headed for the scrubbing board and hidden the boat inside the reeds an hour before rendez-vous time.

He perched the barrel of the Armalite rifle on top of the perspex screen of the open wheelhouse. The boat he had hired was equipped exactly as he had specified. A microphone was close to his mouth. A small megaphone was mounted for'ard. The cabin cruiser's engine had been cut out. For a moment it was very silent, then his voice boomed out over the gentle purr of his own engine.

'The three guards standing on deck will keep quite still. They will drop the guns they are concealing at once. 'Or,' his voice increased in power, 'I'll blow you into the water.' He fired two shots. One bullet, carefully aimed, shattered the wheelhouse window, missing the helms-man. The second bullet thudded into the deck.

'Drop the bloody guns!' Marler yelled.

The three men froze, uncertain how to react. Then one man dropped his weapon. A moment later the other two followed his example.

'Free the hostage's hands!' Marler thundered.

A third bullet hit the deck close to one of the guard's feet. Merged behind the reeds, Marler was that most unnerving of terrors, an invisible target. The guard alongside Paula took out a key, unlocked the handcuffs. Paula stretched her aching arms, waved both hands aloft.

On the platform Butler shoved his Luger inside his belt, produced a penknife, reached under the scarf, slit the cloth binding Drayton's wrists. Seconds later the gun was again pressed against her side as she waved her free hands.

'Bring the cruiser slowly up to the platform,' Marler commanded. 'Try and run for it and you're dead . . .'

Another bullet through what remained of the glass backed up the threat. The cabin cruiser's engine started up, the vessel moved slowly forward, its hull bumped the edge of the platform, the engine was cut.

'The exchange takes place now,' Marler called out in a confident tone. 'You may all live to see another sunrise if you don't play tricks . . .'

A further bullet thudded into the deck. Marler reloaded the weapon, peered through the 'scope. Paula stepped on to the platform, passing Drayton who stepped aboard. Neither woman gave the other as much as a glance.

Sonia Drayton was hurried below decks as the engine was started up. Grabbing Paula by the arm, Butler hurried her off the platform towards the tangle of undergrowth. She took long strides, easing movement back into her legs.

'Can you ride a bicycle?' Butler asked.

'To get away from that lot I'd ride a penny-farthing.'

A lot happened so fast it was a blur of movement. Newman was dragging the three bicycles Marler had hidden in the undergrowth into view. The cabin cruiser was speeding out across the sea. A motor cycle appeared, a Honda ridden by Pete Nield, a long chain with heavy iron links looped over his handlebars. He had hired it earlier in the evening on Tweed's orders.

Marler watched as they cycled off up the road, Newman in the lead, Paula behind him, Butler bringing up the rear. Paula was pedalling furiously, ramming down her aching legs. She cycled in London frequently from her apartment to Park Crescent: it was quicker than using a car and sitting in a traffic jam.

A brown Buick raced into view down the road from the north. Full of men, it turned to pursue the cyclists, to run them down. Nield rode his Honda alongside the car, threw the chain just ahead of a front wheel. The chain coiled round the wheel, the Buick swung round in a crazy circle, stopped, as Nield followed the cyclists. Marler aimed his Armalite, found he couldn't target the man getting out of the Buick: the tangle of undergrowth masked his view.

The man outside the car swore foully as he fought to free the chain too quickly, then took more care, pulling the chain loose, hurling it towards the scrubbing board. The cyclists had disappeared, turning right up the hilly road past several foreign embassies. As she pedalled after Newman Paula sensed there was a new emergency: she had heard the car's tyres screech as it revolved in a circle.

'Keep moving!' Newman shouted over his shoulder. 'We haven't much time left.'

She didn't answer, saving her breath for her exertions. Newman reached the top of the hill, saw the BMW parked off the road, heard the Buick coming up behind them. He leapt off his bike, let the machine topple, grasped Paula's arm as she left her own machine, half

387

dragging her into the section of the weird Kalastajatorppa complex on the side of the road nearest the sea. On the opposite side of the road where the BMW was parked was the other section of the hotel. The Kalastajatorppa was an architect's fantasy, a series of stone block-houses which seemed to grow out of the granite it was built on.

Newman and Paula, followed by Butler, were disappearing inside the hotel when the brown Buick topped the hill summit and screeched to a halt. Slumped behind the wheel of the BMW, a cap pulled down over his head, Tweed sat quite still as he watched four men pile out of the Buick, run inside the hotel. He switched on the engine, sat up straighter, gripped the wheel, waited.

Inside the hotel Newman led Paula to a flight of steps leading underground. At the bottom a nightmare tunnel stretched into the distance. Its walls were covered with white polystyrene, carved into shapes like ice. Paula recalled the claustrophobic atmosphere when she had explored the underworld beneath the Rhône glacier in Switzerland. The tunnel ahead was deserted, the atmosphere horrific.

'What the hell is this?' she gasped as she ran alongside Newman.

'Tunnel for guests linking both complexes. Goes under the road, emerges inside the other section of the hotel. Keep moving . . .'

They were three quarters of the way along the tunnel, Butler at their heels, when they heard the urgent clatter of feet running down the steps leading to the tunnel behind them. Newman ran faster, forced Paula to keep up with him, still grasping her arm. She was almost out of breath when they reached the second flight of steps. She glanced back, saw men coming down the tunnel.

They rushed up into the large reception hall, ran across it out into the open. Newman guided her to the BMW, threw open the back door. She stumbled, trying to get inside too quickly. In his wing mirror Tweed saw the four men emerge, run to the Buick. He was worried. He had hoped they wouldn't have to use the second contingency plan he had worked out with Marler and Newman, who knew the layout of the hotel – that they could have jumped inside the BMW as soon as they reached the top of the hill. The arrival of the Buick had forced Newman to use the diversion. As Paula managed to climb into the rear, followed by Newman, Butler dived into the front passenger seat. Tweed saw the Buick was already moving towards them to block their escape.

'We'll never get away,' said Paula, looking through the rear window.

The Buick had been driven forward at speed, was now turning through ninety degrees to ram the side of the BMW. Tweed watched it, his foot on the brake. The Buick rushed towards them, Paula braced herself for the moment when it would slam into the side of their car. Tweed glanced to his left at the massive granite boulder he was parked alongside, timed it carefully. Foot off the brake – thank God the BMW was automatic – foot hard down on the accelerator, gear in reverse. Paula watched in horror as the huge brown projectile hurtled towards them. Tweed backed swiftly. The timing was in fractions of a second. The BMW cleared the boulder. The Buick's driver saw what lay ahead too late. Almost scraping Tweed's front bumper, the Buick roared at top speed, slammed with great force into the granite. The impact was so great the vehicle shuddered.

Tweed turned the wheel, drove on to the road, down the hill towards Helsinki. Behind him Nield skidded to a halt in front of the crumpled Buick, held the Browning, borrowed from Paula's room, by the barrel in his left hand. He smashed the butt against the windscreen. The shatter-proof glass crazed, making the world in front of the driver opaque. Nield raced off at speed, huddled low in his saddle.

389

38

In his bedroom at the Hesperia Tweed told Dillon what had happened. The American had earlier become aggressive in his attempt to join them. Tweed had been firm, brusque.

'The Deputy Director of the CIA risking exposure? If it all goes wrong, exposure of your presence in Finland to Mauno Sarin? The answer is no!'

'But it's all right for you to go? Deputy Director of the SIS?'

'It's my girl they've got . . .'

Now Paula was relaxing from her ordeal in a bath while Newman, at her request, sat in her bedroom. She had felt the need for company, for someone to talk to beyond the half-open door.

'It's been one hell of a day for you,' Newman commented. 'First the flight to the Institute, the scene in the Level Four garage. You must be just about at the end of your tether. And then the grim experience of being kidnapped.'

'The bath is helping. I appreciated the way you let me watch while Marler retrieved his knife from that guard. I know he told me not to look, but he didn't expect me to take any notice of him. I appreciate the way you both treat me as a member of the team.'

'You are a member. Fully paid up.'

'And you left that bit out when you told Tweed.'

'Deliberately. Marler and I decided that beforehand – we both felt Tweed would have disapproved. And Tweed has amazing reflexes. The way he timed backing out of the way of that Buick. And cool as a cucumber on the way back here.'

'Talking about the kidnapping . . . No, Bob, it will help me to get the experience out of my system, the trauma. Looking back on it, I don't believe Adam Carver had a clue about what was going to happen. I think they used him.'

'I rather agree with you. I found him in a bar after we knew they'd grabbed you. At the Intercontinental of all places. I half-throttled him to screw information out of our smooth-talking vice president. I'd say he's pretty strong but he didn't resist. Seemed in a genuine state of shock.'

'What do you make of him?'

'I'm not sure, but he doesn't seem to fit in to that outfit as a banking chief. He's a bit of a mystery to me, something there I can't put my finger on.'

Midnight. An hour later, it was dark; the brief two-hour night Helsinki experiences in July had begun. Everyone was assembled in Tweed's room. Dillon, Paula, Newman, Butler and Marler, who had taken the power boat back to its mooring in North Harbour.

No one felt like going to bed, keyed up by the events of the day. Tweed had ordered ham sandwiches, mineral water and champagne from room service. Paula was keeping going on sheer nervous energy. Tweed swallowed the last of a sandwich and spoke.

'That kidnapping – and the swift way Hauser decided to release her – may be a significant turning point.' He looked at Paula. 'I'm appalled you had to go through that experience but, if it's any consolation, it tells us something we might not otherwise have realized.'

'And what is that?' Paula asked.

'Hauser is on the eve of launching some major operation he couldn't afford to have interfered with. Sonia Drayton may know something vital to his plans.'

'So the usual waiting period while you accumulate data is over?' she suggested hopefully.

'I think it is. Time we organized our bogus film unit and paid a visit to that so-called Meteorological Institute. And this time you stay home, Paula.'

She was about to protest when the phone rang. Everyone stiffened, looked at each other. Who could be calling at this hour? Tweed picked up the phone, the operator said she had a Mr Smith on the line for Mr Baker.

'Put him on.'

'I think you'll recognize who this is speaking,' a familiar voice said. Rebet. 'I hope I haven't woken you up but it's an emergency. We need to meet. Urgently.'

'When?' Tweed asked.

'Tonight. Or rather, this morning. Within the hour. I will be waiting in a black Saab at the top end of North Harbour.'

'At what time?'

'Are you dressed?'

'Yes.'

'Can you make it by one o'clock?'

'Yes.' It sounded like General Rebet but Tweed was in a cautious mood. 'Mind telling me the name of the hotel I stayed at when later there was a reception, followed by a banquet?'

'The Moskwa,' the voice answered immediately.

'See you at one o'clock.'

Tweed put the phone down. The others watched him curiously. The conversation had been so monosyllabic. Paula assumed it must be one of his secret informants, identity known only to Tweed. Newman reared up violently as soon as Tweed announced what he was going to do.

'I have to leave you. Please stay here, finish your meal, finish off the drink. God knows you've earned it. I'm driving myself to an appointment – just made on the phone as you heard.'

'What appointment? Where?' demanded Newman, standing up.

'As it happens,' Tweed told him reluctantly, 'at the top of North Harbour where they hold that market in daytime.'

'Great!' Newman put his glass on a table. 'Same place as where Ed Riverton was murdered, garrotted, also in the middle of the night.'

'My contact is trustworthy,' Tweed replied stiffly.

'Well, you're not going alone.'

'I think my contact would expect me to be alone . . .'

'Doubtless he would.' Newman was strapping on his shoulder holster, checking his gun. 'We've run enough risks in the past twelve hours or so. So have you. You're supposed to arrive alone. Fine. You drive, I'll hide in the back of the BMW.'

'It's parked at the rear of the Intercontinental,' Nield informed them. 'I moved it there. No point in advertising our presence.'

'Got the car keys, Pete?' Paula enquired, standing up. 'Good. Toss them to me.'

She caught them in mid-air. Staring at Tweed, she handed them to Newman. She brushed her hands together, as though to say: that's that.

'I've been through enough myself today,' she snapped at Tweed. 'Now you'll do as you're told. Bob goes with you in the back.'

'I used to think I was the boss,' Tweed lamented in a mock timid tone. 'I appear to be out-voted.'

'You goddamn well are,' Dillon told him gruffly. 'Night assignations are always dangerous.'
'

At 12.30 a.m. the streets of Helsinki were traffic-free except for a solitary cream BMW, occupied apparently only by the driver, who turned into the tree-lined

Esplanade. The street lamps cast a weird glow, creating large areas of shadow where anything might lurk. The driver's window was open, as were the rear windows on both sides. Newman wanted to hear, to see, to be able to shoot, if necessary. Tweed cruised slowly along the deserted street. Not the sign of a living soul anywhere.

He was almost thirty minutes early for his meeting but Newman had insisted they arrived in the vicinity well before time.

'If anyone is waiting to surprise us we'll surprise them,' he had ordered.

Tweed crept the car away from the Esplande and along the waterfront. At Newman's whispered command he stopped, left his engine running. Moored round the waterfront were many vessels, lights at their mastheads swaying gently. There was always a wind at North Harbour. Sometimes a raging gale, sometimes a gentle breeze as there was tonight. Newman told him to turn off the engine, listened.

He heard the sea lapping against the quayside, a creaking from several wooden boats. Quiet sounds in the otherwise sinister silence. Tweed glanced round like a man out for a breath of fresh air. He couldn't see any out of the way movement.

'Start the engine,' Newman whispered. 'Drive around the side streets up towards the cathedral. If you see anything, warn me. We have time to check out the whole area.'

Tweed turned left up a one-way street, continuing to cruise. He bumped over a tram line. The side streets were darker, shrouded in the deepest shadows beyond the pools of light cast by street lamps. For Tweed this was a novel experience – the dark. Ever since arriving in Finland he had gone to bed by daylight, woken up to it.

He completed a slow circuit of the old buildings, drove back on to the waterfront, checked the time by the dashboard clock. 1 a.m. A black Saab was parked by the quay, its engine turned off. Without turning his head – hardly moving his lips – he reported to Newman.

'My contact has arrived.'

'Is he alone?'

'Appears to be. I think he'll keep his word.'

What bothered Tweed was the Saab was parked by the quayside steps leading down to the landing stage where he had been hijacked by Rebet before being taken to Leningrad. He pulled up alongside the Saab, a few feet away so the driver couldn't see inside the rear of the BMW. He was careful not to use a name as he called out to General Rebet.

'Move your car away from the quayside. Park it on the far side of the market area. Then we can talk.'

Tweed had surveyed the harbour and could see no moving vessel but was taking no chances. He drove on slowly, watched Rebet in his rear-view mirror as the Russian moved the Saab across the wide concourse, parked it in the shadows of a building. Tweed performed a U-turn, drove towards the Saab, stopped close to the wall of the building.

'Leave the engine running,' Newman whispered.

'No. He has to trust me.'

Rebet was walking towards him, wearing a sports jacket and slacks. Tweed left the car quickly to meet him, to keep him away from the BMW. In his pocket he carried the photographs Nield had taken of the third man aboard the *Alskär* during the chase through the Turku archipelago into the open sea. When Nield had brought the developed and printed pictures to Tweed he had grinned, holding them behind his back.

'Write down on a bit of paper who you think the third man is.'

Tweed had obliged, Nield had handed the pictures to him. As Tweed looked at the prints Nield had chuckled.

'You guessed right . . .'

Tweed did not shake hands with the Russian and they began to stroll up and down the cobbled open space. Tweed took the initiative.

'What is this emergency? And where have you been hiding yourself?'

'In a safe place here in Finland.'

Which meant the heavily guarded Soviet two-hundred-man Embassy on the way to Brown Park, Tweed thought. The Russian, taller than Tweed, looked very slim in his well-cut outfit, younger in his roll-top sweater.

'The emergency,' Tweed prodded.

'You heard about the explosion on the Trans-Siberian Railway? We haven't caught those responsible but we know the saboteurs were infiltrated across the northern border.'

'Northern?'

'The Finnish frontier. A thousand miles or so long. Finland has a small population, a vast land area. And the explosives came in the same route the saboteurs used – via Lapland. We think we know where. We hear a huge consignment of more explosives is due to cross the border tomorrow. That is, today. It's after midnight.'

'How on earth does someone smuggle in explosives in large quantities, into Finland?' asked Tweed.

He knew very well. Newman had discovered the route when he visited Porvoo with Paula and Marler, when he heard about INCUBUS's factory ship operating outside the coastal waters. He was testing the Russian's knowledge.

'Probably through the archipelago,' Rebet replied. 'It wouldn't be too difficult – it's an incredible labyrinth of islands. The Finnish authorities could never guard the whole area. That we understand.'

'How can you be sure about this explosives consignment? About the precise timing – tonight?'

'I'm not identifying him but we have an agent inside the so-called Meteorological Institute east of Kemijärvi. He reports a great convoy of trucks with guards – who are undoubtedly also saboteurs – will slip across the border tonight. And this links with another movement. One of the three Angel suspects is touring the northern frontier on his way to Murmansk.'

'This man?' Tweed asked quietly, producing the photos.

Rebet examined them under a street lamp. He looked at Tweed in surprise.

'You know? We can't be sure. His presence could be a coincidence.'

'No coincidence,' Tweed said briskly.

Without naming Nield, he told Rebet how a member of his team had tracked the third man through the Turku archipelago, aboard a fishing vessel obviously heading out to transfer their secret passenger to a Soviet ship bound for Tallinn.

'And you guessed who Angel was in Leningrad when you watched Dikoyan, Kazbek and Marshal Zaikov talking separately to Hauser?'

'Yes. Some day I may tell you why.'

'We thought the Red Army was restless about *perestroika* and *glasnost*.'

'We may be able to give you some help with the operation from the Finnish side . . .'

Tweed explained in detail the plans of the fake film unit which would be travelling to Lapland later that same day. Rebet listened as Tweed told him a few members of his team would be armed.

'We are leaving the Soviet border open to let the convoy through,' he warned. 'Your team should all wear white coats. I now reveal a top secret since you have co-operated so fully with me. You will be careful who knows this?' Rebet stressed.

'Of course.'

'Soviet paras will be waiting for that convoy. Your team could cross into Russia without realizing it. I am catching the first Aeroflot flight from Helsinki to Leningrad this morning. I shall then fly on to the north opposite Lapland. I will warn our troops to watch out for men in white coats, that they are friends.'

'Who knows? We may help to drive them into your arms.'

'That is what I am hoping.' Rebet stopped walking, turned to Tweed, held out his hand. 'Do not forget, Soviet paratroopers, an élite force. It could be very dangerous.'

'I think we've coped with our ration of danger so far.'

39

Dawn spread its eerie light over Helsinki shortly after 2 a.m. Tweed, leaving Newman to park the BMW, returned to his room to find everyone waiting for him. Paula, keeping herself awake by sheer will power, stifled a yawn. Tweed appeared still fresh.

'Who doesn't need sleep?' he asked cheerfully, glancing round. 'There's a job to be done. Keep you up until the morning.'

'It is morning,' Paula commented.

'I meant until eight or nine ack emma.'

'What's the job?' asked Marler. 'I can get by without sleep for two days.'

'And you'd be ideal for the job.' Tweed was moving about, full of bounce now action was imminent. 'I want

398

someone to watch INCUBUS Oy's HQ. There could be activity. You know where to watch the place from.'

'I'll do it . . .'

'Draw me a plan,' Dillon interrupted, 'and I'll keep an eye on them. I've been out of things all day.'

'Not you, Cord,' Tweed said. 'Not for this surveillance job. You could do it. Don't doubt it for a moment, but for a while longer you have to stay under cover. Remember your instructions.'

'Keys, Newman,' Marler said, holding out his hand as the reporter arrived back. 'You parked the BMW out back?' He looked at Tweed. 'I'm on my way. Report back about ten?'

'Not a moment later. We're leaving aboard the chartered plane for the Arctic Circle.' He continued giving orders as Marler left. 'Butler, Nield – I want you up at six. Come to my room. We have to drive in your hired Saab to the warehouse to collect the equipment for the film unit. As soon as Stockmann's is open one of you buys seven white coats. Better get some shut eye, all of you. You may soon feel a bit tired after yesterday.'

'A bit?' Paula remarked, standing up. 'You must be joking.'

'Sorry. I wasn't including you. You've had the toughest day any one of us has gone through for a long time. Get off to bed. Sleep well.'

Newman waited until they had all gone. He had the stamina of an ox, still didn't feel like sleep. He poured some mineral water for Tweed out of a bottle which had rested in the ice bucket alongside the champagne bottles.

'We were lucky during the hostage exchange,' he observed as Tweed drank. 'At that hour there were no guests from that hotel with the unpronounceable name floating around down by the scrubbing board. And none in reception when we rushed through it to reach you – even the receptionist was absent.'

'Lucky,' Tweed agreed. 'Paula seems OK. At nine this morning I have to soothe Dr Winter who came to check Paula. Says he never got near her.'

'No time,' recalled Newman. 'We were too busy escaping. And Paula looks pretty good.'

'I'll keep Winter quiet with a large fee,' Tweed decided. 'He's one of the few English doctors in Helsinki. I'll tell him it was an operation the police want kept quiet. Which is why nothing will appear in the press.'

'I think sending Marler out to INCUBUS at this hour is a waste of time. The place will be shut up. What's the idea?'

'First, Hauser moves about a lot, jets all over the world. He's spent far longer in one place – Helsinki – than he normally does. I got this from the data Monica fed to me. He could be moving on. Second, he's near the end of a risky and sensitive operation in Finland. I'd expect him to clear out in case it blows up in his face. Literally.'

Without revealing Rebet's identity, he told Newman what the Russian had explained to him. What they might face if they were close to the border, the precautions he was taking. The only factor he omitted to mention was the existence of Angel.

'Today,' Tweed ended, rubbing his hands together, 'will be one of frenetic activity.'

'That's nice. Yesterday you'd call a rest day?'

Inside his penthouse office at INCUBUS's HQ Hauser was supervising the removal of all key files locked away in steel cabinets. Each was labelled with a coded designation of its contents. Male staff were heaving cabinets out of his office towards the elevator.

It was 2.10 a.m. For a moment Hauser glanced at Carver and Galvone, then looked out of the picture window. The rising sun was casting a pearl-grey light on the

400

smooth sea which made it look like a leaden lake.

'I'll miss this view,' he said nostalgically.

'I suppose someone will let me in on the secret of where we're going to when they feel like it,' Carver commented ironically.

Hauser closed the door behind the last workman who had temporarily left the office. He poured a large glass of mineral water, drained it.

'OK, boy,' he said to Carver, 'time to let you in on the secret. We're moving our centre of operations to the HQ in Stockholm.'

'Nothing is labelled with its destination,' Carver pointed out.

'For security reasons. Addressed labels are prepared, will be attached while the trucks are en route to the airport. Attached only by trusted staff. You know how I operate. I turn up where I'm least expected.' He swivelled his gaze. 'Frank, hadn't you better be leaving to take charge of Operation Urals?'

Hauser waited until he was alone with Carver. The president of INCUBUS had his shirt sleeves rolled up above his elbows. He was personally supervising the movement of top secret filing cabinets. If you wanted a job done properly you had to do the goddamn thing yourself.

'Adam, you fly today to Stockholm aboard the Lear jet. It will be carrying the key filing cabinets. I'm making you personally responsible for supervising the unloading and transport of them to the vault at our Stockholm HQ. The Lear lands at Bromma Airport – away from prying eyes.'

'We'll need a vehicle to carry them from Bromma . . .'

'All arranged. A truck will be waiting. You take them to our HQ in one of those high-rise office blocks on Sveavägen – high-rise for Stockholm.'

'I didn't see any identification to separate the key cabinets from the others.'

Hauser clapped a hand on his shoulder. 'All taken care of. Green labels will be attached aboard the truck for the jet downstairs. The rest of the stuff travels air cargo by scheduled flight.'

'When are you coming? You are travelling to Stockholm?'

'I travel incognito under a different name aboard another scheduled flight later. I have to be out of Helsinki by midday.'

'What is this Operation Urals?'

'Questions! Questions! Haven't I told you before you ask too many? Get down to the garage area and make sure those jerks attach a green label to every cabinet. On your way.'

Hauser inserted a cigarette into his holder as Carver left the room. Hauser radiated confidence but he was a worried man. The plan to rescue Irina Serov, to hold on to their own hostage, had gone badly wrong. Tweed had foreseen his strategy, had out-manoeuvred him with superior strategy. Hauser shrugged his massive shoulders. So Tweed had scored a brownie point.

He smiled as he thought of his opponent's chagrin when he eventually discovered the entire INCUBUS apparatus in Finland had disappeared. Oh yes, he could out-smart Tweed.

Sitting inside the car perched in the trees above INCU-BUS's HQ, Marler watched through the viewer of his camera. At three in the early morning, now broad daylight, he studied the intense activity.

Men in overalls carried filing cabinets to one of the waiting trucks parked in the compound outside the garage area. There seemed to be some division of labour. Adam Carver was standing by one truck as cabinets were heaved inside.

402

Other men were lugging cabinets to two other trucks and Carver appeared to have no interest in these vehicles. Marler twiddled an unlit king-size between his lips and waited.

Occasionally he sipped water from a plastic bottle. He could do without food but already it was very warm: had it ever cooled down? Marler settled in for a long wait. He had infinite patience, had learned to develop that virtue as a marksman waiting for his target to show.

Nearly two hours later, at 5 a.m., Carver climbed into the cab beside the driver. The vehicle drove forward, the automatic gates in the wire fence opened, the truck came out, turned in the direction of Helsinki.

'You're for me, Laddie,' Marler said to himself.

He started the engine, drove down the road out of sight of the HQ, joined the main road. Keeping well back – there was no traffic to speak of at that hour – he kept the truck in sight. Soon he realized it was heading for the airport as the truck barrelled along the highway between the granite outcrops.

Marler was driving the hired Saab. The opposition would be familiar by now with the cream BMW. He arrived at the airport as unloading was beginning. Driving past, he pulled in at the kerb, locked the car, strolled inside the concourse.

Even at that hour there were a number of tourists waiting for flights. Mostly young back-packers, sprawled in seats, fast asleep, a growth of stubble on the men's chins, the girls in crumpled denims and creased blouses.

Marler picked up a brochure from a pile on the counter, pretended to be studying it. A wheeled trolley laden with filing cabinets marked with green labels was pushed past him. The presence of Carver outside did not bother him: so far Carver had never seen Marler.

Through a window he watched the trolley being propelled out to the waiting Lear jet. The men in overalls had a hard job manoeuvring a cabinet up the retractable steps inside the jet. Marler decided it would be too risky enquiring where the jet was bound for. He heard another truck arriving.

Half an hour later the cabinets aboard the second truck were being handed over to Cargo for transport aboard a scheduled flight. Marler waited until the team went back for another load, approached the cargo supervisor.

'I have a consignment arriving a bit later for you. I hope it arrives in time. Can I check departure time of that plane you're loading?'

'For Arlanda, Stockholm? Departs 7.30 a.m. Will be on time.'

'Thank you,' said Marler.

He walked outside and a third INCUBUS truck was drawing up at the kerb. He paused to light a cigarette. Two men jumped out of the cab, ran to the rear, unlocked the doors. A team inside began unloading at once. Conducted with military precision, Marler thought as he climbed behind the wheel of the Saab and drove away.

Tweed was freshly shaven, fully dressed, when he opened his bedroom door to Marler. In a chair sat Paula, also dressed for the day. Marler swallowed a yawn.

'You people don't get much sleep, do you?'

'Too excited,' Paula told him.

'I have to leave for the warehouse with Butler and Nield,' Tweed said briskly. 'What have you found out – if anything?'

'Hauser is evacuating the Helsinki HQ . . .'

He described what he had seen, kept it short, to the point. Tweed was drinking mineral water as he finished.

404

He put down the glass, walked to the window. It was going to be another glorious day. The metal mobile sculpture was motionless. Not a breath of wind. It was going to be bloody hot.

'Stockholm,' he said after a moment. 'I thought he might be running for it, dissociating himself from Finland considering what will soon be happening in the Arctic Circle.'

'I am coming with you all,' Paula said firmly.

'No, you're not,' Tweed informed her. 'Change of plan – because of Marler's news . . .'

'Because you think this expedition is too dangerous for a woman,' Paula blazed.

'Because,' Tweed countered calmly, 'I now have a job for you which could be even more dangerous. Because you know the area. Because I know you would never let me down.'

'What job?'

'I want to be sure you can disguise yourself. You may be travelling with members of the opposition who know you – who have pictures of you. In short, I want you to fly to Stockholm, preferably aboard the 7.30 a.m. flight, providing you can get a seat. If you do board that flight, wait at Arlanda, wait when you arrive. Before you leave Helsinki phone one of the twenty-four-hours-a-day hire firms, arrange for a car to be waiting for you at Arlanda. After they've unloaded the cabinets Marler has told us about, follow them to their destination.'

'I'd better get moving . . .'

'Wait. First, go to your room, disguise yourself. Come back and let me see how you look . . .'

Within minutes she had returned. Tweed and Marler stared at her. Paula had tucked most of her hair under a tight-fitting straw hat, had changed into a grey skirt and a long-sleeved cream blouse. But the greatest transformation was the pale shade of face powder she had applied, the large pair of horn-rim spectacles she was wearing. And no lipstick.

Marler chuckled. 'God! You look like a schoolteacher.'

'That's the general idea,' Paula snapped.

'I congratulate you,' said Tweed. 'When you arrive in Stockholm book rooms for all of us at The Grand Hotel, if they have the space. If you have to fix us up elsewhere, leave a message in a sealed envelope for me.'

'The Grand?' Paula objected. 'Bob and Cord Dillon stayed there with me when we were on our way here.'

'No matter. If Hauser checks, finds we have arrived on his heels, so much the better. Pressure, that's what I'm putting on him from now on. Pressure and more pressure. Better get moving.'

Marler waited until she had rushed off. 'It is a dangerous assignment you've given her. Is that wise when she's recovering from her kidnap ordeal?'

'One reason why I asked her – apart from the fact that I do need her to do the job. She'll be working on her own – which she's very good at. That alone will help the ordeal to fade.'

'And now we're heading for the Arctic Circle. It could be quite a battle.'

'A ferocious battle.'

40

The heatwave was scorching London. At Park Crescent Monica had all the windows open. It made no difference: the air was still, not the ghost of a breeze came inside. She was sitting with Howard, explaining her extensive research on INCUBUS and Franklin D. Hauser.

'I had trouble locating this house he has in Sweden close to Norway in the western archipelago – that's north of Gothenburg. Most people outside Scandinavia think there is only one, the archipelago outside Stockholm.'

'I do know some geography,' Howard bridled.

'Good for you.'

Howard smiled. With so many of his key staff away the barriers between himself and Monica were coming down. As a major concession to the heat Howard sat in shirt sleeves, an informal state of dress Monica had never known before. She ran a hand over her bun of grey hair and continued.

'It is a large house, very remote as far as I can see. I had to get this chart from a contact at Lloyd's to locate Skalhamn.'

'What's that?'

'The tiny cove below where the house stands.' She pointed to the chart. 'There it is. Well out of the way. My contact at Lloyd's phoned a friend in Sweden. Apparently the house looks like a major communications centre. A tangle of weird aerials on the roof, plus a satellite dish.'

'Where does that get us?'

'If you'll wait till I've finished. Hauser also has based there a large yacht – the kind of boat Onassis used to live on. The *Washington IV*. When he's not jetting across the world Hauser travels around a lot in that vessel. And it is equipped like a floating communications platform.'

'Hauser is in Helsinki so far as we know,' Howard objected.

'But I've checked his movements in recent years as far as I can. He jumps all over the globe like a grasshopper – so he may leave Helsinki. Tweed will want to know about his haunts.'

'And that's it?'

'Heavens, no! The best is yet to come. He has offices in

407

Oslo, Stockholm, Copenhagen, Amsterdam, Brussels, Frankfurt, Paris, Geneva, Vienna, Madrid, Lisbon, Milan, Athens. Also in Singapore, Auckland, Sydney, Montreal. And in South America and Japan. Do you want me to go on?'

'That is the best?'

'No, I've been saving the gem for last. Livingstone Manor in Suffolk. Apart from Boston, New York, and a host of other cities in the States. Livingstone Manor *is* the gem,' she repeated.

'What about the place?'

'It appears to be the real HQ from where he controls and directs his world-wide empire . . .'

'Sounds most unlikely.'

'That's the clever part. It's supposed to be his country home in Britain. Who would suspect it was the centre of the INCUBUS spider's web?'

'I wouldn't, for one. What is all this?'

'Livingstone Manor is very large, has extensive grounds. Underneath the ground floor is a labyrinth of converted cellars. They're like catacombs. The whole area was reconstructed, the security is tight. He has installed the latest sophisticated cipher and coding machines. A very advanced telephone scrambler system has been secreted in one huge room. More sophisticated than the hot line between Downing Street and the Kremlin.'

'How on earth do you know all this?' Howard asked in an incredulous tone.

'I have a friend in an insurance company who covers the equipment. He only gave me the tiniest hint but I followed it up.'

'And how did you do that?'

'I obtained from the same friend the name of the electric company who had installed it.'

'Don't tell me he spilt all these beans to you.'

408

'No. I didn't even try that route. Instead I phoned one of Tweed's close friends in Special Branch. He owes Tweed. It's all the old boys' network. You use it yourself at that club of yours.'

'Never mind about that. Go on.'

'I gave the Special Branch man the name of the electrical firm and he went to see the managing director. I gather he had to twist his arm, but I didn't want to know about that. Guess what?'

'I'm not partial to guessing games,' Howard retorted, for a brief moment his old stiff self.

'The Special Branch man obtained from this managing director a complete specification of what they had installed at Livingstone Manor. He, the managing director that is, became worried he had broken some regulations. He came up with the information I've supplied.'

'And they installed the cipher machines?'

'No. They must have been made inside INCUBUS' laboratories in Boston on what used to be Space Highway. But one of the top electrical supervisors wandered round this underground labyrinth beneath Livingstone Manor. He was at Bletchley during the war – working on the ENIGMA cipher machine the Nazis were using. He found a steel door open and looked inside. No one was about. He saw the cipher machines, reported what he'd seen to his managing director.'

'I see.'

Howard was impressed, almost appalled. Bloody nerve. In the middle of the English countryside. And in Suffolk – where he had his own country retreat on the rare occasions when he paid his obligatory visit to his wife, Cynthia.

'Nothing illegal about it, I suppose. Unfortunately.'

'No,' Monica agreed. 'But highly significant. As I said earlier, I'm convinced Hauser has moved his operational centre from America to Livingstone Manor . . .'

She broke off as the phone rang. She listened for a short time, put a hand over the instrument.

'We have two unwelcome visitors. Chief Inspector Buchanan and Sergeant Warden. They're waiting downstairs and have asked to see Tweed.'

'Tell them to go away, that he's not here.'

'Not wise,' Monica said firmly. 'We ought to find out what they want. Forewarned is forearmed.'

'Oh, all right, if you say so . . .'

Howard himself was surprised at the transformation in the relationship between himself and Monica. He had always before regarded her as the ageless woman who looked after the files. Now he was treating her as an equal.

Buchanan was at his most official when he entered, Sergeant Warden was his normal poker-faced self. Howard did not stand up. Dismissively, he waved them to sit down.

'I'm Howard, Tweed's superior. Tweed is away. If you can make it brief I would appreciate it. We are rather busy.'

'Aren't we all?' Buchanan, appearing not to notice Howard's lack of welcome, and relaxed, crossing his long legs. Warden took out his notebook, rested it on his lap.

'Anything said at this interview is off the record,' Howard snapped. 'Kindly remember where you are.'

'Oh, we're very conscious where we are,' Buchanan told him amiably. 'But I would remind you, Mr Howard, since I am confident you must have heard, that I am investigating a particularly brutal murder. Namely that of Sandra Riverton in Suffolk.'

'And I read in the paper,' Monica chimed in, 'that you've caught the Camden Town murderer.'

'Quite correct.' Buchanan politely swivelled in his chair to address her. 'So all our energies are now released to continue the investigation into the Sandra Riverton case.

410

Not that we ever ceased our interest.' He paused. 'Did you know that Evelyn Lennox, Sandra's sister, has been attacked in her cottage at Walberswick?'

'What on earth has all this to do with us?' Howard demanded.

'I'll explain,' Buchanan continued patiently. 'The person who discovered Sandra's body hanging from a bell tower was Robert Newman. You know where he is at this moment?' he asked suddenly.

'No idea,' Howard snapped. 'No contact for some time.'

'The point is,' Buchanan went on relentlessly, 'within twenty-four hours Ed Riverton, Sandra's brother-in-law, an American, was also brutally murdered in Helsinki. And I detect a similarity in both MOs. Murder by garrotting the neck, murder by hanging from the neck.'

'Fail to see the connection.'

'I'm coming to that. Sandra Riverton had worked for INCUBUS, who have an office in Norwich. She had resigned two weeks before she died. Ed Riverton was a top executive with INCUBUS. Evelyn Lennox also worked for INCUBUS.'

'How is she?' Monica asked. 'Is she seriously hurt?'

She felt illogically conscience-stricken. At Tweed's request she had withdrawn Harry Butler from Walberswick and his job had been to protect her.

'She was lucky.' Buchanan changed his phraseology. 'She was resourceful, plucky. It was evening. A masked intruder appeared in her hall. He must have picked the lock to get into the place. They grappled in the hall, Miss Lennox was bruised but broke free. She fled into the kitchen where she had some water boiling in a pan. She threw it at her attacker, at his masked face. He screamed, ran for it. Lennox thought from his build he might be a man called Steve who visited her some time ago at her Wandsworth home.'

411

'He works with a man called Papa Grimwood,' Monica told him.

'And how do you know that, if I may ask?'

'Bob Newman told me . . .'

'Lennox gave us a good description of her attacker's build,' Buchanan added. 'It also pretty well fits Newman's.'

'That's ridiculous,' Monica burst out.

'It would be,' Buchanan agreed, stretching out his legs, 'if I knew Newman was a long way from the scene of the attack at the time.'

So that's what you've been building up to, Howard thought. He waved a hand.

'So far as we know Mr Newman is out of the country.'

'So far as you know? That's not good enough.'

'It will have to do for now.'

'Chief Inspector,' Monica broke in to divert him to another subject, 'is Evelyn Lennox under police protection? Whoever did this awful thing might come back.'

'Yes, he might. The local police have agreed to your suggestion. The trouble is all they can spare is a PC who visits Walberswick on his bicycle, that he will call in at Rose Bower to make sure Lennox is all right. I'm afraid it's rather a flimsy form of protection.'

'Then find Papa Grimwood and this man, Steve,' Monica said.

'We're looking. So far no trace of them.' He handed Howard a card. 'When Newman gets back from wherever he is I'd appreciate it if you'd give me a call.'

'Why can't he give you a call himself?' Howard suggested in a bleak tone.

'Better still.' Buchanan stood up, Warden followed his chief's example. 'Thank you for your co-operation, sir. Perhaps now you can see the connection?'

'Not entirely,' Howard responded. 'Thank you for calling.'

412

'That's all right. And we can find our own way out . . .'

'Don't forget to hand in your passes. Or otherwise even you won't get past the guard,' was Howard's parting shot.

Monica could hardly contain herself until they were alone.

'You see! I was right about Livingstone Manor. It's in the same area as Walberswick where that girl was attacked. Sooner or later the action is going to move back to Livingstone Manor.'

'I do wish Tweed would get in touch,' Howard said irritably. 'I wonder what he's up to now?'

41

'He's an expert executioner,' Hauser said.

In the turret room at his house overlooking the park he was taking files from a wall safe, stuffing them inside a briefcase. The files were records of various key industrialists who owned companies he was determined to buy up in Britain and Europe. The files had been compiled by Sandra Riverton and Evelyn Lennox pretending to compile profiles for the American magazine *Leaders of Mankind.*

His reply had been in answer to a question posed by Iris Reynolds, the girl sitting on the edge of a couch while she watched him.

'Why have you decided to fly Ion Manescu to Stockholm?' she had asked him. 'I thought he was going with Galvone and Ziegler to see the explosives convoy safely across the Soviet border.'

Iris Reynolds was the new identity given to Irina Serov

by Hauser. She had arranged her bleached blonde hair so it framed her face. Combed down over her forehead, it changed her appearance from the woman who had visited Tweed at the Hesperia. She wore a flowered print dress, a wide-brimmed straw hat, flat-heeled shoes – reducing her earlier heights by inches. She looked very English and carried a doctored British passport.

'Manescu,' Hauser went on as he slid more files into the case, 'is travelling by scheduled flight to Arlanda. I'd like those photographs now.' He put them inside a cardboard backed envelope, inserted the envelope in the case.

'The only member of the opposition we haven't pictures of now is the man on the motor cycle who helped to foil our trap at the scrubbing board. You'll travel aboard the Lear jet with me. When we reach our destination you can help produce an Identikit of Tweed. As you saw, we have photos of the man who guarded you standing on the platform. The schmuck was filmed from the cabin cruiser with a telescopic lens. There may be others but they'll be back here, trying to locate us.'

Irina marvelled at the American's energy. He now had shown full confidence in her after the long apprenticeship: it was the first time he had let her know his identity.

'One thing I don't understand,' she said carefully, 'is why I'm not yet being sent into Russia to run Operation Urals.'

'You've phoned your agents in München, the Free Ukraine movement. Your agents are placed in Poland and Czechoslovakia. They'll all be crossing the border into Russia, they know where to pick up the explosives, the targets.' He paused briefly, stared hard at her with his icecold eyes. 'That is a fact, I hope.'

'I have done all that,' she assured him.

'Then maybe later we'll fly you to Istanbul so you can slip across the Turkish border to keep them active.'

414

'One more point,' she ventured. 'That attractive girl you exchanged me for. You think she'll stay here?'

He grinned cynically. 'Could you imagine Tweed having the audacity to send her after me? Bearing in mind how many pictures we have of *her*?'

Waiting aboard the Lear jet at Helsinki Airport, Adam Carver checked his watch again. When was the damned thing going to take off? They were hours behind schedule. He swallowed some more mineral water. The jet was air-conditioned but the heat seemed to penetrate inside the aircraft.

A small canvas-covered truck drove towards the jet. Carver frowned. All the cabinets had been put aboard ages ago. What could be coming out to the jet now? The truck arrived, turned a half-circle, backed to the foot of the steps. Carver stared in disbelief. The canvas flap had been lifted from the rear, two people appeared, boarded.

Hauser wore a peaked cap of the type once favoured by German students, a British sports jacket with a small check design, a pair of well-creased grey slacks, dark glasses. He parked the unknown girl with him in a seat at the front of the jet, walked back to settle in an armchair next to Carver.

The step ladder had been retracted, the door closed; the jet engines were growling, building up power. Hauser clutched the bulging briefcase in his lap. It contained enough information to blackmail over thirty industrialists and copies of the earlier reports by Sandra Riverton and Evelyn Lennox. The profiles on firms already swallowed up, details of the techniques used. A briefcase of dynamite.

'It's mid-afternoon,' Carver protested. 'And I'd no idea you'd be travelling with me.'

'Now you know.'

415

Hauser grinned to himself. Keep them all off balance – and it was good security not to let even his closest associates know what was happening next.

'I suppose we are going to Bromma?' Carver asked as the jet moved down the runway.

'Bromma is our next destination,' Hauser agreed.

He turned away to conceal his wolfish smile. Well, they were at least putting down at Bromma for a few minutes. And he had fooled that bastard Tweed.

'At last we have some questions we can put to Hauser. To grill him,' Mauno Sarin said with satisfaction to Karma.

It was the news from the Finnish traffic police about the brown Buick wrecked at the Kalastajatorppa which had given the Finn the lever he had been looking for. Sarin had told them to leave it where it was, had driven at speed with Karma to the scene of the 'accident'.

'Surely someone must have witnessed this,' he said when they stood looking at the vehicle, its bonnet telescoped against the granite boulder.

'I haven't found anyone,' reported Karma who had arrived earlier. 'The guests were enjoying themselves at a dinner dance in the main restaurant across the road. But I found this taped to the underside of the front passenger seat.'

A Luger. Fully loaded. In Finland you don't travel with handguns. Karma had used the hotel phone to check the registration number on the intact rear plate. The Buick was registered to INCUBUS. Sarin wasted no time.

'Drive me to their headquarters. Fast . . .'

Arriving at the tall circular building they were surprised to find the automatic gate open and no sign of a guard. No sign of any staff. The switchboard was unmanned.

Sarin had pressed the elevator button for the penthouse floor. As they stepped out he was struck by the silence.

416

His long legs took him swiftly to Hauser's office. Opening the door he walked inside, stared.

The furniture was still in place. What attracted Sarin's attention were rectangles of dust-free marble on the floor against the walls. Spaces where filing cabinets had stood. He opened several drawers in the outsize desk. Empty. He looked at Karma.

'If that phone is working call the airport. Hauser has a Lear jet.'

Karma found Hauser's personal phone was still connected with the outside world. Probably a private line which bypassed the switchboard. Sarin walked rapidly through the other offices, returned as Karma put down the phone.

'The place has been evacuated,' Sarin commented.

'And the Lear jet took off mid-afternoon after being in a holding area all night and since early morning.'

'Destination?'

'The flight plan was for Bromma Airport, Stockholm.'

'So he's run for it. I wonder why? You may as well know I told the Minister about the Semtex Marler says he took from an INCUBUS truck north of Porvoo, and the second lot from a truck in an alleged hidden garage at the Institute.'

'How did he react?' Karma enquired.

'At first he said he'd take it under consideration. In other words, do nothing. Or so I thought. Yesterday I heard the government had turned down Hauser's offer of the three million dollars for a new icebreaker. That was signalling to Hauser he'd better be more careful.'

'Could be the reason he's left Finland.'

'Unless there's a more sinister reason. Assemble a team of men to fly to the Arctic Circle. I'm going to take a look at that Institute for myself.'

'Half our people are on holiday – it is July,' Karma warned. 'It will take time.'

'So have the team ready for tonight.'

*   *   *

Newman was disturbed to discover the plane Tweed had chartered was a Fokker, a machine powered by propellers. He sat alongside Tweed as it took off from Helsinki Airport in late afternoon.

'Sounds like a bloody sewing machine,' he commented.

'It was the only machine I could get,' Tweed responded. 'And it's large enough to take all of us in comfort – plus the equipment.'

Marler sat opposite, staring out of the window. His Armalite was easily concealed among the fake film unit's load of cameras, lights and canisters of film. Butler and Nield sat beside each other near the front of the aircraft. Cord Dillon sat alone, his craggy face grim as the machine soared into the sky, heading north.

There had been an animated argument between Tweed and the American alone in Tweed's room at the Hesperia prior to departure for the airport. Tweed had marshalled all his reasons why Dillon should not go.

'You're the US President's personal representative . . .'

'And he sent me to Europe to get enough evidence to destroy Hauser in the courts back home. What could be more damning than proof he's transporting explosives into the Soviet Union? Goddamnit, hear me out! I'm coming with you if I have to shove this Luger in your back . . .'

Eventually Tweed had given in. Dillon's case for joining them was overwhelming. Reluctantly, he had agreed.

One thing which worried Tweed as the Fokker continued to climb, leaving Helsinki far behind, was the few weapons they carried. Dillon had his Luger; Marler his Armalite; Newman his Smith & Wesson. That was it. No, there was another weapon: Marler had given Butler the Mauser and the spare mags taken from the second guard at the Institute. One rifle, three handguns. A meagre strike force.

Before leaving for Stockholm Paula had offered her

418

Browning. Tweed had insisted she kept the weapon. It was bad enough sending her off on her own on a dangerous mission. At least she should be armed.

On two empty seats at the rear of the machine were six white coats purchased from Stockmann's. And those, Tweed reminded himself, were vital life savers to identify the fake film unit. His mouth tightened at the prospect before them on the Finnish border. Operating just over that frontier: Soviet paras.

Due to the regulations the Fokker had to land at Oulu on the coast of the Gulf of Bothnia. Tweed peered out of the port window. A small airfield. No sign of the town. Just one tiny airport building designated *Oulu* over the entrance. No other aircraft. Butler returned from the pilot's cabin with the bad news.

'The pilot says we have to wait here. Weather conditions. A storm is coming in fast. It may be for a while.'

'How long is a while?' Tweed demanded.

'No idea. Oh, he also had a met. report from Rovaniemi. Temperature 33°C. That's 91°F.'

'But that's hotter than Helsinki,' Tweed protested to Newman. 'Rovaniemi is north of the Arctic Circle.'

'Didn't anyone tell you?' Newman replied with a droll smile. 'It often is hotter in the Arctic Circle.'

'Charming. Meanwhile we're stuck here. Might as well eat while we're stationary . . .'

He had hardly finished the sentence when the storm broke. Beyond his window forked lightning flashed non-stop. The spectacle was punctuated by tremendous thunderclaps which seemed to shudder the aircraft. Sheets of tropical-like rain hammered the tarmac, bouncing off its surface, flooding the area. Rain lashed the windows like a flail of whips.

'Just what we needed.' Tweed sighed.

Butler and Nield acted as stewards, serving ham sandwiches from coolbags. Tweed was ravenous. With his sandwiches he drank mineral water. Dillon, holding a paper plate piled with sandwiches, left his seat, walked up to where Tweed sat.

'This delay going to screw up our schedule?'

'The beach buggies waiting for us at Rovaniemi airport will just have to move faster,' Tweed told him.

'Ever tried to drive one of those things? Tried to make them move faster?'

On this optimistic note he returned to his seat. There was no point in continuing the conversation – thunder crashed like a continuous banging of giant cymbals, rain was still streaming down in sheets, more like a cascade from a deep waterfall. Lightning flashes flared as Tweed finished his meal, checked his watch.

'Has to stop sometime, I suppose,' Newman remarked.

Tweed grunted, closed his eyes for a nap and fell fast asleep. He was woken by the starting up of the motors. He looked out of the window and it was a bright summer's day. The Fokker moved forward, gathered speed, took off and turned in a circle. Through the window Tweed saw a vast distance – out across the sea to the west was the coast of distant Sweden. The plane continued climbing, heading away from the sea north-east for Rovaniemi.

'Are you satisfied with the arrangements?' Newman asked. 'This is going to be a tricky operation.'

'The Admin. Officer at the Institute is a Mr Palonen. Paula had a long talk with him on the phone yesterday. Gave him the impression we are filming for a TV documentary. They always fall for TV. Palonen said the Institute had just been closed for redecoration . . .'

'That would be Hauser. Trying to keep people away from the place while the convoy of explosives is moved.'

'Exactly. Paula went on talking, said would it be OK if we took pictures of the outside and the surrounding countryside. Palonen agreed to that. So he is expecting us.'

'And supposing we need to make a quick getaway? Hardly a situation for beach buggies.'

'Which is why when I chartered this machine I also fixed up for the hire of a Sikorsky and a pilot. An S61. Takes eighteen passengers.'

'So why didn't we travel in that?'

'Because it wasn't available until this evening. I also obtained from them a Verey pistol with orange flares. Marler has it. If we're out in the wilderness – which I suspect we shall be – we can signal to the S61 where to land to take us off.'

'You seem to have thought of everything,' Newman commented as Tweed peered out of the window at a blue rope which was a river winding its way across the flat sun-bleached plain far below.

'Except for the unexpected. Thank God Paula isn't with us.'

Hours earlier Paula sat in her hired Volvo outside Arlanda airport. Knowing it would take time to unload cargo from the aircraft which had flown her from Helsinki, she had not hurried with the courier who handed over the car to her.

Now she sat peering from under the brim of her straw hat at the waiting INCUBUS AB truck. The heatwave was burning Sweden and she had all the windows open. An hour later she saw trolleys stacked with filing cabinets being trundled towards the truck where the automatic rear platform had been lowered to street level.

Half an hour later the truck was belting down the highway through open country towards Stockholm. Paula was careful to keep some distance back: it was a good three-quarters of an hour's drive from Arlanda into the city centre.

The highway reminded her of the drive into Helsinki from the Finnish airport. It stretched into the distance between limestone outcrops until she reached the outskirts of the Swedish capital. She closed the gap.

Sveavägen. Near the end of the wide street was Sergels Torg. A few hundred yards before reaching that notorious square where on their outward journey Newman had purchased weapons, Little Manhattan sheered up to her right just beyond where she was parked. Five nineteen-storey slabs of white stone; the tallest office blocks in Stockholm.

Paula watched as the filing cabinets were moved inside one of the towers. Over the entrance was the logo INCUBUS AB. She sat behind the wheel as though waiting for her boy friend. The charade was not difficult to keep up as several Swedish youths approached one by one and chatted her up.

Paula began to worry as the elevated platform was raised, the truck drove away. Delivery completed. If those cabinets were so important why weren't they accompanied by a top executive?

I'm missing something, she kept thinking. What is it?

Then she remembered Bromma, the small airport the other side of the city Newman had driven her to when they were in Stockholm on their way to Finland. Paula had a flair for recalling routes. She drove through the city, headed along the highway to Bromma.

The airport seemed as quiet and lifeless as it had when she had last explored it. Parking the Volvo, she walked inside, across the deserted concourse to the window she knew overlooked the airfield. She stood stock still for a moment, hardly able to believe her luck.

'Bull's-eye!' she said to herself.

Extracting the small pair of binoculars she always

422

carried in her shoulder bag, she focused them. The Lear jet stood in almost the same place it had been parked before. And along the fuselage stood out the logo. INCUBUS.

She moved to one side of the window, raised her glasses, waited. The door was open, the retractable staircase was leading to the ground. Five minutes later she saw a man appear, walk stiffly down the steps. A large man, he wore a peaked cap, a British-type sports jacket, grey slacks and dark glasses. It took Paula a moment to recognize him. More something about his movements than his mode of dress.

'Good God! Hauser!' she said under her breath.

Hauser was stretching his arms, walking up and down, when a second man appeared. Slimmer, he ran down the steps, paced slowly up and down alongside Hauser. Paula had no trouble recognizing him. She pursed her lips.

'Mr Casanova himself. Adam Carver.'

She lowered the glasses, slipped them back inside her bag, waited. It was obvious they were not waiting for a car to take them into Stockholm. Marler had told her enough about Hauser's meticulous organization and timing for her to realize a limo would have been waiting *before* the jet landed. Mopping her forehead with a handkerchief, she prepared to wait some more.

'I thought when you said we were flying to Bromma we'd be occupying the Stockholm HQ,' Carver said as he strolled alongside his chief. 'What's next on the menu?'

'The cargo of filing cabinets which travelled by scheduled flight to here are routine. Tweed seems good at gathering information. His job, I guess. So we let Mr Tweed think we have flown to Stockholm when he wakes up to the fact we're no longer in Finland. Let him waste his time, not mine.'

'Well, if it's not a state secret, what is next on the menu? Where are we going?'

'To somewhere, boy, Tweed knows nothing about. Time we got aboard. The pilot should have checked that flashing light by now.'

He hauled his bulk back up the steps, walked inside the cabin, sagged into his arm chair. Jesus Christ! It was bloody hot.

'So make it a mystery tour,' Carver said irritably as he sat beside him.

'Gothenburg, boy. That's where we're going to. Gothenburg on the west coast of Sweden.' He lifted a hand as the pilot appeared at the exit to the control cabin, waved it forward.

'Get this hunk of scrap metal off the ground,' he growled.

Inside the airport building Paula watched as the jet became airborne. She waited until she saw the direction it was taking. West.

She was walking out of the entrance when she heard a shutter being pushed up. Swinging round, she saw the reception counter had just opened. A fair-haired and good-looking man in his thirties was arranging some papers. She rushed across the concourse as though she had just arrived.

'Is Mr Hauser's jet still on the ground? The INCUBUS Lear jet.'

'Just took off. You missed him by minutes.'

'Oh, Lord! I have a vital file he thinks he has with him outside in my car. I'm Peggy Vanderheld, his PA. I'll have to fly after him. He'll go crazy when he discovers he hasn't got it. And the hell of it is I got to the office late on Sveavägen so I don't know where he's off to now.'

'I shouldn't disclose flight plans, lady.' He was examining her with more than a little interest. 'Will you

424

be coming back to Stockholm? Maybe we could have a drink together one night?'

'Well ...' She gave him a winning smile. 'I'm just arrived from England. I don't have many friends. So maybe yes. But first I have to catch up with Hauser.'

'I never said anything to you.' He leaned over the counter, his face close to hers. 'Gothenburg.'

42

It was midnight north of the Arctic Circle in Lapland and broad daylight. The sun would remain above the horizon for twenty-four hours a day between June 16 and July 18. Tweed found the incredibly clear and ghost-like illumination weird.

The three beach buggies with their huge tyres were moving at speed through the wilderness. The manager of the firm Tweed had phoned in Rovaniemi had said he might be able to supply machines with souped-up engines. He had succeeded: the three cumbersome-looking buggies rocked from side to side as they plunged down an arid slope.

Newman and Marler were in the first machine with Newman behind the wheel, driving full out. In the second buggy, following him, Tweed sat beside Butler who was driving at the same teeth-shattering speeed. Behind them followed Nield, driving with Dillon seated alongside.

'This is like Macbeth's blasted heath,' Tweed shouted to make himself heard above the roar of the engine.

'It is blasted rough country,' Butler retorted. 'I hope Newman is heading in the right direction.'

'The man who hired out these things supplied a compass as I requested. Marler has a map.'

'I wonder if he can read a map?' Butler queried sarcastically.

Butler didn't too much like Marler. Tweed stared round as the file of machines raced on, holding on tight. The light was like high-powered moonlight and the country like a moonscape. The ground was covered with rocks protruding from its surface, rocks coated with lichens. A few stubby trees were little more than undergrowth growing in small miserable clumps. A wilderness. No landmarks. Low bare hills rose ahead.

'Why didn't we use the Fokker to fly us to the airfield at the Institute?' Butler called out. 'We'd have made much better time.'

'Because I couldn't persuade the pilot to fly on without referring back to Helsinki air control. That might have been dangerous. And in any case he had total interference with atmospherics on his radio.'

He stopped talking as the buggy began to climb the slope of one of the low hills. More rocks. More stunted trees. The ground covered with shrivelled moss. Tweed thought the world might look something like this after an atomic blast. Ahead of them Newman had stopped just below the summit, was standing up to peer over the top. Butler drew up alongside him, followed by Nield's buggy. Tweed stepped down on to spongy ground thankfully as the engines were switched off. He stretched his cramped legs, his aching arms, mopped his sweating forehead.

'And to think, we're only four hundred kilometres south of the Arctic Ocean.'

'I haven't done too badly,' Newman commented, binoculars pressed to his eyes.

'Let me have a shufti,' said Marler and took over the binoculars.

'What can you see?' Tweed asked as Dillon stood beside him.

'The Institute – a long way behind us. I bypassed it deliberately. We were way behind schedule. Take a look yourself when Marler has torn himself away from my binoculars. And the target is in sight . . .'

Tweed ignored the offer of binoculars. He had exceptional eyesight. With Dillon, Butler and Nield he walked the few paces to the summit, looked down over a vast landscape. The white buildings of the Institute complex were standing at a far lower level to the west, reminding him of their toy-like aspect Newman had described returning from his earlier visit.

What excited him was the convoy of ten trucks wending its way along a track to the east. He took the binoculars Marler handed him, stared through the lenses. Inscribed in Cyrillic along the sides of each truck were the words *State Transport*. They had located the INCUBUS convoy on its way to the Soviet Union. Tweed was appalled as he considered the amount of explosives, the havoc it could cause. Hauser was planning on creating a state of total turmoil and destruction so later he could walk in as a saviour. On his own terms.

'See that prominent hill,' Marler said, checking his map. 'It is 656 metres high – and inside Russia.'

'We are so close?'

Tweed was startled. He could see no sign of fortifications, no indication of where the frontier ran. Except for that prominent hill. Gazing at the luminous light he knew he shouldn't be here, so near to the border. And neither should Dillon. Howard would have a fit if he had known. But Tweed was enjoying the experience. Back in the field after many years. It took him back to the old days when he was a field agent. Then he frowned. The convoy had halted. Why? Had something disturbed them?

He swept the general area of the border again. Nothing

which betrayed the presence somewhere of Soviet paras from even this height. His binoculars picked out an unmanned watchtower. He could see inside the cabin perched at the top of the stilt-like support legs. Empty.

'Something is going wrong,' Newman said grimly. 'That convoy is still on Finnish soil, looks as though it may not be going any further.'

'Maybe we ought to encourage it,' Dillon suggested, producing his Luger. 'To keep moving.'

'So long as someone is waiting for it,' Tweed replied.

Troubled, he wondered if Angel had succeeded in his task. Maybe the frontier *was* wide open for the trucks to move into Russia and disappear to their various destinations. Marler had no such doubts.

'Time we got after that convoy, prodded it into moving. A few bullets flying round their cabs should encourage the drivers no end. Tweed, may I suggest you drive your buggy? Butler has the Mauser. Nield can stay behind his wheel – Dillon has his Luger.'

'And what about us?' Newman snapped. 'I have a Smith & Wesson. In case you've forgotten.'

'Never forget anything, chum,' Marler replied. 'But I have the Armalite. You stay with the wheel.'

'Let's get moving,' Tweed ordered. 'The first two buggies drive along the right side of the convoy when we catch it up. Nield drives along the left side – trap them in a crossfire, make them panic . . .'

Tweed settled himself behind the wheel as Butler jumped into the passenger seat. Newman was already rocking and slithering down the steep eastern slope at speed as Tweed started his engine, followed. It was the worst ground they had crossed. The slope was littered with boulders. Tweed avoided many of them, weaving in and out, but there were some he couldn't avoid. Only the enormous tyres of the buggies could have negotiated such territory. Frequently he had to wipe a damp hand on his white coat. His body was streaming with moisture – the effort of driving the buggy, the Arctic heat, above all the fact that the white coats were of the type worn by house surgeons. Too heavy.

The convoy was still stationary. They were approaching it from the rear as they reached the lower part of the back-breaking slope. With luck, Tweed thought, they won't see us until we're on top of them. The element of surprise was even more likely to cause panic.

'Aim to miss, for God's sake,' Tweed warned. 'We want the drivers alive to get those vehicles moving east.'

Butler had hauled out his Mauser, holding it in one hand to check it while he used the other hand to grip a bar. There was every chance that otherwise he would have been hurtled from the buggy which was swaying and bucking like a ship in a storm.

'Got the message,' Butler shouted back.

Newman's buggy was slowing down. Tweed realized he was doing this to mute the roar of his engine as they came closer to the tail of the convoy. Tweed reduced speed.

Still perched above the vast spread of landscape although now much lower on the long slope, Tweed was surprised at how close they had come to the prominent 656 m high hill. Inside Russia. He realized the lead vehicle in the convoy had stopped just short of the frontier.

He also had a good view of the track which continued on over the border with no apparent barrier, an equally good view of the terrain inside Russia. Very small scrub covered hills, deep rocky gulches and narrow crevasses just beyond either side of the track. Still not a sign of any human being, of Rebet's paras. Again he wondered had Angel tricked his own people, even tricked Rebet?

'I'm going to let rip in a minute,' Butler said.

'Not until we're alongside the lead vehicle. And miss the petrol tank, we want the trucks kept moving,' Tweed warned.

'I do know my job,' Butler protested mildly. 'That is exactly what I planned to do.'

In the third buggy Dillon, like Tweed, was frightened and exhilarated at the prospect of some active service once more. Better than sitting behind a desk in Langley, Virginia, sending out one poor schmuck after another into the firing line.

In his wing mirror Tweed saw Nield peeling off over to the left to take the convoy from the far side. Tweed checked his watch. He was thinking of the Sikorsky he had arranged to fly into the area to take them out. It was going to be a damn' near-run thing. Marler could be up to his neck in action when he should be signalling the pilot with his Verey pistol.

Newman opened up his engine, raced forward at all-out speed, racing past the first nine trucks of the convoy. Tweed saw Marler, holding the Armalite, bracing himself for his first shot. He raced his own buggy forward as Butler held on to the bar with one hand, rested the arm holding the Mauser across the bar, the muzzle jumping up and down. How the hell could he hope to aim a shot in the correct direction?

Newman rammed on his brake as he drew alongside the cab of the first vehicle, turned the wheel. The buggy skidded in a half circle, stopped. Marler was now facing the two men inside the driver's cab. He aimed his rifle, the two men ducked, he fired, high and at an angle. The windscreen shattered, spilt glass over the bonnet. Newman drove slowly back along the convoy, swerved to avoid Tweed's buggy while Marler continued firing the Armalite over the roofs of the trucks.

Nield arrived on the far side of the lead vehicle as the driver started his engine. Dillon loosed off one shot from his Luger, aiming above the two men's heads through the cab which had both side windows down to counter the heat. Nield drove on, turned on to the track to spin

430

round. His engine stalled. The lead truck picked up speed, rumbled towards Nield to slam into the buggy. Nield tried twice to start the engine, got it going at his third try, drove off the track seconds before the truck crushed him. Dillon loosed off another shot.

From Tweed's buggy Butler was firing his Mauser as the other truck engines started up, aiming across the bonnets as the whole convoy began lumbering forward. Tweed suddenly observed Newman's buggy driving straight for the frontier, the foot of the 656 m high hill.

'What the devil is the crazy fool doing?' he burst out.

'Someone on that hill,' Butler said laconically. 'And no one is shooting back at us from the convoy. Didn't expect that . . .'

'None of those men aboard the trucks will have arms – they're probably dissident ex-KGB men who slipped out of Russia soon after the new president took over. Now they're going back as trained saboteurs. So no arms – in case they're stopped later and searched. What man on the hill?'

'Pull even further away from the convoy and you'll see him. A little way up, standing in front of a huge rock and waving a white flag. I saw him for a few seconds when you were turning . . .'

Tweed drove the buggy away from the track. Stopping it, leaving the engine running, he stood up to get a clear view. The last truck of the convoy was crossing into Russia. A hundred feet or so up the side of the hill stood a man waving a white flag. He lowered the flag and at last Tweed understood why the convoy had waited.

It had been waiting for the all clear signal, the waving of the flag. Marler was running forward to the base of the hill, reached it, began climbing, carrying his Armalite in his left hand. Butler saw Tweed lean forward, stare fixedly.

'Oh, my God!'

431

'What is it?' Butler asked.

Out of one of the rocky gulches close to the last truck a group of men were springing to life. Men in army camouflage. The Soviet paras. The large man on the hill stooped, straightened swiftly, holding a machine pistol. He aimed it at the paras directly below him. It would be a massacre.

The man was large, looked huge even at a distance, a man with a mane of thick black hair, a black beard. Viktor Kazbek, the Georgian, the Minister of Communications. He raised the barrel of the machine pistol, hugged the stock into his massive shoulder.

A single shot rang out, echoing in the sudden silence of Lapland as the engines of the trucks died. The engines of the beach buggies had been turned off. Kazbek swayed, a second before he could press the trigger, sending a lethal fusillade down on the unsuspecting paras below. Kazbek stiffened, seemed about to step back from the edge, then his huge flamboyant figure toppled, fell down the sheer face of the hill, crumpled over a jagged rock on the ground. Marler removed the Armalite from his shoulder, scrambled back down the hill, walked with a jaunty step back to the beach buggy where Newman waited.

Butler looked behind the buggy into Finland. He stared for a moment, gripped Tweed by the arm. Tweed looked in the same direction. In the distance a vehicle very like a Land Rover was stationary on the track. Two men. One standing up, holding something to his eyes. The strange light flashed off something. Binoculars.

As he watched, Newman drove his buggy back with Marler by his side, stopped next to Tweed's machine. He pointed to the Land-Rover. Tweed nodded, seemed indifferent.

432

'They could be some of Hauser's men, watching how the operation went,' Newman asserted.

'They undoubtedly are.'

As he spoke the standing man sat down. The vehicle performed a U-turn, built up speed, racing back westward towards the Institute. A dust cloud floated up from the sun-scorched track, hiding the Land-Rover.

'Shouldn't we get after that?' Newman pressed.

'No.'

'But they will report to Hauser the operation had failed.'

'Which is exactly what I was planning on,' Tweed replied enigmatically. He turned to face east. 'I think I see a familiar figure. All of you wait here.' He looked at Marler. 'I congratulate you on your marksmanship. You brought down your target just in time.' He jumped out of the buggy.

'I'd better come with you,' said Newman.

'No, this is a rendezvous I must keep alone . . .'

General Valentin Rebet was wearing full military uniform as he beckoned Tweed forward, staying on his own side of the border. He must be sweating like a bull, thought Tweed. Rebet held out a hand.

'So it was Kazbek. How did you know in Leningrad?'

'Quite simple. So obvious you missed it. Hauser talked at the reception before the banquet with Dikoyan, with Marshal Zaikov, with Kazbek. But when he was with the first two he was in a middle of the room, surrounded with people. For his chat with Kazbek they moved into a corner. That huge Georgian hugged him. Undoubtedly Hauser slipped something to his Angel. Money? Details of the operation inside Russia? We'll probably never know. I thought it significant Kazbek was Minister of Communications.'

'Why, if I may ask?'

'You may. The most effective way of throwing the

433

Soviet Union into chaos is to disrupt communications. The telephone system. Radio stations. Above all, the railways which are so important to you. Hence the first explosion on the Trans-Siberian Railway.'

'I am grateful to you, Tweed. We are checking the trucks. So far every container opened has been full of explosives. That convoy must hold enough to blow up half Russia.'

'And don't forget, some must already have been smuggled in. You will have trouble for a while. Has Hauser concluded any trade deals with Moscow?'

'Yes. At the conference held secretly in Turku. He is opening banks, supermarket chains.'

'Close them down. Have nothing to do with him. I must go now.'

Tweed had heard the chug-chug of an approaching chopper. Over his shoulder he saw Marler firing his Verey pistol, saw the orange flare explode. The S61 was descending rapidly, close to where the beach buggies were formed up in a laager formation.

'Please give my warmest thanks to your marksman,' Rebet said quickly. 'He saved a whole unit of paras. Kazbek would have massacred them. Of course, we had back-up units further behind the frontier. And welcome to the Soviet Union. You have one foot on our territory!'

Tweed withdrew his right foot, shook hands, ran back to where the Sikorsky had landed, its rotors slowing, then stopped. Tweed noticed there were two pilots for the large machine. Marler came forward.

'You might like to know I trained my binoculars on that Land-Rover. The man standing up was Frank Galvone.'

'Who probably directed the whole operation. Who will report back to Hauser it was a fiasco. Everything now is working out as I hoped.'

'What does that mean?' Newman demanded.

'The kidnapping was significant. To be precise the easy

434

way they released Paula. That told me something big was afoot. My strategy has been to drive Hauser out of Finland. No more questions. Board the machine . . .'

The spacious cabin which could take eighteen passengers gave them plenty of room. Marler sat next to Tweed who was gazing out of the window as the Sikorsky lifted off, turned away from the border. He borrowed the binoculars from Marler. It was a relief to be aboard the chopper, away from the drumming beat, the vibrations of the beach buggy.

'What are you looking at?' Marler asked.

'We left just in time. Several beach buggies full of men are approaching those we left behind. I can see Mauno Sarin in the lead vehicle. I have saved him a great deal of trouble.'

'How do you mean?'

'Finland naturally treasures its neutrality. If a huge quantity of explosives – so easily smuggled in ashore from Finland's long coast – had been discovered, it would have compromised their relations with Russia. And there is enough turmoil across the Baltic without Finland being dragged into the inferno.'

'What next? Newman is sitting all by himself. Why?'

'He's thinking about who murdered Sandy. I'm thinking about destroying Hauser. Maybe the two objectives are linked.'

PART THREE

Whirlpool of Terror

43

'I've just heard, Adam, that cretin Steve did a screw-up with Evelyn Lennox.' Hauser clenched a beefy fist, punched the air in the huge living room as though felling Steve. 'The Norwich HQ tells me he attacked her in her cottage at Walberswick, bruised her, and she got the better of him. Now he's had to go under cover – the police are after him.'

'Unfortunate,' Carver commented.

They were sitting in the L-shaped living room of Hauser's house perched on a small clifftop at Skalhamn - Shell Bay – in the western archipelago of Sweden. Landing in the Lear jet at Gothenburg, the waiting limo had taken them north, followed by a truck transporting the secret filing cabinets.

The weather had changed drastically. The big picture window at the end of the room looked out over the Skagerrak and the North Sea beyond. A storm was raging. An army of thirty-foot waves was rolling in, crashing against the rocks below the house, splashing the picture window with brown spume.

'Dramatic, isn't it, Adam?'

Hauser walked over, glass of bourbon in his hand, to get a closer look at the turbulent sea. Offshore, the anchored *Washington IV*, an enormous white cabin cruiser, pitched and tossed as the giant waves swept under it. The window was also L-shaped, continued along the southern wall. Hauser looked down but the projecting clifftop masked his view of tiny Skalhamn where a powerboat was moored safe from the storm.

'Evelyn Lennox,' Hauser continued. 'I think you ought to go see her again, persuade her to sign the pension agreement, solve the problem. She's a hole in our defences.'

'I thought we were sailing to Harwich. We won't make it until the storm abates. You want me to fly over from Gothenburg?'

'The met. forecast says the storm may move on. We'll wait it out a day or two . . . Who the hell can that be on the phone?'

Hauser stood to take the call. Adam straightened out a crease in his trousers, shot his cuffs to display the gold cuff-links, then watched the American. Hauser's eyes behind the pince-nez were bleak, his mouth a tight line. His reactions were monosyllabic.

'Yes, Frank . . .'

'No . . .'

'No . . .'

'OK,' he concluded. 'Get your ass over here to Skal-hamn. For Chrissakes, it's my house north of Gothenburg. Catch the first flight. Bed down at an airport if you have to. Get over here yesterday . . .'

He slammed down the phone, drank more bourbon, refilled his glass. Carver kept quiet as his chief paced up and down the long living room, expression grim, big feet hammering into the pile carpet. He sank into a chair.

'Operation Urals is a bust.'

'What operation is that?'

'None of your goddamn business. Frank says Tweed is responsible. How the hell he got into the act I'll never know. But I do know we're going to have to do something to discourage that guy.'

'And how do we go about that?'

'*We* don't get involved. That's Frank's territory. We'll sail for Harwich soon as Frank gets his carcass into this house.'

'The storm may still be raging. Look out of the window.'

'I've looked. The storm will have stopped by then.'

Hauser spoke as though he could command the waves. He tilted his jaw, his mind racing. He'd decided by the time he'd put down his glass.

'We'll definitely sail for Harwich. Then to Livingstone Manor by car. That old English country house is my most modern and advanced communications centre in the world. Tweed will never guess I've moved back on to his own doorstep.' He waved his cigarette holder. 'Equally important, all communications can be sent via the cipher machines. There isn't a code-breaker on the planet who can penetrate the system.'

'You seem to have Tweed on the brain,' Carver ventured.

'Hell, no! Tweed is just one more opponent to be outwitted, outmanoeuvred.'

Hauser perched his large buttocks on the arm of a chair and smiled. It was an effort. Carver had hit a sensitive nerve. Hauser was undergoing an experience he had never known before. Tweed was becoming an obsession with him. Only to himself would he admit it was Tweed who had driven him out of Finland, had made him flee like a fugitive to the west. Well, Livingstone Manor was one place Tweed would never dream of locating him. Come to that, the bastard would never find Skalhamn.

'They won't be moving any more of those filing cabinets out to the *Washington IV*,' Paula said to Linda. 'Not while this weather keeps up . . .'

The two girls were crouched together in the cleft of a rock above Shell Bay. Both wore yellow oilskins with hoods pulled well down over their heads. So far they had served as reasonable protection against the lashing rain. The rock face, looking inland, afforded further shelter against the fury of the storm.

Paula had travelled a long way and fast since seeing the

441

Lear jet take off from Bromma. Driving back to Arlanda, she had handed in the Volvo, bought a ticket to Gothenburg, caught a flight to Sweden's second city and west coast port. She could hardly believe her luck when as the SAS plane came in to land she saw the Lear jet parked at the fringe of the airport.

Arriving in Gothenburg, she had booked a room at the Sheraton, a very modern hotel with a vast interior and rooms on several floors looking down on the restaurant at ground level. She had been lucky again when she phoned one of Tweed's network of informants and researchers spread over Europe.

Linda Sandberg had left her apartment nearby and reached the hotel as Paula finished unpacking. Paula had taken to Linda, a tall slim girl in her late twenties with a waterfall of golden hair framing her excellent bone structure. They had talked for half an hour.

'. . . so I do know about this Franklin D. Hauser,' Linda had said later. 'Not many people know he has a super house at Skalhamn. That's a tiny place even a lot of Swedes don't know exists, but I drive round the coast of the archipelago when I get time off from my job with the advertising agency. Skalhamn is way up north, well on the way to Norway . . .'

Linda's car had been in a garage awaiting maintenance but she knew a car hire outfit close to the hotel. She had warned Paula a storm was predicted so while Paula hired a red Mercedes Linda had gone to a shop, purchased sweaters and oilskins.

It was early evening when Linda drove along a winding road through wild country where brown stone cliffs rose in the distance with dense black fir forests scattered at frequent intervals. They had turned off at a lonely signpost with the legend *Skalhamn* along a narrow road when Paula saw the INCUBUS AB truck ahead.

'Slow down,' she warned. 'This could be dangerous.

442

Are we far from this Shell Bay?'

'Pretty close,' said Linda as she slowed the car.

'If you can, park the car out of sight when we're within walking distance . . .'

Linda had parked the Merc inside a forest and they had walked the last half mile when the Swedish girl pointed to the upper half of a house showing at the top of a small cliff. As she pointed, a black limousine appeared near the cliff edge, vanished.

'That's Hauser's house,' Linda said. 'And it looks as if he might be inside. I once saw him arrive at Gothenburg airport and a car like that picked him up from his jet. The chauffeur has just moved it into the garage. I think the storm is about to break . . .'

They were walking along a very narrow winding road hemmed in by rocks. Linda grasped Paula's arm, put her other hand to her mouth for silence. They crept forward, peered round a rocky bluff and Paula had her first view of Shell Bay.

The anchorage was tiny, scooped out of the brown rock rising up on both sides. Shaped like a sea shell it had a neck-like entrance, a minute stone jetty with a power boat moored below an iron ladder attached to the jetty wall. The INCUBUS truck had backed close to the ladder and men in overalls were lowering a steel filing cabinet held by ropes into the power boat. Paula thought she saw a green label attached to the cabinet. A second cabinet was lowered and this time Paula was certain it had a green label. Two men shinned down the ladder as the ropes were released. The engine of the power boat purred into action, the craft was steered slowly through the entrance.

Linda pulled at Paula's arm, guided her up a narrow defile out of sight of the anchorage. Suddenly they were looking out at the open sea where a big white cabin cruiser rode at anchor. The power boat picked up speed, left a white wake behind its stern, headed for a platform

443

and staircase slung over the hull of the cruiser. They watched as the cabinets were transferred aboard.

'Time to put on our oilskins,' said Linda. 'I felt spots of rain. It's starting.'

Over the sea the sky was black as ink. The full fury of the storm broke suddenly. Lightning flashed. Thunder pealed like the drums of some celestial orchestra. The clouds opened and Niagara flooded down. The power boat, returning to the anchorage, had trouble manoeuvring back behind the shelter of the jetty. It just made it as the wall-like waves started sweeping in. Paula lowered the binoculars she carried in her shoulder bag, shoved them inside, closed the flap. Through the lenses she had made out the name of the ship. *Washington IV*. That was when she made her remark:

'They won't be moving any more of those filing cabinets out to the *Washington IV* . . .'

'Better get back to the car,' said Linda.

They ran all the way, saved from being drenched to the skin by the oilskins. When they had stripped them off and Linda was settled behind the wheel, she turned on the ignition. Nothing happened. She tried six times to start the car and each time the engine died on her.

'Great. Maybe the engine's overheated. We drove here at quite a lick.'

'I'm sorry,' Paula told her, 'it could be dangerous staying here.'

'You said that before we started out. It's more fun than writing advertising copy. Let's eat those sandwiches you got the hotel to make up. We could be stuck here.'

In the living room Hauser had the radio turned on low, waiting for the next met. forecast. Adam, who insisted on regular meals, hating the American habit of gobbling down fast food snacks, was eating the dinner prepared by

444

the housekeeper. He wondered who the second place was laid for. A slim girl with bleached blonde hair walked into the room and Hauser introduced her as Iris Reynolds. She wore a tight blouse which hugged her figure and a mini-skirt exposing shapely legs. Adam stared at her in open admiration, grinned at her as she pulled back her chair at the table.

'Take that look off your face or I'll kick you in the crotch,' she said pleasantly.

Adam nearly choked on his food. Attractive women didn't talk to him like that. He glared at her across the table and their eyes locked. Iris held his stare, no longer smiling as the housekeeper laid her meal in front of her. Adam was disturbed: the eyes seemed to stare right through him, like a hangman measuring him for the drop.

Hauser was amused. 'Iris is coming with us to our new headquarters.' He looked at the housekeeper. 'Bring me a hamburger wrapped in paper. I'll eat it with my hands. And plenty of fried onions.'

'Who,' asked Adam, to change the subject, to ignore Iris, 'if anyone, will be travelling with Frank? Or maybe I shouldn't ask?'

'Goddamn well shouldn't ask. Told you before – you ask too many questions. I can't figure out why.'

Hauser was continuing his usual tactic of letting executives know only as much as they needed to. Ion Manescu would be flying with Galvone. The two men would then fly on from Sweden to London Airport. Who would dream of looking for an ex-*Securitate* chief – or an ex–STASI leader – inside an old English country house? And Galvone would bring Helmut Ziegler with him.

Adam Carver seemed at once to read his mind. 'If Frank flies here we may be gone when he arrives.'

'We will be. So I leave a note for him with the housekeeper. "Contact Dr Livingstone immediately." That will give him the message.'

'A bit of a long way round for him to get there.'

445

'So he has some exercise. Do the schmuck some good . . .'

An hour later the storm subsided as suddenly as it had broken. Through the picture window the sight was spectactular. The huge waves became smaller, the late evening sky lightened, the surface of the sea became an oily calm. Hauser ordered the loading operation to be resumed.

'We sail tonight to Harwich, we keep moving . . .'

Inside the Merc, under the cover of the fir forest, Linda lowered a window. The storm had gone away, the air was very cool. Paula found it a strange experience after the heatwave to feel almost cold and shivery. She pulled over her head the sweater Linda had bought.

The silence of the forest was unnerving. The only sound was the steady drip of raindrops from the spreading branches which reminded her of the wings of some huge evil birds. Linda turned the ignition key. The engine burst into life first time.

'I'm going back to take a final look,' Paula said. 'Now, no protests! You stay with the car, keeping the engine ticking over. And one person is far less likely to be seen. I do know the way now . . .'

She walked along the road which was no more than damp: most of the downpour had drained off the cambered surface into the fields on either side. Unencumbered by the oilskin, she climbed agilely up the rock cleft to the point where it overlooked the sea. She whipped out her binoculars.

The power boat was moving out from Shell Bay, heading across calm water which resembled a vast endless lake. Besides the helmsman the craft carried three passengers. She easily recognized in the lenses the bulky figure of Hauser, the far slimmer Adam Carver. The third passenger was a woman. Something about her seemed

446

familiar, then she got it. Her mind flashed back to the horrific episode when she had been exchanged for another hostage on the scrubbing platform. This was the woman she had been exchanged for. As they approached the landing stage slung over the side of the hull she switched her gaze to the ship.

At the masthead on top of the huge control cabin a flag was being lowered, the flag of convenient Panama. As soon as it had been hauled down a fresh flag was hoisted. The Red Ensign. Paula had seen enough.

She scrambled down the rock cleft, ran back along the deserted road to where Linda waited anxiously in the Merc. The Swedish girl waved as Paula approached her, opened the front passenger door.

'God! Am I glad to see you safe and sound.'

'That's nice of you,' Paula jumped into the car. 'I'm OK. Could you drive me straight back to the Sheraton? I have an urgent phone call to make.'

44

Tweed seemed tireless. Even Marler marvelled at his endless stamina as he sat with the others in Tweed's room at the Hesperia. Newman and Butler sagged in armchairs; Cord Dillon was asleep on a couch. Only Pete Nield also looked fresh as he gazed out of the window. In the late evening, tourists in shirt sleeves, the women clad in dresses creased by the heat, trudged wearily along the Mannerheimintie. With the windows open the atmosphere was still torrid. The metal mobile drooped stationary as Tweed listened on the phone, taking notes.

He was talking to Monica who said she had been trying to contact him for hours. He listened without interrupting, occasionally reassuring her.

'Yes, I'm still here. Go on . . .'

Monica was showing great ingenuity in passing information to him, wrapping it up in seemingly innocuous data about insurance. Eventually he thanked her, put down the phone, turned round.

'Bob, Chief Inspector Buchanan is on your tail again. He called on Monica and Howard, wanted to know where you were. Apparently he's cleared up another murder case and is now concentrating on the murder of Sandy.'

'About time he damned well did . . .'

'Wait, there's more. Evelyn Lennox, the girl you interviewed in Wandsworth – and later was being guarded by Butler in Walberswick – has been attacked.'

'And Buchanan suspects me? Why on earth . . .'

'Do wait till I've finished. Lennox was attacked in her cottage by a masked figure but she fought him off. She thinks it was a man called Steve . . .'

'That thug?' Newman made a gesture of disgust. 'Surely the Yard can track him down.'

'He's gone under cover. What we have to do concerns me – and it's a lot. I hope you haven't forgotten Peggy Vanderheld, maybe *the* key witness. Butler, your next job is to fly to Arlanda, hire a car, drive to the island of Örno, pick her up, take her back to Arlanda, fly with her at the earliest to London, take her to Park Crescent, leave her with the guard in the hall, pick up a gun, drive her to Walberswick to Evelyn Lennox's cottage. You know where it is. Guard both women. They may have interesting things to tell each other.'

'I'd better get my ticket for the first flight tomorrow now.'

Butler was on his way out when Tweed stopped him. He included all his team in the next order.

'Everyone, including you Butler, has to get rid of all the weapons. Dump them in the harbour, anywhere. But get rid of them.' He nodded to Butler. 'All right, you can go now. And I'll visit Walberswick myself to question Vanderheld. By then she will be thoroughly frightened.'

'Why?'

Butler paused near the door. Tweed's mind was moving like lightning. He had thought of something else.

'Because Evelyn Lennox will have told her of her own experiences with INCUBUS. She'll be more than ready to talk to me.' He looked across at Nield. 'On second thoughts I want you to go with Butler. Lennox and Vanderheld are the only two witnesses who may be able to bring down Hauser.'

'Let's hope Evelyn Lennox is still alive,' Newman said grimly. 'Is she under guard? Surely Buchanan has thought of that.'

'He's done his best. The local bobby on his bike is calling in on her.'

'Heaven help us,' Newman commented. 'We're dealing with pros. Let's hope you get there in time, Harry.'

'You have a point, Bob,' Tweed decided. 'So Butler, you fly to Arlanda, pick up Vanderheld. Nield, change of plan. You fly direct to London, go to see Monica. She will show you the location of Lennox's place in Walberswick, Rose Bower. Then drive straight there. Bob, can you give Pete a brief letter identifying him to Evelyn?'

Dillon sat up. 'I heard what you said about weapons. I'm wondering how to get rid of this Luger when I don't know Helsinki all that well.'

'I was about to suggest something,' Marler intervened. 'It's almost as difficult to get shot of a gun safely as it is of a corpse. If everyone hands me their hardware I can do the job.'

'How?' Tweed demanded.

'I still have hire of that power boat I used when Paula

449

was kidnapped. I'll put them in a hold-all – including my own dismantled Armalite – and weight it with a length of chain or something. I take the power boat well out to sea, drop the hold-all overboard.'

'The best idea,' Tweed agreed. 'Don't forget spare mags.'

Dillon handed over his Luger and ammo; Butler his Mauser; Newman the Smith & Wesson. He held on to it for a moment.

'Tweed, the people we're up against will be crawling with guns. Why leave us naked now?'

'I'll explain that later.'

'As Paula would say, be cryptic.'

Marler put the weapons in an empty drawer, left the room, was back in no time with a leather hold-all. He placed the guns inside, zipped it up, sat down, lit a cigarette.

'What's next on the agenda?'

Butler and Nield had left the room. Tweed checked his watch. It was later in the evening than he'd realized. They had landed at Helsinki Airport on their return from Lapland early that morning, had flopped into bed as soon as they reached the Hesperia and The Palace. They had slept until almost midday: Tweed had told the operator at the Hesperia not to put through any calls before struggling into his pyjamas. An almost unprecedented action.

He had let his team alone during the afternoon, summoning them to his room late in the evening. Now he had been fooled by the fact that it was still daylight. He opened his mouth to reply to Marler and the phone rang. He replied as he reached for it.

'We're flying to Stockholm. That's where you reported those INCUBUS filing cabinets were being flown to . . .'

The caller was Monica. Again he listened for several minutes. This time he took no notes. He thanked her,

450

said he'd call her back, replaced the receiver, looked at his team.

'Fresh change of instruction. Cancel Stockholm. What I thought might happen has – Hauser, Adam Carver and the girl who tried to kill me have sailed from the west coast of Sweden. Undoubtedly heading for England. I'll check in a minute. Paula has done a magnificent job . . . .'

He gave them the gist of Monica's report. Paula had called her from the Sheraton in Gothenburg, had described what she had seen at Sveavägen in Stockholm, her trip to Bromma, and her experiences with Linda Sandberg at Skalhamn.

'. . . so,' Tweed concluded, 'we can now assume my plan worked better than I could ever have hoped.'

'What plan?' Newman demanded. 'Tell us this time, for God's sake.'

'We were always handicapped coming to grips with Hauser in Finland – because of its understandable desire for absolute neutrality. I aimed all along to frustrate any operation he was carrying out – to drive him west. Into Sweden I expected, but the plan worked even better. We have driven him back to England – where he is under British jurisdiction.'

'You wily bastard,' was Dillon's comment.

'But are you sure?' Newman pressed.

'With luck I shall be during the next hour. The Harbour Master at Harwich, a Jonas Heathcoate, is a friend of mine.'

'Where does that get us?' protested Newman.

'Paula has reported seeing Hauser, Adam Carver and a girl I suspect who tried to murder me here boarding Hauser's millionaire's cabin cruiser. I mentioned that before – but not that Paula had seen it with her own eyes. It is a question of geography. The port closest to Livingstone Manor where such a ship – the *Washington IV* – could dock is Harwich.'

451

'He could have sailed off anywhere,' Newman persisted.

'Except that earlier Monica phoned, told me her researches had revealed Livingstone Manor is equipped with some of the most modern communications equipment in the world. Including cipher machines. Hauser is getting wary – he needs a foolproof method of communication we cannot penetrate.'

'You never told us about this earlier call from Monica.' Newman snapped. 'All this data about Livingstone Manor.'

'I don't believe I did.' Tweed smiled drily. 'But when I first knew all this Hauser was in Finland.'

'So,' repeated Marler, 'what's next on the agenda? As if I didn't know,' he added.

'I'll tell you after I've phoned Jonas Heathcoate. Just contain your impatience.'

He took out a small notebook with an index, turned to the letter 'H', dialled a number, waited. There was an atmosphere of growing tension in the room. Newman as well as Marler had guessed what he was checking. Tweed had to speak to several people before he reached Heathcoate. He identified himself, reminding the Harbour Master of the last time they had met. Newman leaned forward, his hands clasped tightly together. Livingstone Manor . . .

'. . . yes, Jonas, that's the vessel,' Tweed continued. 'The *Washington IV*. A big white cabin cruiser. It belongs to the banker, Franklin D. Hauser. What was that? Could you repeat it? The line isn't good. The *Washington IV* docked at Harwich early this morning? And Hauser was met with a black limousine? That's a dangerous habit of his – he's setting himself up as a target. Bullet proof, you said? It had better be from his point of view. Thanks, Jonas. I owe you one.'

Tweed put down the phone, wiped his clammy hand, looked at the others.

'You heard all that, I imagine? He must have arrived at Livingstone Manor hours ago.'

Marler whistled in admiration. 'How do you do it? You wouldn't have an informant planted inside INCU-BUS?'

'I have taken a lot of trouble to think myself into the mind of my opponent. To foresee his every move. I sense he's doing the same thing with me. So why should I need an informant?'

'And next on the agenda?' Marler repeated for the third time.

'Obvious, isn't it? We all fly back to London tomorrow, plan the next stage of our campaign against Hauser. He has walked into my cage.'

The following morning at Livingstone Manor Hauser was leaving the cipher room when he found Adam Carver in the corridor. He pushed his pince-nez further up his strong nose and his mouth was pouched unpleasantly.

'What the hell are you doing poking around down here?'

'I came to find you.' Carver, immaculate in a light-weight pale grey silk suit, was poised and confident. 'I have the balance sheet figures of Egon – or rather, now Dieter – Schmidt's bank we bought in Frankfurt. You said you wanted to see these figures.'

'Later.' Hauser slammed shut the security door leading to the cipher room. 'How did you get down here? There's a security door at the top of the steps. You don't have a key.'

'Someone must have left it open. I'll be ready to show you these figures when you are.'

Hauser waited until Carver had strolled off up the cellar steps out of sight. Dressed in short sleeves and slacks, he took out a bunch of keys, opened the door to the suite next to the cipher room, walked inside, closed the door.

The suite was luxuriously furnished, had a living room, a bedroom, a bathroom. It was also air conditioned. On a couch was sprawled Ion Manescu. It was doubtful whether his old *Securitate* associates in Bucharest would have recognized their ex-chief.

Manescu had had his hair trimmed very short before he had flown from Helsinki with Galvone. He had a pair of large horn-rim glasses perched on his beaky nose which gave him a professorial look. He was smoking a cheroot as he swung his legs to the floor, clasped his strong bony fingers, waited.

'Frank says you left him at London Airport, that you hired a car. You arrived here half a day after Frank. So what the hell did you think you were doing? Where did you go?'

'I drove up into Suffolk, didn't I? Before I came here I cruised, stopped at a few English pubs, listened to the locals, picked up a little more English accent.'

'English pubs where?' demanded Hauser.

'Lavenham, Southwold . . .'

'You went into that area? Are you crazy? I told you to avoid that part of the world. Why did you do it?'

'I've just told you.' Manescu had no intention of being intimidated by the American who stood over him. 'And no one took any notice of me. I can pass. Isn't that what you wanted?'

'You took a helluva a chance going into that area. Don't do it again unless I tell you to.'

His manner changed, became affable. It was these switches in mood the Romanian found it difficult to adapt to. And Hauser had the habit of assuming his genial personality when issuing important – even dangerous – instructions. When he had finished talking Hauser turned to leave the room, spoke once more as he unlocked the door.

454

'OK what I told you? And don't discuss the problem with Carver or Galvone.'

'OK,' agreed Manescu.

Time to light a fire under Galvone. Hauser locked the door leading to the cellar complex. Clenching his fists, he walked into the big living room with the arched window at the front. Galvone was standing, gazing out of the window. The sun was burning Suffolk as the heatwave went on. The storm at Skalhamn had been a freak, Hauser was thinking. He looked at the glass in Galvone's hands.

'Bit early to start getting smashed. You're going to need a clear mind, for God's sake.'

He had been looking for something to set the tone. Walking to the cocktail cabinet, he poured a large glass of mineral water to ram the point home.

'You screwed up with Manescu at London Airport. Christ, Frank, can't you even escort sensitive material?'

'I was amazed at how different he looked. He was keen to merge into the Brit background. That's what we want, isn't it?'

'I'll tell you what I want, Frank,' Hauser roared. 'I want people who aren't laid back about their jobs. When I give an order, you carry it out. I want men who wake up in the morning ready to bite the ass off a bear. Talking about bears, you really screwed up in Lapland. Did those explosives get through or didn't they?'

Galvone paused, feeling he was walking on a quicksand. He had felt compelled to report to Hauser what he had seen from the Land-Rover. You didn't lie to Hauser – if you wanted to survive. But under pressure you could shade the truth.

'Most of the trucks had crossed the border before I saw signs of the intervention . . .'

'Intervention! Soviet paras you said earlier. Don't play

455

word games with me. They were waiting for that convoy. Who tipped them off? My best bet is that bastard, Tweed. It's lucky we smuggled a big consignment through earlier.'

'You've seen the newspapers?' Galvone asked, hoping to divert his chief. He pointed to the *Daily Mail* on a table with its shrieking headline. 'That really is sensational.'

Hauser nodded. He looked down at the paper, his arms folded across his chest. That did give him some satisfaction.

KGB HQ IN KIEV BLOWN UP. UNREST GROWING.

'What is the plan?' Galvone enquired.

'You've read the story, I guess. The blue and red flags of an independent Ukraine are flying everywhere. No sign of the Soviet flag. The UTS – the Free Ukraine movement based in Munich – is active. What is the master plan, you meant?'

'That's what I meant.'

'I have a vision. One day not long from now, the dollar will be the world currency. The dollar will replace the rouble. Hell, any tourist to Moscow will tell you the locals pester them for dollars. They even have bars in Moscow where some of the ten thousand prostitutes look for customers – providing they can pay in dollars. Prostitution isn't illegal in Russia. It's their largest growth industry. They even have police girls dressed in civilian clothes, often sitting on a stool next to a call girl in these bars in the top hotels.'

'But you said it was legal,' Galvone pointed out.

'Your hearing is improving. The police girls are simply there to make sure there's no trouble for foreign tourists while they take their pick. Dollars, Frank – the key to a home for human beings stretching from the Pacific coast of the States to the Urals.' Hauser puffed at his cigarette,

456

waved the holder, changed the subject in the swift way Galvone found disconcerting.

'Talking of money, has that private bank, Street & Braithwaite, down in Southampton, decided to sell out to us?'

'I called the Norwich HQ. They said Leopold Street said no. Apparently there's an empty shop right next to the bank. Easy to break into.'

'Then maybe Mr Street needs a little encouragement. We have that load of Semtex in the basement here for cases like that.'

Galvone stood up. 'You want me to organize a sweetener for the guy?'

'Why the hell do you think I raised the subject? Wait a minute,' he called out as Galvone strode towards the door. 'Another bone I have to pick with you. How did you get here so quick? I told you to go to the house at Skalhamn.'

'Oh, that.' Galvone made a throwaway gesture with his large hands. 'Knowing how you jet around, change your plans, I called the house from Helsinki Airport. The housekeeper opened the envelope you'd left for me, read out the message. The reference to Dr Livingstone told me you'd moved on here. So we flew direct to London Airport – myself, Manescu and Ziegler. You've hidden Ziegler away somewhere here?'

Hauser flushed with fury. He bit hard on the holder to regain self-control. Seeing his expression, Galvone stood stock still. Hauser strode forward, a thick index finger pointing, jabbing.

'You could be on your way out. The hard way. I've told you before, you obey my orders. Don't start thinking, taking your own decisions. Ed Riverton did that and someone did me a favour. You delivered Ziegler. That's the end of it so far as you're concerned. Adam Carver knows how to do what he's told.'

'Adam knows his job,' Galvone agreed in a conciliatory tone.

'And Adam is doing a job at this moment.' Hauser smiled. 'But sometimes I wonder about Adam. Better collect that Semtex, drive down to Southampton.'

'I suppose it's OK to use a bomb? We are in Britain.'

'Jesus!' Hauser clapped a hand to his forehead. 'Do I have to do everything myself? Call in at London Airport on the way. Wait for an Irish to check in at the Aer Lingus counter, pinch his passport. You started out in Chicago as an expert pickpocket. Leave the passport in the shop. The Brits will think it's the IRA.'

Alone in the living room, Hauser smiled with satisfaction. The Evelyn Lennox problem would be solved soon now.

45

Panic!

Evelyn Lennox stared out of the mullioned window in the living room at Rose Bower. She could hardly believe her eyes. A red Jaguar had pulled up by the front entrance at the end of the garden.

'It's Adam Carver! You said he was in Finland . . .'

'He was,' Butler replied tersely. He looked at Pete Nield. 'Hustle Peggy upstairs. Stay with her in her bedroom . . .'

Nield was moving, taking Vanderheld by the arm, hurrying her into the hall, up the narrow staircase. Butler moved away from the window, walked quickly to an open door. He turned before he went into the next room.

'I'll leave the door open a crack. I'll be able to hear all that's going on. Don't let him know we're here – and not a word about Vanderheld. You've no idea where she is. Can you handle it?'

Evelyn nodded. 'Yes, I can . . .'

'Of course you can. Let him talk. If you're alarmed, say something about Southwold. I'll be in here in a flash . . .'

Evelyn took a deep breath. The door bell was ringing. She smoothed down her mini-skirt, glanced at herself in a wall mirror, fiddled with her hair, went to the door, opened it.

'Surprise!' Carver grinned. 'Hope it's not the wrong moment to call. I tried to phone but you're not in the book.'

'Ex-directory.'

Evelyn swallowed. She thought Adam had never looked more handsome. His face and hands were tanned brown. He wore a smart beige silk suit, a blue striped shirt, plain blue tie, matching display handkerchief, hand made brogues. The tan emphasized the perfect bone structure of his face. He held a small posy of flowers.

'These are for you. Although I expect you've more than enough flowers.' He glanced back at the hedges of wild roses bordering the path. 'I just wanted to bring you a little something.'

'They're lovely. Thank you so much. Come into the living room. That chair is comfortable.'

She carefully didn't look at the door leading to the small study cum library where Butler was hiding. She knew he was armed with a Smith & Wesson. He had showed her the weapon to reassure her when he arrived. And upstairs Nield was carrying a Browning .32. The weapon he favoured most, like Paula.

The posy was a problem. Normally she would have taken it into the kitchen, filled a vase with fresh water, but she dare not leave Adam alone in the living room with

459

Butler so close. Picking up a vase off the table, she took out the flowers it held, dumped them on the hearth, arranged the posy in the same vase.

'I'll put fresh water in later. What would you like to drink?' she hurried on. 'Orange, lemon, lime juice? Or something stronger?'

'Lime juice will do very nicely. I've got a thirst like the Sahara. Are you all on your own here?'

'Yes, but I enjoy the peace and quiet. There was one rather nerve-wracking incident . . .'

She handed him his drink, sat down, crossed her legs and told him about the masked attacker without mentioning the resemblance to Steve. He had trouble tearing his eyes away from her legs and then listened with a grave expression, holding her eyes with his own.

'That's quite dreadful,' he said when she had finished. 'Surely you reported it to the police, asked them for some protection?'

'Yes, I did. But all they could spare was the local bobby who cycles here occasionally and calls in to see I'm all right. I probably disturbed a burglar and he lost his head. Not to worry.' She smiled. 'Ancient history. How is the banking business?'

'Oh, we're still taking over everyone in sight – that is, everyone who wants to meet our price. It's becoming a mania with Hauser. Buy, buy, buy.'

'You don't like the Americans?' she asked quietly.

He hesitated. 'Well I do find them rather brash. They seem to think they do everything better than anyone else can. Which isn't the case.'

'If you don't like them, why do you go on working for them?'

He gave her the disarming smile which always made her feel weak and yielding. 'Frankly, for the money.' He moved his fingers as though counting banknotes. 'Where else am I going to get a job which pays that sort of money?'

'Money isn't everything.'

'Wasn't it Rockefeller who said that?' He smiled again. 'Look, I really came here to ask you out to dinner one night. Maybe at The Swan over at Lavenham. It's not so far – that Jag eats up the miles. I'd drive you home afterwards, of course. I'm trying to persuade you.'

'I know you are. When?'

'That's great. What about sometime next week? Thursday any good?'

'It might be. All right, I'll say yes. On one condition.'

'Name it.'

'If something crops up I may have to delay it. So I need some way of getting in touch with you. A number I can call. Where are you based now?'

He hesitated again, briefly, took a card from his wallet. Scribbling a number on the back he handed it to her.

'There was one other thing before I go. The Pension Fund. I've been asked by Equality and Fraternity whether you'd now sign the agreement . . .'

'Hence the briefcase.' Evelyn indicated the case he had perched against the side of his armchair. 'So now we come to the real reason for your visit.'

'No!' Adam was vehement. 'I was coming to see you for my own personal reasons, to ask you out to dinner. I had to tell Hauser where I was going – he keeps us all on a tight leash. He shoved the papers at me, told me to ask you while I was here. I don't give a tuppenny damn myself. Incidentally they've upped the amount payable each month.' He wiped his moist forehead. 'Wish I'd never brought the subject up now. And I don't like that insurance outfit any more.'

'Why?'

He leaned forward. 'Because I was always told it was an independent company. Recently I discovered by accident it's a subsidiary of INCUBUS. More of Hauser's business trickery.'

461

'You can leave the agreement with me. I'll have to consult my accountant.'

'That I can't do.' His tone was apologetic. 'If I don't return with the agreement I'll be scalped. Let's forget the whole idea. Dinner's still on?'

'Unless I call to say I can't make it.' She looked at the calling card for the first time. 'I see you are based at Livingstone Manor now. I thought that was one of Hauser's country homes.'

'He's fitted it out as a business headquarters. I suspect he likes playing the squire of the manor. Which is amusing considering he's a billionaire.' He checked his watch, stood up. 'I think I've taken up enough of your time. Hope to see you Thursday next week. I'll call for your about seven.'

'We'll see.' Evelyn smiled as she escorted him to the front door. 'Your Jag will be pretty hot by now.'

'You're right.' Carver pulled a pair of kid gloves from his pocket, slipped them on. 'The wheel especially will be burning hot for the first few miles. See you . . .'

She waited until the car had disappeared before closing the door. Butler was waiting for her in the living room. She poured him a cooling drink.

'What do you think?' she asked. 'Was the real reason for his visit that beastly pension?'

'Oddly enough, I don't think so. He had some other reason for calling on you.'

'Being as cynical as I can, I agree with you. Strange the way he showed hostility to Hauser – almost as though he was sending me a message.'

'I'm going to call Tweed immediately, report the incident.'

At Park Crescent Tweed took the call from Butler, listened, thanked him for calling, put the receiver down.

462

His room was so crowded extra chairs had been brought in.

Paula had just finished telling them in detail about her experiences in Sweden. Starting with her arrival at Arlanda, watching the filing cabinets being unloaded at INCUBUS' HQ on Sveavägen in Stockholm, her drive to Bromma, her later arrival with Linda Sandberg at Skalhamn and what she had seen there.

She had an attentive audience. Monica took notes. Newman and Marler sat listening. But the man who sat quite still, his grey eyes never leaving hers, who listened most closely, was Chief Inspector Roy Buchanan. Beside him Sergeant Warden took his own notes. Tweed was the first to speak when she had finished. He told them about Carver's visit.

'. . . but what was even more interesting was what Butler told me about Nield. Pete travelled up to Walberswick on a motor bike. Yesterday he was driving slowly round the beach area. He's worried someone could come in by sea. On his way back to Rose Bower he saw a Ford Cortina dawdling past the cottage. It then did a U-turn, drove back towards the A 12. Nield followed at a discreet distance on his Honda. Later the Ford was stopped by lights in open country and Nield drew alongside it, got a good look at the driver. He swears it was Ion Manescu.'

'The terrorist you told us about,' Buchanan commented.

'More a saboteur than a terrorist. Like all of us, Nield has studied those pictures Marler took of Manescu leaving INCUBUS in Helsinki. He didn't twig immediately, but the driver glanced at him before driving off and then Nield was sure. Says the Romanian has had his hair cut much shorter, was wearing large horn-rims.'

'Any idea where he drove on to?' Buchanan asked.

'That's interesting too. Nield followed him when the

463

Ford turned on to the A1120, through Yoxford. Then he turned back, afraid Manescu would spot his tail.'

'If I remember rightly,' Buchanan suggested, 'Livingstone Manor is located further along the A1120.'

'It is,' Tweed agreed. 'Which makes the direction Manescu was driving along it significant.'

'I'd like to get the position quite clear in everyone's mind,' said Buchanan. He stood up, began walking between the chairs, addressing no one in particular, rattling loose change in his pocket. 'At the moment I am investigating three murders, albeit one out of my jurisdiction – in Finland – but I'm convinced the same hand committed all of them.'

'Three?' Tweed queried. 'Which three?'

'First that of Ed Riverton in Helsinki, second that of Sandra Riverton in Suffolk, and third that of the man called Steve who accompanied the man called Papa Grimwood when they visited Evelyn Lennox in Wandsworth.'

'So you found the thug, Steve?' Newman asked.

'Yes, but a very dead Steve, unfortunately. We traced him through underworld informants to the East End of London. Specifically to an address in the Mile End Road. We were just too late. The body was secreted behind the locked door of a disused cellar.'

'And the link is he was employed by INCUBUS?' suggested Tweed.

'The link,' Buchanan continued as though no one had spoken, 'is the cause of his demise. He had been garrotted.'

He paused. There was dead silence in the turgid atmosphere of the office. Buchanan wore a grey business suit and seemed unaffected by the heat: the temperature had risen into the eighties. Buchanan leaned against a wall, folded his arms, continued.

'Every killer – assassin might be a better word in this case – inadvertently leaves behind his trademark. Here

464

we have a killer who always goes for a particularly vulnerable part of the human body. The neck.'

'I think we get the drift,' Tweed said, anxious about what he might say next.

Buchanan went on remorselessly. 'The American in Helsinki, Ed Riverton, was garrotted.' He stared at Newman. 'Sandra Riverton was hung by her neck until she was dead.' It was a brutal thrust and Newman froze. 'And now we have this Steve, also garrotted. I have little doubt that when we identify the murderer of one of those three victims we shall have found the murderer of all three. That is the present position.'

He sat down, stretched out his legs. As he waited he was watching Tweed.

'I think my next move,' Tweed began, 'is to travel up to Walberswick. I want to have a long talk with Peggy Vanderheld. She will know more about people connected with INCUBUS than anyone we can get at.'

'I would like to be present,' Buchanan said simply.

'If you promise to keep quiet. Not otherwise. And only if Vanderheld agrees to your being present. Since she is an American citizen you have no jurisdiction over her. Come to think of it, neither have I. Certainly we have no evidence she is guilty of any crime. I can only hope to coax her into talking.'

'And you are experienced in interrogation,' Buchanan remarked. 'Not only in your present position. I do know that before you joined this organization you were one of the most successful Yard superintendents with Homicide.'

Tweed smiled wryly. 'That was a little while ago. Are you agreeable to come under the conditions I laid down?'

'Quite agreeable.'

'May I come too?' asked Paula. 'The presence of another woman might help. If she bridles I'll leave you with her immediately.'

'Again, on that condition, yes.' Tweed's manner

465

relaxed. 'My interview with Vanderheld could be the turning point in what started out as an investigation into INCUBUS, an attempt to trace what had happened to missing members of one-time Communist secret police services like the *Securitate*. Now it is a murder investigation.'

'A triple murder case,' Buchanan emphasized. 'We are hunting a mass murderer.'

Cord Dillon, seated on a chair tilted against the wall in a corner, had remained silent. Introduced to Buchanan as 'Mr Dexter, an official of the State Department', he spoke for the first time.

'And I need evidence to put Mr Franklin D. Hauser out of business.'

'Maybe the solution to Chief Inspector Buchanan's problem will turn out to be exactly what you also need,' Tweed said. 'Any more comments?'

'I rather think it might be an amusing idea if I drove up to Suffolk by myself,' interjected Marler. 'Nothing exciting – just to mooch around Livingstone Manor. After dark, of course.'

'Be very careful,' Tweed warned. 'I have the strongest foreboding Hauser is about to strike back. The trouble is we don't know what he will choose as his target. I think we should now leave for Walberswick.'

46

Hauser crashed his clenched fist on the desk in his large study overlooking the grounds at the back of Livingstone Manor. His eyes glowed with rage and frustration. Facing him, Carver wondered whether this was another exhibition staged by a natural actor.

'Why couldn't you persuade the Lennox bitch to sign the agreement?'

'She said she wanted time to think it over. If I could have left the agreement with her she might have changed her mind.'

'You know we never leave documents like that lying about for prying eyes. God knows who she might have shown it to.'

Carver, seated erect in a hard-backed chair, kept quiet. He didn't think it wise to let Hauser know Evelyn had proposed keeping the agreement to let her accountant examine the papers. Why add fuel to the flames?

'Well, there we are.' Hauser smiled, tilted his jaw.

'Why is Evelyn Lennox so important?' Carver asked.

Was Hauser a schizophrenic? he was wondering. His changes of mood were bewildering. Hauser was beaming now, leaning back in his executive chair as he waved his hand.

'There you go again, boy, asking questions about departments of INCUBUS which don't concern you. Maybe I'll send one of our female staff to have a word with Evelyn. Woman to woman. Might work,' he went on genially. 'Who can tell how women will react? They don't even know themselves. Would you have a map of that area. Adam?'

'Yes, I do.' Carver extracted the map from his breast pocket, handed it to his chief. 'Suffolk is a complex area. It's easy to get lost.'

'No, spread the map out. Mark on it with a cross in pencil where Evelyn Lennox lives. Then the young lady I send can find her way there. That is, if I decide to send anyone. You haven't a pencil? When I was young and starting out in California I always carried a pencil and a rubber. Here you are. You're a well-educated guy. I'll bet

467

you've got three or four gold pens on you but no pencil. Shame on you.'

Carver disliked the patronizing tone Hauser liked to adopt. He bent over the map, marked the location of Rose Bower with a pencil cross. He had no inkling that his chief's banter was to cover up the significance of the pencilled cross. Afterwards it could be rubbed out – a vital piece of evidence destroyed.

'Thank you, Adam.' Hauser folded up the map. 'No sign of anyone else at the cottage while you were making up to Evelyn? No? I just wondered.'

Carver was startled, kept his expression blank. How the devil could Hauser have guessed he had asked Evelyn out to dinner? The man was a mind reader. It was unsettling, worse than when Hauser was in a rage. Hauser came round his desk as Carver stood up, clapped him on the shoulder.

'Later I may have a serious mission for you. You do it right and there's a big bonus coming. Off you go, play with your bat and ball . . .'

Hauser waited until Carver had left and his expression was grim. Taking out a bunch of keys, clutching the folded map, he walked from his study down the long hall, entered the living room, inserted a key into the locked door leading to the cellar complex.

Irina Serov looked up from the English novel she was reading as Hauser entered the suite next to where Manescu was quartered. Elegantly stretched out on a couch, she let Hauser have a good look at her legs before she stood up.

'I have a difficult job for you,' Hauser began, spreading out the map on a table. 'See that pencil cross? Take this rubber with you. When the job is done be sure to erase the cross, throw away the rubber. A girl lives at Rose

Bower in a hick place on the coast called Walberswick. The cross shows Rose Bower – crappy name – which is where she lives.' He straightened up, smiled down at her. 'And that is the problem – she's still living . . .'

Irina, driving a hired Ford Escort, turned off the A 12 on to the B 1387 where the signpost carried a single word. *Walberswick*. She was carrying a driving licence in the name of Iris Reynolds, a calling card with the same name and her occupation. *Beautician*.

The card had been printed in one of the rooms in the cellar complex at her suggestion before she left Livingstone Manor. She guessed that a lot of INCUBUS employees were carrying cards with fake names. And in the heat the ink had dried quickly when she had left it face up in the passenger seat.

She also had perched on the same seat an expensive-looking wine-coloured executive case. The necessary ingredient had been supplied from the pharmacy in another cellar room which, like the other rooms, always had the door locked. Which was a good idea, Irina thought as she drove along the deserted country road. They had enough stuff in that so-called pharmacy to poison the whole of Suffolk.

She slowed down as she passed the first house, slowed a little more as she drove out of the sun glare into the shade of a tunnel of trees. She was checking the name of each residence as she crawled through the tunnel. She nearly missed her target because this name was almost covered in creeper. *Rose Bower*.

She continued to crawl as she glanced up the path between hedges of wild roses, checked the windows downstairs and the dormer windows in the thatched roof. No sign of life. Still cautious, she drove on, checking both sides of the road for hidden watchers. Hauser had said the girl lived alone. But Hauser hadn't visited the place and she didn't trust that fashion plate creep, Adam Carver. She had seen him when she had peered from her cabin door aboard the *Washington IV* during the night crossing from Skalhamn to Harwich. Carver had not seen her but as he had walked down the companionway she had heard Hauser call out. 'Adam, I want to talk with you . . .'

She reached a point where a panoramic view of the glittering sea appeared. In the distance a man and a woman stood on a shingle bank, staring out to sea, their backs turned. She swung the wheel, drove back to Rose Bower.

Butler was in the lavatory, coping with a bout of constipation, when Evelyn saw the small slim girl walking up the garden path. She dashed from the living room to the door, peered through the spyhole. She saw an attractive face framed with blonde hair. Before the visitor could ring the bell she opened it on the chain.

'I am so sorry to bother you,' Irina began, 'but I am lost. I must have taken the wrong turning. Have you a map you could show me? This heat is getting me down.'

Evelyn slipped off the chain, invited her inside, took her into the living room. On a sideboard stood a large jug of punch, freshly made. Butler had told her Newman was coming to see her. 'With some friends . . .'

Evelyn had decided she must have some refreshment to offer. After the long drive from London in this heat the visitors would probably appreciate a pick me up. Irina settled back in a chair, her handbag on her lap, the flap undone.

'I've been driving round for hours,' she explained. 'I don't supposed you could let me have a drink of something? I'm almost dehydrated.'

470

'I've just made some punch. Or you could have a fruit drink. Lime juice . . .'

'A small glass of punch would be wonderful. Providing you're joining me.'

'Well, a small glass for both of us. Where are you trying to get to?' she asked as she poured from the jug, then placed it back inside the ice bucket.

'Southwold. I suppose I'm miles away.'

'No, you're very close. If you drove down to the end of this road to the sea and looked north across the entrance to the harbour you could see it in the distance. But driving there is a bit complicated. Let me show you on the map . . .'

She traced the route for her guest. Irina nodded, smiled.

'That's very clear. Thank you so much . . .'

Settled back in the armchair she stiffened suddenly. Evelyn was still standing as she spoke.

'Oh, Lord! I'm a beautician. Don't think I'm trying to sell you anything,' she added hastily. 'Not after your helpfulness. But I've left my case of samples outside your front door. I put it down by the door to ring the bell . . .'

'I'll get it. I'm sure it will still be there.'

Evelyn left the room. Irina lifted the flap of her handbag, took out the white paper packet, emptied the cyanide powder into Evelyn's glass, lifted the spoon Evelyn had left on a plate, quietly stirred the drink. When her hostess returned she was flopped back in her chair.

'Here is your case. It's very smart-looking. You don't want to lose that.'

'How kind of you.' Irina lifted her glass to drink, smiling again. 'Cheers!'

Evelyn reached for her glass of punch, changed her mind, picked up another half-filled glass.

'I'll finish my lime juice, then enjoy myself. I feel like something with a bit of a kick.'

Irina drank her own punch, put down the empty glass. She opened her executive case, took out a small box, handed it to Evelyn. Closing the case, she stood up to go.

'That's a little thank you present. I could have been driving round in this heat for hours. I must go now.'

'Chanel No. 5!' Evelyn was looking at the small box. 'This is quite unnecessary . . .'

'Don't you like it?' Irina asked moving towards the door. 'They are free samples for special customers – and I rate you in that category.'

'I still think it's too generous, but thank you – and it is my favourite perfume.'

She opened the door and began walking down the garden path with her departing guest. Suddenly there was an ear-splitting barking of such savagery Irina jumped and looked to her left. At the border of the garden a strong high wire fence divided off the two properties. The barrier continued at right angles halfway down the next front garden, turned again to form a box. Behind the wire crouched a large dog; an Alsatian? The animal, teeth bared, was foaming at the mouth.

'Don't worry,' Evelyn reassured her, 'it's well fenced in. The owners have gone to fetch the vet. He's going to put it down. It's gone mad. Could be the heat . . .'

She stood by the gate as her guest drove off towards the A 12 in her Ford Escort. Evelyn peered over the gate towards the sea. Pete Nield had taken Peggy Vanderheld for a walk along the sand dunes. The American woman seemed restless, had to have regular walks.

Going back inside, Evelyn closed the door, remembered to attach the chain. Even that brief sojourn in the heat of the day had made her thirsty. She went into the living room, picked up her glass of punch. I need a pick me up myself, she thought, as she raised the glass.

*   *   *

Newman was grim faced as he drove his Mercedes 280E along the A1120 heading for Yoxford. Beside him sat Tweed and in the back the only other passenger was Paula. Tweed glanced at Newman, saw his expression, guessed accurately what he was thinking, kept silent.

They were approaching Livingstone Manor's long drive to their left. Already Newman could see the old church perched on the hill with its isolated bell tower, the place where Sandy had died horribly. He reduced speed, began to cruise at thirty miles an hour.

'Coming close to Livingstone Manor, are we?' Tweed asked.

'Yes.'

'If there are guards at the entrance lodge they may spot us.'

'Let them.' Newman's tone was cold, remote. 'Let the bastards know we're coming after them. They've walked into your trap. Let them sweat.'

'Oh I'm sure they're doing that already,' Tweed replied, trying to lighten the atmosphere, 'in this heat sweating has become a way of life.'

'That's not what I meant.'

'We know,' said Paula quietly. 'We do know, Bob.'

A hundred yards behind them, adjusting his speed to Newman's, Chief Inspector Buchanan drove a Volvo station wagon. He liked plenty of room for his long legs. Beside him sat Sergeant Warden in his shirt sleeves. For Warden this was a great concession to the heat.

Newman slowed the Mercedes even more as they began to pass the sprawling estate of Livingstone Manor. At the lodge gate a guard was wiping his wet forehead. The car meant nothing to him. Paula looked to her left and beyond the closed grille gates she saw several vehicles drawn up near the front of the mansion with the central arched window.

'One red Jag,' she said. 'One cream Cadillac. And one

473

stretched black limo. Mr Franklin D. Hauser must be in residence.'

'Three cars, I know,' said Tweed.

Paula blinked. She had not seen Tweed move his head one inch as he stared ahead along the road. But she had experienced this before. Tweed seemed to be able to see more out of the corner of his eyes than most people observed staring straight at something.

'Pity that mansion is spoilt by the load of communications equipment on the roof,' he remarked. 'Monica was right – or rather, the electrical supervisor grilled by Special Branch was right. That place has as much sophisticated communications junk as we have at Park Crescent. Alarming thought.'

'At least it confirms it is a key headquarters,' Paula remarked.

Tweed checked his watch. 'I just hope nothing has happened to either of our witnesses at Walberswick.'

'How could it?' snapped Newman. 'With Butler and Nield on guard.'

'I'll just be glad when we get there and find they're all right. How much longer before we do get there?'

'Roughly half an hour,' Newman said and lapsed into silence.

Butler hurried into the living room. He had thrown on his jacket to conceal the holstered Smith & Wesson. As he entered Evelyn raised the glass she was about to drink from in a salute.

'I heard voices,' Butler said. 'I got here as soon as I could.' He looked at the empty glass on the table. 'Who came? Where are they now?'

'A girl who had lost her way. A beautician. The heat was getting her down. She left her samples case outside the front door. I fetched it for her. She was genuine. She even gave me this bottle of Chanel No. 5 . . .'

'*Don't drink that!* Now, put the glass down carefully on the table. Tell me exactly what happened . . .'

Butler's normal poker face had a concentrated look as he listened to her account of the visit, his head turned to one side as he visualized everything which had happened.

'. . . so you see, she was quite harmless,' Evelyn concluded. 'And, as you can see, she drank her own punch . . .'

She broke off as the Alsatian next door began snarling, barking its head off. She grimmaced at the sound.

'I told you the people next door have gone to fetch the vet to put down that dog. It gets on my nerves.'

'Have you a shallow bowl? The sort of thing a dog could drink out of?'

'Yes. Why? Sorry, you must have a reason. As a matter of fact I kept the one I had for my own dog. It got run over and I couldn't bear to have another one in the house.'

Butler grasped the handle of the coal shovel lying in the hearth. In his other hand he carried her glass of punch and followed her into the kitchen. She was just putting a plain white shallow china bowl on the table. He poured half the contents of the glass into the bowl.

'I'm going out of the back door. Could you go into the front garden and distract that animal, keep it there for a few minutes. For heaven's sake keep well back from it.'

He stepped out of the back door where the high wire fence continued along the border of the garden next door. He walked half-way along the lawn, bent down close to the wire, placing the bowl by his side. The dog was shrieking its head off at the front.

The ground was so hard, so sun baked, it took him several minutes to shovel a shallow hole under the fence – shallow but deep enough to push the bowl through to the other side. Standing up, he rattled the metal shovel along the wire, back and forth. The sound of the dog barking stopped for a few moments, was resumed as Butler continued scraping the wire. He jumped well back from the barrier as the Alsatian appeared.

Evelyn came rushing back through the front doorway, shut the door, fixed the chain, ran along the passage into the kitchen and out through the back doorway. Butler gestured with the shovel.

The Alsatian, dripping foam, glared at him with startling red eyes, bloodshot. Then it saw the bowl. It sniffed at the intruder, stood for a short time staring at the liquid. Then it bent its huge head, began lapping up the contents. Suddenly it jerked its head up, a shudder ran through its body, it opened its jaws, gave one muted howl, stiffened from head to tail, fell over sideways, hitting the ground with a heavy thud. It lay quite still, the sun shining down on it, roasting the corpse.

'Oh, my God!'

Evelyn's right hand flew to her mouth. She stood still for a moment. Butler took her arm, guided her inside the house. She thanked him, walked like a zombie to the living room, collapsed into a chair, staring up at Butler.

'That could have been me.'

'But it wasn't.' He gave one of his rare smiles. 'You and I have to come to an arrangement. You promise never to let anyone into the house yourself – or I'll stop going to the toilet . . .'

She laughed, with only the faintest touch of hysteria, then giggled. Jumping up, she threw her arms round him, hugged him. He gripped her shoulders reassuringly as she released him.

'We have a sample for the Forensic merchants left in the glass. Now I'm going to empty the jug of punch you so carefully prepared down the lavatory.'

'And after all the trouble I took to concoct it.'

That was when Butler knew she wasn't going to slide

into a state of shock. He had emptied the jug, was flush-
ing the toilet, when the door bell rang. Evelyn ran into
the lavatory, playfully tugged at his arm.

'Someone at the door. Do your duty, Harry.'

Peering through the spyhole, he saw Nield standing
arm in arm with Peggy Vanderheld, looking at the rose
hedge while they waited for the door to be opened.
Standing in the entrance, Butler stared cynically at their
posture.

'Enjoying yourself, Pete?' he enquired.

Even though tanned, Nield flushed. Peggy disengaged
her arm and gazed boldly back at Butler. Clad in a form-
fitting skirt and a short sleeved blouse she looked sexy
and knew it.

'All's well?' Nield asked in an over-hearty tone.

Butler's mind moved like lightning. Tweed was coming
to interrogate Vanderheld, should arrive soon. Maybe a
jolt would help to loosen the tough American woman's
tongue.

'Oh, sure,' he replied. 'Everything's fine. Of course we
had a little bit of excitement. A girl called while I was in
the loo and tried to poison Evelyn. Go through to the
kitchen and take a peek out of the back door – see what
happened to that mad dog next door when I fed it the
drink meant for Evelyn. It's quite an education . . .'

47

Tweed stepped out of the Mercedes Newman had parked
in front of Rose Bower. He scanned the area, his experienced eye judging the security – or lack of security – of

the location. Newman locked the car and waited as Tweed walked back to where Buchanan had stopped his Volvo.

'I'm going in now. I'll do my best to persuade her to let you be present but I guarantee nothing. Someone will come shortly to let you know.'

'It's up to you. I'll wait here,' Buchanan replied.

Tweed looked at Warden who was about to get out of the car. He already had his notebook in his hand.

'I don't think your presence will help the interview at all,' he said crisply.

'You mean you want me to stay in the car like a guard dog?'

'If you wish to put it that way, yes.'

As he strode away Tweed was sure Buchanan had suppressed a smile. Butler had emerged from the cottage, was talking to Newman. He listened while Butler told him about the attempt on Evelyn's life. Outwardly he seemed unaffected by the incident.

'Where is Peggy Vanderheld?'

'Nield has her in the guest bedroom at the back upstairs,' Butler told him. 'They are expecting you.'

'Then I'd better get on with it . . .'

The living room door was closed as he entered the cottage, ran up the narrow stairs. Nield met him at the top, pointed to a closed door.

'She's in there. You've heard about the attempt to kill Evelyn Lennox this afternoon? Good. And,' he lowered his voice, 'that Butler told Vanderheld. Thought it might soften her up for you. She's a pretty gutsy lady.'

'You stay on the alert here on this landing but not near this door. I'm expecting another attempt – maybe on the lives of both women, once they know Evelyn is still alive.'

'How can they know that?'

'No idea. But they will . . .'

Tweed knocked on the closed door. A soft American

voice called 'Come in', and he entered a small bedroom with an angled and beamed ceiling, closed the door. Whatever he had been expecting it was not this. Peggy Vanderheld was reclining on a double bed, her shapely legs stretched out below her mini-skirt, her breasts tight against a close-fitting white blouse, the first three buttons undone. She appeared to be wearing nothing but her skin under the blouse. Perched up against a pillow, she studied Tweed through half-closed eyes. Her thick, jet black hair was splayed over the pillow. She's trying to sex me up, Tweed decided.

'My name is Tweed, Chief Claims Investigator of General and Cumbria Assurance. I'm probing into the death of Ed Riverton in Helsinki. He carried a very large policy with us. Also into the death of Sandra Riverton, who also carried a policy with us. May I sit down?'

'Perch on the edge of the bed if you like.'

'I think a chair might be more comfortable. Thank you.'

'How do you think I can possibly help?'

'The investigation has widened its scope. To get at the truth we're having to investigate the company you once worked for. INCUBUS. Incidentally, in a car outside is Chief Inspector Buchanan of New Scotland Yard. He is in charge of the Sandra Riverton murder case. I would like him to be present, if you agree.'

'Wheel him in. If I don't like him I'll tell you and he can piss off.'

'He won't ask you any questions.' Tweed opened the door, called out to Nield, went back into the room. Vanderheld had slid off the bed, was standing in front of a wall mirror, brushing her hair. She straightened her slip of a skirt, sat in a chair, crossed her legs as Buchanan strolled in.

'This is Chief Inspector Buchanan,' Tweed introduced. 'He is here strictly as an observer.'

For a moment Buchanan stood still, his grey eyes meeting Vanderheld's, then he walked forward, held out his hand. 'Miss Vanderheld.' Her shapely hand was surprisingly cool, her grip firm.

A formidable woman, Buchanan thought as he chose a chair in a corner, out of her direct line of vision. She had the most compelling dark eyes and when she spoke he found her voice very feminine, enticing. Her unbuttoned blouse emphasized her beautiful neck but Buchanan also noticed the excellent bone structure, the strong chin.

'So you're investigating the whole INCUBUS apparatus,' she began, addressing Tweed. 'In that case I may have interesting facts to tell you. Hauser runs the entire world system. Personally. If that bastard goes, INCUBUS collapses.'

'What about his top executives?' Tweed asked.

'Messenger boys with big titles.' Her full lips curled. 'Take Adam Carver. Vice President of Banking Operations! He can't buy a hot dog stall without Hauser's say-so. He is a front man who smooth-talks through a deal already set up by Hauser. And for that he's paid $300,000 a year. Another thing about Adam – Hauser likes having a well-educated Englishman at his beck and call. Why? Because Hauser came up from nothing in California, had little formal education. Sometimes I wonder how Adam spends his days when he's not seducing some floozie.'

Her tone was vicious. Tweed wondered whether Adam hadn't paid sufficient attention to Vanderheld.

'What about Frank Galvone?' he asked.

'Frank!' Her voice dripped contempt. 'Did you know he was scum on the streets of Chicago when Hauser hired him?'

'Yes. Occupation: professional pickpocket, strong-arm man.'

Vanderheld looked surprised. 'You seem to know a lot. You wouldn't have a man on the inside?'

'Unfortunately, no,' Tweed responded immediately. 'But I've done my homework. Please go on – you were talking about Galvone's background, his work at INCUBUS.'

'Officially he's Vice President of Strategic Planning. The titles change at Hauser's whim. Another $300,000 a year for another messenger boy. He's Hauser's hatchet man, but again he can't take a shower without the nod from Hauser. He flies about the world a lot. Sandra Riverton told me that when he visited the Norwich HQ everyone was shivering in their shoes. He puts on the pressure, keeps the staff working all-out.'

Buchanan leaned forward. 'If I might ask a question?'

Vanderheld looked at him, gave him a slow smile. 'Depends on the question, Buster.'

Tweed heaved an inward sigh of relief. Obviously she approved of the Chief Inspector's polite, quiet manner.

'You mentioned Sandra Riverton just now. Was she visiting Helsinki when you had this conversation with her?'

'No. It was over the phone. She'd had a long session with Frank. She told me she was limp with exhaustion after the experience. In Norwich, that was. He'd fired questions at her non-stop about her job, whatever that was. He stayed several days but I don't think she saw him again.'

'Thank you. I wish everyone I met answered with such precision.'

He settled back in his chair, withdrawing from the discussion. Tweed's technique of interrogation intrigued him: the way he was playing on her fury at being summarily dismissed, a fact he cleverly had not referred to. He relaxed again, listening as Tweed put his next question.

'In Helsinki you mentioned a Mr Popescu to Bob Newman.'

481

'Nicolae Popescu is a creep. I only saw him once when he had just arrived in Helsinki, months ago. I was coming up to the penthouse floor in the elevator, the doors opened and I saw him. Hauser moved in the way to conceal him and I pressed the "down" button before Hauser saw me. I don't know why, but I felt I wasn't supposed to see him.'

Tweed produced an envelope, extracted a number of photos he had previously shown to Buchanan at Park Crescent. He handed them to Vanderheld and she pulled her chair forward so their knees were almost touching. Buchanan watched the effect of their proximity on Tweed. Not a blink. She looked through them, quickly. All her movements were brisk.

'This one,' she said handing back one print.

'You're sure?'

Tweed held up the photo so Buchanan could see the one she had chosen. The picture of Ion Manescu.

'Positive. I said he was a creep. He was creepy. Not someone I'd like to meet in a dark alley.' She paused. 'Look, when this interview is over does the protection for me continue? Specifically, will Pete Nield stay with me while Hauser remains free?'

'Yes,' Tweed said promptly. 'You have my personal guarantee. What made you ask?'

She reached under the counterpane covering the bed, pulled out a large polythene wallet containing a green file. She handed it to Tweed.

'I took out some insurance when Hauser fired me after all those years. That is a photocopy of the file on Popescu. Ridiculous name, but he's anything but ridiculous. When Hauser gave me the file to put in the vault he said Popescu was Austrian. I ask you! Austrian – it sounds one helluva more like Romanian to me. That file records he speaks good English, that he was an attaché at some embassy in London for a year. Nationality of the embassy is deleted.

482

You see now why I checked on the protection?'

Tweed smiled, looked at her dark eyes which stared straight back at him. Almost hypnotic.

'You wanted to be sure of me before you gave me the file. Very sensible.' Despite the heat inside the claustro-phobic bedroom, he kept his voice casual. 'Just as a theory, let us suppose Hauser was capable of organizing a murder. Would he hire an outsider, a professional assassin?'

'You think he's done that?'

'At the moment it is a theory.'

She sat back in her chair, kicked off her shoes, grasped both arms of the chair with her hands, crossed her legs and one of her feet brushed Tweed's trousers. He pre-tended not to notice. Her face had become like carved stone.

'I'm not answering any more questions. This is getting me in too deep. I thought that Robert Newman was going to be present. That was the message Pete gave me.'

'What has gone wrong? Tweed asked quietly.

'You have. You're some kind of insurance man – if that's what you really are.' She glanced at Buchanan. 'Sitting over there is a high-ranking detective. Now you're talking murder. If a reporter was present – someone really from the outside world who can't be intimidated – then I might talk. Put up or shut up.'

'Give me a moment,' Tweed said amiably. 'We thought you'd feel overwhelmed with three people.'

He went to the door, opened it. So Vanderheld could hear he called out to Nield to fetch Newman immediately. He waited until Newman, wearing his shirt open necked, his sleeves rolled to the elbows, appeared. He ushered him inside without a word.

'Hello, Peggy,' Newman greeted her with a droll smile. He leaned against a wall, folded his arms, crossed his ankles, the soul of relaxation.

'Give me a cigarette, Bob,' Vanderheld said. 'And maybe you'd light it for me.'

Newman obliged, handed her the cigarette. She took a long drag, blew out a smoke ring.

'Now I'm relaxed.' She looked at Tweed. 'You were saying?'

'Assuming Hauser wanted to organize a murder – or a series of murders – would he hire an outsider, a professional assassin?'

'No. Never. He'd keep it in the family – a phrase he often uses referring to INCUBUS. Maybe a top executive, maybe someone professional but on the payroll. That way he keeps complete control – because he's paying them a fortune. Definitely someone on the inside, close to the top.'

'So,' Newman intervened, 'I'll ask you again the question I asked in your apartment in Helsinki before we moved you out to Örno, with a guard, and probably saved your life. Remember Anna Jarva, the poor woman murdered on the scrubbing board, the woman who happened to be dressed just like you, who travelled on the same No. 4 tram.'

'What question?'

All her attention was on Newman now. Her full red lips were slightly parted, showed the tip of her tongue. My God! Buchanan was thinking, you do like to arouse men, to make sure you still have the power to do so.

'Can you check from your records,' Newman asked, 'who was present in Helsinki the night Ed Riverton was murdered. Who – providing it's the same man – was *absent* from Helsinki the following night when Sandra Riverton was murdered in Suffolk. Or are the records, maybe your diary, still locked away in that Helsinki bank you told me about?'

'I don't need written records.' She leant back, arched her chest. 'I have a photographic memory. That was why I lasted with Hauser five years. He couldn't abide a PA who had to look things up in files.'

'I'm still listening,' Newman assured her.

'Adam Carver fits. He was in Helsinki the night Riverton was garrotted. The following day he flew off somewhere. No idea where.'

'Anyone else?' Newman pressed.

'Frank Galvone. I remember when I left the building I saw a light in his office. Said he was working late. The following day he was away for forty-eight hours. He looked bushed when he got back.'

'That's the lot?'

'No, it isn't. Nicolae Popescu was sacked out on a bed at Level Five. His door was open a fraction – it was a cold night, ice cold. The heating in the corridor was going full blast. I caught a glimpse of him as I took some files to the vault.'

'And the following day?' Newman persisted.

'I had to deliver some important papers to catch a flight from Helsinki airport. I saw him queueing up to catch the direct flight to London.'

'Peggy, your memory is quite extraordinary. You are sure of these facts?'

'That's right, Buster. That's what they are. Facts . . .'

'Leaves us just about where we were,' Tweed said as he descended the staircase. 'Three possible suspects.'

'Not quite,' said Newman grimly. 'I can't prove it but I think I've identified the killer.'

'And how have you done that?'

'Since I can't be sure yet I won't say any more. I can be cryptic too, Tweed.'

Paula met them in the hall. During the drive to the cottage Tweed had persuaded her too many people might overawe Vanderheld. Which wasn't his real reason: he had suddenly realized the presence of another attractive woman might make Vanderheld bridle. After his visit to her at the Helsinki apartment Newman had described Vanderheld as 'a powerhouse of sex . . .'

'How did you get on with her?' Paula asked, excited.

'So, so,' Tweed replied. 'I sense you have something else on your mind . . .' He broke off as Butler appeared from the living room.

'Harry, I want you to tell Chief Inspector Buchanan all about what nearly happened to Evelyn. Take him out into the back garden. Then show him the state of that dog – and give him the sample for his Forensic people.'

He nodded to Buchanan who had followed them slowly down the stairs, slotting into his mind the general layout of Rose Bower. As Butler led the way to the kitchen Tweed followed Paula into the living room. Evelyn, who had heard their voices, was filling glasses with lime juice.

'I am bone dry,' Tweed admitted as he sat down. 'Thank you. Are you feeling better after your nerve-wracking experience? My name is Tweed.'

'Much better, Mr Tweed. If you'll excuse me for a moment, I want to fetch some more lime juice. I've been taking glasses out to Sergeant Warden.'

'What is it, Paula?' Tweed asked when they were alone.

'I want you to show her that picture of Irina Serov you wouldn't tell me where you got it from.'

Tweed drank more lime juice, considered her request. He had been given the photo in confidence by General Rebet during his stay at the Hotel Moskwa in Leningrad. Because the dissident had been a colonel in the KGB, Rebet had wanted the defection kept quiet. Very Russian.

'Why to Evelyn?' he asked.

'Because we've been chatting about her ordeal while you were upstairs. Something about the description she gave me of the fake beautician made me think of that photo. She doesn't need to know who it is.'

'I'll think about it. I can't see Hauser risking bringing someone like that into this country. Buchanan mustn't know about that picture. I've been careful that he didn't see it. Lord, I hope you're wrong.' He lowered his voice. 'Vanderheld told us Manescu has visited Britain more than once. A frightening thought.'

He stopped speaking as Evelyn reappeared with a jug of fresh lime juice. He let her refill his glass. Talking a lot was a thirsty business in the late afternoon heat.

'Miss Lennox,' he began, 'I have a photo here I'd like you to look at. You might just have seen this woman in the vicinity of Walberswick at some time.'

Paula stood beside Evelyn as she examined the print. She frowned, puckered up her mouth, held it further away.

'I don't think so,' she said eventually. 'Although there is something familiar.'

'Place the print on that drum table,' Tweed suggested. 'Then use your fingers to cover the dark hair so you can only see the face.'

He drank more lime juice. Even inside the shaded interior the temperature was high. He looked round the comfortable room, furnished with chintz-covered chairs and matching curtains. Normally he disliked the material but it suited the beamed ceiling, the large brick alcove fireplace.

'I'll be damned,' exclaimed Evelyn. 'Now I'm certain it is that awful beautician woman who tried to poison me. It was the bleached blonde hair which fooled me – makes her look quite different. Who is she?'

Tweed was prepared for that question. 'A woman wanted for involvement in insurance swindles. This is the first time she's resorted to attempted murder. You haven't taken out an insurance policy on your life recently, have you?'

'No, I haven't. How on earth do you think she came to pick on me?'

'Maybe there was something in what she said. She was lost, came to the wrong address. And I'd appreciate it if you didn't mention this to Peggy Vanderheld. We can't be sure of anything so it's important to keep her nervous – alert. Of course, that fake beautician might have come from INCUBUS's insurance outfit, Fraternity & Equality.'

He wished he'd thought of that explanation earlier. The heat must be fogging my brain, he thought. Buchanan came into the room followed by Newman.

'Don't worry, Miss Lennox,' he assured her, 'I'm not here to ask a lot more questions. Only one.' He produced a large button, showed it to her. 'You worked in Helsinki for quite a time, as I understand it. I sent back Sergeant Warden to search the messy floor of the bell tower where Sandra Riverton was murdered. You can see threads attached to the button. It has the Daks symbol on it. I suspect it was torn from a British warm while Riverton was struggling for her life. Anyone you knew in Helsinki who wore a British warm?'

'Hauser does in winter. He buys a lot of British clothes. And wasn't it bitterly cold here when my sister died?'

'It was,' Newman intervened bleakly. 'Can I look at that button? Thank you.'

'Someone else wore a British warm in Helsinki,' Evelyn recalled. 'Why do I think it was a foreigner?'

'You tell me,' Buchanan suggested.

'No good. It won't come back to me.'

'It is the only solid item of evidence,' Buchanan remarked, taking back the button. 'I didn't ask Vanderheld – she's American and I'm not sure of her. She talked just a little too much. If you do recall the owner of another British warm perhaps you'd call me at this number.'

488

He gave her a card, walked down the garden path towards his Volvo. Tweed drank some more lime juice, thanked Evelyn, walked out into the heat.

'I'm worried,' he told Newman as they strolled between the hedges. 'Nield reported identifying Manescu in that car he pulled up alongside on his motor cycle. Now Evelyn has positively confirmed the presence of Irina Serov in the area. Hauser is preparing something very nasty indeed.'

He asked Newman the question nagging at him as they drove back to London followed by Buchanan and Warden in the Volvo.

'You said you'd identified the assassin among those three suspects Vanderheld listed. May I ask what gave you the clue – always assuming you're right?'

'Something Buchanan said at Park Crescent before we left for Finland. You pride yourself on your memory, so just play back that conversation in your mind.'

48

IRA BOMB MISSES SOUTHAMPTON TARGET.
Hauser read with satisfaction the headline in the late edition of the *Evening Standard* Galvone had bought during his drive back from the Hampshire city. The story below told how the bomb had been placed in an empty shop next door to the private bank, Street & Braithwaite. The assumption was they had hoped to blast a way inside the bank and make off with a large sum of cash to swell IRA funds. The reporter theorized the bomb had detonated not close enough to the adjoining bank's wall.

'You've done good, Frank,' he said, throwing the paper on to his desk in his study at Livingstone Manor.

'Must have scared the shit out of the bank's directors,' Frank agreed smugly.

'You've not finished yet,' Hauser snapped as Galvone started to leave the room. 'But first come down with me to the map room . . .'

Inside the cellar labyrinth he unlocked a door, beckoned Galvone to follow him. The room was empty as he walked over to a huge wall map of Europe and Russia. Red pins were stuck into different cities. Warsaw, Budapest, Sofia, Belgrade and Bucharest . . .

'That shows where the next major explosions will detonate. The outfits I want to take over will be anxious to sell to me before they're blown up. We have to create turmoil before we can establish American control.'

'Why Belgrade?'

'You really must keep in closer touch with the situation, Frank. That is, if you're going to continue to be of any use to me.' He smiled. 'I never have this trouble with Adam. Yugoslavia is falling apart. The province of Slovenia is screaming for independence. Always keep the pot on the boil.'

He spoke as though it was a normal business deal. The fact that the bombs would be timed to explode at lunchtime on weekdays – when maximum casualties would be caused – was for Hauser an obvious ploy to bring about more chaos.

'The other job you have,' he went on, 'is to double check the security here at Livingstone Manor. I've a feeling that Tweed will get to know I'm here. He's dangerous – well, so am I. Move the big feet, Frank.'

It was probably just as well that Marler was immune to the heat. He spent an active day preparing for his

490

exploratory assault on Livingstone Manor.

He planned to penetrate the defences at three in the morning. Morale was always at its lowest ebb, guards on duty would be weary. He spent a long time in the East End of London. At a none too salubrious address off the Old Kent Road he met Alfred Higgins by appointment.

Alf Higgins, as he was known to his mates in the underworld, owned a small watch-maker's establishment. He did just enough legal business to make it impossible for the police to haul him in for questioning. Alf's real skill lay in his up-to-date knowledge of alarm and security systems. He was also an expert locksmith, which was a euphemism for picking locks and opening the doors to houses and safes which were supposed to be impregnable. Marler had used his services on several illegal occasions before and knew he was a slippery customer. He also knew he'd have to listen to the same lecture.

'Sit yourself down in that armchair. Real comfy, Mr 'Enderson,' Alf greeted his client. 'Not your real monicker, 'Enderson, I'll be bound.'

Marler took one look at the decrepit armchair in the dimly illuminated room – dimly because of the grimy windows. He perched himself on a polished wooden stool instead, folded his arms.

'Henderson I said, Henderson it is. Just like last time. I want you to break into a large country mansion which is heavily guarded. By men, by the latest security systems . . .'

'Installed by who?'

'A British firm. They really know their stuff.'

Alf, seated in an ancient rocking chair, scratched his thatch of grey hair. Needed a trim, Marler thought – made him look like a farm labourer. Which was all to the good since they'd be travelling together in Suffolk. He was a small man with skinny arms and legs. His face was like a walnut, wrinkled and brown. Age, impossible to

491

guess – somewhere between forty and sixty. His best feature was his hands with long sensitive fingers. The lecture came.

'You said, "I want you to break in." You know my rules, Mr 'Enderson. I never goes inside. That way I've never gone "inside", if you gets my meanin'. All right?' He chuckled at his little joke. 'I make sure you get into this mansion. I loan you the equipment you'll need to open any lock easy. But I stays in the car while you're breakin' the law. I'm law abidin' and wouldn't dream of bein' found on private property.'

'Understood,' Marler said brusquely. 'What equipment? I emphasize the place will be like a fortress.'

'Costs more, does a fortress. We can talk about the dibs later. Want some beer? Bloody 'ot.'

'No, thank you,' Marler replied, observing the greasy glass Alf was drinking from. 'What equipment?' he repeated.

Perched on the stool rather like a pixie, Marler was wearing an old lightweight navy blue suit. It didn't show the dirt. He glanced round the room full of junk. The room had probably once been a bar. A stained wooden counter ran behind his host, the counter almost covered with old clocks, none of which appeared to be working. More clocks and old watches were piled on the shelves behind the counter. The floor was covered with spare parts, boxes of tools with the lids open. Hardly a square foot of free space. Which would make it almost impossible for the police to search the place. Like sifting through a council rubbish dump.

'There's two kinds of security lock,' Alf said suddenly. 'These security burks think if they make a lock complicated they've kept everyone out. Just the opposite. If they used lots of bolts they might earn their big fat fees. There's the combination lock – what you get when you come across most wall safes. Come to that in a mo' –

let's see what we do with deadlocks first.'

Higgins was wearing a surprisingly clean linen jacket with large pockets. He delved inside the right-hand pocket, brought out three apparently ordinary keys of different sizes. Only the colour was peculiar, had a fluorescent tinge. He nodded towards the door leading direct to the street.

'Take these, open the door. And they ain't the proper keys for that door.'

Marler looked at the heavy wooden door. It had three locks. Higgins believed in his own security. But there were also four large bolts which had been shot closed after Marler had entered the premises. He took the keys, looked at Higgins.

'How then?'

'You're 'oldin' magnetic keys. One of them will slide inside any security lock. Fiddle the key gently, see what 'appens.'

Marler shrugged, dropped off the stool, walked up to the door. First he opened the four bolts. Taking the three keys, he held each one close to the top lock, found one which seemed the right size, inserted it, fiddled it gently as instructed. He heard the lock opening. He chose another key for the second lock, performed the same action, again heard the lock open. The same key worked on the lowest lock. He turned the handle and the heavy slab of wood opened.

'Lordy!' he said under his breath.

'Better lock up,' Higgins said, leaving his rocking chair.

He held a bunch of keys, attended to the locks, shot the bolts back in to the closed position. Moving light-footed in his trainers, he bent down at the far end of the counter, pushed aside a heap of boxes, exposing a large safe.

'Keeps all my money in that, don't I? You can 'ave it if you open it. This might 'elp.'

From his left-hand pocket he produced a small circular

instrument with a thick base. He showed Marler the other end. It was hollow, appeared to be fitted with a series of flanges of diminishing size. Higgins handed it to Marler.

'Try your luck, matey. Insert the hollow end over the combination. Again be gentle when you fits it. When you feel it lock on, press the button in the base and wait. And that safe 'as the latest combination lock. The company what makes it guarantees security. Stupid burks . . .'

Marler crouched down, studied the instrument for a moment, carefully slipped the hollow end over the combination lock, felt a slight pull as it locked on. He pressed the button in the base, clasped his hands, waited crouched on his haunches. He heard faint clicking noises. Very rapid, one after another. Then silence.

'Well, get on with it,' urged Higgins. 'You're where you're not supposed to be. Don't 'ang around.'

Marler turned the safe handle, pulled the door open and stared at the contents. Nothing. It was empty. Higgins bent beside him, closed the safe, twisted the instrument slightly to the right to release it, dropped it in his pocket.

'Those three keys . . .' Marler began.

'Magnetic, like I tell you. Sucks the tines of the lock open. The security lot make their locks of metal, think that makes it safer. Those keys are my own invention. Made them meself in a friend's engineering shop. Sometimes I thinks I ought to patent them.' He chuckled again.

'And the combination thingumajig?'

'Ah, that.' Higgins looked sad, drank more warm beer. 'Like to tell you I made that. Be a lie. Got it off a Yank friend I'd done favours for in Philadelphia. Very expensive to buy, I'd say. If you knew where to buy it from. 'As a tiny built-in computer in that base. It's battery operated. I'll fit a new battery so it's nice and fresh for you. Eight hundred nicker the whole job,' he said quickly.

'Eight hundred pounds! You must be joking.'

'And no rough stuff. You'll 'ave to 'andle any of that.'

'I can. I will. Four hundred pounds. And it's getting damned hot in here, so make up your mind. I could go elsewhere.'

'Don't be barmy. And get keys like I got? And the thingumajig?'

'Five hundred. In cash as last time.'

'Only deal in cash. You knows that. Tax people can read cheques. Can't read cash – not if they can't find it. Six hundred nicker. Final offer. There's the door. I'll even unlock it for you.'

'All right, Scrooge. Six hundred nicker. Oh, there will be alarms. Electronic beams. I'm sure of it.'

'I'll handle them. All included in the six hundred nicker. Only 'cos I like the look of your face. When?'

'Tonight. I'll call for you at 11.30. After dark. In a blue Ford Cortina. Don't keep me waiting. Here's four hundred in fifties on account. And don't forget to bring *all* the equipment. Now unlock that bloody door before I suffocate.'

Marler's brief call at Newman's South Ken flat in Beresforde Road turned out very differently from what he had expected. Newman listened to him, heard about his plan to break in to Livingstone Manor:

'. . . so as you visited Hauser there back in February, I hoped you'd be able to give me some idea of the layout inside. Maybe draw me a plan of the part you saw.'

'Yes, I will do that.' Newman lifted his glass of fruit juice and then grinned. 'On condition you let me come with you and this Alf Higgins.'

'That wasn't on my agenda . . .'

'It is now. If you want that ground plan. And I noticed some of the security system.' Newman's manner changed, his voice became sombre. 'Don't forget my girl friend,

495

Sandy, was killed by one of Hauser's men in an especially horrible way. And I'm convinced now since Tweed told me what Vanderheld said before I sat in on the interview – convinced that Hauser gave the order for Sandy's execution. Because that's what it was.'

'Tweed would say you were too personally involved to get mixed up with me on this trip.'

'I'm personally involved up to the hilt. Take your choice. I can draw that plan, tell you something about the security, maybe save your life. We're not dealing with pussy-cats.'

'I had realized that.'

'So do I draw the plan?'

'Yes, please. And I agree, this may take two of us to do the job. Even then, it will be dangerous.'

Marler wandered to the large bay window at the front of the large Victorian living room. Beyond the net curtains was the church of St Mark's, the trees and the grass in the garden surrounding it. Not a normal London view.

'This is the plan,' Newman said after a few minutes. 'I can only give part of the ground floor. Hauser's study appeared to be at the back – I saw a door open at the end of a long passage. The key is probably the huge living room. When I was talking to Hauser I noticed Galvone leaning against an almost closed door in the inner wall here . . .' He pointed with his pen. 'He quietly closed it. I think that leads down to the cellar complex Monica described to us during the meeting with Tweed this morning.'

'I was going to drive up for a quick recce of Livingstone Manor, but you've been there. They have guard dogs patrolling the grounds?'

'No, I don't think they do. They seem to rely on human guards. The windows are wired up, but I couldn't see any security round the heavy front door. Mind you, it has three locks.'

'Any bolts?'

'No, why?'

'Just wondered. This chilled champagne is good. Lanson? Your favourite brand?'

'I find it goes down well. One more serious factor. I'm proposing to go armed.'

'Sensible chap,' Marler drawled. 'So am I. Not the Armalite for this job.' He opened his tropical drill jacket, showed the butt of the .32 Browning nestling in his hip holster. Pulling up his left trouser leg, he exposed the strapped sheath, the handle of a hunting knife protruding. Reaching into a pocket he took something out, slipped it over the fingers of his right hand.

'Knuckle dusters?' Newman queried. 'You're expecting close-quarter combat.'

'If we meet anyone they have to be eliminated quietly.'

He slipped off the knuckle dusters, dropped them in his pocket, raised his glass.

'Here's to success.'

'To survival,' Newman amended. 'And the obtaining of evidence to bring down Franklin D. Hauser.'

As they drank Newman reflected the normal hostility between himself and Marler had vanished. For the moment. Maybe it was the hot weather? The phone rang. Marler picked it up as Newman nodded. It was Tweed.

'Put Newman on, please.'

'And what can I do for you?' Newman asked.

'Whatever you're planning you're on your own. Remember that. And take care. I predict we're approaching the final crisis.'

'Tweed sends his love,' Newman joked as he put down the phone. 'When exactly do we launch this break-in operation?'

'Zero hour 3 a.m. On the dot, if you please . . .'

'What are you up to now?' Paula asked.

She was wearing a pale fawn mini-skirt, pale red tights

and a short-sleeved white blouse as she perched on the edge of her desk. The atmosphere inside Tweed's Park Crescent office was torrid. He replaced the receiver.

'Just checking. Marler *is* with Newman at Bob's flat.' He looked at Monica. 'Rather obvious – Newman draws a Smith & Wesson with his certificate of use from the armoury. Marler takes a .32 Browning. And they're together.' He glanced at Cord Dillon perched on a chair in a corner. 'You need evidence, solid evidence, against Hauser.'

'I sure do. Something the Justice Department can nail him with forever. I hope these two ladies realize that officially I don't exist this side of the pond?'

'Both are trustworthy. The question is unnecessary.'

'When did you realize Marler was also up to something?'

'As soon as Monica told me he had been here early this morning. That he had extracted from her all the information she had obtained about the cellar complex at Livingstone Manor.'

'You could have stopped them,' Paula accused.

'They can look after themselves.' Tweed's voice hardened. 'Hauser breaks every rule in the book. Terrorizes companies he wants into selling out. Transports explosives into the Soviet Union. We're not going to outwit a man like that by playing it strictly legal. And he's a world menace.'

'You sound unusually vehement,' Paula commented.

'Look at these newspaper reports, for God's sake.'

He spread out different papers over his desk. He jabbed a finger at the headlines.

BOMBS EXPLODE IN BALKANS.

CAR BOMB KILLS LEADING ROMANIAN LIBERAL.

CHAOS IN BULGARIA.

YUGOSLAVIA BREAKING UP.

BOMB AT KIEV KGB HQ KILLED TWENTY.

498

'Since the lid was taken off by the Soviet President all stability has gone,' said Tweed. 'Europe has become a whirlpool.'

49

'Evelyn Lennox will be one stiff corpse by now,' Irina reported. 'What is my next assignment?'

'You've seen the newspapers.' Hauser waved a hand towards the papers spread out over the living-room table at Livingstone Manor. 'You're just completed a task which worried me for quite some time. Your next assignment? To stir up the cauldron boiling over in Europe and Russia. Specifically, I'm flying you to Münich in the next few days. From there you control the assault on the Ukraine.'

'And until then?'

'You stay under cover in your suite.'

'Hauser took out his bunch of keys, walked to the door leading to the cellars, unlocked it, led the way down. On his return he pressed a switch on his intercom.

'Frank, get your ass in here. Inside thirty seconds.'

He unfolded the piece of paper Serov had given him. On it was noted the phone number of Evelyn Lennox. Earlier they had found she had an ex-directory number. While in the hall of the cottage Irina had observed the number. Hauser held it out to Galvone as the American, dressed in a T-shirt and slacks, hustled into the room.

'Frank, call this number, ask to speak to Evelyn Lennox. It probably will get you no place. She's dead.'

'Then why am I calling?'

'You really aren't too bright sometimes, Frank. To make sure she is dead.'

'And if she isn't and comes on the line? She'll recognize my voice. She did work at the Helsinki HQ.'

'Frank, amazing as it may seem, I do remember that. If she did come on the line, recognized you, OK. It steps up the pressure. Now, call a dead lady . . .'

Galvone dialled the number. It rang for some time before it was answered.

'Yes, who is this?' a woman's voice enquired.

'I wish to talk with Evelyn Lennox.'

'You're talking to her. Who *is* this?'

'We're not selling anything,' Galvone said quickly. 'We are operating a survey on the Greenhouse menace. You live near the coast. What are your views?'

'I'd first like to know who is calling, please.'

'I can't hear you too well. Atmospherics. It's a very bad line. I'll call you back . . .'

Galvone rammed down the receiver. He looked grimly at his chief. Hauser was not a man who liked bad news.

'That was Evelyn Lennox I just spoke to. I recognized *her* voice. She's about as dead as I am . . .'

'Maybe less so,' Hauser snapped viciously. 'You're quite sure?'

'I told you. I know her voice.'

'Then we'll have to do something very final about her. I want you to organize a squad of four men – no, six men – in two cars to visit Rose Bower in the middle of the night. She may have protection. The squad is to be armed with the weapons the IRA often use. Kalashnikov automatic rifles – and tear gas pistols.' His voice was rasping. 'Assault that goddamn Rose Bower. You don't go. Choose a tough squad leader. When they've done the job set the place on fire. Take gasoline. Rose Bower goes up in flames. Get on it, Frank.'

'Six men away from here will dilute the security – you told me to double it.'

'Do what you're told!' Hauser jabbed a finger at

Galvone. 'You think I want an argument from you? I can get that from other cretins.'

'Then can I bring in some dogs to patrol the grounds during the night? I know a guy in Norwich who could supply . . .'

'Frank! I've told you a dozen times before. Use dogs and the guards rely on them. All intruders need are hunks of poisoned meat and all *you've* got are dead dogs. I want human dogs who stay alert and hungry. Why are you still standing there?'

Hauser felt restless when Galvone had gone. He also felt harassed and harried. Why? The Lennox problem would be solved in the night. He was launching the most ambitious campaign of his career, the campaign to control a 'home' from the Pacific to the Urals, a campaign which was well under way. So why?

He inserted a fresh cigarette into the ivory holder, lit it and left the room. He walked down the passage to his study, walked inside. To alleviate the heat of the afternoon the French windows were open to the vast spread of grounds at the back. He walked outside, down the steps from the wide stone terrace on the lawn.

The grounds were surrounded with a wall of fir trees. At the end of the lawn was a circular concrete helipad. A small Sikorsky helicopter stood on the helipad, fully fuelled at all times with a roster of pilots on duty round the clock.

Behind him along each of the perimeter paths armed guards followed the bulky figure at a discreet distance. Hauser reached the Sikorsky, boarded it and the two guards ran to join him. One sat at the front, the second made his way to a seat at the rear. Hauser occupied the single armchair as the pilot appeared for orders.

'Hank,' Hauser instructed, 'fly this thing over a place called Walberswick. A hick village on the coast north of here. Circle over it until I tell you to fly back here.'

501

'Yes, *sir*!'

Hauser had at last put his thick finger on what disturbed him. There had been no reaction anywhere from Tweed. So what was the bastard up to? He was becoming obsessed with his antagonist.

Sergeant Warden dashed into Chief Inspector Buchanan's office at New Scotland Yard. He clutched two documents in his hand and his manner was triumphant.

'It's all right, sir.'

'What is all right? And you shouldn't rush about in this heat.' Buchanan leaned back in his old wooden swivel chair, clasped his hands in his lap and continued in a dry tone. 'Sit down, compose yourself, tell me about it.'

'I've got the two search warrants. One for Adam Carver's flat in Chelsea, the other for Frank Galvone's pad in that de luxe block near Regent's Park. We could go there now.'

'Hardly to both places at once. There is a distance between them.'

Buchanan opened a drawer. He took a plastic bag from it, extracted a large button with the Daks symbol and several strands of black thread entwined inside the metal shank at the back. He held it up to the light.

'Our only clue to the murderer of Sandra Riverton. I wonder.'

'Don't follow you, sir.'

'Sandra Riverton was murdered close to dawn on a bitter February morning. That sort of weather the murderer might well have worn a British warm. But that coat, if it still exists, might well be in Helsinki.'

'Only one way to find out,' Warden said with unusual eagerness.

'Then there is the third suspect Vanderheld mentioned in my presence at Walberswick. Ion Manescu.'

'A Romanian. Surely he'd never possess a British warm, sir.'

Buchanan was amused. 'Because he's a foreigner? Tweed told me Manescu was attached to the Romanian Embassy in London several years ago. What makes a man look more English than wearing a British warm? Only one problem.'

'What's that, sir?'

'I contacted Interpol. They told me Manescu is dead.'

'Bit of a teaser that. Tweed got it wrong then?'

'Possibly. Yet one of his men positively identified Ion Manescu, hair trimmed short, behind the wheel of a car in the vicinity of Livingstone Manor a few days ago. My experience of Tweed is he is usually correct. Time we made the effort. Adam Carver's flat in Chelsea first. And it was Tweed's handmaiden, Monica, who traced both unlisted addresses.'

At Rose Bower Butler made his fifth effort to get through to Tweed on the phone. It was with great relief that he heard Monica's voice, identified himself, heard her say:

'It's Butler. Sounds urgent. He had trouble reaching us . . .'

'Am I glad to hear your voice, Tweed. There's been a couple of important developments. Frank Galvone phoned Evelyn – obviously to make sure she was dead. I let her take the call while I listened on the extension . . .'

Butler relayed the conversation between Galvone and Evelyn word by word from memory. Tweed listened, was not surprised, but kept the reaction to himself. His brain was thinking in top gear, assessing the implications as Butler ended his report.

'Harry, Hauser now knows Evelyn is still alive. Prepare for a much heavier attack on the cottage. I've already arranged with a friend at Special Branch to send a courier by car. He'll be bringing you two machine pistols with plenty of ammo. If you decided to move everyone to a new location, do so. And the courier is also bringing you a mobile telephone – so wherever you decide to go you can contact me.'

'Thanks. That's not all. I told Evelyn to let Vanderheld know about the Galvone phone call. She then told me she had three more files here. One on Adam Carver, one on Galvone and a more detailed one on Manescu. She didn't leave them in a Helsinki bank.'

'Then give the files to the courier. Tell him to drive to Park Crescent immediately on his way back. Will you be leaving Rose Bower?'

'Let me have a quiet word with Pete before I decide.'

'It's your decision. And good luck.'

Paula jumped up from behind her desk. 'I've just remembered something else I saw at Skalhamn. The *Washington IV* had a helipad on the aft deck – and a small Sikorsky parked on it. I don't know whether it's important.'

Tweed reached for his phone, dialled a number. He looked at Paula.

'I'm calling Heathcoate, the Harbour Master at Harwich.' He spoke into the phone, asked for the Harbour Master and again had to wait.

'Heathcoate? Sorry to trouble you again. This is Tweed. That ship the *Washington IV* – has it by any chance a chopper on its aft deck?'

'You do seem well informed. It did have one when it berthed.'

'*Did?* I thought you said a black limousine took Hauser away. Maybe I misunderstood you?'

'You understood me perfectly. I was surprised he hadn't used the Sikorsky. Then later I saw mechanics working on it. Looked as though something was wrong with the engine. It's all right now. Must be. It flew off this morning, hasn't been seen since.'

'Thank you . . .'

'Hold on. Don't suppose you're interested, but I've just been informed the *Washington IV* expects to put to sea tomorrow morning. Supplies are being taken aboard.'

'Thank you again.'

He told Monica and Paula what he had heard. Paula was pouring more tea into his cup. He drank half the contents: his thirst seemed endless.

'Everything seems to be happening at once,' Paula commented. 'The tempo is accelerating all round. Newman and Marler on the move. And I don't like the sound of the situation at Rose Bower.'

'I fear the crisis is very close now,' Tweed said gravely.

50

The Sikorsky flew low over Walberswick, slowly circling the area. Hauser stared down out of the window. Serov had reported she'd killed Lennox. What had gone wrong? What was it about this place?

Impossible to locate the cottage, Rose Bower, from the air. The machine flew over the sand dunes and the beach where tourists gazed up at the chopper. Hauser saw the narrow entrance channel leading to the harbour. Boats were moored a fair way inland: the entrance consisted of wooden piles bordering the narrow neck of the channel. No boats moored there.

He nodded to himself. Once again he had to go and look at the target, to spot the weak point. God knew why neither Carver nor Manescu had reported back the safest way to approach Rose Bower. The sea was calm, small waves lapped at the entrance, rolling into the channel, merging further inland into the smooth surface of unruffled water. He gestured to the for'ard guard.

'Tell the pilot to head back for Livingstone Manor. I would appreciate it if he'd use what passes for his head. Fly direct inland before he alters course, flies south for the helipad. Get to it . . .'

As soon as the machine had landed he jumped out, dipping his head to escape the rotor which was still revolving slowly. He strode back to the study entrance, saw Galvone coming out to meet him.

'Everything is fixed, Chief, for the assault on Rose Bower . . .'

'Come inside. Change of plan. There's only one road in to Walberswick off the main highway.' He sat in his chair, very erect as he stared at Galvone who stood in front of him.

'So, Frank, that means there's only one way out, for Chrissakes. Can't you read a map? The assault squad could be trapped. The obvious approach is from the sea. Cancel the attack overland. Send the squad to Harwich, tell them to board the *Washington IV*. They take the big powerboat – and make sure they have the large rubber dinghy with outboard. They wait till after dark, then move up the coast to Walberswick.'

'Might be difficult to find Walberswick in the night.' Galvone suggested.

'My God! Do I have to draw a blueprint with every tiny detail? The skipper provides them with a chart. With the six-man squad travels one of the seamen who knows the coast. I've cruised along it often enough.'

'They're still waiting to leave.' Galvone checked his watch. 'I'd better send them off by car so they do have plenty of time.'

'By car?' Singular? You're a case for brain surgery. If six men turn up at Harwich together, board the vessel as a team, they may be spotted by the Harbour Master. They are a tough-looking bunch.' He smiled, not pleasantly. 'So Frank, they travel to Harwich at intervals, in three cars, two men to a car. Got it?'

'Sounds sensible.' Galvone, about to leave, hesitated.

'You've something on your mind. Spit it out.'

'All that explosive – the Semtex – we have in the cellar. Shouldn't we shift it away from here?'

'Why? It's the last place anyone would think of looking. And I carry clout here. The factories I've built in depressed areas provided employment. We move it out as it's needed in Europe – stashed in frozen food containers. The Brits are watching for drugs and explosives coming in, not going *out*.'

'It was clever bringing in the stuff gradually from Libya in private luggage from the *Washington IV*.'

Galvone had decided it was time to soothe Hauser. Once again he had miscalculated the psychology of his boss.

'Sure it was clever, Frank. Something you'd never have dreamed up. Which is why I'm a billionaire and you're getting by on $300,000 a year. Now go organize the new plan for that squad. And remember, they're strong-arm men, so not too bright in the head. Spell it out very clearly.'

Alone in his study he strolled restlessly. He had been careful not to let Galvone know the *Washington IV* was due to sail early the following morning. There should have been someone snooping round Livingstone Manor by now, maybe even calling on him. The apparent inactivity of Tweed was getting on his nerves.

Inside Newman's South Ken flat at Beresforde Road Marler sat up on the bed in the small room at the front leading off the living room. He had just woken from taking a catnap. He swung his legs on to the carpet, stood up, tucked his shirt back inside his slacks, went into the living room en route to the bathroom.

Newman was walking round the large room, hands in his trouser pockets. He checked his watch as Marler appeared.

'You should get a bit of kip, chum,' Marler advised.

'Sleeping in the daytime just knocks me out.'

Marler swilled his face with cold water in the bathroom, combed his hair. When he returned to the living room Newman was still pacing. Marler straddled a dining chair, lit a cigarette.

'Your trouble goes back to the days when you were a foreign correspondent,' he observed. 'Always on the move. You're like a caged panther. Relax.'

'Don't feel like it. We'd better have something to eat. There's a hotel nearby where we can get a near edible meal. You wouldn't want to sample my cooking – not that I feel up to boiling an egg in this heat.'

'And since I'm not partial to food poisoning, I agree. We go out.'

Marler was aware of the tension inside the flat as he put on his jacket. Newman was wondering what might be waiting for them at Livingstone Manor.

Chief Inspector Buchanan made a detour before visiting Adam Carver's flat. He was intrigued by the difficulty of tracing Papa Grimwood, the man who had accompanied the dead Steve to the original interview at Evelyn Lennox's flat in Wandsworth.

He parked on a yellow line in the side street off Shaftesbury Avenue in front of the entrance to the only INCU-BUS offices in London. Warden made his obervation as Buchanan locked the car.

'We're on a yellow line.'

'I had noticed. Where else do you suggest we park? We're not causing an inconvenience in this quiet street. Let us see whether we can dig up some information here. When you called you said they'd never heard of Fraternal and Equality.'

Buchanan showed his warrant card to the rather dim-looking girl receptionist. He spoke to her as he might to a sixteen-year-old, but politely.

'I want to see the managing director of Fraternal & Equality Insurance. If you've never heard of it I'll see whoever is in charge here.'

'That's Mr Humble. Only appointed a few weeks ago. I'll tell him you're here.'

Buchanan followed her as she knocked on a door with the top half an opaque window of glazed glass. Everything about the place had an old fashioned, run-down atmosphere. A deliberate ploy?

He walked in behind the girl and a middle-aged man wearing gold rimmed glasses glanced up from behind his old wooden desk, frowning at the intrusion.

'It's all right now,' Buchanan told the girl, 'I'll take over from here. If you'd be good enough to close the door and go back to reception.'

'You can't come in here like this.'

Humble was an appropriate name, Buchanan decided as he again showed his warrant card. The managing director had a squeaky voice. Trying to show indignation, he sounded ridiculous. Buchanan hauled forward a rickety chair, sat down cautiously. Warden, notebook in hand, leaned against a wall.

'I don't understand what you could want,' Humble went on. 'We haven't had a break-in or anything like that. Perhaps you have the wrong address?' he added hopefully.

'Company records in the City show this address as the registered office of Fraternal & Equality Insurance. So

509

you must be managing the company,' Buchanan said, framing the statement positively.

'It is a small part of our business, as I understand it. I'm new here . . .'

'Papa Grimwood is one of your chief operatives. He goes round with a man we've identified as Steve Reilly.'

'I've never heard of either of those names.'

'Then you won't mind our looking at your employment records, I'm sure. Of course, you can refuse. But then I would obtain a search warrant – and inform Mr Franklin D. Hauser of my action.'

'I've never seen Mr Hauser. I'd sooner you didn't communicate with him.' Humble was agitated. 'Certainly you can examine the employment records. No search warrant is necessary. I am only too anxious to co-operate with the police. But it could take you some time. There are a lot of ledgers.'

Buchanan glanced at Warden who had just finished scribbling in his notebook. The sergeant nodded, confirming that he had carefully recorded the managing director's statement.

'A lot of ledgers,' Humble repeated. 'The one thing I know about Mr Hauser is he doesn't trust computers. He says they can be "hacked" – I think that's the word. We store them in this back room. Please come with me . . .'

Beyond the doorway Buchanan and Warden stared. The room was lined with wooden shelves. The shelves were jammed with ledgers, wall to wall. Humble excused himself, left them alone. Buchanan stripped off his jacket, placed it over the back of a wooden chair which had seen better days.

'Come on, Warden. We'd better make a start. At least the spines of the ledgers have a description.'

'Funny, sir,' said Warden, following his chief's example, 'I thought INCUBUS was one of the most modern organizations in the world.'

'It is. This is just a front outfit, but from the few spines I've read so far it's Fraternity and Equality . . .'

It took them ages to locate the Executives ledger. Buchanan found Leopold Grimwood. With an address in Pimlico. Warden noted down the details.

'Why is Grimwood so important?' he asked.

'From what we've heard this so-called pension fund is a form of blackmail and extortion. If we can break down Grimwood we may just get the evidence for a case against Hauser. I stress the word "just".'

'Where to now?' Warden asked as Buchanan settled behind the wheel of their car.

'Carver's flat in Chelsea first. Heaven knows when we will reach Galvone's apartment near Regent's Park. And after all that work, radio in Grimwood's address – with a request that a couple of men are sent to bring him in for questioning.'

Warden was reaching for the microphone when the message from Tweed transmitted via the Yard reached Buchanan.

For the fifth time Paula stood up from her desk and gazed out of the window at the night, her arms folded. Tweed looked up from the old file on his desk.

'You're restless.'

'I know.' Paula swung round as Monica watched her. 'I can't keep still. Surely there's something we can do – instead of just sitting around waiting.'

'It's getting to you, isn't it?' Tweed smiled. 'So if it's getting to you what effect do you think it will be having on Hauser? I've been on his tail ever since I arrived in Finland. He'll guess I've tracked him back to England by now. He's smart. So he'll expect me to do something. Instead nothing happens. It's what one of our famous generals once called masterly inactivity.'

'It's driving me up the wall,' Paula snapped.

'So let's hope Hauser is up there with you.'

An hour later the Special Branch courier arrived with the files Peggy Vanderheld had handed over to Butler. He apologized for the long delay. Traffic jams, the traffic solid during the holiday season. Tweed opened one file, his mind elsewhere.

He was worried about Newman and Marler. He took the decision suddenly. Picking up the phone he dialled Buchanan's number at the Yard. A policewoman answered and Tweed thought the voice was familiar.

'Sergeant Murray-Browne speaking. Can I help? Who is calling?'

'My name is Tweed . . .'

'Hello, Mr Tweed. I came with Chief Inspector Buchanan to see you once when Sergeant Warden was off colour. Is there something I can do to help?'

'I need to speak to the Chief Inspector urgently.'

'I'm afraid he's been out on a job for hours. I might be able to contact him. He has a radio in his car.'

'The message is urgent. He knows the Chief Constable of Suffolk. I don't know the new man. Could he contact the Chief Constable, ask him to send as many patrol cars with armed officers as he can muster to the vicinity of Livingstone Manor? No screaming sirens. A silent approached is vital.'

'I'll pass on the message as soon as I can reach him on the radio. Is that all, Mr Tweed?'

'That's all. Emphasize the officers should be armed.'

He turned his attention back to the files. He was skip-reading the last one when Cord Dillon came into the office. Monica asked him if he'd like some coffee and he said he'd be grateful. He sagged into a chair. Tweed handed him the files.

'These came in from Vanderheld. She's been holding out on us. They're fascinating, but I can't see anything which could put Hauser in the dock, here or in America.'

'I can tell you that would be near impossible without reading them – although I'm going to do that. Hauser has so many judges in his pocket I doubt we'd ever get a conviction. But I'll look . . .'

Five minutes later the phone rang. Tweed picked it up, wondering who it could be at that hour. It was Marler.

'I'm calling just before we leave Newman's flat. He's in the loo. Have you got – or do you think you'll ever get – evidence to put Hauser behind bars?'

'Odd you should ask that now. You must be psychic. Is there a reason?'

'I always have a reason for asking a question. Are you going to answer it? And I'm in a hurry.'

'Hold on thirty seconds.' Tweed looked at Dillon. He knew the American had taken a fast-reading course. He was already scanning the remaining pages of the last file. 'Cord, what do you think now you've looked at the files?'

'What I thought before. One or two things stand out – but a smart attorney could rubbish them. And Hauser has the best attorneys in the States on his payroll.'

Tweed took a deep breath, removed his hand from the phone.

'The answer is no.'

'Thank you.'

The connection was broken. Tweed put down the receiver, stood up. He looked at Paula.

'I'm driving out to Suffolk myself now. You can come if you want to. I don't want to get back and find you swinging from the proverbial chandelier.'

'Action at last.'

Paula opened a lower drawer in her desk, took out her bag, slipped her .32 Browning inside with spare mags

513

under cover of the desk. As she stood up she saw Tweed checking his 7.65 mm Walther automatic. She had hardly ever known him to carry a gun. He slipped it inside his jacket pocket as Dillon also stood up.

'And I'm coming with you folks. No argument. Something is breaking. I can smell it.'

'Will we arrive soon after Newman and Marler?' Paula asked.

'Not by a long chalk,' Tweed told her. 'Not the way Newman drives.'

51

At two-thirty in the morning Hauser was working in his study, checking the clauses in the agreement for the sale of the Street & Braithwaite bank in Southampton. He had been careful not to let either Carver or Galvone know that he was sailing aboard the *Washington IV* by 7.30 a.m. Destination: Boston.

He couldn't be sure why his instinct told him it was time to leave Britain. He disliked the decision: his HQ at Livingstone Manor was ideally equipped. But he had survived so far by always obeying his instinct. He pressed the intercom switch.

'Adam, come and see me. My study. Now.'

Another inconvenience was having the French doors shut and locked. It was becoming unbearably foetid inside the room. But with only four guards available he had sensed it would be foolish to leave those doors open.

'What can I do for you, sir?' Adam asked as he stood in front of the desk.

514

He noticed Hauser was freshly shaven, had changed his clothes. He assumed it was the heat. Hauser pushed the sheaf of papers across the desk.

'Make an appointment to meet with Street today. See him while he's still shocked by that IRA bomb. Don't come back without his signature on the agreement.'

He studied Carver. The Englishman was clad in one of his silk suits, a pale blue check. No wonder he could make it with almost any woman. Well, he was going to have to do without his dinner date with Evelyn Lennox. Unless he wanted to dine with a corpse.

'I'll take this into the living room, master it before I get a few hours' kip.'

'Use the library upstairs. Not the living room. I want to use it myself for a conference. Get moving.'

A conference? At this hour? Carver shrugged to himself as he climbed the wide winding staircase from the hall. The billionaire seemed to live without sleep. The secret of his success, Carver thought as he closed the library door, settled himself in a chair and began studying the agreement.

The phone rang just before Hauser left his study. He let it ring several times. He wasn't expecting a call at this time of night. He picked up the receiver.

'Who is it?'

'Mr Franklin D. Hauser, I believe. This is Robert Newman. Hope I'm not disturbing your beauty sleep – I thought there was something you ought to know.'

'Say your piece, then drop off a cliff.'

'I thought you'd like to know a vital clue has been discovered in the investigation into the cold-blooded murder of Sandra Riverton. A button torn from a Daks overcoat. From what we call a British warm. The button carries the Daks symbol.'

'Are you drunk? What the hell is this?'

'I found the button among the straw at the bottom of

the bell tower where she was murdered. I've left it there. It's evidence for the police to find when daylight comes. Sleep well . . .'

Hauser cursed as the connection was broken. He stood for several mintues thinking, then walked rapidly down the long passage to the hall. Turning into the living room, he unlocked the door, closed it behind him, ran down the steps and along the flagstones of the cellar passage floor. Opening the door to Manescu's suite, he walked inside. The Romanian was again stretched out on the couch, reading a newspaper. As Hauser came in he was loosening his necktie, taking it off to combat the heat. He stood up slowly while Hauser waited: he expected swifter demonstrations of respect from his minions.

'Some problem?' Manescu enquired.

Waiting for an answer, he played with the necktie, twisting the cloth into a rope-like skein. His swarthy chin was disfigured with a dark stubble.

'Get a shave,' Hauser snapped. 'That's your first problem. And I've had a phone call from that crazy reporter, Robert Newman. Says he's found a button torn from what he called a British warm inside the bell-tower. So, when it's daylight, maybe you'd better poke around, see if you can find any button. And then later in the afternoon you're flying to Belgrade. Keep the cauldron on the boil. Your ticket is in the pseudonym you're operating under at the moment.'

He threw down the airline folder on a coffee table. At the door he turned round.

'I'm leaving this unlocked. Don't start prowling inside the house.'

Continuing along the passage, he unlocked the door leading to Irina Serov's suite. She was fully dressed, seated in front of her dressing table mirror. Dropping her lipstick, she jumped up to face the American.

'Change of plan. Like Manescu, you're leaving earlier –

516

this afternoon. You catch a flight for Munich. Here is your ticket. You know what you have to do. Set the Ukraine ablaze. And this door will stay unlocked. You leave at eleven in the morning.'

'Understood . . .'

She was talking to the air. Hauser had gone. He climbed the steps, closed the door, walked to his desk in the living room, pressed the intercom switch.

'That you, Frank? Get down here. Adam, you heard what I said? Why aren't you here then?'

Hauser was seated behind his desk when the two men entered. He wiped the back of his thick neck with a handkerchief. How did Adam Carver keep so slick-looking in this heat? But it was good to have someone around who kept himself smart. Galvone was freshly shaven, but otherwise he looked a crumpled mess in his soiled shirt and denims.

'I just had a phone call from Newman,' he told them. 'In the middle of the night. He's crazy as a coot – I think he was bluffing too. Said he'd found a button torn from a British warm on the floor of that bell tower. That he'd left it there for the police to find in the morning. A pretty feeble war of nerves. But that tells me Tweed is back. So what the hell is he and his gang of killers doing?'

Adam Carver thought that remark was priceless – coming from Hauser with Galvone standing in the room. Hauser looked at Carver.

'You've got your red Jaguar fuelled up with gasoline for your trip to Southampton in mid-morning?'

'A full tank,' Carver assured him.

'Frank, you're flying back to Helsinki. To open up that HQ again. Tweed will never guess I'd make it operational so soon. There's your ticket. Don't miss the flight. Now, leave me alone, both of you.'

Fetching a jug of ice water from the fridge built in with the cocktail bar, he poured a large glass, drained it. He

517

checked his watch. He'd dealt with everything now. No, there was one more vital detail to check. He walked down the passage into his study, unlocked the French windows, nodded to two guards as he hurried across the lawn to the chopper stationed on the helipad.

'That machine OK?' he shouted up to the pilot.

'Ready and rarin' to go.'

'Show me. Lift off, then land again.'

The rotors spun, the engine throbbed, the chopper elevated, circled over the grounds, made a perfect landing on the helipad. The pilot slid back the window, grinned.

'Satisfied?'

'Take that smirk off your face. Complacency I can do without. You'll be flying me to the *Washington IV*?'

'Sure thing, sir. Just came on duty. Met. reports indicate a smooth flight.'

'It had better be.'

Off the coast of East Anglia the powerboat was stationary. The helmsman waited as six heavily built men put the big dinghy with the outboard over the side, transferred to it weapons with silencers, tear-gas pistols loaded with lethal nerve gas shells, then climbed aboard themselves.

The squad leader carried a map of Walberswick with Rose Bower marked with a pencil cross. They'd moor the dinghy to the harbour entrance, make their way across the sand dunes to The Street, the country road where Rose Bower was located. Do the job, set fire to the place with the cans of gasoline already stashed aboard, head back for the dinghy. He estimated the job would be accomplished in thirty minutes. At the outside.

The man at the stern started up the outboard. He steered the dinghy for the harbour entrance. It was a moonless night. That would just help a little more, the leader of the squad thought, as the dinghy rode the small waves and the wooden piles came closer.

Marler had lied to Tweed when he told him Newman was in the loo. Newman had earlier driven to the Old Kent Road to collect Alf Higgins. As soon as the Mercedes had arrived back Marler, carrying a large canvas satchel with an adjustable strap, had climbed in beside Newman. Higgins, hands clenched tightly, sat silent in the back for most of the journey.

They were driving across Suffolk before Newman asked his question in a whisper. The headlight beams, undimmed, illuminated a traffic-free road lined with hedges. For the last hour they had not seen a single other vehicle.

'What are you carrying in that heavy satchel?' Newman asked.

'A couple of gadgets Alf gave me,' Marler whispered back. 'Plus some toys I brought back from that explosives course I attended at the country house near Amersham.'

'You're expecting to use that stuff?'

'No idea. Until we get there, see what the set-up is. Be prepared is my motto. Didn't know I was once a Boy Scout, did you?'

'A less suitable member I can't imagine . . .'

He slowed down as they came within a mile of Livingstone Manor. The clock on the dashboard registered 2.30 a.m.

'We're nearly there,' he told Marler.

'I know. Didn't I tell you? One evening after we returned from Finland I drove out here alone on a recce. It was after Monica told me about the cipher machines and all that equipment she'd found Hauser had installed.'

'What kind of a recce?' Newman pressed.

'Oh, the normal kind. After dark I penetrated the

519

grounds, circled Hauser's Georgian mansion. I counted nine guards. We'll have to tread a little carefully. And if we meet one of those guards leave him to me. I called in at a sleazy night club on my way to your flat. The type of place the so-called aristocracy patronizes for their illegal kicks.'

'What the devil are you talking about?'

'With luck you'll never know. We should park the car – turn in to that field behind those trees. We're close. Take a deep breath, Newman, it's starting . . .'

Butler had led Evelyn and Peggy to the bottom of the back garden behind Rose Bower. Now their eyes had become used to the dark they could see where they were placing their feet safely. Each woman wore a high-necked overall supplied by Evelyn. Over their heads they had pulled pale grey waterproof hoods Evelyn used for gardening in damp weather.

'Find some protective clothing if you can,' Butler had asked Evelyn earlier. 'And two pairs of slacks – if you think one of yours would fit Peggy . . .'

Both women now wore slacks under the overalls as Butler held up a hand to halt them. It was the appearance of the helicopter flying low over Walberswick which had warned both Butler and Nield that they might all be in mortal danger before the night was out.

Butler, wearing gardening gloves, carefully parted clumps of brambles at the edge of the garden, held them while the two women passed through. They waited on the verge of a field and Butler showed them their hiding place.

'There's a large ditch almost covered over with grasses. I want you to lie down in it, pull the grasses over your-selves and keep very quiet. Even if you hear men coming don't move a muscle. And you may hear bursts of gunfire.

That will be me shooting at them. Whatever you do, don't get curious, look up to try and see what's happening . . .'

He waited until both women were stretched out inside the wide ditch. Leaning down, he pulled more grasses over them. There had been no rain for weeks so the ditch was bone dry. The only problem was it could be crawling with insects. He hoped the protective clothing would shield them from any creepy-crawlies.

'Where is Nield?' Evelyn whispered.

'He's out front, keeping watch. I'll be nearby. You may be there for quite a time. Try and relax.'

'Maybe you'd like us to go to sleep?' Peggy called out ironically.

'That's right,' Butler told her. 'Have a nice nap.'

He crept back along the side of the garden, stopped at a point half-way to the house. Looping his weapon over his back, he climbed an old oak tree he had discovered earlier. Perching himself in a crook between two thick boughs, he checked his field of fire. From here he was able to cover the entire back garden. Any men exploring the back garden would be point-blank targets for his gun. He settled down to wait.

Marler was also high up a tree he had climbed at a corner of the spacious grounds. Before leaving the Mercedes he had stripped off his jacket and donned a boiler suit of a neutral colour which merged with the foliage. From one of the capacious pockets he had extracted binoculars and he was scanning the grounds close to the mansion.

He had sat on a branch for over half an hour and was puzzled. During the whole of that vigil he had only seen three guards patrolling. They moved round the house separately and so large was the mansion each man

521

reappeared at intervals of ten minutes.

During his previous recce he had counted nine guards. At that time they had patrolled in pairs – two couples moving close to the mansion while the rest prowled across the grounds, frequently walking the perimeter. One man had passed under his tree, but no one ever looked *up*, a phenomenon he had observed in the centre of cities.

Where the devil were the other six guards? Marler doubted that they were all inside. If so many men were available the smart thing was to position the majority outside. *If* they were available.

It was then he noticed the absence of something. There were only three cars parked on the gravel circle by the far corner of the house. A red Jag. A stretched black limo – undoubtedly Hauser's. And a red Cadillac. When he had watched before he had counted nine cars of various makes. Marler's patience was endless: to make sure he waited a little longer.

Inside the Mercedes Newman's patience was anything but endless. He sat with all the windows open, drumming his fingers on the wheel, checking his watch every five minutes. In the back Alf Higgins stirred.

'These jobs take time,' he observed. 'Can't rush 'em. That way you get caught. Mr 'Enderson knows his stuff.'

'Glad to hear it,' Newman said brusquely.

'Knew a chap like you once,' Higgins went on obstinately. 'Was doin' a job in Lunnon. I told 'im 'e was in too much of a bloody 'urry. Case the place proper, I says. Wouldn't listen. Know where 'e is now? Servin' a ten-year stretch in Strangeways.'

'A very comforting thought at this moment.'

'Just tryin' to be 'elpful. Why not get out, walk about a bit? Some people gets stiff, sittin' in a car.'

Newman decided he would take this bit of advice. Opening the door, he stepped out on to the grass. He walked slowly back to the road, listening for any sound of

522

traffic coming. And Marler appeared, having approached without making a sound.

'Time you started working for your living, chum,' he told the irate Newman.

52

Pete Nield stood outside Rose Bower, holding a large briefcase he had borrowed from Evelyn. It was very quiet in The Street, so quiet he could *hear* the heavy silence of an early morning when the air was still turgid with the heat of the previous day.

He looked back at the cottage he was supposed to guard. There were no lights, the front door was locked and bolted. Nield was fighting with his instinct. He had followed it so often before and been proved right.

Taking a firmer grip on the briefcase, he left his post, began walking rapidly towards where the village ended, towards the sea. As he turned on to the track leading to the wilderness of dunes and grasses a hint of a breeze touched his face. He quickened his pace, leaving behind the darkened houses.

He stopped suddenly, undecided. Butler was relying on him to provide back-up. And the two men had been partners in more than one desperate situation. It seemed like an act of desertion. As he stood there, about to turn back, the only sound was the gentle whisper of the grasses, moved by the breeze. The only sound? He waited a moment longer, certain his ears had deceived him.

Then he heard it again. The faint sound of an engine. From the direction of the sea, the enemy. Since his first exploration of Walberswick as a refuge he had always been convinced the sea was the enemy. He moved off the track, plodding as fast as he could across the rough territory of the dunes, the treacherous powdery sand. He climbed one dune to try and get a view over the long barrier of the shingle bank.

He blinked, closed his eyes, opened them again quickly. Above the barrier a belt of calm sea stretched away. He caught the wisp of white as the faint engine sound died. The wake of a powerboat? Or was it all his imagination? He looked back. Butler would be on his own if they came by car, pulled up outside Rose Bower and rushed the cottage.

Much against his will he plodded on over the dunes, the tang of salty air much stronger. Then he was climbing the slippery shingle bank overlooking the beach and the harbour entrance. He stood there, alone in the world of the night and the sea, staring out to catch a glimmer of navigation lights. Nothing. He waited, checked the illuminated dial of his watch. It had taken him ten minutes to reach this spot from the cottage. He would wait three more minutes and then run all the way back, stumbling over the dunes.

He heard the faint burst of the engine starting up – but it had a different sound from the earlier one. He sat on the shingle bank, decided he could still be seen as a silhouette through night glasses, huddled down behind the top of the bank.

A fresh burst of another engine starting up, which promptly died. What the hell was going on? Now he could identify the chug-chug of an outboard motor approaching the harbour. The skipper of the powerboat, the mother ship, had tested his engine, switched it off. But the chug-chug was growing louder.

Now he could see the growing arrow wake of the incoming boat. From his jacket pocket he hauled out the night glasses Tweed always insisted his men carried. Crouched out of sight, he focused them just in front of the wake. God! It was an outsize rubber dinghy. Powered by an outboard. Six men aboard. All wearing what looked like pea jackets, peaked caps. Carrying what looked like automatic rifles.

Nield felt a surge of exhilaration. He had guessed right. The attackers were coming in from the sea – as he had always predicted they would. If they were hostile. Nield was in a dilemma. It was summer. Tourists sometimes liked a novelty. Sailing across a millpond sea in the middle of the night. And he couldn't feel sure they were carrying automatic rifles.

The dinghy loomed larger, seemed to be heading straight for the harbour entrance. Nield gritted his teeth in frustration. How to be sure they were not getting ready to sail down the entrance between the piles, aiming for their berth further inland after an evening cruise up the coast? Then he remembered the powerboat.

He stood up in full view, cupped his hands, bellowed at the top of his voice:

'Cut your engine immediately or I'll blow you out of the water . . .'

He dropped flat behind the bank as he ended his warning. And as he dropped the bullets began to fly from the dinghy, a steady fusillade which was alarmingly accurate. One silenced bullet winged past the right side of his skull as he disappeared below his makeshift parapet. He heard others hammering the shingle in front of him. One pebble whipped into the air, spun down within inches of his left foot.

Nield hauled the Uzi machine-pistol out of the briefcase. The weapon, brought by the Special Branch courier, held a magazine of forty rounds, fired at a rate of six hundred rounds a minute. Nield rested the muzzle on top of the shingle bank, aimed at the lower hull of the rubber dinghy, pressed the trigger. A hail of bullets hammered into the craft, above and below the waterline.

Nield rammed in a fresh mag, saw the dinghy topple to starboard, empty the six men into the sea, capsize, vanishing below the surface. He fired again, aiming above the bobbing heads, some of which were swimming towards the shore. They reversed course, began swimming out to sea, in the hope of reaching the distant powerboat, no more than a speck to Nield's eyes.

He inserted a new mag, opened fire again, aiming always over the bobbing head, the flailing arms. He saw two heads sink without resurfacing. Not from his fire – must be poor swimmers.

He stood up to get a better view. Four heads now, then another one sank into oblivion. Nield shoved the Uzi back inside the briefcase. Time to get away from there quick. He took one last look out to sea. Only two of the bobbing heads remained in view. Nield turned away, shrugged.

'So what?' he said to himself. 'They were all killers, bent on massacre.'

When he entered the back garden of Rose Bower, in search of the two women, Butler jumped down from the oak tree.

'You look tense,' he commented. 'Run into anything?'

53

Marler, Newman and Higgins crept along the front of the mansion close to the wall. They had climbed the same tree, dropped over the wire fence surrounding the estate, approaching Livingstone Manor from the outer perimeter.

Marler had given the go-ahead after seeing a guard disappear round the side of the building. They had ten minutes to get inside before another guard appeared. The windows they were passing faced out from the living room: Newman recalled this fact from his visit in February. He whispered the information to his companions.

'I'll check to see if there's any one in there,' Higgins whispered back.

From his pocket he produced an instrument like a stethoscope, plugged one end against a pane of glass, listened through the earpiece at the other end. Newman checked his watch. They were way behind schedule: Marler had taken so long before returning to the Mercedes. And now Higgins was taking up more time. He pulled gently at the rubber sucker, freed it from the glass.

'No one in that room.'

'How can you be sure?' Newman demanded.

'Very sensitive, this gadget. Can pick up a man turning the pages of a newspaper. Shifting 'is position in an armchair. I guarantees it. No one in there. Now open that front door,' he told Marler. 'Don't 'urry it . . .'

Newman swore inwardly. They'd had an argument earlier before leaving the Merc. Higgins had insisted the front door was the place no one expected a break-in. He examined the solid slab of wood, the edges with the aid of a pencil flash.

'No alarms. Get stuck in.'

Marler confronted the three locks, selected a key for the lowest lock, inserted it slowly, cocked his head to listen. He heard the lock opening. He had the other two locks open faster than he'd expected. Higgins handed a small torch-like instrument to Newman. He whispered the warning.

'That's the little jigger I tells you about in the car.

527

Detects electronic beams. Switch it on and it kills the beam for thirty seconds – and no alarm goes off.'

'And you're coming in with us . . .' Marler began.

He was too late. Higgins had sprinted past the curtained windows masking the lights behind them, was taking off his jacket as he ran. Presumably to form a cushion when he scaled the wire fence, climbed back into the tree.

'I'll take over,' Newman said. 'I know the layout.'

He held his Smith & Wesson by his side in his right hand and hoped to God he wouldn't have to press the trigger. Its silent use as a blunt instrument was a different matter. He turned the handle slowly, eased the door open. Well oiled, it made no sound. The gap widened and he had a view of the large hall, the deserted staircase curving upwards, the long passage leading to another room at the back. The door to the room was open and there was a light on inside.

He checked his watch. Nine minutes. A guard would come round the front very soon. Jerking his head to Marler, he stepped over the doormat – in case there was a pressure pad underneath. He closed the door very carefully as Marler stood against a wall, his right hand by his side, his left concealing a small canister. Both men were wearing rubber-soled shoes as Newman crossed the hall, peered inside the living room. Higgins had been right: it was empty.

Leaving the door open, he went inside. There were no electronic beams in this room: he had observed that on his previous visit. He gestured towards the door let into the inner wall. Marler studied the lock, tried one key. No result. Selecting another key, he fiddled it, again heard nothing. The third key was too large. Newman reached past him, turned the handle slowly, pushed. The door opened, exposing a flight of stone steps leading down into the cellars.

'Let me do a quick recce,' Marler whispered.

Newman waited in the shadows at the head of the steps as Marler crept down them. The stone-flagged passage was illuminated by overhead fluorescents. Holding the 'torch' in front of him, Marler moved down the long passage, passing several alcoves and side passages in darkness.

The guard walked out of a room ahead of Marler, stood, stared at the intruder as Marler slipped the torch inside a pocket. The man was a giant, well over six feet tall, built like a quarterback. In his early thirties, he had his hair trimmed to a stubble. Ex-Marine, Marler thought.

The guard, wearing a singlet and slacks, grinned as he looked down at the small, compact Marler. Eat you alive, he was thinking. He walked forward, huge fists clenched, a holstered gun on his left hip. He expected Marler to back away. Marler ran forward, his right hand with the knuckle dusters over his fingers slammed up, crashed into the large jaw. The guard staggered, dazed, dropped his head as Marler skipped to one side, brought his stiffened left hand down in a chopping movement against the side of the guard's neck. The guard toppled forward, his jaw smashed into the flagstones. He lay still.

Newman ran forward. Marler was checking the neck pulse. He looked up.

'Dead as a doornail. He hit the floor like the Empire State falling. Help me drag him into a side passage . . .'

They had hidden the guard inside the darkness when Marler reached into his pocket. He brought out a small packet, stuffed it inside the guard's trouser pocket.

'What's that?' Newman asked.

'Crack. I bought several packets of the filthy drug at a night club. If he's found while we're still down here it will be assumed he was on drugs, took an overdose, fell and smashed his jaw on the flagstones.'

'Let's explore,' Newman said.

They were further along the passage when they heard the sound of a door opening behind them. Marler had his satchel close to his back on a shortened strap. He followed Newman into the gloom of a side passage. Voices. Feet walking away slowly. Newman peered out. A girl and a man. Faces turned towards each other as they talked. He had studied their photos. Irina Serov and Ion Manescu.

'How do they keep this place so clean?' Manescu asked.

'Servants from the outside. Locals. But they're here in the daytime only. Hauser won't let them live in . . .'

They walked up the steps. Sounds of the door opening and closing. Newman realized why the door wasn't locked. For some reason the two terrorists – saboteurs, to use Tweed's description – were free to roam around tonight.

'We'll explore some more,' said Newman.

Half-way down the long passage they detected a beam. A red light flashed on in the top of the torch. Marler switched it on. They walked past electronic eyes embedded into the stone walls at ankle height. Just beyond was a locked door.

Marler only succeeded in opening this lock with the third key. They walked into an arched cellar. Stacked along both walls were familiar boxes stencilled with the words 'Frozen Fish'. Marler opened the lid of one box, stared at the grey dough-like substance. Newman lifted another lid. More of the grey dough.

'Semtex,' said Marler. 'I phoned Tweed before we set out. He told me no one could bring Hauser to justice.' He swung his satchel round to his chest, unfastened the strap, placed the satchel on the floor, opened the flap. 'You go outside, close the door, hide in the passage opposite, watch my back.'

'What are you going to do.'

'Move, we're short of time . . .'

Newman went outside, closed the door, slipped inside the dark side passage, waited. He seemed to wait for ever and kept checking the illuminated dial of his watch. He heard Manescu and Serov walking back down the passage. Serov was talking, her voice surprisingly feminine and seductive.

'That walk in the grounds was a relief. Now for sleep. We have flights in the afternoon and I want to arrive in Munich fresh. I'll be radioing instructions from there well into the night . . .'

Newman heard one door close, then another. They had separate rooms. He checked his watch again. What the hell was Marler taking all this time over? Newman was determined to be well away from Livingstone Manor by dawn.

The door opened, Marler paused, satchel slung over his back, waited until Newman emerged and beckoned. Closing the door, Marler used the same key but found he couldn't relock it. Something he had forgotten to check with Alf. He glanced further down the passage.

'That door is open a bit,' he whispered.

'Time we left . . .'

'Only take a moment to have a peek inside.'

Marler pushed the door open wider, saw the room was deserted, walked inside. Newman followed, stared at the huge wall map of Europe and Russia, the red pins stabbed into various famous cities.

'My God!' he explained. 'These are the targets for the bombs going off all over Europe. You read the papers.'

'Sometimes. I see there's a pin for Kiev. KGB headquarters was blown up the other day. At least twenty dead.'

'Hauser is a monster,' Newman commented. 'Nothing stands in the way of his pursuit of power. Destabilize,

531

then move in to rebuild on the ruins – rebuild American-style.' He looked at Marler. 'What's that thing you're holding? Looks like a mobile pocket telephone.'

'Complete with press button numbers. Designed by our boffins in the Engine Room at Park Crescent.' He pulled up an aerial. 'They're clever johnnies. This chap is a radio transmitter to detonate a bomb. And there's rather a lot of explosive, I'd say, in that cellar next door. I press the numbers for the right code – in this case 142 – and the radio signal is transmitted to the bomb.'

'You fixed all that up while you were in the cellar?'

'Not quite. I had a device inside my satchel. Involved a certain amount of advance preparation. You've forgotten the Semtex I pinched from the truck north of Porvoo, then later from the Lapland Institute. Hadn't we better take our leave of this de luxe millionaire's property, as the estate agent chappies say?'

'Immediately. What is that transmitter for?'

'Purely a precaution. In case we meet a little opposition on the way out. When I've explained the position I think they'll be happy to escort us off the premises.'

'Then let's move. Now!'

Tweed drove the new Volvo station wagon Howard had sanctioned at speed along the winding road. Beside him Paula clung to the hand grip as he swerved round a long bend. In the rear seat Cord Dillon sat chewing an unlit cigar.

'I think we're pretty close to Livingstone Manor now,' Paula said. 'I recognized that bend you've just flown this aircraft round.'

'I'm worried,' Tweed snapped, keeping up the same speed. 'We haven't seen any police patrol cars. They should be in position by now.'

'They may be concealed,' she mused. 'Although the

way you're driving I'd have expected one to stop you.'

'Lord knows what risks Newman and Marler are taking – and Hauser is totally ruthless. You're right, we're very close. I'll turn into this field, park behind the copse of trees over there.'

Paula sat up straighter. Tweed had parked, switched off the engine.

'Look, there's Bob's Mercedes . . .'

She jumped out, ran to the stationary car. A figure stirred in the back, opened the door, stepped out. He touched his forelock.

'Mornin' to you, ma'am. George Budge at your service,' said Alfred Higgins. 'Just 'aving forty winks. Stupid to drive at night when you're tired. Your feller doesn't 'alf get a move on . . .'

Many miles behind Tweed, Chief Inspector Buchanan was also exceeding the speed limit. It seemed to Warden seated beside him that they were negotiating dangerous bends on two wheels.

'We'll get there eventually, sir,' he ventured.

'*Eventually* may be too late. I took too long persuading Tweed's assistant, Monica, to tell me where she thought Newman had gone. He's a man motivated by revenge for the murder of his girl friend, Sandy. I think he's identified the killer.'

'You can't be sure of that, sir.'

'I'm not sure, I'm certain. So was Monica. It's that damned coat button.'

'Well, you're behind the wheel.'

'Your powers of observation astound me,' Buchanan responded and rammed his foot down further.

54

Marler and Newman had almost got clear of Livingstone Manor when they ran out of luck. Marler had climbed the tree at the corner of the estate, dropped to the ground. Newman was following, climbing the trunk from branch to branch when he heard the sound of automatic rifle fire. He glanced back. One of the guards had appeared, must have seen the movement of the foliage, had perhaps found the front door unlocked.

Bullets spattered the foliage as Newman desperately moved faster. A shower of leaves whisked across his face. That was close. He reached the overhang branch, risked a final look back. A second guard held a rifle to his shoulder. As he dropped the foliage was shattered with a hail of gunfire.

'Across the road,' Marler shouted as Newman dropped beside him. 'The ground rises. There's another tree copse. If we can reach that we can mow them down as they cross open ground . . .'

They ran across the hedge-free road straight into a field of wheat, ran uphill planting their feet flat to avoid turning an ankle. Marler moved like a four-minute miler with Newman close behind, climbing all the time. They dived inside the copse, Marler looked up, chose an exceptionally tall chestnut, began to shin up it with the agility of a monkey, his satchel flapping against his back.

As Newman climbed after him he heard a car start up from the direction of Livingstone Manor. It drove closer, then moved further away for a short distance. Newman heard the engine sound change and not far away it seemed to be driven on a course parallel to the one they had taken running up the hill. He paused, tried to see the car, but the foliage smothered his view. The engine stopped as he followed Marler who was climbing an incredible height.

He found Marler straddled across a branch with an open view clear down the hill, over the grounds and beyond the roof of Livingstone Manor. Marler had binoculars pressed to his eyes. Newman perched on the same thick branch, leant against the trunk of the tree.

'Hauser is running for it,' Marler warned. 'He's got a small chopper, Sikorsky, I think, at the end of the estate. He's boarding the bloody machine.'

'He's going to get away. The top man always escapes,' said Newman.

He leaned forward. Police patrol cars had appeared out of nowhere. One was approaching the open grille gates as a guard ran out. The guard aimed his automatic rifle at the car, shattered the windscreen. The offside door opened, a policeman jumped out, steadied himself behind the boot, fired twice. The guard was thrown back against one of the stone pillars, leaned there for a moment, sagged to the ground. Other policemen were jumping out of cars as another guard appeared, raised his weapon. One shot rang out. The guard dropped his weapon, slumped to the ground.

The firing ceased, was replaced by another sound, the whirring of the chopper's rotors. The machine elevated slowly from the ground, hovered, then turned south towards Harwich. It was then Newman noticed Marler had his radio transmitter in his hand. The helicopter was passing over Livingstone Manor as Marler punched out the numbers. *142.*

Newman had just checked the time. 5 a.m. Dawn would break at any moment. But first a false dawn broke. The

chopper was still flying over Livingstone Manor when the
world erupted. A tremendous BOOM murdered the last
of the night silence, disturbed now only by the steady
chug-chug of the chopper. The mansion came apart, was
hurled upwards in flying chunks of masonry. The
shockwave of the detonation shook the helicopter, which
suddenly seemed to hover. A flaming curtain of red
soared upwards, enveloping the machine. Newman saw it
sink into the shattered relic of the mansion which now had
only two walls standing. He thought he saw Hauser's
chopper hit the ground a second before one of the walls
crumbled inwards, burying it. Then the smoke came,
blotting out the carnage.

'This little jigger has a range of over two miles, I'm
told,' Marler remarked. He looked where the mansion
had once stood.

'In any case, it was second-rate Georgian architecture.'

Newman was clambering down the tree, smashing off
twigs in his rapid progress. Marler stared down, called
out.

'Where are you going?'

'I have an appointment. With a murderer.'

55

It was going to end as it had started. In the same place. At
the bell tower. For several days Newman had thought it
would be like this. What he was not prepared for was how
like February it would be.

Dawn was breaking in the east, bands of deep blue and
gold. Another heatwave day. Toiling up the track he

stopped, almost transfixed, disbelieving. Parked near the gaunt bell tower was a red Jaguar. Just as Sandy's red Jaguar had been parked when, buoyantly on a bitter frosty February day, he had strode up this same track to meet her.

He shook himself, like a man emerging from a nightmare. Tired, dirty, clothes torn, hands bleeding from twigs which had grazed his hands, he took a deep breath, strode faster up to the bell tower.

It was the same, but it was different. Before it had been winter, now it was glorious summer, a summer Sandy would have loved. He flexed his aching fingers as he came over the last rise, saw inside the bell tower. Moving on to the grass verge, he advanced silently.

Inside the bell tower a man was on his knees, his back to Newman, scrabbling among the straw, searching for something. Newman was within two yards of the bell tower when the man glanced over his shoulder, jumped to his feet.

'What was that terrible explosion?' asked Adam Carver.

'You've messed up your nice silk suit,' Newman said in a cold voice. 'Would this be what you are looking for?'

He held up the button he had torn from his own British warm, the button carrying the DAKS symbol. Carver waved both hands in a gesture of incomprehension.

'What are you talking about? Why should a button concern me?'

'Because Sandy tore this button from your coat when she struggled for her life before you hung her like a common felon from that beam up there. Up there, Carver. Above your head.'

Instinctively Carver glanced up. Newman moved forward. Carver looked for escape, stared through one of the arched openings, saw the car approaching, bumping up the track. He turned, grasped the sides of the ladder, ran

537

up it. Newman reached for his ankle, missed it, began mounting the shaking ladder himself.

Looking up he saw Carver's foot aimed at his head, ducked just in time. Carver continued his climb, reached the wooden platform close to the hanging beam. He was in such a rush he slipped on the straw scattered across the platform, sprawled full length.

Newman stepped on to the high platform as Carver jumped up, faced him. Newman showed him the button a second time. Both men stood quite still for several seconds.

'You're Hauser's hired assassin,' Newman told him. 'You killed Ed Riverton, garrotted the poor bastard, then threw him into the ice of North Harbour to be crushed by the icebreaker. You're a fast mover, I'll give you that. You next caught a plane to London, drove up here after making an appointment with Sandy for dawn. You want to know how I eventually knew it was you – not Galvone, not Manescu?'

'All right, Brain Box,' Carver sneered. 'How *did* you know it was me?'

'Because,' Newman said, hiding his sadness, 'it had to be someone with an appearance, a personality she would trust. That ruled out Manescu and Galvone. You've a way with women, you louse. Under that nice silk suit you're pure filth.'

'Jealous, are we?'

As he spoke Carver stooped swiftly, scooped up a handful of straw, threw it in Newman's eyes. Newman was blinking when Carver rushed him. Instinctively Newman grabbed Carver round his body with both arms to save himself. Both men were so intent on their struggle they failed to realize the car approaching the bell tower had reached it. Buchanan had grabbed a British warm off the back seat, had run inside the bell tower in time to hear the conversation, Carver's admission. He stared up as

538

Warden followed him. Cupping one hand, Buchanan called up to Newman.

'We have Carver's coat minus the missing button. Forensic confirmed the button's from his coat. He'll stand trial . . .'

Grim faced, he saw the grapple continue on the rickety platform constructed of single wooden planks without any protective rail. Carver hooked a foot behind Newman's ankle to trip him. Newman hung on, freed his right hand, thrust it under his opponent's jaw. He jerked his hand up savagely. Carver toppled, recovered his balance, not realizing he was at the edge of the platform with an abyss below. Newman kneed him in the groin. Carver grunted with pain, loosened his grip, clenched his right fist to slam it into Newman's throat. His feet slithered over the edge. His right hand grabbed for Newman's throat. He dropped off the platform as Newman countered the grab by grasping his arm.

Carver fell, almost dragged Newman with him. Newman had braced his legs to take the strain, crouched, still grasping Carver by the right arm. Only Carver's body above the shoulders was level with the platform. The greater part of his body hung suspended in space. Newman gazed down into the terrified eyes of the killer.

The silk sleeve began to come apart at the shoulder. Newman continued holding on to the right arm, feeling the material slowly slithering through his grasp. His eyes were cold, almost devoid of expression as he watched the sleeve ripping loose stitch by stitch. There was a long moment when it looked as though Newman might haul the hanging man back on to the platform. Then the sleeve parted company with its owner. Carver let out a high-pitched scream as he plunged down. His body performed a semi-somersault in mid-air, then like a swimmer he dived down head first. Buchanan heard the awful sound of the skullbones smashing against the flagstone floor of the tower. Carver lay sprawled motionless, like a broken rag doll.

Newman stood up slowly, holding the sleeve, walked forward with an effort of will, forced himself to descend the shaking ladder rung by rung. At the bottom he stood quite still, not looking at the corpse. He was gazing at the red Jaguar, the spitting image of Sandy's.'

'I'll drive you back to where Tweed is waiting by your car. Let Tweed drive you back,' Buchanan said.

'I can drive myself . . .'

'But you won't. That's an order. And I'm sure Tweed won't let you. This is Carver's coat. We found it at his Chelsea flat. One button missing. Strange that he never realized how incriminating a missing button could be.'

'Strange,' Newman agreed and let himself be led to Buchanan's car.

His mind was so dazed he had no idea what Buchanan was talking about.

Epilogue

'I've come to say goodbye.'

Cord Dillon held out his hand to Tweed in the Park Crescent office. Tweed paused, shrugged, shook hands without enthusiasm.

'You've guessed it?' Dillon suggested.

'Guessed what?'

'Why we wanted Hauser finished. His whole apparatus wiped out. Which is what will happen now he's gone.'

'Go on.'

'The infrastructure of the Soviet Union is on the verge of collapse. The railways are crumbling for lack of maintenance. The telephone system hardly works – a lot of their equipment was installed before 1918. Try to make a call from Moscow to Leningrad and you'd better allow a day to get through. Then maybe you won't.'

'So?'

'The subway in Moscow, once their pride and joy, is also crumbling. Stand on a station platform and watch water dripping through the cracks in the walls. Do I have to go on?'

'The whole place is collapsing?'

'Exactly. And Hauser – after scaring them to death – was going to rebuild Russia into a new America. You think we want that? After seventy years of Communism? Russia is going off the map. Will become a Third World country.'

'And that suits you?'

'Down to the ground. No more worry as to who takes

over. Makes no difference. Hauser was going to spoil all that. Now we can just sit back and watch it happen. You knew?'

'I guessed. Because all the time you were with me your function was mostly that of observer. You didn't do all that much to help. Isn't it time to catch your flight?'

'Guess so.' Dillon looked across the room. 'Goodbye to you, Paula.'

'Goodbye,' she said.

'Is that a good idea?' she asked when they were alone.

'It wasn't a good idea to let Hauser take over,' Tweed replied.

'I mean to let Russia collapse,' she persisted.

'If it does we'll have an even grimmer situation to cope with.'